QUIRKE
A NOVEL OF LOVE, LAW AND MAGIC

by

KAYE REEVES

To my good friends and colleagues at the court, about whom this book is not.

ISBN: 978-0-9963568-0-0: (paperback)

Cover by Mark Ziemann (markzman@markzman.com)

TABLE OF CONTENTS

Chapter One   7

Chapter Two   21

Chapter Three   28

Chapter Four   37

Chapter Five   49

Chapter Six   57

Chapter Seven   63

Chapter Eight   70

Chapter Nine   74

Chapter Ten   84

Chapter Eleven   89

Chapter Twelve   96

Chapter Thirteen   108

Chapter Fourteen   114

Chapter Fifteen   120

Chapter Sixteen   125

Chapter Seventeen   131

Chapter Eighteen   138

Chapter Nineteen   145

Chapter Twenty   151

Chapter Twenty-One   158

Chapter Twenty-Two   162

Chapter Twenty-Three   165

Chapter Twenty-Four   168

Chapter Twenty-Five   176

Chapter Twenty-Six   181

Chapter Twenty-Seven   184

Chapter Twenty-Eight   187

Chapter Twenty-Nine   194

Chapter Thirty   201

Chapter Thirty-One   211

Chapter Thirty-Two   219

Chapter Thirty-Three   **222**

Chapter Thirty-Four   **237**

Chapter Thirty-Five   **240**

Chapter One

August 15, 2014, 4:15 p.m.

Justice Conal Quirke poured Cristallino Brut into red plastic party cups and handed them out to his staff, who had gathered around the conference table in his comfortably appointed chambers at the state Supreme Court. Margie, his judicial assistant, flushed pink already, before having taken even a sip, and the extern was grinning a little too widely, making sure to show his awareness of the historic nature of the moment. Three of the four staff attorneys—Sadie, Freddie, and John—appeared relieved, for their own careers depended—for the time being anyway—on the judge's. And Lucas, the fourth and head staff attorney, was indulging him by dispensing, for once, with his usual nervous superciliousness and looking mildly pleased.

"Got the papers right here, comrades," the judge said, indicating a large manila envelope on the table. "They'll be fedexed to the Secretary of State tonight."

"Not a moment too soon, Judge. Deadline's tomorrow," said Lucas.

"I'm well aware of that. You weren't worried I'd change my mind, were you?" Everyone laughed a little too heartily. The subject of his retention had been an unmentionable yet obsessive topic among them for the last several months. Quirke's current term was due to expire at the end of the year, and the state constitution required him to file for a spot on the November ballot if he wanted to be retained on the court where he'd sat for the last three years.

And he did, more even than he thought he would when he was first elevated three years previously from the Court of Appeal. Although he could have decamped, as his predecessor, former Justice Frank Carraway, had done, to an arbitration and mediation firm, or become a rainmaker at any number of big law firms, Quirke's heart was with the court. The chance to do something with potential long-term significance and the intellectual challenge posed by most of the cases that came before the court, along with the absence of timesheets, made it the best job he could imagine having, despite the flak his wife gave him over having chosen public service over joining her father's growing business empire after law school.

His staff, too, helped make the job a pleasure, apart from Lucas, who always talked as though Quirke were hard of hearing and frequently looked at him as though he'd just emitted a rude noise. Constraining Quirke's generous impulses, the chronically threadbare state budget hadn't permitted staff raises for the last seven years. He'd have to find other ways of showing his appreciation.

John at last spoke up, raising his plastic cup. "A toast and a prediction: To the well-deserved upcoming electoral success of Justice Conal Quirke and a fruitful and happy new term."

"Here, here," they chorused, raising their cups.

"Thank you, one and all," Quirke said. "Drink up. This stuff is tolerable chilled, but medicinal at room temperature."

Following his own advice, he drained his cup and started pouring another round. Margie demurred as always on festive occasions, hastening back to her filing and taking the precious election papers with her to dispatch before the deadline. After one more drink, the extern likewise excused himself, saying he had to study for an intellectual property exam.

The four attorneys lingered, Freddie and Sadie refilling each other's cups, John and Lucas beginning to argue over an opinion Justice Hetford had circulated in *Amar v. County of San Eligio*, involving attorney's fees in qui tam actions. Sometimes it seemed half the cases before the court involved attorney's fees. This was a subject Quirke knew all too well lay close to the legal community's heart but one that, truth to tell, did not make his top ten. John was urging him to dissent in *Amar*; Lucas was hectoring him to sign the majority opinion.

"I'm really going to have to focus on that one soon," the judge acknowledged as Lucas, exiting the party, shot him a glare. "It's got to file by the fifteenth of September or none of us gets paid."

"By 'us' you mean you?" asked Freddie.

"Yes, the court, of course. You guys get paid no matter what. Not that that makes up for the lack of a raise again this year."

"Kind of you to say it, Judge," said John. "I wish the Chief saw things your way. It's getting so I have to consider a part-time job to make ends meet. My kid's tuition only goes up, you know."

Margie popped her head in the door. "Mrs. Quirke on line one."

"What did I do now?" said the judge, simulating mock terror and feeling a more than a trace of the real thing as he reached toward the phone, which was nestled between half-empty bottles of Cristallino on the conference table. Then he reconsidered. "Tell her I'll get back to her."

Staff eyed him with unconcealed worry. He never injected his domestic issues into chambers, but they were all aware that Eleanor Quirke had what in a four-year-old would be called a spirited personality. More than once she'd marched into his office, slammed the door, and read him that ancient piece of legislation called the riot act, after which for several days the judge had crept around, unlike himself, silent and moody. This time, however, perhaps because of the bottle or so of Cristallino he had on board, he wasn't letting himself feel demeaned or guilty. She was but a distant irritant, and would not be allowed to spoil the party.

"Everything all right, Judge?" John asked.

"Never better. Anybody up for the Inns? I'm buying." As the attorneys knew, he was referring to the dive known as the Inns of Court across the street from the state building. Back in the day, judges and their staffs knocking back martini lunches there was a common sight. Latterly, however, a more abstemious culture prevailed at the court, and now the bar was frequented mainly by a more down-market crowd consisting of workers' comp attorneys and their maimed clients. But tonight, it would serve well enough for his staff appreciation gesture.

"I'll have one with you, Judge," Sadie said, with a warmth that set off, in the back of his mind, a quiet alarm. In their little chambers universe, he'd always known, somehow, that Sadie put him first and took unalloyed pleasure in doing so, though why she did was a mystery to him. Other staff attorneys around the court, as a rule, never let their judges forget to whom they owed their well-crafted legal prose, and left the care and feeding of the judge to the judicial assistant. Besides Sadie's impeccable legal work, there were all the little things she did: giving him a bright smile on tedious afternoons, sharing her home-baked cookies (too often, his expanding waistline testified), bringing him lunch on days when he couldn't get away from his desk.

Although sorely tempted, he'd never allowed himself to become accustomed to her kindness. Not that she might misinterpret his employerly gratitude, unlike what had happened on a few unpleasant occasions in other work settings in the past. He knew her well enough to know that, at least. It was rather a matter of his tendency to develop feelings, the way a seed that's way postmortem will suddenly sprout a tendril, and ere you know it, you have a field full of kudzu or some other ineradicable menace. But before awakening to the alarm's full implications on this festive and well-lubricated occasion, he had pressed the mental snooze button.

"Good! Guys?"

"Sorry, Judge, we have tickets to Salome tonight, and Derek'll have a fit if I show up pickled," said Freddie.

"Too bad. Say hi to your husband for me," Quirke said. He'd been the first justice at the court to solemnize a same-sex marriage, between

Freddie and his long-time partner, right after the court declared the ban unconstitutional. Despite his own marital misery, Quirke seemed to have done an adequate job joining Freddie and Derek, as they remained to all appearances still devoted to one another after nearly three years. "John— you gotta come out."

"Judge, Helen'll kill me—she's been cooped up in the house with the twins all day and if she doesn't have adult contact by six o'clock she goes a little insane."

"Just one? Help me celebrate?"

"I'd better not this time."

"You're fired. Kidding," Quirke hastened to add. He never lost sight of the fact he was dealing with lawyers, and his jocular comment technically violated at least three statutes that he knew of.

"Well, one, then. *Only* one."

"Of course, only one. Sober as a judge, that's my motto. We have to avoid the appearance of impropriety, after all, and you never know when a reporter's going to leap out of the shrubbery."

"Should I see if Lucas wants to come along?" John asked.

Quirke couldn't tell whether John wanted the answer to be yes or no. Either he was looking forward to further skirmishing on the *Amar* case or he was hoping to avoid it. Regardless, Quirke thought it unwise to drink with his terminally buttoned-up head of chambers—he might say something he really meant. "Normally I'd say that's an excellent idea, but Lucas seems to have gone back to work. Imagine that! A head of chambers at his desk after five o'clock. What would we do without Lucas? All right, let's go before the Inns get so crowded we can't hear ourselves think."

The lawyers' favorite local drinking establishment was even darker and greasier than Quirke remembered it. The walls still bore the caricatures of silly, bibulous-looking British judges in their robes and frothy wigs; bowls of peanuts dotted the bar, shells carpeting the floor; and the stolid bartender in his plaid yoked shirt and white apron sipped tonic through a mixing straw as he surveyed the day's legal newspaper, left behind by a lunch patron. The sound system delivered one eighties stadium rock anthem after another. Quirke breathed deeply, feeling his gut muscles relax for the first time all day. The place felt more home than home.

Sadie slid into an empty corner booth and called to John. "Get me a glass of red, would you please?" Starting toward the bar, John asked over his shoulder, "What'll it be for you, Judge?"

"Whiskey sour, double," Quirke nodded, sliding in after Sadie. "And see if we can get a bowl of peanuts. Here, I told you I was paying," he said, handing his attorney a couple of twenties.

"Done," said John.

"So, Judge," said Sadie, turning up the thermostat of her smile once they were alone, "are you planning on doing much campaigning?"

"None at all, if I can help it."

"I suppose it can be pretty boring."

"Oh, I don't mind pressing the flesh. When I was a youngster, I did a little retail politics—helped on a gubernatorial campaign or two. The problem is that people don't understand what appellate justices do and how we do it. Explaining why we can't promise never to spring a criminal or rule for a human being against a business, or why it's impossible to decide death penalty appeals in a month, is harder than you might think. I suppose I should be noble and think of it as educational outreach."

"I see what you're saying. Still, though, if anything comes up that you need to respond to—"

"What are you thinking of? I guess I'd better Google myself and find out what the opposition knows. Wait, what opposition?"

"There won't be any, I'm sure of it. You're a wonderful judge, and I'm not saying that because you're my boss and I write your opinions. It's just that everything's so polarized these days. Every campaign seems to bring out the worst in the media and draw all the extremists out of the woodwork. I'm afraid your idealized view of a judicial election may be outdated."

"I can only hope you're wrong. But don't let it worry you, because I certainly intend not to let it worry me."

John returned with their drinks, a laminate bowl of peanuts in their shells nestled in his arms. Sadie relieved him of the bowl and set it down in front of Quirke.

"You have to help me with these," he told his attorneys. "I shouldn't be eating this stuff anyway."

"Too much sodium?" John asked.

"That and this," Quirke said, straightening his tie over his incipient paunch, which strained the fabric of his Bengal striped shirt, before proceeding to attack the nuts. "We were looking at some pictures of my confirmation hearing the other day and Eleanor informed me I've gotten fat in the last few years. She's not overly endowed in the tact department, but

I do need to lose weight."

"Oh, not necessarily," Sadie said.

Quirke shook his head. "Your loyalty is touching, but don't make me happy; what I need is the truth. 'Judge, you need to lose twenty pounds,' 'Judge, you need to figure out where you stand on the *Amar* case,' 'Judge, you need to get off the dime and file your damn election papers'—that's the kind of thing I need to hear. Truth hurts, as they say."

"Nobody needs that much truth from a spouse," Sadie said.

"Eleanor can't help it; she's a pathological truth-teller. But enough about her." For a while they chatted idly about neighborhood trivia—the new Burmese restaurant in the next block of Lamden, the alarming recent Health Department rating of the Vietnamese place from which they'd often bought takeout—until Quirke noticed they had all finished their drinks. "Can I buy you another round?" he asked.

John shook his head. "Sorry, Judge, I really do need to get home, or Helen's going to turn into a pathological truth-teller herself, and I'm not nearly as stoic as you are. See you both on Monday morning." He gathered his jacket and messenger bag and waved at them as he cut through the patrons now starting to throng around the bar.

"I don't mind taking you up on that drink offer, if it's still good," said Sadie, taking off her jacket as if planning to stay a while and smiling at him in a distinctly off-duty manner.

The mental alarm awoke from its snooze with a buzz almost too faint to hear, but before he could think about it he'd pressed the button again. "Well, of course. I'm gratified that at least one of my staff doesn't mind celebrating with me. Hang on, I'll get them this time. Stay right where you are."

Quirke maneuvered his way to the bar, drew himself up to his full height, and fixed his features into the most distinguished-looking mien of which he was capable. As he stood trying to attract the bartender's attention, he caught a glimpse of himself in the mirror behind the bar. He supposed what gazed back at him was pretty well preserved for fifty-two, Eleanor's opinion to the contrary notwithstanding. There was still more pepper than salt in his thickly waving hair and Van Dyke whiskers; the dark blue eyes behind the horn rims were clear enough despite his worrisome daily bourbon intake; and the advantage of the extra avoirdupois Eleanor had chided him about was that his cheeks remained smooth, unlined and rosy.

And Eleanor made sure he dressed the part of a justice: navy wool flannel Armani suit, Ferragamo necktie, Crockett and Jones wingtips. He could still take a decent picture for a mailer if the reelection committee could come up with the scratch for it. Assuming he needed to, of course; there was, now, little reason to think he'd have to work that hard to capture fifty percent plus one of the voters who bothered to work their way to the nether regions of the ballot, where the judicial candidates lived.

"Double whiskey sour and a glass of Chateau Civic Center red," he said when the bartender finally turned to him.

"Is that really—Justice Hetford?" At the sound of Quirke's voice a slightly inebriated man at his right elbow, a beer-stained set of briefs spread in front of him, piped up.

Typical, thought Quirke. *Even lawyers can't tell us apart.* "Sorry, no," he replied.

"You're joshing. I'd recognize you anywhere. I argued in front of you once, you know."

"My apologies, counsel; after a few thousand oral arguments, I'm afraid I'm not placing you."

"Hal Driggs, Your Honor. *Bickenstaff v. Blackacre*? Recreational immunity? Very, very important decision, absolute landmark. High point of my legal career. Though I must say, Your Honor, in all honesty I preferred your colleague Justice Quirke's dissent."

"Ah yes, Quirke's dissent. There was much merit in it. It very nearly persuaded me."

"Wish it had, then. My client would have come away a lot happier."

The bartender set the whiskey and wine in front of Quirke with a wink and a cheery, "Good to see you, Judge. It's been awhile." Quirke winked back.

"Maybe I'll have the sense to listen to Quirke next time," he told the lawyer. "Good evening, Mr. Driggs."

※

"So, tell me, Sadie." Back in the booth, Quirke set the glass of wine in front of her and quaffed his own drink. He had hit that sweet, unsustainable state of mild intoxication wherein anything seemed possible, including that his staff attorney—who, he now perceived, was quite pretty in a Joyce Carol Oates sort of way—could illuminate all mysteries. "How is it you seem so happy most of the time?"

Her dark brown eyes radiated a warmth he couldn't remember recently being directed at him by anyone else, and she touched her glass to his.

"To your health. I seem happy most of the time?"

"Yes. What's your secret? Is it magic? Well, that was tactless. Eleanor's rubbing off on me. If there's one thing that's been drummed in, it's not to ask staff about their religion."

"No offense taken, but let's save that topic for another conversation, if you don't mind. Now I get to ask you a question: Are you happy? I can't help worrying about you sometimes."

"About me? No one's ever asked me that before. What would I have to feel unhappy about? I've been pretty lucky." Skirting the truth always made him feel uneasy, but the prospect of self-revelation to her was even more so, and he changed the subject. "You know, the Chief just appointed me to another of her committees. Something about self-represented litigants, God help us. Just what I need with the election coming up."

Sadie laughed. "I thought you weren't planning to campaign. You should have plenty of time to figure out ways to help self-represented litigants."

"Watch out or I'll have you appointed, too. In fact, I think I will. It's just the sort of thing you'd be really good at, with your sunny disposition and patience and mastery of the rules of court and all that."

"I see I've somehow managed to keep you fooled. But if you're not kidding, go ahead and put me down. Call me a masochist, but I've always wanted to be on one of the Chief's committees, and I'd love to help you out."

Underscoring her sincerity, she let her hand rest casually on the sleeve of his jacket. This was a gesture he couldn't remember a staff attorney ever previously making, although, under the influence of the whiskey, the stadium rock, and her smile, he couldn't see why this was so. An answering current of need and urgency passed through him, making his pulse pound so hard he was afraid she might hear it. They had now arrived at a place where the safe thing to do was to act as though nothing had happened, and he wasn't yet drunk enough to realize he had a choice in the matter.

He finished his drink in one gulp and stood awkwardly. "That's very generous. Why don't you remind me about it next week? Right now, I ought to get back to work. Or pick up some papers and go home and try to read. Or something productive like that."

"I'll walk back with you," she said, taking a last sip of wine.

The evening air had turned misty and cool, softening windows and streetlights in white haze. Traffic was already thinning out and the nighttime denizens of the Civic Center were beginning to arrive, pushing their shopping carts, claiming their accustomed doorways, lighting up their cigarettes and joints and pipes. Making room for them, the last workers were hastening to the subway. Quirke and Sadie walked against the tide of exiting personnel into the state building. The darkened Clerk's Office was locked and vacuum cleaners droned faintly from within the interior hallways.

She slipped a hand under his elbow as they tiptoed over freshly waxed terrazzo, and his face must have registered his surprise at her touch. "I hope you don't mind. Slippery floor," she explained.

"Not in the least," he said. *Something only seems to be going on here*, he told himself, trying to focus on the driest imaginable subjects—Article 4 of the Uniform Commercial Code, the court's mileage reimbursement rules—as they entered the elevator. She had not let go of his arm, and he felt her heat through her black jersey dress.

"It was fun," she said. "Thanks for inviting me to celebrate."

"I'm glad you could come. I don't know why we don't do it more often. We're far too monkish at the court. Maybe we'd have more unanimous decisions if we'd all go out and tie one on now and then."

"I'm down with that," she laughed.

She followed him into his office, and he knew he didn't want either to go home or to start in on one of the many memos awaiting his attention in their neat piles on his desk. They would be there next week, next month, next year; right now, he needed to spend a few more minutes in her company.

An idea occurred to him. "Oh, look," he said, indicating the conference table, laden with leftover Cristallino. "It would be a sin to throw that out." He took one of the bottles and emptied the contents into two clean party cups.

"Not too medicinal at this point?"

"Good for what ails you." He considered. "Maybe nothing ails you."

"I've no complaints at the moment." As she leaned back against the conference table her dress clung to her slim figure in a way that pulled him closer. Her eyes were so bright, so inviting. Now actively fighting desire for her after three years of an entirely blameless employment relationship, he tried to will his pulse back down to a moderate tempo, drank a cup of Cristallino, and poured another. She likewise drank, and held out her empty cup for a refill. Pouring, he reflected it was a good thing he had so much practice at containing this sort of momentary hopeless longing, or the evening's outcome would be unpredictable.

"Then there's no impemident—impediment—to your staying to polish this off?" he asked, handing her the cup.

"There's nowhere else I need or want to be." She put the cup on the table and leaned back further. He wondered if she was trying to tell him something, then dismissed the thought. She was, after all, a young and attractive woman, she must have dozens of young and attractive boyfriends, and theirs had always been strictly a working relationship. Still, he mused; still...

He drank down his cup at one go and stood over her. As Eleanor was his own height—taller in the heels she wore everywhere except to bed—looking down into the diminutive attorney's face induced a novel vertiginous sensation. "I probably shouldn't have had that last one," he muttered, swaying slightly and blinking. He tried to focus on her bewitchingly warm dark eyes, whose depths he was seeing as if for the first time, and not solely due to the doubling effects of the alcohol he'd put away. "And so, what's next, Sadie?" he asked, simultaneously hoping and fearing she'd tell him. " 'Should I stay or should I go? Should I cool it or should I blow?' Indecision in a judge is a terrible thing." He braced himself against the conference table, from which he suddenly noticed something seemed to be missing. "Hang on a sec; where did my keys go?"

Her mouth formed an irresistible pout. "I suppose this evening, like all good things, had to come to an end. So, if you need to leave, I'll call you a cab."

"No need for that. I'm perfectly capable of driving if I could only kind my fees. Find my keys."

She shook her head. "Judge, I can't believe I'm saying this to you, and I'm really very sorry, but you need to sober up a little before you go anywhere near a steering wheel." She was holding something, which he suspected were his keys, behind her back. He tried reaching around her waist to retrieve the thing, and she deftly moved aside just as he made contact with her ribcage. The evasive action saddened him—that was a place he'd have liked to investigate. But what was he thinking? She was his staff, after all—untouchable. As a matter of law.

"You're right," he conceded. "Tomorrow's headline would set the legal world agog: 'Supreme Court Justice Kicks off Retention Campaign with a Deuce.' Hetford would never let me forget it. And Eleanor would have my guts for garters. Probably not worth it."

"Definitely not worth it. If you like, I'll keep you company until you're good to go."

"You wouldn't mind staying? If you say I have to stay, then I want you to stay, too. We can have a pajama party—no, no. Kidding. Not that I want to, but when would I be good to go?"

"Here, I can tell you." She fished around in her purse and brought out her mobile phone. "There's an app for it. Let's see—how much do you weigh?"

"Oh, about a hundred and seventy-five."

She scanned him from head to toe with an incredulous smile. "I mean what you actually weigh, not your driver's license weight."

"All right, a hundred and ninety-six. Is there a lie detector app on there, too?"

"And you had how much?"

"Just a little more than usual, say a bottle and a half or two of wine and four shots of whiskey."

"Wow. Over something like an hour and a half." She finished entering the numbers. "So, if you were pulled over right now, you'd blow a very impressive point one eight. More than twice the legal limit."

"No way. Really? So, the best I could hope for would be to plead to a wet reckless."

"And that's only if the DA were feeling charitable. So, unfortunately, you won't be legal to drive until around breakfast time. Don't worry. I won't hold you captive all night, but I will call you that cab."

"Not yet." The thought of leaving her company to return to the palatial prison he called home depressed him, and he found himself grabbing her upper arms for emphasis. Somewhere in his brain it registered that she did not stiffen or pull away, that she remained receptive to him, and he relaxed his hold, while absentmindedly massaging her arms.

"You have really nice triceps, Sadie. Firm but somehow soft at the same time." Hearing what he'd just said, he shook his head. "I'm sorry, that was way out of line. I don't want you to think I'm trying to—Christ, what am I trying to say? You're right, I'm in no condition to drive. I'm probably not in a condition to go anywhere."

"It's okay. Everything's going to be fine," she was saying, gazing evenly into his eyes, her hands now gently squeezing his forearms. "We'll be laughing about this by the time you get over your hangover."

"I hope you're right, but I have a feeling I'm making an ass of myself. But all the same, I'm not going home yet."

"Then let's sit down and talk some more. Shall I make us some tea?"

He considered the possibility, absent-mindedly reaching for the cup of Cristallino he'd poured for her. "What I could really go for is a pizza."

She nodded, taking the cup from him and setting it on the table with a dazzling smile that made him forget how he hated anyone cutting him off. "That's a great idea, you should eat. It'll help. I'll order it right now." Out came the phone again. While she made the arrangements, he went into the en suite restroom, considered forcing himself to vomit, and then rejected the idea in favor of drinking a glass of water.

Waiting for security to announce the arrival of the food, she made him walk arm in arm with her up and down the building's block-long hallway, past their colleagues' empty offices and the locked-up courtroom, back to his chambers and forth again. At first, he expended all the effort he was capable of in keeping his posture from betraying how drunk he was. But then he remembered she already knew precisely how drunk he was, and so he let himself lean into her. The sensation of her lithe, warm body against his felt so good after the years-long famine of intimacy he'd endured in his marriage that soon the thought of breaking physical contact with her became unbearable. Meanwhile, she made charming conversation, but in his preoccupied state he couldn't remember from one end of the hall to the other a word she said.

At last she pulled him into the chambers kitchen area and made him stand there, reeling slightly, while she brewed a pot of coffee.

"That's Justice Wiggins's coffee," he said. "She'll be upset."

"You're so rule-bound," she said, laughing. "Are you starting to feel a little bit soberer?"

"I think the worst is over," he replied.

When security called about the delivery a few minutes later, she had him take off his shoes and sit on the sofa in his chambers. "I'll just run downstairs and get the pizza," she said. "Promise me you'll stay here till I get back?"

"Promise me you won't seize your chance and escape? On second thought, that's so unfair of me. Why on earth would you *not* want to do that?"

"I'll tell you when I get back. Wait right there."

Remaining conscious until Sadie returned now assumed paramount importance. He got down on the floor and managed three pushups, crawled back up onto the sofa and tried to whistle, and finally resorted to pinching himself. At last she appeared bearing the food. Her smile was worth a hundred—no, a thousand—such ordeals.

"This should perk you up," she said, setting the box on the coffee table and sitting beside him on the sofa. "The grease in the cheese alone should soak up a lot of the booze you've got in your system."

"If you put it in those terms, I'll probably throw up," he said.

She laughed. "I'm so sorry. Here, let's make you more comfortable. Why don't you take that lovely tie off so you don't get tomato sauce all over it?"

"You're brilliant; I'd never have thought of that. Eleanor would be pleased you appreciate her taste." After a few fumbling attempts he let her loosen and pull off the tie and undo his top shirt button.

"Now the belt. You can do it," she encouraged him.

He leaned back and complied with some effort. "But how do I know you won't take advantage of me?" he asked archly. "Oh my God, I've stepped in it again, haven't I? Please don't take it the wrong way."

She smiled, leaning close and, reaching toward him again, laid the back of her cool hand against his cheek.

"There is no wrong way," she murmured.

It took him a second to grasp her meaning. Then their lips met and he knew he needed her almost more than air. They kissed long and searchingly and, hardly believing she was allowing him the liberty, he cupped her right breast through the thin fabric of her dress. She was moaning a little under her breath, and inwardly he thanked Almighty God that he was still capable of having such an effect on a woman—and not just any woman off the street, but this one, who saw him nearly every day and knew his foibles, and apparently wanted him despite them.

They fell together onto the sofa. He slid his right hand under her dress, along the inside of her thigh, beneath her underclothes. She was so hot and juicy nothing mattered but to penetrate her, and the intensity of his need obliterated any prudential considerations. She reached for his trouser button and deftly, one-handedly, undid it.

Just then the stairway door slammed outside his chambers. Dimly he sensed it might be wise to stop what they were doing and pretend to be editing an opinion or something like that, but he was no more capable of it than of making time run backwards.

"Oh, fuck," Sadie whispered.

"I love the way you say that," he murmured back, nibbling her neck, kissing her cleavage. He had just pulled off her underthings in a single motion when—oh nightmare reality!—she began to struggle under his weight.

"Wait," she gasped. "The door—"

For the first time, he noticed that the door to his chambers stood wide open to the hallway, and something flashed along the periphery of his field of vision.

"Jesus, what was that?" he cried, getting off her and trying to put himself back in his clothing.

She rose and smoothed down her dress, padded to the door, and peered in the direction of the staff attorneys' offices.

"*Mer-de*," she said. "Lucas's light is on."

Chapter Two

August 15, 8:35 a.m.

Eleanor Quirke sat at the breakfast table, picking at her cantaloupe with increasing aggression as the minutes ticked by with no appearance by her husband. She knew it was after midnight before he'd gone to his room because she was up once around then and had seen the light still on in his study. Not that he would have been doing much work at that hour—passed out drunk, more likely. His habits were becoming more intolerable with each passing day. No amount of talking to him seemed to have any effect.

She was beginning to think Daddy was right that an intervention was the only prospect of straightening him out. She would have to enlist Quirke's dim-witted secretary and that promising young man he'd kept on, at her insistence, as his head of chambers to find and eliminate his secret supply. They'd have to search his study—she was afraid to think how many empty bottles he might have stashed in the two years since he'd allowed anyone to set foot in there. Maybe if they could get him into rehab quickly it would all blow over before the election. She took up the iPhone beside her plate and texted her assistant to look into residential treatment centers. Or maybe an intervention would induce him to quit being a judge once and for all and get into something more exciting. Daddy might still be willing to give him something to do in Marvelocity Industries if he proved he could be trusted, such as by giving her what she wanted for once. Or quite possibly it was too late for any of that.

At last she heard his slow, heavy footstep on the stairs and his muddling about in the kitchen, after which he sat down across the table from her with his mug of coffee and slice of bread and jam.

"You look like hell this morning," she said.

He wrapped his hands around the mug, giving him the double benefit of warmth and concealment of his morning shakes, and smiled bitterly. "Noted."

"Didn't you sleep at all?"

"A little."

"You're on the way to ruining your health, the way you're living."

"You're probably right." He managed a gulp of coffee and a bite of bread, then yawned and tugged his hair so that it stood straight up.

She fumed at his nonchalance. "Are you even capable of withstanding the demands of a campaign at this point?"

"Don't be ridiculous, Eleanor, I'm not running for president. There won't be any campaigning if I have something to say about it."

"What do you mean? Have you decided not to—"

"I mean I'll get through this nonpartisan, uncontested retention election the same way Supreme Court justices always do—without flinging myself at the voting public like a cheap streetwalker. It isn't necessary and it isn't seemly."

"So, there's really nothing I can say to get you to see my point of view? Have you already—"

"I'm putting in my papers today, and that's final. No appeal, no rehearing. It's my life, Eleanor, and it's what I want to do."

She pursed her lips and gave the melon rind a final stab. "I'll be out this evening."

"That's nice," he said, taking another tentative bite of bread and jam.

"Till quite late, possibly."

"Thanks for letting me know."

When no inquiry as to the nature of her plans was forthcoming, she offered a suggestion. "Perhaps you can get your dinner somewhere. I hope it won't be entirely liquid."

"Too bad, I was planning on a kale-avocado smoothie."

"You wouldn't recognize kale if it wore a sign. Well, the car's waiting, and I need to leave. I'd offer you a lift, but it may be an hour before you're presentable."

"Thanks anyway. I'd rather make my own way to the office."

As soon as she had departed, clouds of Flowerbomb in her wake, he covered his face with his hands and promised himself no more breakfast-table arguments forever.

Eleanor kicked her Louboutins off onto the carpeted floor of the town car as her driver silently navigated the heavy, mizzling air and sluggish traffic. The ride afforded her time to catch up on a few personal calls.

"Joan, it's Eleanor Quirke. I really need to see you today, I feel like I'm jumping out of my skin, really anxious and depressed and just—everything. Can we advance my appointment from tomorrow? See what you can do and let me know. Oh, and I'm running out of Xanax. Call me, okay?"

"This is Eleanor Quirke, and I'd like to schedule a massage with Brandon today...Three o'clock? Terrific. Thanks, see you then."

"Oh, hi, Joan, thanks for calling me back so quickly.... No, I just made another appointment for three. Can we do two?... Well, please at least try, and let me know as soon as you can. Oh, and what about the Xanax? Can't you just...oh, you're great. Thanks so much.... Yes, yes, I'll be sure and do that next time. Call me back about the appointment, all right?... Okay, talk to you soon."

"Carrie? El. Lunch?... Yes, today. I must tell you about a fascinating conversation I had with one of Quirke's colleagues. Do you know Allan Hetford?... I would say one, I'm awfully busy with work, but I already have a two and this is going to take longer than that. So 12:30, Rita's Grill, upstairs. See you there."

"Joan?... Oh God, thank you. I don't know how I'd have made it through the day without you. See you at two."

"Emily? Why aren't you at your desk? Listen, I need you to do a couple of things. One, I need a reservation for two at Rita's today, 12:30. Two, there's a prescription waiting for me at CVS. Would you please run out and pick it up as soon as you have a moment? Thanks."

"Daddy? Hi, it's Kitten. Do you really need me at the nine o'clock with the accountants?... You do? Well, I'm running a little late. Traffic and—well, there was another argument with Quirke over breakfast... yes, pretty bad...and I simply don't know what to do about him and I'm a bit rattled and... Daddy, you're totally a dear... Emily can find the file—it's somewhere on my desk. I should be in by 10, 10:30 at the latest. Love you the most."

"Davis?" she called to the driver. "Don't go straight to the office, please. I want you to swing by Neiman's first and let me off on the Geary side. I've got an appointment with my shopper. It shouldn't take very long, so why don't you just circle around; that way you can pick me up as soon as I come out."

"I'm a little concerned about the time, Mrs. Q.—I have to take the COO to the airport this morning."

"I'll keep one eye on the clock. Nobody's going to miss a flight on my account."

Any resistance Mr. Davis had thought to mount promptly dissolved, as tended to happen with everyone in Eleanor's life except Quirke, the one apparently immovable object she had to contend with. Most people existed for Eleanor only to the extent they mirrored back to her the face she was wearing at the time: the executive ("Special Vice President for Protocol and Communications" was her title at Marvelocity, her father's corporate conglomerate) and the socialite being her two principal masks. It had been a very long while since she'd worn the face of a justice's wife, either publicly or privately.

To wonder why Quirke hadn't already left had never occurred to her; she could not imagine anyone voluntarily dropping out of her orbit, and for Quirke there were financial considerations. By the terms of their prenuptial agreement, in the event of a split he would get no share of the house (which actually belonged to Daddy) or its contents (including, under her interpretation, Quirke's clothes), and she would keep all her premarital investments (ten million shares of Marvelocity Industries and a few other odds and ends), and the beach house Daddy had gifted her. He would also have to repay the cost of the legal education Daddy had provided him, with interest, but would get to keep his judge's pension, amounting to something less than what she spent annually on Louboutins and Birkin bags. Why she hadn't yet divorced him was a mystery she was trying to solve.

She was a very young forty-eight, her complexion peeled, exfoliated, botoxed, filled and hydrated to glowing perfection, her form unburdened by an ounce of excess flesh and sculpted by several decades of Pilates, her features neither beautiful nor pretty, but of which it could be said she made the most. She had an encyclopedic knowledge of certain categories of information pertinent to her station, such as how to instantly secure a reservation at a really hot restaurant, the personal cell numbers of the best caterers and florists for a dinner party, and whether anyone would be wearing lavender next season. The upkeep on such a knowledge base was taxing, and fortunately her hours and duties at Marvelocity were flexible.

The appointment with her personal shopper at Neimans was mutually profitable, although in the course of giving due consideration to a wide and thoughtful selection of shoes, frocks, outerwear, and accessories, she somewhat lost track of time. Nevertheless, her satisfaction at having snagged the perfect pair of grey suede booties and various other accoutrements neutralized the murderous looks Davis directed at her on their way into the office (the COO having been forced to find a different way to the airport).

Eleanor so thoroughly enjoyed the substance of her work—on this day it happened to be reading an executive summary of the annual report of her favorite Marvelocity subsidiary, the clothing designer Ren Jenkins, Inc.— that the moments flew by until it came time to slip out for her lunch engagement with her friend Carrie. The nouvelle Cajun/Creole cuisine at

Rita's was, as usual, exquisite, although an onlooker would have hesitated to attest that either of the two social X-rays consumed more than trace amounts of it. Carrie shared some amusing gossip about the principals at the architectural firm where she worked; Eleanor described the object of her latest flirtation.

"He's nothing like how Quirke's always described him—pompous, overbearing, arrogant. In fact, he's utterly charming. And really hot, I have to say."

"What does he look like?" Carrie asked. "And how did you meet him again?"

"At Rowena and Clyde Forsythe's last weekend. Quirke begged off going—it seems all my friends give him a headache—so I was on my own. Apparently, Allan knows Clyde from prep school."

"Married?"

"Not currently. We talked about mutual friends, the ballet, our favorite places in Paris—we have an unbelievable amount in common—and of course the court. He was the soul of discretion, but I could see he doesn't think much of Quirke's opinions. It soon became obvious that I'm much more sympatico with him than tiresome old Quirke. It was magical."

"And really hot, you said?"

"Oh my God. Well, you know Quirke—not only has he let himself go physically—he barely fits into his clothes anymore—but he smells like bourbon most of the time. Even when he's not drunk he's never quite sober. Allan is slightly older than Quirke, a little taller, lean, muscular, tanned, and just—more virile. *Way* more virile."

"Sounds yummy. Do you think he's attracted to you?"

"Of course, he couldn't be overt in the circumstances, and his manners are impeccable. But I have a feeling he'd be interested."

"So, invite him to lunch and find out if you're right."

"You didn't think I'd waste any time, did you? We're having dinner tonight."

※

August 15, 3:00 p.m.

"Come in, Eleanor. Tell me how things are going for you right now."

Joan Marchgrave, Psy.D., sat in the overstuffed chair alongside the fireplace in her office as Eleanor dropped into the leather sofa on the other side of the antique Tabriz rug. A sense of dissonance arose as Dr. Marchgrave compared her client's current cheery, even exhilarated, demeanor with the anguished-sounding woman who'd called earlier in the day.

"It's like you're always saying, self-care is so essential. Today started out so badly, but I was able to use the tools we've talked about to help myself feel better."

"I'm glad to hear that. What caused you to become so depressed and anxious this morning, and how did you get things to turn around?"

"Well, I'm not sure I want to plunge back into it, but this morning I felt completely disregarded. Quirke made it absolutely clear he didn't care how I felt, he was going to go through with the election."

"So that I have the facts firmly in mind, this is your husband's judgeship we're talking about, and his term is expiring, so to continue being a judge he has to run in the election this fall. Is that right?"

"Correct. And, as I've told you more than once, he's going downhill in so many ways. He's not the man he used to be when we met. He hides himself away in his study and drinks. Constantly. Physically, he's a disgrace, unlike the other men his age or older that I know who still keep fit, and he doesn't seem to care. He never wants to do anything. He picks fights. He's falling apart, and it's so not pretty. I don't think I can stand to watch."

"How does he pick fights?"

"Well, like today, he doesn't respond when I try to engage him; instead, he comes up with some judge-y, noncommittal response until I feel like I'm talking to the wall."

"He picks fights by being noncommittal."

"And we haven't had sex in you wouldn't believe how long."

"Yes, you've mentioned that. Have you tried any of the usual recommendations—date night, you taking the initiative, and so on?"

"It's crossed my mind, but then I can't help thinking how pathetic he is, and pity's no aphrodisiac."

"Of course, it isn't. Well, these issues sound quite serious in terms of whether your marriage has any hope of being mended. What's kept you in it up till now? In other words, what's made it worth enduring despite your dissatisfaction?"

"That's what I've been asking myself. You know, just to change the subject, I met someone."

"I doubt you've really changed the subject if we examine it closely enough, but tell me about this person."

"He's fantastic—friend of some friends of mine, a bit older than Quirke, really sexy, and I think he's interested. We're having dinner tonight." Eleanor laughed. "Quirke would have an absolute fit—they're colleagues."

"So, you're contemplating having an affair with someone your husband works with."

"That's putting it so coldly. I'm...I just think it's time I got some enjoyment out of life, and if the opportunity presents itself, I don't see why Quirke should be an obstacle."

"Could you talk with your husband about the feelings you're having?"

Eleanor shook her head and hugged herself. "I'm afraid he'd go off the deep end."

Dr. Marchgrave sat forward. "Are you afraid for yourself—your safety—or his, or both? Or the colleague's? Are you concerned he might react violently?"

"Nothing's impossible, though Quirke's such a nebbish it's pretty farfetched. He'd probably only drink himself to death. Still, any man could react badly to losing something so precious, especially when the collateral consequences would be so extreme, and I have no plans to say anything to Quirke about Allan until there's really something to say."

"What extreme collateral consequences are you referring to?"

"Let's just say Quirke's lifestyle would change abruptly and dramatically if he didn't have my resources at his disposal."

Dr. Marchgrave tapped a pencil against her notepad. "Does he see anyone?"

"Who? Quirke? I can't imagine who'd be interested in him, and I certainly haven't seen any indication—"

"I'm sorry, I was being cryptic. I meant does he see a therapist? From what you've said, he may be in the grip of a major depression, as well as the obvious alcohol abuse problem, which could both get even worse if your life takes a different direction, as you've been suggesting could happen."

"Do you think I should tell him to see a shrink?"

"I wouldn't put it quite so baldly. But it might not hurt to broach the subject if you see a suitable opening."

Chapter Three

October 30, 1995, 4:50 p.m.

In the ninth-grade classroom where Leila Henningsen and Peter Blake team-taught language and visual arts, desks for three dozen students were pushed together in clumps of four, their corresponding chairs inverted atop them, all resting on the scarred speckled green linoleum; clotheslines crisscrossed overhead, hand-drawn and -colored cartoons clipped to them; racks of tattered paperback novels stood in the corners of the room and shelves housing textbooks lined the western wall under windows that were now admitting the fading afternoon sunlight.

Ms. Henningsen's desk faced the room from in front of the chipped green boards displaying classroom rules and encouraging slogans in faint, feathery chalk. Trolleys full of art supplies were moored here and there among the desks. The two teachers sat at one of the clumped tables over a troublesome but nonetheless riveting document, and agonized over what to do about its precocious author.

"You have no doubt this is all true, right?" Peter asked. "You satisfied yourself Sadie's other stories were all autobiographical?"

"I've no doubt. She confided to me her creative writing assignments aren't particularly creative. She just writes what she knows—so she says."

"Is she really on probation? Despite the—for lack of a better word—slutty look she seems to favor, she doesn't really seem like the JD type."

"She told me she's been picked up for petty theft a number of times. But unlike other juvenile delinquents she's not taking tapes, videos, jewelry, that sort of self-indulgence; she's stealing groceries from mom and pop corner stores. No one's providing for her, poor little thing, so she has to boost her dinner. Clearly not a viable long-term survival strategy, since mom and pop are starting to call the cops as soon as they see her coming. But you're right, there's a sweetness, a sadness, about her that's nothing like the hard bravado you see in the other so-called 'bad' kids. How long it's going to be there, I don't know. That's what I'm worried about. That, and her physical safety, since I read this latest story of hers."

"Yes, it's disturbing. Unless she did some incredible research, or talked to someone who's been through it, I don't know how she could write with this level of detail and feeling about these sexual experiences, partial miscarriage, and D and C, unless she'd been through them herself. Nothing remotely like it should be happening to a girl just out of middle school."

"And we know Laudie Norrell's capable of anything, like the mom in the story," Leila said, and the teachers fell still for a moment.

"We have to talk with her about it," Peter said. "Or you talk with her, anyway—I'll be on the other side of the room organizing my supplies and straining my ears. If she sounds at all receptive, go ahead and pitch your idea."

"And if she isn't—?"

"We're mandated reporters. We have no choice but to go to the police. It'll be up to the juvenile court what to do with her, but she'll end up in a foster home at best, a group home at worst. Her mother's parental rights will probably be terminated and, although that'd be all to the good, if that's what does happen no one will really be responsible for Sadie. Most kids in that situation never graduate from high school, let alone college. I know we'd both hate to see her promise die like that. Then she really would be at risk."

"So, you're prepared to personally step in? With me?"

"I'm prepared to carry out our plan. Look, I'm thirty-three years old, never been married, never had a kid. This is my last year of full-time teaching; it's time for me to try and make it freelancing. I'm just not in a position to have the day-to-day custody of a teenage girl right now, more for her sake than mine. But I know St. Anstrudis School for Girls, and they'll take good care of Sadie until she's eighteen, just like they did my little sister. Okay, I know what you're thinking. I'm a ceremonial magician. If the Mother Superior knew what kind of mass I attend on Sundays, if she could see me evoking Goetic demons, she'd freak. On the other hand, she might really dig the angelic magick we practice, I don't know. What I do know is that, for a bunch of Catholic nuns, they're broadminded and caring women who'll instill a sense of order in the chaos of Sadie's life. And then, after she graduates, she can come and live with me, and I can correct any bizarre notions she might have acquired from the nuns. I'm not sure where I'll be at that point, except it won't be here. Above all, she'll be safe from her mother. Which she wouldn't be if she were to stay here in town with you."

"It's settled, then. At least as far as you and I are concerned. I have the guardianship papers here—my lawyer friend drafted them pro bono, and she'll go to court with us when the time comes. Are you ready?"

He nodded. "Let's do this."

The artist opened the classroom door and surveyed the hallway of Ceres High School. The school's life, in all its hormone-driven diversity, was on display: kids sitting, legs splayed, on the floor doing homework; kids making out on the stairs; kids cartwheeling and practicing backflips; kids selling raffle tickets to their peers and teachers; kids sticking up newsprint banners advertising the homecoming dance.

The din was numbing, except for a zone of stillness surrounding a short, undernourished girl who was slowly dialing her locker combination just outside Leila's classroom. Her frizzy red hair appeared unconstrained by the laws of gravity; her black-rimmed eyes told of a long string of late nights; and her black dress, beginning mid-chest and ending mid-thigh, looked scarcely big enough for a third grader. But for the overstuffed book bag slung over her right shoulder, she looked like an underage streetwalker fallen on hard times.

"Sadie," he called.

She turned a wary face toward him. Her features were delicate and rather pretty, although an excessively free hand with cosmetics had veiled their charms. At odds with her slutty appearance was an air of wanting to escape notice. Yet, at the sight of him, she brightened slightly.

"Got a minute? Ms. Henningsen would like a chat."

She followed him into the classroom and approached the cluster of tables where Leila was sitting. Peter busied himself arranging his supplies at the opposite end of the room. He caught only the occasional word or phrase of their murmured conversation. Glancing over surreptitiously, he saw Sadie nod or shake her head as Leila's voice went lower and lower, more and more quietly emphatic. At last Sadie shrugged, as a fracas erupted on the other side of the door.

He decided to check it out, closing the door behind him so Leila could continue trying to sell Sadie on her own salvation undisturbed. In the hallway, a portly couple in matching school sweatshirts were yelling furiously at a trollopy thin woman in a black leather miniskirt, fishnet tights and black leather spike-heel boots, a revealing purple top with exaggerated shoulders, and white sunglasses. The thin woman, none other than Laudie Norrell, was giving as good as she was getting, and Peter feared one side was about to take a swing at the other. An assistant principal was trying to sort things out and being roundly ignored. Pretty Kelly Flaherty, the couple's fifteen-year-old daughter, a cheerleader and member of the homecoming court, stood at their side, her face an amalgam of horror, shame and disbelief. Mrs. Wong, the algebra teacher, broke away from the cluster of students she had been whispering excitedly with and approached Peter.

"They say that woman's trying to pimp out Kelly Flaherty," she said. "Telling her she'll make good money. Can you imagine? Kelly's uncle is my priest!"

"Her parents must be ready to call the cops. If not, somebody should."

"I think they're on the way."

Indeed, at that moment a siren, winding down to a stop, was faintly audible in the parking lot beyond the exit, and seconds later a uniformed police officer strode down the hall as the students witnessing the exchange stood aghast.

"Excuse me," said Peter. "Mrs. Wong, would you let me know how this turns out? I'll be in Ms. Henningsen's classroom."

Knowing they hadn't much time, Peter immediately approached the table where Leila was still coaxing the skeptical-looking Sadie and squatted beside her.

"Sadie, there's a problem outside that involves your mother, and I think you're going to want a place to stay tonight."

"If that's true, Sadie," said Leila, "you're coming home with me. What's going on?"

"It seems Sadie's mom's trying to recruit one of her classmates for a prostitution venture. Neither the young lady nor her parents is thrilled. The police are here. I doubt Sadie's mom will be, much longer."

Sadie put her forehead down on the table. "How could she do this to me again?"

"Has she talked about involving you in—in sex work?" Leila asked.

"Sure, but she'd prefer girls with bigger tits. Is it Kelly?"

"Why, has she talked about Kelly before?"

"She...noticed her the other day."

Peter smiled sadly. "This is your chance to escape, Sadie. Leila's told you what we're going to do, provided you agree. We can see that you get a chance to finish your education and, more importantly, that you always have a safe place to come home to and people who care about you. You'll be far away from here. But you'd have to be willing to keep a distance from your mother, at least till you're legally an adult. No matter how awful she's been, that might be harder than you think."

"If I don't want to do that—?"

"Unfortunately, then it'll be out of our hands. You've been in foster care, right?" Peter asked. Sadie nodded. "Ever been in a group home?" She shook her head. "It'd probably be an improvement over your current situation, but—"

"You don't have to paint me a picture," Sadie said. "I've heard about them."

"Then will you—"

Mrs. Wong entered the room, waving her hands, speaking breathlessly. "The police just took Sadie's mom away. She was punching and kicking them, so I think there's going to be a resisting charge along with the—uh—sex trafficking thing. Maybe child endangerment, too."

Sadie stood up. "Let's go. I want to go right now. Is there a different exit or do we have to go past them all?"

Peter smiled. "Good girl. Let's sneak down to the other end of the hall and go out the door by the counseling offices."

"I'll lock up and be right behind you," said Leila.

※

November 4, 1995, 10:20 a.m.

The juvenile court, Judge Desmond Riordan, was the same one Sadie had appeared in front of on her petty theft cases, but he explained to her this proceeding was different. "This isn't about anything you did, Sadie, unlike delinquency court, where you and I've seen each other before; now I'm sitting as a dependency court, which is for kids whose parents aren't able to take care of them. Same judge, different statutes, different considerations. I have in front of me a petition for guardianship filed by Peter Blake and Leila Hennig—Henningsen?"

Leila's lawyer friend rose. "Sally Hartford on behalf of petitioners. Yes, Your Honor. Mother, who's in custody awaiting trial on various charges, has filed a stipulation to the guardianship."

"While we're at it, can we have the rest of the appearances, for the record?"

One by one the attorneys stood. "Martine Eldridge, Deputy County Counsel."

"Amanda Serrano for mother, Lauds Mary Norrell."

"Okay, so what are the charges?" Judge Riordan asked, thumbing through the file.

"Resisting arrest and procuring a child, PC 266j."

"And what kind of time is she looking at?"

"The midterm on the procuring is six years; three, six, eight. We have no information at this point about any possible plea deals."

"Is mother here today?"

"She was noticed but declined transportation."

"Hmm," said Judge Riordan. "Ms. Serrano?"

Amanda Serrano stood again. "Mother acknowledges she's unable to care for the minor until her criminal case is resolved, and given there are no close relatives she agrees the proposed guardianship is in the minor's best interests."

"And does she stipulate to the protective order the guardians are asking for?"

Ms. Serrano pursed her lips. "No, Your Honor. Our position is that it's excessive. That mother should be permitted to write and phone the minor, and visit when she gets out of custody."

"The court's inclined to issue the protective order, but I'd like to hear from the social worker."

The court clerk administered the oath, and Jessamyn Janeway took the stand. Under direct examination by county counsel, she began to recite the bare facts of Sadie's life to date. Born to a fifteen-year-old Laudie; father not identified, but possibly a soldier who died in the invasion of Grenada; maternal grandparents long out of the picture following allegations the grandfather sexually molested mother; lengthy criminal history on mother's part, escalating from shoplifting to drug dealing and many other offenses, culminating in a prior prison term during which Sadie was placed with a foster family for a year.

"The court would like to hear a little more about how that went," Judge Riordan interrupted.

Janeway nodded. "When Sadie was nine, mother was convicted of grand theft and Sadie was placed with Mr. and Mrs. MacRae. Her adjustment was rocky at first, but she appeared to be thriving when mother was paroled to a halfway house and a visitation schedule was started. Within weeks minor was asking to leave the foster family and resume living with mother. Based on minor's strong preference, and against my better judgment at the time, I went along with termination of the placement."

"That's not really how it went," Sadie interjected. "I loved the—"

"I'll give you a chance, too," said Judge Riordan. "Let's let Ms. Janeway finish her report."

"Since that reunification, mother's criminal involvement has continued, but until now she's managed to stay out of custody. Our office has received numerous calls from concerned neighbors and regarding possible abuse—of Sadie by mother and mother's boyfriends; also of mother by the boyfriends. Laudie simply can't or won't protect Sadie."

County counsel Eldridge pressed on. "Can you describe the most recent report of abuse—that is, tell the court basically why we're here today."

"On Monday the 30th, I received a call from Ms. Henningsen."

"Objection, we're getting into hearsay," Serrano said.

"If counsel prefers, I'll call Ms. Henningsen to the stand," said Eldridge.

"Since your client stipulated to the guardianship, I'm going to allow the testimony, at least until it's clear where we're going with this," Judge Riordan said. "Proceed."

"Ms. Henningsen advised that, in some nominally fictional writing assignments in class, Sadie disclosed that she'd been raped repeatedly and, as a result, had been infected with sexually transmitted diseases. And that she'd also become pregnant but had miscarried and required medical treatment. Sadie later confirmed to Ms. Henningsen that these experiences in fact happened to her."

"And where did the rapes occur?"

"In her mother's trailer home. By a meth customer waiting to make his purchase. Sadie added that she'd been fondled many times by other men in her mother's residence, that she had access to alcohol and drugs, and that both her mother and visitors to the residence possessed weapons. Knives as well as firearms of various kinds. Ms. Henningsen said that, prior to these disclosures, she and a co-teacher, Mr. Blake, had been contemplating seeking guardianship because it appeared Sadie wasn't being cared for. They went ahead and filed the petition immediately after mother was arrested on the current charges."

"Ms. Serrano, cross-examine?"

Amanda Serrano stood, flogging her palm with a pen. "When you say it appeared Sadie wasn't being cared for—?"

"She indicated Sadie seemed poorly nourished and not to be getting adequate rest, that she was having to steal to meet her basic needs."

Judge Riordan was growing uncharacteristically disturbed. "The court's beginning to see Sadie's delinquency proceedings in a whole new light. All right, Sadie. It's your turn. To expedite this, the court will be doing some questioning on its own, and then I'll let the parties follow up if they need to. Will the clerk please swear the minor." Sadie promised to tell the truth and took the seat next to the bench in the witness box that the social worker had just vacated.

"Now, first of all, Sadie, how would you feel if the court were to make Mr. Blake and Ms. Henningsen your guardians? They, and not your mother, would then be responsible for making decisions about your life until you turn eighteen."

"I trust them. It's cool."

"Good. Second, I sense you'd like to correct some of what Ms. Janeway said earlier."

"Okay, well, first off, she implied that I wanted to live with Laudie, that I didn't want to stay with the MacRaes. That wasn't it at all. I loved Mama and Papa MacRae. I wanted them to adopt me. But Laudie was playing a game. She acted like she wanted Mr. MacRae, and he got stupid. She would have torn them apart. I had to get out of there so she'd leave him alone. The only thing I could think of was to say I wanted to live with her. But I didn't."

Judge Riordan pondered. Amanda Serrano stood up, as if to question Sadie, but the judge waved a hand and she resumed her seat. "When you say Mr. MacRae got stupid, what do you mean?" he asked.

"I don't want to say anything bad about him. He was like a real dad to me, even if only for a while."

"I understand your reservations, Sadie, but I'm afraid I need a clear record. He thought Laudie was seriously interested in him, and would have allowed his feelings for her to break up his family?"

Serrano objected weakly. Judge Riordan overruled her.

"Yes. I tried to tell him what she was up to. He got mad at me, the only time he ever did."

"You were how old at the time?" the judge asked.

"Nine. Now I see now how impertinent I was; I don't blame him. The other thing is that I wasn't raped. The guy was sort of like my boyfriend."

The judge closed his eyes and rubbed his forehead. "I'm glad you didn't feel forced, but—how old was he?"

"Twenty-eight, I think."

"Okay, you were what's sometimes called jail bait, and he was more than twice your age. You understand what I'm getting at. Unless there's cross-examination, I'm prepared to rule."

Sensing there was nothing she could accomplish, Amanda Serrano stayed in her seat and shook her head.

"The court finds it in Sadie's best interests that the petition for guardianship be, and it hereby is, granted, and Mr. Blake and Ms. Henningsen are appointed as co-guardians. The application for a protective order is granted. Mother's to have no contact with minor. Ms. Serrano, you're ordered to inform your client. Sadie, I'd just like to say I'm sorry. The court hereby dismisses on its own motion the wardship petition, number... Miss Clerk, could you look up the number? What this means, Sadie, is that you're no longer under my jurisdiction as a delinquent. But I'll expect annual status reports from your guardians, as required by law, and I look forward to hearing about all the good things that are going to be coming your way in the days and years ahead. Stop by and say hi if you're ever in in the neighborhood, okay? The court is now in recess."

Chapter Four

August 20, 2014, 3:30 p.m.

As soon as the judicial assistant nodded to go ahead, Lucas rapped on the doorjamb and proceeded into Justice Allan Hetford's chambers. "Got a minute, Judge?" he asked, approaching the enormous mahogany desk behind which Hetford sat playing with a cigar. Seeing Ward Freitag, the court administrator, sitting in one of the guest chairs in front of the desk, Lucas stopped. "Sorry to interrupt; Tracy told me to come in. I'll come back when you're free."

"Not at all, Lucas. Ward and I were just shooting the breeze. What can I do for you? Is this about *Amar*?"

Lucas took the other guest chair. "No, not *Amar*; I'm still working on the judge. See, it's like this: I find myself in a bit of a dilemma and was hoping for some advice."

"And you came to me instead of your boss?" Hetford asked.

"My dilemma sort of involves him."

"You intrigue me. Sit, and do tell."

"First," said Lucas, getting up and backing toward the door, "may I shut this?"

"Now you're really starting to intrigue me."

Lucas shut the door and sat down again. "Yes. I don't want this going any further than the three of us, if at all possible. It's highly sensitive."

Freitag cleared his throat. "I take it this is a confidential personnel matter?"

"Oh, boy, is it. So, the other night—it was the night I came up to see you about...the other matter, Judge—I was here late. It was the same day Justice Quirke finally decided to put in his election papers, and he'd had a little celebration in chambers and invited the staff to the Inns to continue it. I didn't go with them; I had too much work to do. When I went back down to our area on the third floor after being up here talking with you, Judge, the light was on in Justice Quirke's chambers. I heard some distinctive sounds coming from the sofa area."

"You're going to have to be more specific," said Hetford. " 'Distinctive' covers a lot of ground."

"Well, not to be too indelicate, they were sounds of an amorous nature."

Hetford hooted. "I'm not asking for a demonstration, but how could you tell? The walls are pretty thick in this old building. Unless—"

"As luck would have it, someone forgot to shut the door, and—"

"And so, you were confronted with the spectacle as you exited the stairwell?"

"Exactly."

"And I take it the other party to this little frolic was one of our colleagues?"

"It was. Staff, of course," Lucas hastened to add, lest they suppose it might have been the Chief Justice or Justice Wiggins cavorting with Quirke.

Hetford whistled, moving the cigar up and down in the circle of his left thumb and forefinger. "Oh my. Quirke shtupping his secretary? One is inclined to be outraged."

"No, no, no, no, no. It was one of my fellow staff attorneys. I'd prefer not to identify the party in the interests of privacy."

"Oh, come on, Lucas. It's not like we can't figure it out by process of elimination. I very much doubt John Hendershott would have any sexual interest in your mutual boss, and Quirke's not really Freddie Osorio's type, so that leaves...that odd little person, Sadie what's her-name. Dresses like a witch. I keep looking for her broomstick in the garage."

"Norrell. Sadie Norrell."

Hetford and Freitag mulled over this piece of intelligence.

"The thing is, I'd just taken the sexual harassment training, and it seemed prudent to ascertain whether there was anything coercive going on. On the face of it, I couldn't be sure."

"No cries for help or anything like that?"

"Not really, but he was practically smothering her—and she's so tiny anyway—it wasn't clear to me she would have been able to summon help in any case. You understand, it was the totality of the circumstances—the location, the hour, the fact they'd been out drinking—"

"I'm reliably informed Quirke has a pretty serious habit, by the way," Hetford interjected, looking at Freitag.

"So, I lingered for a second in the interest of eliminating the ambiguity, one way or the other. And in fact, I'm sure she said 'Stop,' or 'Wait,' or something like that. But at just that moment they seemed to become conscious of my presence and, like, froze, and so I merely memorialized the scene and went to my office and turned on the light. I waited there a while in case she wanted my help, but soon after that I heard them leave."

"When you say you memorialized it, you mean—"

"I took a photo."

"So, as it stands you have—"

"Justice Quirke *in flagrante delicto*.   On the Samsung," he concluded, patting his pants pocket.

"If I were you, Lucas, I wouldn't share that with anyone just yet," said Hetford.

"Should I get rid of it?"

"I didn't say get rid of it.   I'd never advise destroying evidence. Just...keep it to yourself for now.   Have you talked to Ms. Norrell since then?"

"Not about that. It's a rather awkward subject, you know."

"There are no awkward subjects, only awkward conversations. But, so, in other words, you have sufficient compunction not to interrogate her about the encounter, but not enough to have refrained from snapping a picture of their intimate moment in the first place?"

"I'm sorry. I know there's arguably something creepy about what I did. I regret it very much if my thinking was off; I was only trying to protect everyone's interests, including the court's. That's why I'm here telling you about it: I just want to do the right thing."

"I'm only playing devil's advocate," Hetford said.   "No one's accusing you of acting badly.   On the contrary, you've shown exceptional presence of mind. Thank you for telling Freitag and me; you were quite correct to do so. But remember what I said: Keep it close."

"Should I try to talk with her?"

"If she approaches you, then yes, of course, and then immediately let Ward or me know; otherwise, I'd say nothing at this point."

"Should I say anything to Justice Quirke?"

"Leave that to me," said Freitag.

"Thanks for your good counsel," said Lucas, rising. "It's a real load off my mind."

"It's I—we—that is, the court—who ought to thank you. Better to learn about this kind of thing before getting served with the sexual harassment complaint than after.   Of course, for the court's sake we certainly hope it never comes to that. Would you close that on your way out? Thank you, Lucas."

When they were alone again, Hetford whistled. "Well, well. Now that's one of the odder couplings one could possibly imagine around here. And you know who Mrs. Quirke is."

Freitag nodded. "Her father's Eugene Scorchner, one of the more socially prominent local billionaires."

"That may exaggerate his wealth slightly, but yes, he's quite well off."

"What else do you know about her?"

"She's a charming woman who's put up with a hell of a lot from our quirky colleague, and I quite like her. I needn't tell you that little jpg Lucas is running around with could be quite useful. I was talking with Stan the other day—"

"The Governor?"

"He'd like to be able to make another appointment before the end of his term. This court's heading in the right direction, and his kind of appointee would go a long way toward keeping us on track."

"But Quirke just put in his papers."

"And now his fate's in the electorate's hands. Do you see where I'm going?"

Freitag involuntarily pursed his lips.

"Well, one can hope to take the high road, but we'd better prepare in case we wind up going the other way."

※

August 20, 2:55 p.m.

"Come on," said Freddie, popping his head in Sadie's office on a slow midafternoon. "You need a break from that sentence credit case, and I need a bubble tea. My treat."

Sadie pushed herself away from her desk with a sigh, draped her sweater over her shoulders, and started down the corridor to the elevator with Freddie. "Gladly. I'm ready to tear my hair out. I just don't see the votes for the right result."

"You never know till you circulate it, though, right? But in the same vein, unfortunately, I think we're going to be giving up the *Marquez* case."

"Damn. So, Wiggins flipped?"

"Yup. Judge is going to be annoyed. Her attorney tells me Wiggins got lobbied hard by the author of the dissenting calendar memo. Which I guess is now about to become the majority calendar memo."

"I'm beginning to totally share the boss's opinion of that guy."

"Oily as he seems, to me anyway, Hetford's apparently pretty persuasive when he wants to be." As they were then passing within earshot of Justice Wiggins's chambers, they fell silent until they had left the building and were crossing the street to Sweetly Tea.

"Speaking of the boss, what's going on with you and Quirke?"

Sadie halted, wide-eyed, in the middle of the street, oblivious of the traffic light, which was just then turning red. Freddie threw an arm around her shoulders and hustled her to the sidewalk opposite. They then continued at a more relaxed pace into Sweetly Tea and got in line.

"Don't ever do that to me again, please. I'd never be able to explain letting you get run over on the way to the tea shop. Here, let me get it. What do you want?"

"Lychee milk with pearls. Thanks."

"And a red Thai for me: a nice fat-, caffeine-, sugar-, and artificial-coloring-rich afternoon pick-me-up. Now come sit over here and tell Uncle Freddie what exactly is going on." They took a table in the corner farthest from the door.

Sadie shook her head. "What do you mean, what's going on? What makes you think there's something going on?"

"Look, I'm not blind—I know you've always had a mad crush on him. But something's changed in the last few days. Unless I'm wildly mistaken—and I'm not—lately he's been doing everything possible, short of quarantine, to avoid being in the same room with you. And when you two are in the same room, I can't help noticing he breaks out into a sweat and keeps his eyes on you as if you were a time bomb he desperately wants to figure out how to get close to without being blown up, something life-threatening and highly desirable at the same time."

"What an amazing imagination you have. If only there were something to what you're saying."

"You're hurting my feelings, girlfriend. You know you can trust me. Something this huge, you must need to talk about it."

The waitress brought their teas, Sadie's milky pale, Freddie's an alarming flame color. Sadie sighed again and began to stir the black pearls around the bottom of her cup with the fat straw.

"I'm sorry. I know you're trustworthy. The actual fact is I have no idea what's going on—he hasn't said a word to me since the night of our little celebration last week. And as you seem to have discerned, I'm going out of my mind wanting to... well, I suppose I'd better tell you everything." She fortified herself with a sip of tea and sucked a boba up into the straw, chewing on it pensively. "So that night we stayed at the Inns for a little while after John went home. Just talking. It was so good being with him. Before that night I don't think we'd ever really had a personal conversation, even though, as you seem to know all too well, I've adored him forever. But then he wanted to leave. Well, I...basically I didn't want to say goodbye to him. So, we came back to chambers. Long story short, he was pretty blitzed by then, I was a bit buzzed myself, and we were starting to, well, act on feelings of mutual attraction, snogging and so forth and so on—in fact, he'd just relieved me of my unmentionables—"

"Oh my," Freddie gasped.

"—when we heard a noise and saw something flash in the doorway."

"You didn't—"

"Yes, I'm afraid I did. I can't believe I was stupid enough to leave the door wide open while the judge and I were on the point of making love, but I was. I mean I did. I could just kill myself. But I wasn't premeditating anything—I swear!—and, you know, things started happening pretty fast, or of course I'd have gotten up and shut it. Plus, who knew that odious little creep would be prowling around, much less that he'd be playing paparazzi at that hour?"

"Who? You mean—"

"Lucas. Our reputations are now in his smarmy little hands."

Freddie knit his brow. "This isn't good."

"You're telling me."

"I mean, who cares if people think you're a slut, but the judge has a retention election to think of."

"That's nice of you, Freddie."

"Kidding, of course. But listen, it's unthinkable Lucas would use that picture. Not even he would stoop that low."

"You're probably right. I hope you're right. It would take the morals of a hyena to..." She shuddered at the thought.

"So, what happened after that?"

"Well, as you might imagine, it kind of dampened the mood for both of us. We put our clothes back on and left. He'd been saying, over and over, he didn't want to go home, so I invited him to stay with me. But he declined, politely and gently, so I put him in a cab and sent him on his way. Freddie, it took every ounce of self-restraint I had not to follow him."

"Why?"

"I'm not sure. You've never seen him so...vulnerable, so sad. He might just be one of these melancholy drunks, I don't know, but my heart was breaking to say goodnight."

"Are you in love with him?"

She lowered her eyes for a moment. "I've tried not to be; it makes everything so complicated. But...yes, hopelessly."

"Okay. And it's painfully obvious how he feels about you, so—when's the wedding?"

"For fuck's sake, Freddie, he isn't even speaking to me. And then there's that little technicality: The judge is already married! To a woman scary enough to be the reason, I'm sure, why he didn't want to go home that night in the first place. Not to mention he doesn't know the first thing about me, and do you really suppose once he does he won't want to run the other way?"

"Give the man a little more credit than that. And yourself."

"And, furthermore, I don't particularly want to find a new job. I like this job. Most law jobs suck."

"One step at a time, honey. Love sorts everything out."

※

August 21, 1:30 p.m.

"Hi, Judge. Margie said you wanted to see me?"

"Thanks, John. Shut the door, would you? Don't worry, it's nothing bad. I just need your help with something."

John Hendershott complied and sat down, at Quirke's gesture, across the conference table where they'd recently celebrated the judge's electoral announcement. An untouched sandwich and a can of Diet Coke at his elbow, Quirke was looking edgy and exhausted.

"OK, here's the deal: I need you to review Sadie's work before she turns it in to me. All her memos, draft opinions, and so forth. I realize you already have too many things to do, and I apologize for commandeering more of your time, but I wouldn't ask if it weren't important."

Having anticipated something more along the lines of a directive to write a dissent in *Amar*, John sat processing Quirke's request for a moment. Then he asked, "I'm not aware of any deficiencies in Sadie's work, Judge. Is there anything specific? Am I supposed to be looking for some particular problem?"

"Not at all, no. I love Sadie's work. I've always loved her work. She's great." Quirke mopped his brow with a handkerchief, pulled at his collar, and put his hands, which had begun to tremble slightly, under the conference table.

"And anyway, wouldn't Lucas be the more logical person to—"

"No, no, no. No. He's got a lot on his plate, and I don't want to interfere with his getting the *Jackson Jones* memo done. The judgment in that case dates back to the mid-eighties, and we need to set it for argument before the guy dies of old age on death row. The court gets a lot of criticism for delays in capital cases, you know."

"Sure, but...well, if you want me to look over Sadie's work, of course I will. Have you told her about this?"

"Not yet, but I will. Probably today. Definitely today. Well, thanks very much, John. This is tremendously helpful. Sorry to hit you with the extra work, and I appreciate everything you do."

"No worries. Did you want me to send Sadie in?"

Quirke paled. "What for?"

"So, you can let her know?"

"No, not right now. I need to get ready for conference. I'll see her later, and thanks again."

Alone once more, Quirke sipped his Diet Coke, wondering if the caffeine were contributing to the jitters he was feeling. In the five days since the Inns and his encounter with Sadie in the office, he'd been stone sober—his longest period of abstinence, as far as he could recall, since reaching the age of majority—and his initial assessment was that sobriety wasn't all it was cracked up to be. He was sweating constantly, his head hurt worse than it had most mornings when he was drinking, the thought of food disgusted him, and his sleep patterns were a jangled mess. Still, as unpleasant as the withdrawal process was, he was frightened enough to think that drying out, on a trial basis anyway, might be indicated. He had never gotten drunk with, much less tried to make love to, any member of his staff, and he wondered if after all those years of abuse, alcohol had finally destroyed his better judgment. And, too, there was the nagging worry that, in having the phenomenal luck to pass by the doorway at the very moment he was tearing Sadie's clothes off, Lucas had succeeded in taking a recognizable photo of the two of them and was even now putting it to some ruinous use.

But his overarching concern was that he could not put two thoughts in sequence without Sadie being at least one of them. He found himself constantly distracted by her face, almost hallucinatory in intensity, in his mind's eye; he felt continually the memory of her smooth, warm flesh; and he mentally rehearsed, in an endless loop, all the jokes, observations, ripostes and clever thoughts he longed to share with her. When he opened his mouth, however, such thoroughly tossed word salad emerged that he dared not speak to her for fear she would see what a basket case he had become and turn away repulsed. And not only she, but his colleagues and the rest of his staff, must doubtless be thinking he'd developed a wet brain—those who hadn't already thought he had one, that is.

As for his home life, an eerie quiet had descended. That fateful night, after saying goodbye to Sadie—were those really tears in her eyes? Could she possibly care that much about him?—he'd directed the cabbie down to the waterfront. There, while tourists eddied around him, laughing and enjoying themselves, and neon reflections from the garish shops danced on the waves in front of him, he sat on a bench until midnight, growing soberer and more despondent with each passing hour. Finally, after the fog had insinuated itself into every hole and corner, and the last tourists and even the mimes and street musicians had sought shelter for the night, he rose, stiff and cold, and made his way up the hill to the marital tomb he shared with Eleanor.

She was out, as he then recalled she'd said that morning she would be. Giving wordless thanks at not having to make contact with her, he fell into bed and a disordered sleep. In the morning, she was gone before he rose, and in the succeeding days he caught only fleeting glimpses of her, if she were on the premises at all. His relief at her absence was commingled with a growing apprehension that she might be planning some cruel and novel punishment for him. He scarcely dared hope she merely intended to make this silent coexistence the new normal *chez* Quirke.

At the court, his staff all seemed to have agreed, tacitly or otherwise, to pretend nothing had changed. Lucas, for his part, betrayed no sign of having seen anything untoward, likely because he was less than proud of having spied on them. John was apparently still in the dark, judging from his reaction to Quirke's request concerning Sadie's work, but if he had any suspicions he was gentleman enough to keep them to himself. Darling Sadie kept trying to catch his eye, no doubt to tell him, with complete justification, what a jerk he'd been but, he fervently hoped, not to inform him she was planning to sue. Or worse, quit. He assumed she'd confided in Freddie because they were such close friends, but Freddie, ever the soul of discretion, said nothing and only cast him a sympathetic look now and then.

The day after the near seduction, he realized he'd lost all objectivity where Sadie was concerned, and with it any ability to intelligently review her work, when he became convinced a six-page memo she'd written on the topic of sentence credits under Penal Code section 4022.9, subdivision (g), was the most profoundly brilliant piece of legal scholarship since Hale's *Pleas of the Crown*. Even in his besotted state he could see this was improbable. He trusted her work and she had never disappointed him, but he knew he needed a clearer head to vet it before he could circulate it to his colleagues. He prayed she'd understand. John was of course right that he should tell her about their arrangement, and Quirke knew he also had to tell her why it was necessary. That, however, would mean essentially declaring his love for her, and he was terrified of how she'd react. And so, he put it off, thinking the right words would surely reveal themselves.

He awoke to a gentle pressure on his shoulder, and instantly sat up, peeling his right cheek off the pile of conference memos in front of him. Sadie was standing at his side, a quizzical smile on her face.

"I'm sorry, Judge. I thought you might want to be awakened, since the door's open. Would you like me to shut it?"

"Oh my God, yes. Please. Haven't been sleeping very well lately."

Once she'd thus ensured their privacy, she sat next to him at the table and pulled her chair close. "I'd give anything to have remembered to do that the other night," she said ruefully.

"Sadie," he began. "Sadie, I..."

"Yes, Conal?"

He was taken aback. "Nobody except my mom has ever called me Conal."

"Would you rather I called you something else? I'd never do it in front of anyone else, of course, but 'Judge' seems a bit formal under the circumstances, and I can't call you 'Quirke'; it's too...dismissive."

"Please do. I need someone to call me by my name."

She clasped his hand. "How are you feeling?"

"Okay, I guess. I'm on a new regimen—haven't had a drop to drink since that night." He reconsidered. If there was even a slim prospect of a relationship with this adorable woman, it would have to be founded on honesty. "Actually, I'm not okay. I'm far from okay. In fact, between this DIY detoxing and being unable to get you out of my head, I'm a complete wreck. It's pretty obvious, I imagine, only everyone's too well-trained to say so."

"You don't have to white-knuckle it, you know. Please tell me you'll go see your doctor and follow his advice until you get through this, please? And anyway, why didn't you call me? It's my fault you're in this state. But that sounds so presumptuous—am I mistaken?"

"As far as getting medical advice goes, I'll think about it, but I'm afraid it would only mean a long stretch in rehab. Eleanor's threatened me with it on a few occasions. And this time I wouldn't blame them, but there's a pretty good chance it would torpedo my electoral chances. Can't you just see the headline: 'Supreme Court Justice Seeks Treatment for Alcohol Dependency and Your Vote on November 4th.' Is it your fault? No, you're not the cause of my being a mess. Actually, yes, I think you are responsible. I don't mean that in a blaming way. But without you I'd still be—what am I saying, 'without you'? As if I have you in some sense. If only. I should say, before you woke me up to what I was becoming. Or what I hope not to be becoming. God, I sound like day one of an ESL class. This is what I was talking about, Sadie, this helpless incoherence I'm experiencing. What I'm trying to say is, before I realized how much you mean to me, I didn't even know I was barely alive. Now that I know it, I...I'm exhilarated and terrified at the same time. Something real is happening here. Something's tearing me apart and trying to remake me. I don't know where it's going, and I can't think of a reason not to just let it happen if you're a part of it somehow. Please don't tell me you won't be, unless—unless I was mistaken the other night and you don't want it."

"You're right, it's real. I do want it, I want you, more than anything." She put her arms over his shoulders and kissed him in proof, at last saying: "We don't need to figure it all out yet."

Tingling everywhere she'd touched him, Quirke tried to catch his breath. "Dearest, I need to figure something out before I lose it completely here. To the extent you could say I ever had it, that is. You can see I'm barely functioning. How in hell am I going to get through oral argument next week? Can you picture me asking intelligible questions in the multistate tax compact case? Just putting two coherent words together is a challenge, let alone making some kind of sense about apportionment formulas and the Contracts Clause."

"As the police officer said, you have the right to remain silent. Well, it works for Clarence Thomas."

His smile gave way to a frown. "That reminds me of something I need to tell you. Please don't hate me."

"There's no danger of that."

"I've asked John to look over your work."

"—Because—?"

"Because my ability to judge it went out the window when I fell in love with you. I never really understood what a conflict of interest is until now. Maybe I'll regain my capacity for rational thought at some point, and we can go back to doing things the way we did them before. But right now, I can't imagine anything being as it was before."

She began to stroke his thigh, making his heart pound. "I don't in the least mind having John edit me," she said, "but it's not a realistic long-term strategy. My work is your work, and if you can't look at it objectively, well—"

"I know. Believe me, I understand what this means."

"Should I look for a new job?"

"If you leave me, they'll *have* to lock me up. Maybe it's I who should leave. But I can't think that far ahead right now."

"I love you, too, Conal."

Kissing her was the only reply of which he was capable. After a few moments of this sublime contact, Sadie slipped out of his office, leaving Quirke to try to referee the warring factions of hope and terror within his own heart.

Chapter Five

August 21, 4:45 p.m.

After Sadie left his office—he made a mental note to ask her how she managed to stay productive at work if love, for her, felt anything remotely like the mental torture he was now undergoing—Quirke made but stuttering progress in preparing for the following day's petition conference. In light of his ongoing internal upheaval—which made the earth's geomagnetic reversal seem to him trivial by comparison—he was in a distinctly review-denying mood. Thus, he was only too ready to lay aside the pile of memos when, once again, his fitful labors were interrupted by a knock at the door and Ward Freitag's burly form loomed at the threshold.

"Judge, my apologies for intruding. I wonder if you've got a minute."

"Sure, Ward, come on in." From the vertical grooves between the clerk-administrator's eyebrows and the slope of his mouth it appeared Freitag wanted to be anywhere but where he was standing. This did not bode well. "Go ahead and shut the door if you like."

"I think I'll do that, thanks." Freitag moved over to the adjacent seating area and stood scrutinizing, as if searching for trace evidence, the sofa that had lately served as the scene of Quirke's romantic rebirth.

"What can I do for you?" Quirke asked, interposing himself between Freitag and the furniture. "I'm not Acting Chief, am I? Need me to stay something?"

"No, Farley's Acting. You're up next month. I just wanted to chat about a little something I heard the other day."

"Of course, sit down," said Quirke, sprawling on the sofa and motioning Freitag toward the guest chair. "Can I have Margie make some coffee?"

"Only if you're having some yourself. I hate having to bring this up, and there's no easy way to say it, but—"

"Did I fill out my travel voucher wrong again? Maybe I need a remedial class."

"No, your vouchers have been flawless lately. I just think you'd want to know—I would if I were in your position—that rumor has it there's a picture floating around of you and someone on your staff in a rather...compromising position."

"Floating around? Care to elaborate?"

"I can't, as a matter of fact. I haven't seen it. But I'm told it exists."

Quirke closed his eyes and breathed for a few seconds, trying to stop his voice from shaking. "I'm not going to sit here and deny such a thing might exist. But rest assured the court's not going to get sued. Anything that may have happened was one hundred percent consensual."

Freitag smiled sadly. "I had no doubt of that. From a court liability perspective, it's all copacetic. From your own personal perspective, well, I simply note it to you as a contingency you may want to anticipate having to address."

Quirke's chest felt about to explode. "Are you telling me my own head of chambers is going to blackmail me?"

"Not per se, no. I don't think Lucas is of a mind to make anything at all out of this little dalliance or whatever it was."

"That's not what it was," Quirke interjected sharply.

Freitag lifted his eyebrows and drew a deep breath. "If I understand you, then maybe it's even more of a problem than I thought."

"I'm afraid I don't understand *you*. Would you kindly enlighten me?"

"I wish I were at liberty. Let me just say it's possible to imagine channels through which that photo could reach people who'd rather not see you retained in November. People who might not wish you well."

"Look, Ward, if you have any concrete information, I'd appreciate you coming straight out with it. Someone's going to dupe Lucas into turning that picture over to political enemies I don't even know I have, is that it? Or are you saying it's going to wind up in Eleanor's hands and cause her to throw me out the door and blast it all over social media that I'm some kind of drunken adulterer? Of course, that's exactly what I am, I'll plead guilty to that charge, but does anyone really care nowadays about public figures divorcing? Something's not adding up here."

"I wish I could say more. You've always been a breath of fresh air here at the court, and I'd hate to see you out after the election. Or maybe it's that I'd hate to see who might be appointed to replace you. Now I've already said too much, so I'd better get out of here. But before I do, take this," he said, handing Quirke a business card. "Give this guy a call and tell him I sent you."

" 'Bobby James, Elections Consultant?' "

"He's saved more than a few judges' bacon in his time. Good luck, Quirke. By the way," Freitag said, reaching for the door handle, "the divorce: is it public?"

Quirke's heart sped up abruptly, leaving him breathless. His saying the word had made the prospect suddenly inevitable, and he hadn't made any sort of plan. An exhilarated fear gripped him, and he floated off the sofa and began to pace. "She doesn't know yet."

Freitag gave a half-smile and patted him on the back. "It won't be easy, but no doubt it's for the best. If you don't already have an attorney, I can recommend Mary Jane Lewis—she did my last divorce. I have her card somewhere. And come on by if you ever need moral support. I've been there."

"Thanks, Ward. I appreciate it."

For the first time in days, Quirke managed to focus his whole attention on something other than Sadie: Freitag's implications. The clerk-administrator, who, as the public face of the court and an old hand in the judicial branch, was acquainted to one degree or another with everyone worth knowing, and who was the repository of many confidences—including, now, Quirke's—was clearly aware something was up. Quirke viewed Ward as a friend—but how good a friend? Not so good as to disclose everything he knew, or that Quirke needed to know; evidently Freitag couldn't risk anything being traced back to him. That meant someone powerful was using him. Someone with leverage over him—or his job. Someone at the court, in all likelihood.

Quirke knew full well his colleagues saw him as something of an eccentric, a throwback to the court's liberal glory days, and that irritated ultraconservatives like Kroner. And Farley. And Hetford. The bloc, as everyone else called them, in recognition of how they tended to vote on cases. Kroner's term was up, so he too would be on the November ballot, but since the vote would be a simple up or down—they weren't running against each other—there would be no benefit to him in trying to ruin Quirke. Besides, although never known to reverse a death sentence, certify a class action, or rule in favor of a sex offender or against an insurance company, Kroner was personally a decent sort, soft-spoken and generous toward his staff and colleagues, and Quirke had never heard him say an unkind word. No, he just couldn't see Kroner engaging in the kind of Machiavellian intrigue that Freitag had hinted at. Farley? He, too, seemed an unlikely one for dirty work. The Chief had him running himself ragged overseeing the judicial branch's technology projects, including the long-awaited e-filing system that, assuming it was budgeted, and when completed, was going to bring the court right up to the 1990s or so. Quirke thought it unlikely Farley would take time away from his crucial responsibilities to wage a covert campaign against a fellow justice.

That left only Hetford, and clarity suddenly pierced the mental haze of lovesickness and alcoholic withdrawal. Allan Hetford had been a thorn in Quirke's side since his arrival at the court two years previously. Hetford had the Ivy League education and Big Law experience to provide a marginally plausible basis for touting himself as the court's expert in all things civil. He had also served a whole year doing felony trials in superior court before his elevation to the Supreme Court, so from time to time he even imagined he could school the other justices in criminal procedure, even though all (except Quirke, who'd come up through the defense bar) had been prosecutors practically from birth. Hetford asked such long-winded questions at oral argument that lawyers groaned under their breath when he opened his mouth. And, for some reason, Hetford seemed to cherish a specific personal resentment against Quirke, starting from the first opinion he'd authored at the court. In that case—*People v. Worniewicz*—the court construed a statute to reject the defendant's argument that he was entitled to three days' more presentence custody credit against his prison term than the trial court had granted him. Not the sort of issue, one might assume, that would pit jurist irreconcilably against brother jurist, but when Quirke wrote a dissent that peeled off two other justices who'd been with Hetford, almost costing him the majority, Hetford seemed to lose all perspective. He'd initiated a volley of internal memoranda so sarcastic and vituperative in tone that Quirke couldn't simply ignore them; gone around personally lobbying the defectors, plying them with fulsome flattery and attempting the grossest sort of horse-trading; and went so far as to storm out of the postargument conference when the dissenters refused to acknowledge the superior force of his reasoning. The other justices chalked it up to teething troubles but, ever since, Quirke had been a little afraid of Hetford. And now, perhaps, Hetford was taking his revenge.

Quirke turned this possibility over in his mind for some time, but ultimately decided no one, not even Hetford, could be so small-minded as to work to unseat him over a trivial thing like the *Worniewicz* dissent. So, if it was Hetford who was behind this threat, he had to have a darker and weightier motive. This would bear further reflection, but it was after five o'clock and Quirke's brain simply wasn't up to it.

He looked down the hallway to the attorneys' offices. All dark. A pang of disappointment shot through him at seeing that Sadie had left without saying good night. He headed toward the elevator.

When the door slid open at the second floor, an old Court of Appeal buddy of his, Justice Howard Latimore, got in. Latimore had something of a temper, and it had always been fun to see him take apart ill-prepared lawyers during oral argument. He was also almost as fond of his whiskey as Quirke, who sighed to think of the many times they'd headed over to the Inns after a long day.

"Justice Quirke! What's up? Haven't seen you leaving the shop this early in years. You all must stay late thinking of ways to reverse us."

"Only when you publish your mistakes. How've you been? What's the latest news at the CA?"

"You know Jan's retiring, right? Justice Bothwell?"

"No, I hadn't heard. What's she planning to do?"

"She's going to study painting in Florence."

"Italy?"

"No, South Carolina. Yeah, Italy."

"Sorry, Howie. I've been feeling a little exhausted lately."

"No kidding. You look like you could use a long vacation."

"Maybe after next month's calendar."

"How about a quick nip for old time's sake? I'll bet you've been working way too hard to stop by the Inns lately."

Every fiber of Quirke's being sang with the prospect of a whiskey sour, while the sacrifices of the past five days reproached him for even thinking of it. But there was no real contest.

"Come on," he said, leading the way.

※

The first half of the second double had Quirke feeling tiptop again. The Inns were their familiar, spiritually nourishing self, the semi-aphasia of the last few days had lifted, and life seemed once more worth living, even navigable. But this time he was going to drink responsibly. He was going to stop at two double whiskey sours.

Latimore was already starting to make his farewell. "Quirke, it's been great to see you, but I should really be heading home. Alice's sister's visiting, and if I don't make a decently timely appearance there'll be hell to pay."

"You can't leave yet, Howie; you said yourself I don't get out enough. Well, here you can help me fix that. And we've just gotten started. I haven't even had the chance to ask whether you're on the ballot this November."

"No, thank God, that was last time. Got seventy-one percent of the vote," he said, proudly.

"That's pretty good, I suppose. You know, I'm up this time."

"So you are, aren't you? Well, best of luck. At least it's not a presidential election year, and there's no monster proposition on the ballot, so the fringe elements will probably stay home."

"Is that good?"

"Some might disagree, but in my opinion judicial elections aren't the kind of thing that ought to be decided by the occasional voter who's galvanized by a high-profile cause. You know, like tax reform or the three strikes law or abolishing the death penalty. I haven't done a study or anything, but my suspicion is that the less activism incited by the contest overall, the better we—judges—do."

"Interesting theory. Let me buy you another bourbon," Quirke urged. "I want to hear all about it, and your winning strategy."

"I'll take you up on that offer next time I see you," Latimore answered. "We really should do this more often." He stood, gathering his balmacaan and briefcase, and pushed his chair close to the table. "You know, Quirke, you're missed in the CA. There's nobody quite as delightfully wicked as you."

"Coming from you, Howie, that's high praise. Well, if you won't let me corrupt you, then be sure and say hi to Alice for me."

"You bet. And a word of advice: take it easy until you can escape for a couple of weeks. Get Eleanor to take you to Aruba or someplace like that after oral argument next month."

"Excellent idea. See you, Howie."

As Latimore made his way out the door, Quirke's mood took a nosedive. Leaving Latimore with the impression there was the remotest chance he and Eleanor would ever holiday together again made him feel morally filthy, but it was the wrong time to unburden himself to his former CA colleague. And if he kept on telling his acquaintances about the divorce before confronting his wife, she was going to hear it from someone else, and that she would never forgive. Perhaps tonight, if she were home for a change, he would talk to her. Get it all out in the open. Well, nearly all: there was no present need to say anything about Sadie, of course. Yes, he would head straight over. He just needed to fortify himself with a little liquid courage before doing the deed. Under ordinary conditions he'd certainly have stuck with his original plan to stop at the second double, but this was a special case, and he simply couldn't face bearding the lioness in her den while enfeebled by sobriety.

So, he stopped after two more doubles, feeling conscientious, and departed the Inns. Standing on the street in the gathering twilight, he didn't need Sadie's blood alcohol calculator to tell him he had better not try to drive home; his car would have to stay overnight in the state building parking garage again. A cab pulled up to the curb without his even having to wave.

"How did you know I wanted a lift?" he asked the driver, a man of Middle Eastern origin named Wakil Abdul-'Adl, according to the ID clipped to the shade on the passenger side, as he got into the back seat.

"I am gifted that way," the man said, tapping his forehead. "Everyone says so. You have the air of a man about to start a long journey, so I am thinking I may as well be the first leg of it. Where are you going?"

"Can you tell if it's going to turn out well?" Quirke asked.

"This leg, perfect. After that, who knows?"

"Fair enough." Quirke named his address, and the man whistled.

"Nice. I get you there. Your house?"

"Last I checked."

The driver pulled into the sparse traffic and turned up Van Vliet Boulevard. Quirke would have enjoyed a traffic jam or any other happenstance that might have postponed his arrival, but they made disconcertingly good time, and the driver pulled up to the gate within five minutes of leaving the Civic Center. Quirke paid the man the flag plus a decent tip.

"Thank you very much, good sir. Shall I wait?"

"No need. Good evening to you."

"Good luck on the rest of your journey, sir," he said with a little salute. Quirke got out of the cab and watched as Wakil made a U-turn and headed toward the Financial District. He wondered idly if Wakil were a good Muslim, and if so whether he was offended at the cloud of alcohol Quirke and many others must exude nightly into the air inside his vehicle.

He typed the security code on the keypad to let himself in, as he did every night, only nothing happened. Thinking he must have mistyped it, he tried again. Still nothing. A third time, slowly, he punched in the numbers. And still the gate stood silently barring his entrance.

Of course, Eleanor must have changed the code—she did that periodically—and forgotten to tell him. He pulled out his mobile phone and called hers, reaching only her voicemail. He ended the call without leaving a message and tried the landline in her room, then the one in the kitchen. Apparently, she was out again tonight, and the housekeeper, too. Had she said anything about the code or where she would be tonight? He suddenly realized he couldn't remember when he'd last seen or spoken with her. The combined effect of the peculiar circumstances, and the four doubles, was one of acute disorientation. He'd had practically nothing to eat all day and, feeling weak in the knees, leaned against the gate trying to think of the most efficient way to get inside the house.

His phone rang; the number on the display was familiar, but he could not immediately place it. "Hello? Quirke."

"This is Eugene Scorchner," said the caller.

Quirke thought it odd, but perhaps propitious, that his father-in-law would call at just this instant. Gene might know either the new code or Eleanor's whereabouts.

"Hi, Gene. How are you? Funny it should be you on the line. You know, I seem to be locked out of my house. Did Eleanor—"

"Couple of things," Scorchner interrupted. "One, it's not your house. Not even your residence any more. Two, you are not to try and contact my daughter. Three, one of my people will be in touch with you to arrange to have your personal belongings delivered to your new residence. Eleanor is filing for divorce. Four things, rather."

Quirke's legs gave out under him and he slid down hard onto the sidewalk. He could neither breathe nor compose a reply of any kind to Scorchner's announcement. After half a minute of silence, Scorchner terminated the call.

Chapter Six

August 21, 7:20 p.m.

As Quirke sat numb on the concrete, heedless of the consequences to his clothing, a siren sounded not far away. The security camera mounted just to the right of the gate was, he realized, likely transmitting his unmoving image to Scorchner, who presumably lay in wait in the house with some muscular help, ready to have Quirke escorted away if he didn't move along. He therefore got awkwardly to his feet and began to walk down the hill toward the lights of the waterfront.

He knew there would be enough to worry about in the near future, and something whispered to him that a man ought to be angry at being thrown out of his home without color of right or even a warning. But he felt neither worry nor anger at his current plight. Instead, there was only a pleasant emptiness, a nonattachment, a lightness. The houses he passed as he walked down the hill, with the warm incandescence of their shaded windows and the faint sounds of television and kitchen washing-up within, together with the hum of traffic and the crackle of the overhead trolley wires, made up the signature of a world through which he could travel incognito, as nothing special, on equal footing with the inhabitants. It was exactly what he needed.

Down at the aquatic park, the precise spot where he'd sat ruminating after his rudely interrupted tryst with Sadie six days earlier, his physical energy all at once left him and he crumpled onto a bench feeling faint and ill. It seemed he could either do nothing and hope to be found—or not found—before something irremediable happened, or he could summon some kind of help. His mind, working at well below normal speed, mulled over these alternatives, hindered in its decision-making function by the sense this was all happening to someone else, someone to whom, truth be told, he was indifferent.

But not everyone on the planet was indifferent to this self of his. There was one person who would care that he was sitting on a park bench, homeless, unwell and alone. He knew this to be true although she might be disappointed or even disgusted at his falling off the wagon. He could not hurt her feelings by failing to call upon her in this hour of need. So, he took out his phone and, unsure of his ability to make himself understood, shakily texted her: *Sadie need help love Conal.*

A minute later he heard the ping of a reply: *Where r u? love S.*

He used his remaining strength to type: *aquatic park bench bring picnic love c.* Then he lay down on the bench to await her coming, hoping the park police were disposed to leave derelicts like him alone tonight.

The next sensation he felt was of his upper body being enfolded and lifted to a vertical orientation. She was beside him on the bench, looking very worried, adorable in her concern, wrapping his hand around a carton, raising it to his lips. He swallowed the sweet, rich chocolate milk slowly at first, then greedily.

"You saved me," he said at last. "Thank you."

She unwrapped a slice of pound cake, broke off a piece, and popped it into his mouth. "We need to go to the emergency room," she said. "Do you know which hospitals are on your plan?"

"I don't want to go to the hospital. Can we just sit here for a while?"

"Okay, for a while. What are you doing here? If you feel up to telling me." She had been facing him, rubbing his cold hands in her warm ones, but now slid over, tight against him, putting her arms around him. "You haven't been eating, and I can feel you're getting thinner," she said.

"At least there's that. I may have to do this in installments—I still feel kind of woozy, not quite myself. It's a nice feeling, actually." He was silent for a while, gathering his strength. "After telling you I was off the stuff, I had a few drinks tonight. You must hate me. You can do a lot better than a weak old man like me."

"I really wish you wouldn't say things like that. Whoever's been reading you that script is full of shit. You drink or not as it pleases you, not me. Now continue. How did you wind up here tonight?"

He could not let her declaration pass unremarked. "Do you really mean that? You're not going to hector me every day about my drinking?"

" 'Do what thou wilt shall be the whole of the Law,' Conal. I can't be indifferent to the consequences, I'm terrified at the thought of you harming yourself, but it isn't for me to tell you what to put in your body, or not. I also won't tell you to cut your hair. Or not cut your hair. 'O lover, if thou wilt, depart'—God, I didn't mean to get all religious on you tonight."

"Blessed art thou among women, Sadie: I can't seem to help myself, either. I love you with all my heart." He paused, taking deep breaths, and tried to hold back the tears that had begun to spill out, not at his predicament, but at her reckless love for his undeserving self. "I used to live up the hill. In a big house that didn't belong to me." He smiled wanly. "Today I got loaded to find the courage to go home and tell her I'm divorcing her."

Sadie gasped.

"Why are you surprised? You knew I was miserable. I wasn't very good at hiding it."

"You've been unhappy for so long I thought there must be an awfully powerful reason why you kept on choosing it."

"I'm sure you're right, and one day I'll understand what it was. In any event, today I was going to tell her. You never met my wife, did you?"

"Saw her once across the room at a court holiday party. Stayed out of her way the times she descended on chambers. I just didn't find her...alluring."

He laughed despite himself. "She could be terrifying as well as unalluring. So tonight, I got drunk, but not too. I had every intention of having a civilized conversation with her, but—got any more of that pound cake? Thanks. When I arrived at my front gate, I found she'd changed the code—I was locked out. Then I got a call from her father telling me I didn't live there anymore and I was not to contact her. She beat me to it."

"How utterly cruel. And blatantly illegal."

"I'm not sure how illegal, actually, now that I think about it. The house belongs to him; for as it is written, the father-in-law giveth and the father-in-law taketh away. All my things are there, but he said he'd have them sent to my new place. Oh, by the way, in addition to being weak and old and borderline alcoholic, I'm homeless. Had enough yet?"

She stopped his flight into self-denigration with a long, deep kiss. "Does that answer your question?" she asked at last. "And you're not homeless, either. Not as long as I'm paying my rent. Well, what happened to you today would bring anyone to a nervous collapse."

"But there's more. Today Ward Freitag paid me a visit."

"What about?"

"The infamous photo. Of us. It seemed his motives were friendly; he wanted to warn me the picture might be used by people—forces—he refused to identify them—who want me off the bench. Yes, in addition to the above, I'm apparently now at risk of losing my job. And I mentioned to him something about the divorce. Sadie, did words ever come unplanned out of your mouth and create their own reality?"

"Yes, I've experienced it many times. That's one kind of magic."

"Well, as soon as I'd said it, I knew it would happen. It was the weirdest thing. But the point is I'd never breathed a word to anyone before that moment, hadn't actually even formed the whole thought to myself, and only a few hours later I'm on the street. Seems like a dubious coincidence."

"It could be Ward betrayed you. But are you sure she wasn't planning this? Had she been behaving normally—for her, that is—lately?"

"Now that you mention it, recently she's been sort of…absent. For a long time now we've been roommates rather than husband and wife, and I haven't actually seen her or even spoken with her since—I don't know exactly when. God, I guess that only proves what an idiot I am. Apparently, she moved out without my noticing. I was too busy enjoying her not being there. But in my defense, it's a big house."

"You're not an idiot. We simply can't be sure what's going on without more information. How are you feeling now?"

"A little better. Not up to a marathon, but I think I can stand without keeling over," he said, demonstrating. "The chocolate milk was exactly what I needed." He paused, collecting his breath. "I don't know how I could go on without you. Stupid admission in my current state, but there you are. How did I get so lucky?" They stood for a long time embracing, kissing, as a cool wind blew off the bay and encircled them.

"I'm taking you home to bed," she whispered.

He felt a perfect contentment.

※

South of Market Street, she turned her little Fiat into a dark alley bordered on either side by converted warehouses and the occasional factory and a few crepe myrtles and lindens. A garage opened before them, and in a moment's time they were inside an elevator alighting on the top floor.

The vast loft received natural light—moonlight and streetlight, at this late hour—from a wall of windows that told of the building's past incarnation as a working factory. The concrete floor and some of the partitions were painted dark gray; the kitchen in the middle of the space was red enamel and stainless steel. The artwork was monumental, perfectly suited to the place's scale, mostly abstract paintings interspersed with colossal nudes. There were several seating areas occupied by modular leather sofas, a long conference table with ranks of chairs on either side, and floor-to-ceiling shelving filled with art objects and books, with ladders placed handily nearby. A few ficus trees in pots here and there softened the stark angles. Even so furnished, you could have ridden a bicycle for exercise throughout the place.

"My God, Sadie, how do you afford something like this on a judicial attorney's salary?" Quirke asked.

"Well, it's not all mine," she admitted. At that instant, a tall, attractive man who might have been anywhere between forty and sixty years old, barefoot and dressed in jeans and a turtleneck sweater, emerged from the kitchen.

"I hope all is well with your friend," the man said, extending his right hand and meeting Quirke's gobsmacked look with a direct and magnetic gaze.

"Conal, this is Peter Blake. Peter, Conal Quirke. This is Peter's loft, of which he kindly lets me rent that corner over there." She gestured toward the far northwestern end of the place, where he caught a glimpse of furniture screened by a wall of cabinets and draped textiles.

"Very good to meet you at last, Conal. Are you feeling a little better?"

"I think so, yes. It's good of you to ask. And to let me stay here tonight. I find myself unexpectedly liberated from my former home and haven't yet had time to find a new one."

Peter smiled. "Aren't liminal states great? Enjoy it while it lasts. Would anyone care for tea? No? Well, then, I'll get back to my work. See you later, no doubt." Peter headed toward the far northeastern corner of the place, where, Quirke now saw, several easels and tables bearing paints, brushes, knives, and other such painterly equipment stood.

"Who's he?" Quirke whispered. "I suddenly feel superfluous as well as inadequate for all the previously enumerated reasons. Maybe I should find a hotel—"

"No. It's my fault—I should have told you about Peter. But don't worry: Peter is my former guardian, sometime teacher, my landlord, my friend...I suppose you could also say he's my Gorodish, since he helped me out of a fiendish situation a long time ago. Oh, I'll tell you about that in due course, but not tonight, if it's all right with you—it's a long story."

"I wish you would, in due course, whenever that might be. I feel like I've gone down the rabbit hole. But I'd go anywhere with you, even there. Gorodish—as in *Diva*?"

She nodded. "You understand exactly what I mean. But now, unless you'd like me to make you some food—oh, I should warn you I'm not a great cook, but you won't starve with me—there's something I've been dying to do." She interlaced her fingers with his, stood on her toes, and pressed herself against him, kissing his lower lip with a gentle bite.

"What's that?" he interrupted, smiling down at her.

She resumed kissing him and, without breaking contact, walked backward, leading him hand in hand toward her room.

Chapter Seven

August 21, 8:00 p.m.

Checking his reflection one last time in the mirrored wall of the restaurant anteroom, Allan Hetford adjusted his tie and satisfied himself of the perfection of his appearance. It was vital to the realization of one's romantic ambitions to look one's best, he had always found, when one's desired companion was the most susceptible, and he had found that women—men, too, for that matter—whose long-term relationship had just fallen apart were typically at that precise juncture quite vulnerable to his attentions. Eleanor Quirke had called that afternoon, interrupting his workout to insist he dine with her that night. From the flutter in her voice, he inferred her domestic situation had changed radically, as she had hinted it might during their date earlier in the week. He further inferred, to his intense satisfaction, that Lucas must have faithfully followed his suggestions regarding the incriminatory photo of Quirke and his attorney-mistress, at which Hetford had so far declined to look himself. Everything was going splendidly according to plan.

"Mr. Hetford? Welcome to Les Vendanges." The maître d'hôtel approached and bowed slightly. His voice had a plummy quality that was of a piece with the atmosphere of the exclusive place. "I've already seated Mrs. Quirke. Please come this way."

He could not even hear his footfalls on the plushy carpet as he followed his host to Eleanor's table, near the wall under a portrait of a voluptuous eighteenth-century courtesan. She wore a long, tight-bodiced dress of midnight blue silk cut so low it revealed every bone in her chest, and held out a freshly manicured hand to him. He brushed it with his lips, an affectation that always went over well with ladies of a certain age.

"Eleanor, how are you? You look wonderful in that color."

"Thank you, Allan. I'm—I'm in a state of shock, actually. You wouldn't believe what I learned today."

Hetford raised his eyebrows and took her outstretched hand in an anticipatory gesture of comfort.

"Quirke's been having an affair with one of his staff attorneys. Right in his chambers, no less. I'd never have believed it, but I saw the proof with my own eyes. Were you aware? Is this...relationship, if I can even dignify it with the term...being talked about by the whole court? Am I an object of pity or, even worse, a laughingstock?"

"Eleanor, please don't worry on that account. I've certainly heard no one talking about it. How long is this affair supposed to have been going on?"

"Probably for a very long time—it would explain a lot—but at least since last week, when the picture was taken."

"—By?"

"The one person at the court—besides you—who's ever shown me the slightest kindness. Lucas Grieber. He phoned today and broke this horrible, outrageous news in the most sensitive way. The first thing I thought was I'm so glad I'm ending the marriage. I don't know why it's taken me so long. The second thing was that I had to tell you, that you'd help me figure out how to manage this."

"Of course, I will. I hope you know I'll be there for you whenever you need a friend. No request is too onerous."

"Well, here's one. Would you order for us? I'm too distracted to put a meal together properly."

"I'd be delighted." A waiter had laid two leather-bound menus the size of half-folded newspapers on the tablecloth. After a few moments' study, Hetford selected the goat cheese tatin and halibut crudo to start, followed by the duck breast "coq au vin" and côte de boeuf. "This may seem unorthodox, my dear," he told her, "and not in any way to minimize the pain he's caused you, but let's think of tonight as a discreet little celebration, for just the two of us, of your release from marital captivity." To the waiter he instructed: "We'll have the Piper Heidsieck 2002 now, and the Chateau Angelus Saint-Emilion 2005 with the entrees."

"Excellent, sir."

Soon they were raising their flutes of champagne. "To your new life, Eleanor. May it hold every happiness."

Clinking her glass against his, she glowed in the candlelight. "I love your style, Allan. So unlike what I've had to live with. Do you know, I almost began to wonder if there was something wrong with me to make Quirke such a constant pill."

"Some people are simply determined to make everyone around them miserable. Maybe he's one of them. In any event, let's hear no more of there being anything wrong with you. You're the top! You're...the Coliseum. You're the top! You're...the Louvre Museum—"

"Oh, stop," she said coyly.

"You're the smile on the Mona Lisa—"

"Shhhh," she laughed.

"You're a hot tamale—"

"Not really."

"Oh, yes, I'll go so far as to say you're simply too, too, too diveen—"

"And you're…what is it? Ovaltine."

"That's the sweetest thing anyone's ever said about me," he said. She giggled like a schoolgirl as the waiter brought their appetizers.

The excellence of the meal demonstrated why tycoons of industry and other movers and shakers came to Les Vendanges to close deals of all kinds. "The crudo is superb, really outstanding. It melts," he said after a mouthful.

"You must try the tatin," she said, pushing her fork toward him. Hetford dodged it, suppressing a shudder. He had never been one to share utensils or eat off the same plate as an inamorata/o, and was not about to start now, in full view of Les Vendanges' other patrons. With his own salad fork, he scooped a tiny portion of her tatin and tasted it. "Ambrosial! This calls for a little more champagne." A waiter immediately appeared to refill their glasses. "So, my dear, you've asked for my help in managing the stress of recent events. And it's my fondest wish to give you that help." Even in the candlelight, her blush was obvious. "I have a few ideas, but first, of course, you must be clear about your goals."

"Well, to get rid of Quirke," she said flatly. "The sooner the better."

"Indeed." Perhaps a way could be found to elicit more nuance, more poetry, from the otherwise wholly praiseworthy Eleanor. "But to do it in a fashion that spares him as much as possible, or one that lets him experience the full consequences of his conduct?"

"Well, why would I want to let him off the hook? After what I've been through."

"It's only natural to feel that way. Let me ask another question, if I may: do you anticipate a big fight over community property? Obviously, you have resources he doesn't, and although Quirke appears capable of supporting himself in reasonably comfortable fashion, that rarely stops an estranged spouse from trying to get as much as he or she can. Is he, in the vernacular, going to try and take you to the cleaners?"

"He won't bother going after any of my money. In fact, he's going to owe me—or, rather, Daddy—something on the order of a quarter of a million dollars. The prenup's ironclad." Seeing Hetford's confusion, Eleanor elaborated. "When we were married thirty years ago, Quirke was finishing college, I was just starting, and Daddy was struggling to get Marvelocity Industries off the ground. Paying for Quirke's law school education was a significant investment for him in those days—a sacrifice, actually—and

Daddy wanted a guaranteed return. Actually, he wanted Quirke to join the business, but Quirke had other ideas. Why does anyone go into criminal law, anyway?"

"It never held the least attraction for me," said Hetford.

"If only I'd met you at that freshman mixer instead of him," she lamented. "Everything would have been different. So, the prenup was Daddy's idea. No spousal support on either side, I keep all my Marvelocity stock, and Quirke repays the cost of his education with interest. Daddy made sure Quirke had his own lawyer to explain exactly what he was giving up."

"What about the house?"

"It was never ours—it belongs to Daddy. I've moved back to his house, and he may or may not put the other place on the market. I think he's waiting to see if I'm serious about dumping Quirke. Anyway, he told me I had to move out to make it look good."

"Very shrewd. It's not surprising Marvelocity got to be such a huge success with him at the helm."

Eleanor nodded. "He's my hero. So, given the independent advice Quirke got, it would be pretty tough for him to undo the agreement. And it wouldn't make him look very good to try, would it?"

"No. Particularly now, when he's trying to get the voters to give him another term. He needs to seem above reproach. That's going to be hard for him. To the casual observer, it's as if he's trying to throw it all away."

"Do you really think he could lose? I thought judges always win. I mean, how hard is it to win when there's nobody running against you?"

"About a third of voters will vote against any incumbent on principle. So, you have to keep a supermajority of the persuadables. Sex scandals are rarely helpful even for Democrat legislative or executive candidates, and for a justice of the Supreme Court, they're an unmitigated disaster."

"But it's hardly a scandal. You said yourself no one's talking about his tawdry little affair. I don't want to become tabloid fodder, Allan. I want *him* to suffer, not me."

"I see. So, if it comes to it, letting him experience the full consequences of his conduct is a lower priority than staying out of the tabloid press."

"That isn't quite what I meant. I don't mind a little publicity, I mean I'm in the society pages every year for the opening of the opera and symphony seasons and things like that, but I don't want to come off as the pathetic deceived wife. You're awfully good at this cross-examination thing, you know."

"I'm sorry. The last thing I want to do is make you uncomfortable. Here, have a little more of the Saint-Emilion. May I share with you a very real and nagging concern I have about all this?"

"Of course," she whispered.

"It transcends you and me, and even Quirke, with all his attractive imperfections. Oh, yes, as dissipated and out of shape as he is today, you still see the traces of the boyish charm, the sense of humor, the killer blues that made you weak in the knees for him."

She laughed. "I'd almost think you've fallen under his spell, Allan."

It was Hetford's turn to blush, and he was silent for a moment as he drained and replenished his wineglass. "As I was saying, my deepest concern is for the people of this state. Don't they have a right to expect their Supreme Court justices will be men and women of the highest integrity? The idea's enshrined in the canons of judicial ethics. Even if it weren't, it's something people instinctively understand. If the full chronicle of Quirke's transgressions were broadcast on Fox News tomorrow, how many voters would say he ought to be retained? I'm not talking only about the sex in chambers, as unacceptable as I'm sure the vast majority of voters would find it if they knew about it. There's also the question of his basic fitness, when, as you've told me, he hardly draws a sober breath from one day to the next. And if he weren't on the ballot in this election, wouldn't there be good reason to take corrective action anyway?"

"What are you suggesting? What kind of corrective action?"

"Perhaps you've heard of the Commission on Judicial Behavior. It's an agency that polices the judiciary."

"Yes, Quirke mentioned them once or twice when someone he knew got in trouble."

"It starts with a confidential complaint. The Commission investigates and decides whether to institute formal proceedings, which are matters of public record."

She looked at him. "You're talking about ruining him, essentially."

Hetford wondered if he'd overplayed his hand.

"I'm going to be using my maiden name now that he and I are finished," she said after a pause. "Since I won't be wearing his any longer I won't be tarnished if it gets dirty."

"So, protecting the public interest won't harm you. Win-win. There are other little consequences he can be made to bear."

"Such as?"

"Let's talk about them over dessert." To the waiter he said, "The napoleon for me and the crème de violette for Mrs. Quirke. And two glasses of your best Sauternes."

※

After their meal, Eleanor took Hetford to the observation deck at the top of the building. They admired the night skyline from every angle until Hetford made his apologies.

"I've had a wonderful time, Eleanor, but I'm afraid I have to head home to bed. Conference tomorrow morning at 9:30 sharp. The Chief always starts on the dot."

"Oh, I know. Quirke used to complain bitterly."

"No doubt you had your work cut out for you trying to see him out the door on time, given his habits."

"Not at all. If he didn't get up, it was his problem, not mine. I was usually in my gym with my personal trainer or already on the way to my own office before he'd stir. That's just one example of how, for a very long time, we'd been living separately together."

"Poor dear." He made to offer her a comforting hug, but she pressed her groin against his and put her arms around his waist, looking up at him and smiling expectantly. He counted to five before ever so gently breaking contact.

"There's one thing we really must keep in mind," he told her quietly. "If there's any notoriety about your divorce and his...electoral situation, and I think there's going to be some and possibly a lot, it's vital you and I remain circumspect until everything's over and done. Not to put too fine a point on it, no public displays of affection. Retaining the moral high ground is an absolute must. No matter how much we might be inclined to behave exactly as he has."

"Of course, you're right," she said, her smile inverting into a frown. "All the more reason to carry out Plan A, as you suggested, as soon as possible and move on from there. I can hardly wait. I wish I could be there to see Quirke's face."

"As to Plan A, you'll have to consult your lawyers and, obviously, you didn't hear it from me."

"I totally, totally get that. I'll pretend I thought of it. Allan, thank you for tonight. Our time together has been so wonderful and restorative that I simply have to see more of you. So, come to dinner at Daddy's, say, Friday evening? I want you to meet him. I know he'll really like you. The two of you are very similar, actually."

"I'd love to meet your father, and I'm flattered at the comparison." He kissed the top of her head. "Sorry, couldn't help myself. Do as I say, not as I do."

Eleanor beamed.

Chapter Eight

August 24, 2:40 p.m.

Quirke entered the Chief Justice's anteroom and stopped at her assistant's desk. "Good afternoon, Margo. How are you doing today? Say, do you think I could have just a minute of her time?"

"Good afternoon, Justice Quirke. She's got a meeting in ten minutes, but go ahead and knock—I'm sure she'll see you."

"Thanks." Quirke did as instructed. "Chief? Got a second?"

"Justice Quirke, do come in. I've been meaning to speak with you." In spite of the vast assortment of challenges inherent in running the third branch of state government, perpetually having to plug leaks in the budget and ward off legislative encroachments on her authority, along with all the toil involved in managing her share of the court's caseload, the Chief Justice always managed to look like the nicest room mom in school: rosy-cheeked, tidy, and well-dressed without ostentation, bestowing a smile on everyone, from the most obnoxious complainant to the most irrational interlocutor. At the same time, during her years in the Sant' Urbano County District Attorney's Office interviewing confidential informants, she had developed an unerring ability to distinguish fact from fiction. One could not hope to put anything over on the Chief.

He closed the door behind him. "What about, Chief?"

"Ward came by yesterday."

Quirke's heart sank a little. "I think I know why. But let me assure you there won't be any repercussions for the court—it was a purely consensual encounter."

"I don't doubt that, but repercussions of one sort or another are always a possibility. Especially given your situation, being on the ballot and all. I'm hoping you have a plan."

"I do have a plan. I'm getting a divorce. I'll do it as quietly as possible. But I can't say I have full control of the process. The other night, for example, I was locked out of the house. For good."

"I'm sorry to hear that. It's tough. Where are you staying?"

"That's what I came to talk with you about. I don't know where I'll be in the long term, but for now I'm staying with Sadie Norrell. I'll text you her address. This is for your eyes and ears only, Chief. No one else's. Not HR, not Ward, not anyone but you. I will not risk Sadie's privacy, but someone here should know where I'm living now, and you're the only one I trust."

"I appreciate your confidence in me. Is there anything I can do to help?"

"Maybe. Can you tell me who wants me off the bench, and why? If Ward's to be believed, there are forces massing to unseat me."

The Chief frowned. "That's news to me. Of course, I'll pass along anything I hear. Meanwhile, take care of yourself. You've been looking awfully ragged lately, and I've been worried about you. I'm glad you have someone to look after you, especially someone as sweet as Sadie, although frankly I don't know how you're going to be able to maintain the status quo for much longer. Not to put more pressure on you, but you can't really have your lover on your staff. But you know that."

He emailed her at 4:50 p.m. *Please come and see me at 5:05.*

You bet, she replied.

She arrived punctually and shut the door. They melted into each other's arms. Her kisses had become the dominant addiction in his life, and he now indulged guiltlessly.

"Anybody still around?" he asked.

"Only Lucas."

"Just as well, really. I haven't had a chance to sweep this place for listening devices and hidden cameras today. And anyway, we have a place to go to now. A bed to call home."

"Unless you want to go out?"

"I want you to make something I can eat off your bare skin. Nothing fancy, of course. Or I'll cook. I'll bet you didn't realize I know how to cook."

"I didn't, but I'm not surprised. You're a man of many parts."

"All of them hot for you," he said, holding her even tighter.

In minutes they were heading, separately, through rush-hour congestion to the loft. The sooner they could go public with their relationship, he reflected, the sooner they could cease this wasteful solo commuting.

As it happened, neither of them bent over the stove that evening, as Peter, who'd gone out to teach a painting class at City College, had left them the remains of a dish of papardelle with baby spinach and mushrooms that he'd concocted, along with a half-consumed bottle of pino grigio. His generosity enabled them to take to bed earlier than usual, and so, even after making love that left them perfectly weak with satisfaction, showering together and doing it again, they had time to talk as they lay on her feather bed in the near-darkness of evening.

"Would you like to go away this weekend?" Sadie asked him. "Some friends of mine in the Order are getting together at this place one of them owns in the mountains south of Sant' Amaro. There's plenty of room and everyone's nice. I think you'll like them, and I know they'll like you."

He got up, turned on the bedside lamp, and poured a glass of whiskey, only his fourth of the day, from the bottle he kept on her dresser. "Want some?" he asked. She shook her head, smiling.

"I'd like that," he said, and drained the glass. "But oral argument is next week, and I need to prepare."

"There'll be time for that. I should tell you I'll be busy Saturday afternoon."

"Stuff I'm not allowed to see?"

"These particular rituals are only for initiates. Are you…?"

"I think about it. Often." He lay down again facing her, his hand tracing her side and hip. "How did you happen to get involved in magick? Just so you know, I'm mentally spelling it with a 'k'."

"That's so thoughtful of you. How did I get involved in magick? I suppose magick was the logical next step after the nuns."

"I had the nuns; how come I didn't get magick?"

"Assumes a fact not in evidence, that you didn't. So, you're Catholic?"

"With a name like mine, what else would I be?"

"I envied the cradle Catholics when I was at school. They seemed to know where they fit in the world, whereas I—well, before the nuns was chaos."

"The earth was without form and void?"

"And the heavens, they had no light. Really, my childhood was more like Dante's nine circles of hell. I think I told you Peter was my Gorodish; when I was in ninth grade and he was my art teacher, he conspired with my English teacher to save me from my mother. To say she was a career criminal makes my early life sound tamer and more orderly than it was. Peter and Leila became my guardians, and I spent the next four years at a Catholic girls' boarding school looking to heaven in search of God. I loved the place, almost converted, but without quite forbidding it Peter managed to make the Old Aeon religion sound pretty uncool. Then, after I graduated, he spent the next few years making a magician out of me, teaching me to look inside myself, instead of outside, for God."

"Did you find Her?"

"Yes, and She told me to become a lawyer. But I had little faith, and settled for Brighton Law School."

"Should I have heard of Brighton Law School?"

"No, it was never ranked or even accredited, and went out of business some years ago. Luckily, I got enough out of it to pass the bar exam—I still find myself checking my State Bar listing to make sure they haven't had second thoughts about admitting me—and snuck my way into the court, first as an extern, then onto the central staff. I still feel like a bit of a fraud. Your predecessor, Justice Carraway, took me on as a temp when one of his attorneys went on maternity leave, and then almost immediately retired himself. I guess he forgot to tell you I'm not a real chambers attorney."

"You walk and talk and write memos like one. Not for a second have I regretted keeping you on. You have no reason to doubt yourself."

"I've loved working for you. You're the best boss I ever had, and I'm not talking about the way you make love to me. Though there's that, too."

"There's one more thing I'd like to know." He hesitated. "What on earth did you see in me?" he finally asked. "And when did you see it? Because it's taken me these three years to realize you're everything I wanted all along."

"You were standing behind the metaphorical curtain of your marriage. I'll bet you were more or less faithful to her pretty much all along."

"Pretty much, more or less," he acknowledged. "No matter what else you might hear about me."

"Well, I had no barrier like that. The minute you walked in I saw a kind, funny, brilliant, crazy, messed-up, real, wonderful, gorgeous man. But I didn't want to be fired, so for three years I forced myself to keep my hands to myself. Three years of constantly remembering the nuns and making the sacrifice. Until the night that, for whatever reason, you opened yourself up to me. I don't know whether alcohol will prove to be your friend or your enemy—I've already told you it's your decision, not mine, if or how much you drink, so I won't try to coerce you one way or the other, even if it kills me—or kills you—which would kill me for sure—but that night it was my ally."

Chapter Nine

August 27, 12:40 p.m.

Carleton Matthews—goateed and balding, tall, broad, and richly tattooed in visible and invisible places, wearing old cutoff jeans and a T-shirt that read "AC2012"—stood in the leafy sunshine outside his spacious cabin in the Sant' Amaro foothills. Several lodge members had already arrived, and the Fiat crawling up the gravel drive meant Sadie Norrell was the latest to join them. He waved and pointed to the side yard, where three other cars were parked. As the Fiat negotiated its way into a space, he ambled over to greet his guests.

"Ninety-three," he said, as she stretched to give the big man a hug.

"Ninety-three," she responded. She turned toward Quirke, standing beside her with overnight bags on each arm. "Carleton, this is Conal. Conal, Carleton Matthews."

"Welcome. Good to meet you, Con. Okay if I call you that?"

"Sure," said Quirke. "Good to meet you, Carleton. Thanks for letting me join you all. I know you and Sadie and your comrades have important plans for the afternoon, so I've brought some work to occupy myself."

"I appreciate your understanding. We all look forward to getting to know you at the party tonight and beyond. It's a pretty relaxed group, so I hope the idea of hanging out with a magical order isn't giving you difficulty."

"Not at all. Living with Sadie and Peter has taught me you're normal in many respects."

Carleton laughed. "I'll show you to your room, and after you've made yourselves comfortable, feel free to roam around. Everywhere except the temple yonder," he said, indicating a wooden structure about the size of a three-car garage twenty yards from the cabin. "We begin at 4:18."

"Got it," said Sadie, as they entered the cabin.

Their room, paneled with wood painted a cool, pale green, was at the top of the sprawling house, facing west and looking out over miles of hilly forest. The windows had been thrown open and a fresh breeze played with the semi-sheer muslin panels hanging in front of them. The bedstead and rocking chair were made of scrubbed oak, as was the floor, and an old handmade quilt in a mosaic design adorned the bed. Sadie fell backward onto it and spread her arms, angel-fashion. After putting the bags down, Quirke lay next to her, drew a forefinger up her concave belly, and kissed her tenderly.

"Thanks for driving all the way down. I should have taken part of it—you're spoiling me."

"It was nothing."

"This is a wonderful place. I could imagine living here, being a carpenter or something like that."

"Funny you should say that, because that's exactly what Carleton is. He built this house, the temple, and a lot of other people's houses around here."

"If I go down in flames in the election, maybe he'll take me on as an apprentice."

"You could do a lot worse than learning carpentry from Carleton, but you're going to ace the election." She put her arms around his waist and returned his kiss.

Within two minutes, their clothes lay strewn on the floor and they had submerged themselves under the covers. Working down his belly, her tongue began to explore him, and her fingers stroked the length of his penis until he was on the point of exploding in ecstasy, but instead he held back, lifted her onto him, and penetrated her as she gasped and arched toward him. Harder and harder he thrust into her; she rocked with him until he came with a shuddering cry. When they unjoined, she lay down beside him, damp with sweat.

" 'Bliss it was in that dawn to be alive,' " he whispered, after catching his breath.

" 'But to be young was very heaven,' " she responded. "Our love is young, even if we aren't."

"How old are you, anyway? Never mind, what a stupid question at a moment like this."

"No, it's something you should know, I suppose. I'm thirty-four."

"Oh, baby. You look a lot younger. May I ask you another question?"

"Of course, sweetheart. Anything."

He kissed her lips softly and studied her limpid brown eyes as she nestled closer, facing him. "I've noticed," he said, tracing the topography of her waist and hipbone, "we don't practice contraception. Should I be starting a college fund?"

He'd thought it a gentle way to broach the subject, but she fell back, supine, her eyes filling with tears, her forearm shielding them as her chest lifted and sank with the effort to contain sobs.

"I'm sorry, dearest. Forgive me. I didn't mean to upset you. I was only trying in my inept way to let you know that I...please tell me what's wrong," he said, caressing her belly, which heaved with silent weeping.

"I've never used birth control," she said, her voice barely audible. "I've never needed to, since—since I was thirteen and I lost a baby before I even knew. It was because of the STDs that I got from the guy I—who used to fuck me when he came over to buy crystal from Laudie—my mother, that is. He was the one who knocked me up. The doctor who did the D and C told me I'd probably never be able to have children." She regarded him as though from an unbridgeable distance. "Do you want children, Conal?"

He feared the honest answer would cause her more pain, but he could give no other.

"Yes, but if it doesn't happen, you'll still be stuck with me."

"Are you sure you want to be stuck with me? I'm lacking the basic womanly equipment."

"You lack for nothing. I only wish I could put it right for you."

She turned her face away, but let him hold her close.

After a while, she asked, "What time is it?"

He fumbled for his phone on the bedside table. "Twenty to four."

"I need to get ready. First the bath. I'm sorry," she said, as he made to get up with her. "It's part of the ritual   something I have to attend to by myself this time."

"Of course," he said. "I'll find you afterward."

She kissed him once more, rummaged in her bag for a moment and pulled out a kimono, which she proceeded to put on, and draped a long dress of black crepe over her arm. Grabbing underthings and a pair of flats, she was gone down the hall.

Quirke sat at the side of the bed for a moment, then put the room back in order, laying clothes over the backs of chairs, smoothing sheets and quilt on the good solid bed. While everyone else in the place was banishing or invoking or whatever they were doing in the temple Carleton had built, he would try to get ready for oral argument next week. After a few minutes, when the stillness outside their room signaled that the magicians were engaged or about to engage in their mysterious work, he dressed and slipped out, benchbook under his arm.

Rounding a corner on a path in the yard, a black-clad straggler heading for the temple nearly collided with him. "Sorry, dude. You're Sadie's boyfriend, right? I'm Reg," he said, extending a hand. "Sorry, can't talk now, but I'll see you after. Oh, there's beer and stuff in the fridge— through there." He pointed to a dutch door abutting an herb garden at the back of the house as he hastened on his way.

Though Quirke was ordinarily a wine and spirits man, the heat of the late afternoon and his recent exertions made the prospect of a cold beer appealing, and he followed Reg's direction. The rustic kitchen had a beamed ceiling, a wrought iron chandelier, and simple pine cabinets, with a round table atop a red kilim. He opened his book on the table and uncapped a bottle of Three Philosophers, which he'd never tasted but whose name intrigued him.

Perhaps it was the dark, rich ale with its hint of cherry lambic, perhaps it was the persisting sexual afterglow, or perhaps it was the magical atmosphere all around him, but for the first time in weeks Quirke experienced something like mental clarity. Even the multistate tax compact began to make sense, and he jotted down a few questions to ask counsel at oral argument. In less than an hour he felt sufficiently prepared and, after returning the benchbook to their room, he took the remains of the brew to the side yard, where he lay down on an Adirondack chair, thinking he'd meditate, while also—incompatibly—keeping an eye on the temple.

He awoke, confused, to the sounds of a shriek and a series of rapid footsteps—those of Reg, who, as far as Quirke could tell at this distance without his glasses, had burst out of the temple cradling his left hand, which was dripping blood onto the gravel path, against his right as he moved toward an old water pump beyond the house. Another man soon walked briskly out of the temple and followed Reg.

After a second's hesitation, Quirke went to them, his heart pounding at the sudden mayhem. "Need help?" he asked. "That looks ugly."

"Actually, yes," said the man who'd followed Reg. "As long as you're here, would you might running into the house and getting my bag? I'm an EMT, and I've got stuff in there to take care of this."

"Where's your room?"

"It's the one on the ground floor, past the kitchen. The bag's a little grey duffle, about a foot long. I think I left it on the chair."

"Be right back," said Quirke.

He found the room and the bag easily enough and returned to the yard. The EMT had primed the pump and was carefully exposing Reg's wounded hand to a thin stream of water to wash away the blood. At Quirke's arrival, he unzipped the bag and began to dig through his supplies.

"I'm Conal, by the way—here with Sadie. I met Reg earlier. Hope everything's going to be all right."

"Jonah Harrison, hi. Call me Harry. So, you're Sadie's boyfriend? Nice to meet you. Oh yeah, Reg'll be fine. We're not into weird shit—it was just a little slipup with a ceremonial dagger. I told you that thing was too sharp," he said, directing the last remark to Reg. "The worst part of it is Reg is our bass guitarist, and he sure won't be playing for a while." Harry was applying gauze to the wound, which continued to ooze blood. "She got you good, man," he muttered.

Quirke wondered what Harry meant, but didn't dare seek to probe the sanctity of their secret ceremonies. Instead he asked: "You guys have a band? What do you play?"

"Oldies, mostly. Eighties, nineties, classic rock, punk, new wave. Some original compositions and some ritual accompaniment, but tonight we were just going to jam for fun. Guess we'll have to stream music at the party instead."

Something leaped within Quirke, a need akin to the fiery excitement he felt in being with Sadie. A quarter of a century had passed since he'd held a bass guitar, but merely thinking of it sent the old sensation of fret on fingertips coursing through his nerve-endings. He suddenly wanted to get hammered, forget his judicial persona, and play the way he had in the old days, as far back as high school, and through law school when he and a few buddies used to entertain the student body impromptu after the last class on Friday afternoons. Those had been some of the best times in his life, at least up until the recent days and nights spent with Sadie. And not primarily because his lead guitarist and fellow law student, Andy Benfield, later became the governor who appointed him to the Supreme Court.

"Wish I'd brought my bass," he said. *Wish I hadn't let Eleanor get rid of it decades ago.*

"You play, man?" Harry marveled. "Reg, didn't I just say Con seems like a cool guy? Well, I'm sure Reg won't mind you using his."

"I'm not trying to—"

"No argument. We need you," said Reg.

"I haven't played in—since I don't even know when."

"It always comes back. Hey, Reg, when was your last tetanus shot?" Harry finished wrapping Reg's wound, leaving him with a white gauze mitten on his left hand.

"Fuck if I know."

"Then I've got a little something for you," Harry said, pulling a syringe from his duffle. "Con, could you push the robe sleeve up off his shoulder?"

Quirke did as instructed, exposing Reg's right shoulder under the T-shirt beneath the black robe. Harry rubbed alcohol over the lower part of the deltoid muscle, administered the vaccine, and taped a cotton ball over the injection site. "You're good to go, buddy. So, Con, what kind of bass have you got?"

"Had, actually. I had a sweet little Fender Mustang. I'd love to lay my hands on that instrument again."

"Money troubles part you?"

"No, it was an ex-wife's idea of housecleaning."

"I'd have dumped her, too, man, that is so outrageous. Well, you're gonna like Reg's StingRay."

"Wow. You sure it's OK? I feel unworthy. I *am* unworthy."

"Just get baked and practice with us a little, and you'll be fine, you'll see."

"That's another thing I haven't done in a while." Early in the course of his legal education Quirke had thought it prudent to quit smoking marijuana, both to facilitate effective studying and because his father-in-law would have had a cow had he gotten caught with it. Of course, although he hadn't been thinking that far ahead, a drug arrest would also have complicated his admission to the bar and almost certainly aborted his judicial ambitions.

At this admission, Harry studied Quirke. "How do you know Sadie again?"

"Work," Quirke responded, hoping but doubting Harry would find his answer sufficient.

"You a lawyer, too?"

As Quirke was trying to think of a reply that wouldn't potentially subject him to disciplinary proceedings, the temple doors opened and members of the order began to file out. Several approached Reg to check on his condition, and Harry was soon conversing with them. Quirke, meanwhile, went to look for Sadie.

She had gone to their room to put away her robe and was once again kimono-clad, sitting in the rocking chair, rocking abstractedly. At Quirke's entrance, she rose and put her arms around him. He sensed fatigue and regret in her demeanor, and held her silently close for some minutes.

"I gather there was a little mishap in the ceremony, but Reg seems to be fine," he said at last. "Harry took care of him. It sure is convenient to have an EMT around."

"My fault," she said, her voice muffled against his chest. "I didn't mean to hurt him, but I was tired and careless."

"Accidents happen. Everyone understands that."

"Maybe I should take a break from all this," she said.

"Maybe you need a nap and something to eat. It was a long drive and we were up early. Or is it something more? Tell me how I can help."

"By being in my life. I'm afraid I'm going to scare you away, Conal. I can be needy at times."

She looked up at him with uncharacteristic sadness and self-doubt.

There was that feeling again, the uncanny feeling that his words could will a new reality into being. Logic kept muttering about the impermanence of rebound relationships, but something truer and deeper than logic urged him to hold fast to her and his reborn life. "I was going to wait until things get under some kind of control in my life, but on second thought, now seems like the right moment," he said.

"For what?"

"To ask you to marry me. When it's no longer a felony, of course."

"Technically bigamy is a wobbler, but..." She stopped, her eyes widening.

He laughed. "Well, I almost succeeded in leaving you speechless It's OK, don't give me an answer now. Wait till I'm able to do it the proper way, with a big gaudy diamond ring and all that."

His proposal succeeded in lifting Sadie's mood. Although she continued more or less mute, it was a happier muteness, and he had the definite sense she was favorably inclined toward the idea of becoming his wife. At his suggestion, she lay down and soon fell asleep, and he went off in search of ways to make himself useful as evening darkened the skies over the cabin.

Carleton put him in an apron and set him to work manning the grills. Under his supervision, chicken, steaks and kebabs yielded their juices to charcoal and mesquite as the other components of the meal were assembled on tables moved out to the yard for the purpose. Fellow guests helpfully kept bringing him beers until he was feeling decently elevated. About the time Sadie made her appearance, looking refreshed and ravishing in a purple shalwar kameez, the meal was served. They all made a curious declaration over it involving will and great work, and ultimately pronounced it delicious.

She wanted to introduce him to everyone in succession, but Harry intervened, pulling him toward the garage on the other side of the cabin where they were to practice before playing their set. Easing the StingRay's strap over his head and feeling its lustrous, shapely body in his hands stirred long-buried muscle memory. For an anxious moment, Quirke struggled to remember how to tune the bass. Then someone started passing around a bottle of Jack Daniel's, and he had his third moment of clarity of the day. The band got through some old standbys, songs Quirke had played dozens if not hundreds of times back in the day—Black Sabbath's *Paranoid*, Pink Floyd's *Money*, the Kinks' *You Really Got Me Now*, the Clash's *Should I Stay or Should I Go*, Hendrix's arrangement of Dylan's *All Along the Watchtower*, Guns 'n' Roses' *Sweet Child o' Mine,* and the band's signature finale, Iron Maiden's *Number of the Beast*—and Harry deemed them ready to rock (with Quirke trying to ignore his butterflies and private doubts). They set up their amps and speakers at a slight distance from the tables, which had now been cleared of food, and connected their instruments.

"Brothers and sisters," Harry said to the audience, "earlier today we thought for a minute all was lost when Reg had his unfortunate accident, but as luck would have it, we have a special guest filling in on bass. Con," he whispered to Quirke, "what's your last name?"

"Leave it at Con," Quirke whispered back. In case any of the Order ever engaged in such mundane civic duties as voting, he preferred musical anonymity to their recognizing his distinctive name on the ballot.

"So, my friends, give it up for Con and the Aethyrs," Harry yelled, leading straight into the count for *Paranoid*, to raucous applause.

Quirke laughed out loud at Sadie's dumbfounded expression when she finally stopped chatting long enough to look up at the band and noticed him playing. Between the abbreviated rehearsal, revived memory, and some inborn facility at faking when necessary, he held up his end of things adequately over the first couple of songs, even singing along behind Thom, the lead vocalist. Then Harry, their lead guitarist, who played like a professional, paused to light up and passed Quirke the biggest joint he'd ever seen.

On later reflection, what surprised Quirke was how deliberation played no part in his reaching for it, taking a deep drag, and another, and passing it back. Smoking weed—which, after all, was still illegal in the circumstances—should, if done at all, have been the product of a calculated decision, weighing all possible consequences, pro and con. But none of the important things he'd done lately—most notably asking Sadie to marry him—had emerged from rational processes. His intellect seemed to be away on holiday, and something else was in charge.

That something, whatever it was, in any event was a far better bass player than the thinking side of him. The awkward barrier between himself and the music dropped away, and the songs flowed together. Too soon they were driving the opening riffs of *Number of the Beast*, and then their set was over.

As the audience hooted and applauded, Harry slapped him on the back and pressed the neck of the Jack Daniel's bottle into his palm. "You did fine, man. How did it feel?"

Quirke took a gulp of the whiskey, feeling his head start to spin on top of the vibration he was still feeling from the amplifier. "Fantastic. I didn't know how much I missed it," he answered, hoarse from his background vocalizing.

"We've got a gig in San Gregorio day after tomorrow, you up for it?"

"You're kidding."

"Not at all. Reg won't be ready to play for another week at least. Meanwhile, we need a bass player, and you just passed the audition."

"I'd love to, but I'm on the bench Tuesday. It just won't—"

"On the bench? What, are you with the Giants?"

"Sorry, I—"

Sadie had come to him out of the crowd, and before embracing her he gently placed the StingRay on its stand at his side.

"I about fell off my chair seeing you up there," she said after a jubilant kiss.

He laughed. "I noticed that."

"If I haven't told you lately, you're beyond amazing, you're magical. Literally, figuratively, every which way. When did you become a musician? While I was taking a nap?"

"Sometime before you were born, dearest. The guys here helped me remember it. They're terrific. Harry asked me to play with them at some gig on Monday night. I was thrilled to death."

"That would be wonderful—too bad you have oral argument on Tuesday."

"That's what I told him. More or less. Actually, I think he has the impression I play baseball for a living."

Before Sadie could reply, the crack of a rifle shot and an angry yell from within the woods at the margin of the property shocked the party into silence. A few of the men headed in the direction of the sounds, and

Quirke, with a sinking feeling, followed them.

They came upon their host in a clearing, holding a semiautomatic rifle and shouting warnings at whatever was retreating noisily through the brush toward the road below. "Take it easy, Carleton—what's up?" someone asked him.

"Damn media scat," he sputtered. "I built way out here to get away from pests like that. What the hell do you think they wanted this time?"

"Did you hit anyone?"

"If I'd been aiming at 'em, I would've."

"What were they doing, exactly?" Quirke asked.

"Tramping in my woods and taking pictures of my house and my temple and my friends and my party. For all I know, they've been out there all day, goddamn—"

"How often does this happen?" said Quirke.

"Not since...Well, now that you ask, I don't think it's happened before. At the temple in Oakland, once, we had some people picketing us, but never up here."

"Well, it looks like you scared 'em off good," Reg said. "Think we need to post a guard tonight?"

"I'll come out and check later. Okay, everybody, I guess we can relax for now. But keep an eye out while you're here, and check media now and again after you head home. If you see anything weird developing, let me know, day or night."

Quirke returned to Sadie and filled her in. "I may just be feeling paranoid from the first weed I've smoked in thirty years," he said, "but the timing's odd. I'll bet I'm the first Supreme Court justice facing a simultaneous high-profile divorce and election to come up here and hang out with your people, and somebody decides this is the time to snoop around. What I'm trying to figure out is how they would have found me here. I didn't notice anybody following us, did you? Never mind—it's too weird. I'm just cross-faded. Too much beer and Jack and cannabis on top of it. Is there anyone you wanted to introduce me to? Before we turn in?" He held her close, kissing her and squeezing her buttocks.

Coming up for air, she said, "We need to find a regular band for you; playing seems to do you a ton of good. Yes, there's a bunch of people for you to meet—hey, Peter finally made it up here." She waved and called out to Peter Blake across the lawn. "And I need to apologize to Reg. Though without my stupid carelessness, who knows when you'd have remembered you're a great musician on top of everything else?"

Chapter Ten

September 2, 3:10 p.m.

" 'Engaging in sexual behavior in chambers is the height of irresponsible and improper behavior by a judge, and shows disrespect for the dignity and decorum of the courtroom.' I didn't make that up, Lucas—these are the words of the Commission on Judicial Behavior in their decision in a disciplinary proceeding just last week," said Hetford, waving at Quirke's head of chambers the document from which he had just quoted.

"I saw that case, Judge," Lucas replied, shifting in his chair. "There were some fairly significant factual differences between it and the matter at hand, though. For one thing, the judge in that case was doing it on a regular basis with his courtroom clerk. Who was married. And to top it off, he lied about the affair to his presiding judge. From what you're saying, Justice Quirke's never denied anything. And the incident seems to have been a one-off. And Sadie's not married."

"Better to leave it to the Commission in the first instance to decide whether the differences matter. Besides, shouldn't Quirke be held to an even higher standard, as a justice of this court? And you're forgetting one aggravating factor: his substance abuse, which is impairing his fitness to serve. It's fair to call him an alcoholic at this point, I'd say. How would you like being a litigant with a case in front of this court, knowing what you know about his drinking habits?"

"Well, he may be a heavy drinker, or even an alcoholic, I don't know, but I've never seen him drunk on the bench or in chambers. Except that one time, and it was after hours."

"Lucas, I thought we shared a sense of the gravity of what you witnessed that night. I assumed you and I share a mutual value system. That was why I offered to make you my chief of staff, and why I believed you accepted." Hetford rose from behind his desk to lean over the short-statured attorney, who shrank even further in the guest chair.

"It's still true, Judge. I've always admired you and your jurisprudence. I never really fit in, somehow, in Justice Quirke's chambers. But filing a complaint against him kind of puts me in an awkward position."

"Of course, you realize he can't possibly retaliate against you. He's not stupid. And if he tried, you'd make the move to my staff immediately. You're completely protected."

"So, should I tell him?"

"That's up to you. Now why don't you go and take care of it? And while I'm thinking of it, have you gotten him to see reason on *Amar*?"

"He hasn't said anything about it in the last few days; I don't think he's decided."

"Well, move him along—the clock's ticking."

"I'll do that. See you later, Judge."

"Thank you for everything, Lucas. And don't look so glum—the way is clearing before us."

Lucas descended from the fourth-floor chambers of his future boss to the third-floor chambers of his current boss, where everyone was still at work. Passing along the corridor on the way to his office he saw Sadie at her desk, so immersed in the drafting of a calendar memo that she never even raised her head at his footsteps. A spasm of an ancient anger seized him, that she could be so oblivious to him and yet so inappropriately infatuated with the slack and shallow, fat and self-indulgent Quirke. Well, maybe when Quirke's troubles came, and they were surely coming, she'd reconsider where she chose to bestow her feelings. Closing the door, he drew his phone from his pocket and stared, for perhaps the hundredth time, at the photo of her spreading her legs to the man he was going to bring down.

Then he sat at his computer, typed the commission's address into his browser and, after sundry clicking, began to work his way through its online complaint form. He first filled in his name and contact information, and then Quirke's name and court—*'Supreme Court' should get that intake clerk's attention*, he reflected. Next the form asked him to categorize the complaint, offering a dozen options. He was uncertain whether 'Misconduct Outside of Court' applied, given the circumstances, but 'Demeanor/Decorum' seemed to fit, so he checked it as well as 'Substance Abuse.' Then he filled in the box asking for a narrative description of the alleged misconduct, trying to walk the stylistic line between graphic and clinical. In the box for 'Other Witnesses and Evidence,' he typed in 'Ms. Sadie Norrell' and 'photographic evidence available on request.' At the end, he checked the box verifying the truth of his complaint and, before he could have second thoughts, pressed 'send.'

Waiting for the elevator at the close of business, Quirke couldn't help indulging in an air guitar solo. After the weekend with Sadie in Sant' Amaro with its manifold pleasures, he felt he had his old mojo back and was actually looking forward to oral argument the following day. Then his head of chambers exited the security doors and came to stand in front of the elevator bank with him. As always when in close proximity to his birdlike chief lawyer, Quirke felt hulking, even huge, although he was somewhat shy of six feet tall and still, if barely, under two hundred pounds in weight despite a new fondness for beer that he'd brought home with him from Sant' Amaro. Lucas had mostly avoided him since the fateful evening, but tonight he was tolerating, if somewhat warily, Quirke's presence. Quirke was feeling too good to do otherwise himself.

"Hello, Lucas. And how are you this evening?"

"Fine, Judge."

"Look, I know you took an interest in the *Amar* case. I should tell you I'll be dissenting. John's working on it now. Just couldn't see my way to signing the majority. Sorry."

"Sure." For a guy who'd worked him relentlessly for weeks to join Hetford's opinion, Lucas seemed surprisingly indifferent to this announcement. In fact, he appeared preoccupied, paying scarcely any attention to Quirke at all. But just as the elevator arrived and the two of them were getting in, he spoke.

"You're going to hear about it sooner or later, Judge, so I'll just tell you. I've filed a complaint against you with the CJB."

Quirke heard but did not immediately comprehend. Then he laughed involuntarily. "Hello, what?"

"A confidential complaint arising out of your activities in chambers on August fifteenth."

Quirke loomed silent over the bantam attorney on the ride to the ground floor. As the doors slid open, he exited, saying drily, "Do whatever you feel you need to do, Lucas."

※

At the loft, Quirke stalked without a word past a baffled Peter directly to Sadie's room, unscrewed the cap on the bottle of Maker's Mark on the dresser, and drank directly from it, first one gulp, then another, and a third before filling the glass next to it and draining that as well. Sadie, who had been lying prone on the bed, propped up on her elbows reading a book pending his arrival, rolled over and came up from behind to put her arms around him as he refilled the glass.

"Good grief, what's wrong?" she exclaimed.

"He's taking a more direct approach to getting rid of me."

"Who? What do you mean?"

"Lucas filed a complaint against me. With the CJB. Concerning our encounter in chambers. What exactly does he have against sex, anyway?"

"The fact he's never gotten any? What does it mean?"

"I don't know, but the Commission's sure to look into it, maybe do a full-blown disciplinary investigation, and who the hell knows what happens then? They just censured some schmuck down in Jefferson Superior who was boffing his clerk in chambers; it might have whetted their appetite for more morals prosecutions." He emptied the glass and poured another, saying, "Don't mind me, I'm just getting wasted over here."

"So, Lucas told you this?"

"As we were leaving for the day."

"And what did you do?"

Quirke paused, slightly glassy-eyed. "I wanted to crush his smarmy little windpipe against the elevator door. I could kill him barehanded, you know; I'm almost twice his size. But the thought of having to do twenty-five to life in the joint, without you, next to all the guys I've sent up over the years, sort of put me off it."

"No jury would convict you of first degree murder in the circumstances. Second degree, maybe."

"I wouldn't even do it for fifteen to life."

"Not that I'm encouraging you—although someone would be doing a huge public service to eliminate Lucas—but you'd probably get voluntary manslaughter. Good chance you'd get the low term and be out in less than three."

He shook his head. "If I were the trial judge, I wouldn't instruct on voluntary. No legally sufficient provocation."

"Well, if I were the Court of Appeal," she retorted, "I'd reverse you and send it back for a new trial."

"But then the hard-ass DA would retaliate by adding a witness-killing special and trying to put me on death row. No, it's just as well I only told him to do what he needed to do and left him to stew in his own rancid juices."

"Actually, the witness-killing special only covers murdering witnesses to criminal and juvenile cases—not administrative proceedings like CJB. But the whole thing's ridiculous anyway. You can't really be worried. Are you?"

"I don't know whether to be, and soon I'll be too drunk to think about it."

Sadie came around and took his face in her hands. "Conal, my love, don't *you* take poison and expect *him* to die. Let's fuck our brains out instead. Or go to your favorite restaurant. Or see if we can get tickets to the symphony. Garrick Ohlsson's playing the Rach 3 tonight."

"I know you're trying to help, but I'm so furious I can't see straight. Even before I had any of this stuff," he said, shaking the near-empty whiskey bottle. "You know, I never liked him. I don't know why I kept him on. I just wanted to give all of Carraway's people a chance, and see where my sense of fairness has gotten me? I'm undermined and threatened and constantly harassed to sign Hetford's opinions. Trouble is, now I couldn't fire Lucas if he came in and peed all over my set of official reports—it'd be retaliatory. If only he'd find a more attractive alternative to being my head of chambers. But who in the world would want him?"

"I think you should talk to the Chief tomorrow. Maybe she can find a new job for him. Or send him on a fact-finding mission to...someplace the Centers for Disease Control are warning against. Or something."

Quirke wore a far-off look, imagining the squeamish Lucas in a foreign land where ailments for which no vaccines exist are endemic.

Sadie stroked his belly, feeling him relax ever so slightly under the gentle pressure of her fingertips. "You need to eat, darling. Let me take you out. And then let's make an early night of it—you're on the bench at nine sharp tomorrow morning. You know the Chief always likes to start on time."

He exhaled, smiled for the first time that evening, and kissed her. "There aren't words for how wonderful you are."

"I had a boyfriend once who said I was built like a car."

"You got a hubcap diamond star halo, all right. You're dirty sweet and you're my girl."

Chapter Eleven

September 3, 8:55 a.m.

Down a secure corridor inaccessible even to most court staff, adjacent to the courtroom in the old state building, is the Supreme Court justices' robing room. In the modern era, most of the justices prefer to don their robes in their own chambers, so the now inaptly named robing room is largely more of a staging area, the place where they arrange themselves in the proper order to file out and take the bench. Because the Chief always sits in the center of the seven-member court, she is fourth in line, led by the second most junior associate justice, the third most senior associate justice and the most senior associate justice, in that order; and followed by the second most senior, third most junior, and, bringing up the rear, the most junior associate justice. After each session's adjournment, the justices exit the courtroom in the reverse order.

While waiting in the robing room, the Chief can communicate with the clerk-administrator, who is supervising matters in the courtroom, by mobile phone. There is a big-screen CCTV monitor in the robing room, so the justices can see who is in attendance before they take the bench. On the monitor, they can also observe assistant deputy clerks deploying water jugs and glasses and placing their individual benchbooks, with their notes and all the court's internal memoranda pertaining to the cases being argued, at the appropriate spots on the bench. In the center of the robing room, next to a full-length mirror mounted on a walnut base, stands a table bearing a coffee pot with a tray of mugs and cookies. Behind an unmarked door on the eastern wall is a discreet loo.

A notable exception to the trend away from robing in the robing room is Associate Justice Allan Hetford, who, perhaps due to a pardonable, and probably unconscious, desire to display his exceptionally toned physique, has always preferred to strip off his bespoke jacket and put on his robe over his fitted dress shirts while in the company of his colleagues. On the morning of Wednesday, September 3, Justice Hetford followed his usual practice despite arriving relatively late, at 8:55 a.m. As late as Justice Hetford was, Justice Quirke was even later—striding into the robing room, already robed, at 8:58—and therefore missed Justice Hetford's display. That he was aware of having missed anything is doubtful.

What Quirke did not miss was the silence that descended when he entered. Two-thirds of the so-called bloc (Justices Kroner and Farley), who had been talking with each other in a corner of the room, fell still and eyed

Quirke coldly when he approached the mirror to check that his tie was properly knotted. Justice Corcoran, at the opposite end of the room, exhibited the same frosty reaction. And Justice Wiggins made no effort to conceal her disdain as she took a pile of cookies from the tray and began to eat them aggressively, staring openly at him the while. The Chief, on her phone with Freitag checking on courtroom readiness, appeared oblivious to the new dynamic. Hetford, too, was whispering urgently into his phone, glancing at Quirke and moving as far away from him as possible consistent with remaining in the same room.

"Good morning, all," Quirke greeted his colleagues, receiving only a couple of icy nods in return. As a criminal defense lawyer, he had faced some hostile juries in his time, but they all paled in comparison with this bunch. It looked like counsel were going to be in for it today.

Unless something else was going on, and the hostility was in fact aimed at him. The realization hit him like a brick. Of course: His relationship with Sadie must somehow have become public knowledge; this kind of unspoken, unanimous social condemnation could only have been excited by something as deeply abhorred as judge/staff attorney miscegenation. No doubt they assumed he was about to heartlessly dump a loving wife for the younger woman. Had they also learned about the abortive tryst in chambers—was the despicable Lucas spreading the photographic evidence around?

Quirke felt his pulse quicken, his cheeks redden, and sweat start to pool under his arms. He tried to walk rather than run into the lavatory, where he shut the door and began to splash cold water over his face, getting the sleeves of his robe wet up to the elbows in the process but not greatly affecting the hectic blush.

He had not been inside for ten seconds when there was a knock at the door. "It's show time," came the Chief's voice. *Fuck*, he mouthed at himself in the mirror. "Coming," he replied in as pleasant a tone as he could muster. After drying his face as best he could with the recycled paper toweling emanating from the dispenser on the wall, he took a deep breath, emerged from the washroom, and fell in behind Hetford as the justices began to march through the passageway into the courtroom.

Along with the usual assortment of staff, observers and court groupies, a sea of suits confronted them this morning. The multistate tax compact case was the third one being argued, and quite a few corporations with a significant stake in the outcome had sent representatives to see which way the adjudicatory wind might be blowing. First, however, after all the justices had filed in and taken their seats, the Chief called the session to order.

"Today we welcome the eleventh-grade civics classes of Nova Pequeña High School," she said. "Students, I'm sure you'll find this an interesting excursion into the workings of our state government. Our first case this morning is *People versus Orlando Quintillion*, number S344215."

Quintillion was a simple case of statutory interpretation. One subdivision of Penal Code section 288a makes it a crime to orally copulate a person who is incapable of consenting because of unconsciousness. A different subdivision of the same statute makes it a crime to commit the same act on a person unable to consent because of intoxication. So, did Quintillion commit one crime or two when he took forcible advantage of an unfortunate young woman who was passed out drunk at the time? As the court and counsel debated the finer points of the statutory language and legislative history, Quirke hoped the eleventh graders in the audience were pondering the case's broader lessons.

Next was a case in which a motorist, pulled over for suspected drunken driving, failed field sobriety tests but blew an ambiguous breathalyzer test, arguably below the .08 percent blood alcohol concentration that would trigger administrative suspension of his license. The question before the court was whether the Department of Motor Vehicles was entitled to use evidence that the driver had horizontal nystagmus—jumpy gaze, in other words—and did a sloppy job in trying to comply with the highway patrol officer's instruction to walk heel-to-toe along the roadside to make up for the doubtful proof of blood alcohol concentration.

Here, too, Quirke hoped the civics students could see past the narrow legal issue to discern the relevance of the case for their lives. For Quirke, the realization he had enjoyed notable luck so far in avoiding the consequences of his own overindulgence was sobering. Thoughts of Sadie, and of the unknown future between them, kept intruding as he tried to pay attention to the argument.

Last on the morning's calendar was the case most of the audience had come to hear: the multistate tax compact case. He found it easier to concentrate on this abstract question of competing apportionment formulas, which involved nothing more, at bottom, than money. The preparation he'd done in Sant' Amaro paid off, as he managed to get in a couple of questions that cut to the chase while hinting at his inclination to uphold the constitutionality of the formula required under the 1993 amendment to the Revenue and Taxation Code. This suited petitioner's counsel right down to the ground, and Quirke heard verbal bouquets being tossed in his direction. "Justice Quirke's point is well taken," counsel was saying.

He felt Hetford seethe next to him, ominously twisting a rolled-up piece of paper, and Quirke knew he would later have to pay dearly in some fashion. In due course the Chief told petitioner's counsel his time was up, and opposing counsel took the lectern. The suits in the audience continued to scribble notes, and by and by it was time for rebuttal. Still Hetford kept silent. When counsel's five reserved minutes were up, the Chief gaveled the session to a close.

"The matter stands submitted, and the court is in recess until 1:30."

"All rise," Ward Freitag intoned, and the audience stood up as the members of the court began to depart the bench.

A middle-aged man with a conservative haircut and Roy Orbison eyeglasses who'd been sitting in the front spectator row hastened through the gate into the well where the attorneys who'd just finished their argument were gathering their papers. His right hand was extended, and he smiled pleasantly, chirping "Justice Quirke? Justice Quirke?"

For anyone to approach the bench as the justices exited the courtroom was practically unheard of, but the fellow was well-dressed and, although Quirke did not recognize him, he did not appear to be either a lunatic or a terrorist. Stopping, by force of social habit Quirke extended his hand to meet the stranger's. As the man drew within a foot of the bench, his left hand stuck a sheaf of paper into Quirke's outstretched right.

"You've been served," he said.

Hetford, behind Quirke, snorted.

The Chief, noticing the exchange, frowned. The remaining audience members, also noticing, perked up at this interesting development. A few legal blogs would have some juicier than usual material tonight.

The caption on the papers Quirke had just been handed read: 'Marriage of Eleanor Scorchner Quirke, Petitioner, and Conal Quirke, Respondent: Petition for Dissolution of Marriage' and 'Summons (Family Law).' Quirke sighed. "Great. You couldn't wait three minutes until I got back in chambers?"

The man looked even more embarrassed than Quirke felt. "I'm terribly sorry, Your Honor, but my specific instructions were to be sure and serve you on the bench. May I say it was a fascinating oral argument session?"

"We do our best," said Quirke, fumbling in his pants pockets beneath his robe. "Sorry, I seem to have left my wallet in my jacket back in the office."

The Chief, who, contrary to all precedent, had stayed in the courtroom to monitor the turn of events, sought to terminate the encounter by putting her hands on Quirke's shoulders and steering him toward the exit, advising: "You don't tip the process server."

The man nodded. "Madam Chief Justice is correct. My compensation is taken care of by the other party."

"Well, have a nice day, then," said Quirke, acceding to the Chief's pressure and moving off.

"It was a pleasure to serve you, Your Honor," the man called, quivering with suppressed laughter at his own joke.

The other justices and Ward Freitag stood around the robing room, some wondering what had happened in the courtroom after they'd departed and the others whispering excitedly of what they had glimpsed. The Chief, upon entering, held up a hand and spoke more acidly than was her wont. "Ward, the well is for counsel making their appearances and court staff only. I don't want to see any of the audience in it again. I hope I'm making myself clear."

"Of course, Chief; I'm sorry. I'll speak with security. We'll get more bodies in there this afternoon."

"Fine, but this time screen them for consciousness. The court will conference in my chambers in ten minutes." While the associate justices continued to stand around expectantly, the Chief departed down the secure hallway toward her chambers.

Avoiding his colleagues, Quirke followed her out and then peeled off toward his own chambers. He poked his head inside John's office. "Round everyone up, would you, please? I want to meet briefly."

"Sure, Judge." John was already rising from his computer desk and heading toward Freddie's office.

Next Quirke entered Sadie's office and shut the door. She turned an apprehensive face toward him.

"What happened in there? The resolution on the CCTV's so fuzzy I couldn't tell if that guy was a long-lost friend or a would-be assassin."

"The good news is I'm now officially the respondent in Eleanor's dissolution proceeding and one step closer to being free to marry you—if you'll still have me, that is, and if you've had second thoughts, I can hardly blame you. The bad news is she's going for maximum embarrassment, having me served with process in the courtroom with two hundred lawyers looking on and snickering. Oh, and the other bad news is I'm afraid we're no longer a secret. This morning, before we went on the bench, the others were glaring at me as though they'd seen the infamous photo, or heard eyewitness testimony. I'm sorry, Sadie. I never wanted any harm to come to you or your privacy or reputation."

"Don't worry about me. I'm the original libel plaintiff who couldn't prove damages because my reputation already sucked eggs. It's you I'm concerned about."

"Well, never mind now. I only want to tell the staff there might be some turbulence on this flight, and then I have to go conference the morning cases and have something to eat if there's time before the afternoon calendar."

In the staff conference room, all except Lucas had gathered. "I can't find him," said John.

"No matter," said Quirke. "Comrades, in case there's talk, I want you to know what happened in the courtroom just now: I accepted service of Eleanor's petition for dissolution of marriage. I also want to say you may be hearing rumors of a personal relationship between Sadie and me. As I'm sure you're aware by now, it's true. Now, don't go all post hoc, ergo propter hoc on me: one didn't cause the other. That's it for now; I have to go upstairs and conference, and we'll meet and talk about the cases later." Quirke unzipped his robe and threw it over the back of his guest chair, while Margie stood by with a hanger.

After the judge had departed for the Chief's conference room, John and Freddie stood with Sadie in the hallway.

"I'm sorry to have caused you extra work," she told John. "You knew, right?"

"I had a pretty good idea," he said. "I'm glad. You'll be good for him."

Sadie gave a little cry and hugged him. "Thank you, you're wonderful. You and Freddie are both so wonderful. I'll be so sad to leave this place."

Freddie gasped. "You can't! It would kill him. Where are you going?"

"I don't know. And you mustn't say a word until I've figured it out and prepared him. This is the best job I can imagine ever having, and my heart's already breaking at the thought of not seeing him—and you guys— all day long, but things have become untenable. For everyone's sake I have to move on. So, if you hear of any openings—"

She fell silent as Lucas rounded the corner into their section of the hallway.

"We just met with the judge," said John.

"I've been briefed," he replied, with an unaccustomed hauteur. The other attorneys looked at each other.

Chapter Twelve

August 29, 1996, 4:10 p.m.

Laudie had yet to set down her small valise. Instead, circling the great room, wide-eyed, exhaustion showing, she clutched it as if to save it from thieves.

Captain Henry Clayton Forrester (USN, ret.) stood in the center of the room as she surveyed her new home. He faced the French doors giving onto the garden and did not turn along with her but steadfastly awaited the completion of her circuit. His bride looked younger than her thirty years, slender to an extreme and pale on account of having spent the summer behind bars. He intended to put some flesh on her bones and roses in her cheeks with the love he felt for her and with his pure way of living, which he would transmit to her with his seed now that they were united in the eyes of the Lord. She needed to be remade after having been pulled by God's grace out of the criminal lifestyle she'd been embedded in and washed clean in Pastor Rowe's prison ministry baptismal wading pool. She didn't like to speak of the things she'd done, which he took as proof of the sanctifying shame she'd undergone. Now, safe with her new loving husband, she could leave all that error and evil behind and grow in godliness like the good wife he dreamed of during the months he'd waited for her parole.

A knock sounded at the front door, followed by a familiar silky voice, easily heard through the screen. "Are the newlyweds at home? Just checking in to see that Laudie got processed out all right."

"Pastor Rowe is so very thoughtful," she said. She looked expectantly at the Captain, who laughed.

"Well, honey, you're the mistress of the house. Go ahead, answer the door."

She obeyed with her first smile since stepping over the threshold and returned with the tall, dark-haired young pastor, who held a bouquet of daisies he'd likely picked from the front yard of the residence the congregation provided him. "I'll give these some water," she said, heading toward the kitchen.

The pastor stood with the Captain in the center of the room, looking through the glass doors onto the flower beds and tidy lawn, which declined to the weeping willow trees at the far edge of the property.

"God does answer prayers," said the Captain.

"Sometimes in very straightforward ways," Rowe replied. "You recall the concern I told you Mrs. Forrester mentioned in her marriage preparation session?"

"I do, and I'll not forget it. Things she did before she turned to our Lord aren't to be held against her. Forbidden knowledge can't be unlearned."

"And that very knowledge, now that it's separated forever by God's forgiveness from the blameworthy acts that imparted it, may, paradoxically, enrich your marriage. You know what I'm saying, Captain?"

"I may not be what others would call a man of the world, Pastor, but I believe I do."

"You're fortunate God brought the two of you together. And how remarkable she's remained so untouched in her essential goodness by what she endured."

Laudie, bearing a tray of glasses filled with iced tea, reentered the great room. "Gentlemen, would you care for refreshments?" She set the tray on the coffee table, departed once more, and returned with Rowe's daisies in a mason jar, setting them beside the tray.

September 20, 1996, 3:40 p.m.

Pastor Rowe checked in frequently on his newlywed parishioners. He was gratified to see that Laudie seemed dedicated to pleasing the Captain, who, although smitten from the start by her angelic looks, had initially expressed doubt that any human being as inured to the criminal lifestyle as she had been could resist its lure once paroled. On none of his home visits did Rowe see anything in her demeanor or behavior to suggest the Captain's fears were justified. Indeed, she seemed perfect: always modest, soft-spoken, and submissive. A total Christian wife.

Then, one humid late summer afternoon, he stopped by the house to find her crying, alone. At first, she put on a brave front, but—seeing the effort it cost her—he demanded to know what was wrong.

"The Captain...insisted," she said, her eyes cast down. "I wasn't well, but he...forced me..."

Rage swelled upward in Rowe. He was all for wifely submissiveness, but a husband must never take away the wife's choice whether to submit. How could the man he'd thought his honorable friend, who'd waited patiently all those months for her release, rape his cherished spouse? She seemed to fold in on herself, and he found himself holding her as she sobbed.

After a hiccup of time in which he seemed to lose and recover consciousness, he found himself kissing her, touching her, falling with her to the sofa. Bewildered, he forced himself to pull away, but for a few moments could not speak. She was looking at him as though seeing into his soul, laying bare with those beautiful eyes all the desires and fears and regrets he hid there.

"I—I apologize for my monstrous behavior," he said at last. "You confided in me about your husband's violation, and then I went and did the same. It was entirely wrong, and I'll stop inflicting my sinful presence on you right here and now. I'll be ready to apologize to the Captain if he should ever care to look at my face again. Until then, I—"

"No, Rowe...my dear Rowe." Her hand, as delicate as rose petals, caressed his cheek. "Please don't withdraw from our lives. I'm sure there's a reason for this feeling you and I have for each other. I trust it'll all become clear. Don't you? I need you, Rowe. Don't you know that I'd never heard the Word until you brought it to me in my imprisonment? That you opened my eyes and ears to heaven? If you take it away, I haven't the strength to live. What will become of the Captain and me?"

"Don't, Laudie; don't talk that way. I won't let you suffer for my weakness. But what'll I say to him?"

"Why must you say anything? It would only destroy his peace of mind." She slipped her arms around him, and he lacked the will to push her away. Her eyes, gazing up into his, signified perdition; no Christian man needed warning. It was the oddest sensation—like what an alcoholic feels, he supposed, when he sees a bottle of gin, knowing that at the bottom of it he'll find only the hospital, the gutter or a jail cell, and yet craving it no less.

※

November 18, 1997, 11:15 a.m.

"But are you sure? Beyond any doubt? How can you be? I mean, we were together—"

"Of course, I'm sure. A mother knows. Why, she even looks like the Captain."

"All babies look like little old men. What's she going to look like in fifteen years, that's what I want to know."

"Rowe, darling, I'm so certain Zelda's the Captain's daughter that I'd give her to you in marriage without the slightest concern for the genetic consequences. Now stop fussing and hand me that diaper bag, please."

Rowe handed her the carryall and sat down on the rocking chair in the corner of the nursery. "You know, that might not be such a crazy idea."

"I'm glad you approve; I need to change her before she gets a rash."

"No, I mean...me marrying Zelda."

Laudie lay the infant on the changing table and unsnapped her onesie. She undid the old disposable, folded it into a neat bundle, and stowed it in the Diaper Genie as Rowe looked on. Then she wiped the baby clean, fastened a new diaper on her, and dressed her again.

"We'd have a reason to stay close forever," he said.

Laudie straddled Rowe's lap, stroking his hair, inclining her head to kiss him. Her tongue penetrated his mouth as her hand slid under the waistband of his pants and began to fondle him. He closed his eyes, a soft moan escaping him, and lifted her blouse. Her breasts were big and heavy, almost hard. As he squeezed the left breast lightly, a little jet of milk escaped. He tore his lips from hers and sucked her erect nipple; his left hand found its way to her other breast as the milk let down and trickled through his fingers.

Zelda whimpered, sucked her thumb in self-comfort, and drifted off to sleep on the changing table.

※

April 17, 2004, 3:30 p.m.

Just when Laudie, scarcely handicapped by the absence of light, was about to pick the pathetic lock on the drawer where she'd seen Rowe hide his personal journal, she heard footsteps coming down the hallway outside his office. There was never a perfect time for burglary, never a day or an hour when parishioners or other staff might not turn up, and she'd made up her mind to take her chances when Rowe announced he was going to the exegetical conference. Her cover story was that he'd called from the conference and asked her to fax him some notes he'd left behind.

As the footsteps receded, she mentally tucked the cover story away and resumed working at the lock. A gratifying click soon rewarded her efforts, and the drawer popped open. She felt around in it for the limp leather-bound journal and moved to the window. After laying it open on the floor and adjusting the blinds to let in as much light as she dared, she pulled a tiny camera from her coat pocket and began to shoot, working her way through the book page by page. Reaching the most recent entries, she paused to read. Just last week, Rowe had applied for appointment to a church in Tennessee! That was not part of the plan, not at all. The Lord would not be pleased to hear it.

※

April 18, 2004, 7:48 p.m.

"I was praying last night, just before I went to sleep, Rowe, and—this may sound crazy, but the Lord appeared to me with a message. For you."

Laudie and the Captain were entertaining their pastor for dinner, as they often did on Sunday evenings. The cook's crown roast sat resplendent in the middle of the table, surrounded by a piped mashed-potato border and bowls of glazed carrots and peas. A coconut cake awaited them on the sideboard. At Laudie's revelation, both men dropped their forks.

"Why, Laudie, you never told me—"

"You'd already fallen asleep, Captain, and I didn't like to awaken you. He was standing in the corner of the bedroom, in front of the closet, wearing a beautiful robe, purple and flowing, and His face was all lit up by His halo. So kind and loving! I felt so deeply how He loves me. And all of us. He said to tell you, Rowe, don't make that change you're thinking about. It is not His will, He was very definite about it. It would grieve our Lord terribly if you were to do what you're contemplating."

Rowe paled and remained still.

"And the last thing our Lord said to me was, 'I'll be watching over you, Ongle-loss.' What do you think that means?" she asked.

"Beats me," said the Captain. "

" 'Angelos' is the Greek word used in the New Testament for 'angel,' " said Rowe, stunned. "That's the Lord's pet name for you, Laudie. You—you've truly found favor with Him."

"My goodness," she said. "I so don't deserve it."

"Just like my beautiful, modest wife," said the Captain, patting her arm. "Next time the Lord comes to see you, honey, would you ask Him about that mutual fund I've been worrying over?"

"Don't be ridiculous, Captain. The Lord doesn't care about your mutual funds."

"But they're yours, too, Angel. I'm sure He wants the best for you."

"No one could dispute that," said Rowe, "although I share Laudie's skepticism that the Lord would want to spend His infinitely precious time providing stock tips. Well, it seems everyone's finished. May I help you clear the table, Laudie? Or shall I say Angel?"

"You may, Rowe." They left the Captain to his pipe and newspaper as they carried dishes into the kitchen.

As soon as they were alone, Rowe whispered urgently. "Was there anything else?"

Laudie gave him a look of perfect innocence. "That was all the Lord said. If He comes to me again, do you want me to ask Him—"

"Nothing was said—of our sin?"

"Not a word. Maybe He doesn't think it's so very sinful, as sins go."

Rowe hung his head, shaking it a little.

"You don't believe me?"

"I have to believe everything you say, Angel, since God trusts you enough to make you His special messenger."

※

June 14, 2014, 11:10 p.m.

Rowe had occupied the hotel bathroom for the past forty-five minutes, showering until the water started to run cool, then blow-drying his hair on the low temperature setting, and finally shaving for the second time that day. His wedding day. Every time the disgust found an inroad into his consciousness, like a finger of water seeping through a dyke, he tamped it back down. He had endured the whole phony spectacle, a grotesque confection of every imaginable bridal cliché concocted by his new wife and her mother, on sheer nerve. Though he normally abstained, he was grateful when the Captain gestured him over to the hotel bar for a surreptitious bourbon whiskey.

"You look like you need a little liquid courage, son," said his new father-in-law. "It's my baby that ought to be wearing that expression."

"Sorry, Captain. If you only knew...how important it is to me to make Zelda happy, you'd understand my jitters."

"I do understand. But you know she's just a sweet, wholly inexperienced young girl, as determined to make you happy as you are her. In other words, relax, son."

"If intentions count, our marriage is already a success."

"Cheers. I wish you as much happiness as Laudie and I've enjoyed."

The Captain had unwittingly made the most inapt comparison Rowe could conceive of. Unable to respond, he put away the bourbon in one go and tried to smile.

Now he donned clean underwear and stepped into the bedroom of the Hyatt bridal suite to do his duty. Zelda sat on the satin duvet of the immense bed, nibbling from a net bag of pastel Jordan almonds, a wedding favor. At seventeen she was tall, plump and bosomy, with dark, glossy hair so heavy and abundant it bent the faux-diamond clasp that sought to contain it and curves that strained the lacy white chemise and garter belt that must have come from some cheap bridal lingerie website. She looked like the modern incarnation of a fertility goddess, the mirror image of his own Italian mother at that age. Which was unsurprising, since Rowe believed to a moral certainty, despite seventeen years of Laudie's assurances, that he, not the Captain, had fathered her.

Three times, his Lord and Savior Jesus Christ had spoken to Angel, emphatically declaring it to be the will of the Father in Heaven that Rowe and Zelda marry. Rowe had prayed, had mortified his flesh, had spent seven days and seven nights in the desert trying to discern how such a terrible deed, not only a grave sin but a crime under the civil law, could be God's will for him. But, though he entreated Him ceaselessly, no answer came, and the child of his loins was now sitting before him, that enigmatic half-smile on her lips, expecting him to consummate their marriage.

It was beyond him even to approach the marital bed in his current state, and so he veered toward the refrigerator tucked under the counter near the television and raided the mini-bar, removing four airline-sized bottles of Tanqueray and a can of ginger ale, altogether no doubt costing something astronomical.

He finally remembered his manners. "Would you like a beverage?"

Zelda shook her head. "No, thank you."

Her patience astounded and nettled him in equal measure. Having determined to perform according to God's will, in furtherance thereof and while silently begging forgiveness Rowe poured half the ginger ale and half the gin into a plastic cup from next to the sink. He then consecrated it to the mystery he was about to enact, and drank.

"Don't think anything of it," Zelda was saying as she patted him on the shoulder. Rowe, more than a little drunk, was sitting on the edge of the bed with his elbows on his knees, his forehead in his palms. The TV, tuned to a porn channel featuring a clean-cut man industriously fucking a woman who looked more like a thin Zelda than the actresses on any of the other available channels, flickered in the background. "I understand this happens to all guys from time to time."

"Not on their wedding night it doesn't," Rowe said. "I'm so sorry. I thought the gin would help, but I guess I'm not used to it. I'll make it up to you somehow."

"Sure. Just—one thing, please."

"Anything."

"Don't tell my mom I didn't turn you on."

Her request shocked him out of his self-pity. "Zelda, I would never—I could never betray your confidence in that way."

"The two of you are so close. You're like a little universe and Dad and I are the outer planets. She was telling me for months I should lose weight for the wedding, but I'm not like her—it's always been hard for me to resist sweets and stuff. But she was right. I wish I'd listened."

"Hey, stop that. You're a beautiful girl. Don't attribute my performance issues to any deficiency in yourself, because you haven't got any. You're everything a man could want in a wife. I'll make it up to you somehow." He put his arms around her soft, dimpled shoulders and kissed her hair, anointing it with his tears. "Would you like to go to the mall tomorrow?"

She nodded. Her eyes, unlike his, were dry. "That would be nice."

※

August 28, 2:05 p.m.

One day, while Zelda was at school and he was at home, attempting to compose the Sunday sermon, Laudie came by.

Rowe had kept his distance from Laudie for several weeks, hoping the fire in his heart would burn out meanwhile, would consume all the fuel that was his being, and if it left him a scarred husk of a man too dead inside to be a true husband to Zelda, why, then she might all the sooner grow tired of him and go off and find someone better, someone capable of—someone who could even get excited about—having sex with her. Leaving him would clash with the religious principles he and her parents had tried to instill in her all her life, but vegetative Zelda, he'd discovered, wasn't one to worry overmuch about internal moral conflict. Her pure earthiness, and his urgent desire to put distance between them, sometimes made him wish he belonged not to the evangelical Protestant tradition but to one of the more monastic sects of the Romish church, so that he could beat a more or less honorable retreat into a desert hermitage and be done forever with both mother and daughter.

Of course, Zelda had—whether willingly or otherwise, he didn't know—given her mother keys to the parsonage. Laudie often dropped by with groceries, or clothing and makeup for Zelda to try on, and if Rowe happened to be home alone at the time, she had her way with him no matter what defenses he tried to mount. He'd come to the point he deplored in some of the men of his flock who rationalized their transgressions as preventing a greater injury. If he didn't get it off with Laudie once in a while, he reasoned, he wouldn't be able to answer for the blackness of his mood or the sharpness of his tongue, and he might even take to drink, an unforgivable failing in his line of work.

And so, on a warm August afternoon, as the week's gospel text stared back at him from the computer screen, he was suddenly blinded. Two cold, rose-scented hands over his eyes stopped the light, and anger and desperation each fought to possess him. He grasped her hands, trying to pull them off his face, but she had a ferocious strength beneath the genteel façade and held on until he began to fear she'd leave marks he'd have a hard time explaining.

"Laudie—" he began.

"I know her class schedule, and we're safe," she said. "Don't you want me?"

Hunger for her, searing like physical starvation, incinerated his resolve to respect the marriage bond—hers, if not his own—without in the slightest diminishing his anger. He spun around in his chair, gripped her by the arms, and threw her on the bed, oblivious of the effects on her hairstyle and clothing; he pulled up her skirt and tore away her panties, somehow undoing his own belt and zipper in the same instant; and he thrust his hard cock into the tight, wet darkness inside her, pounding her again and again until he came, groaning and shuddering, within a minute, as though this were his first time. Release then began corroding the anger, producing the first stirrings of the return of sanity and guilt.

She lay beneath him, trembling. "Oh, why can't you do it like that all the time? And why have you ignored me for two weeks? You aren't falling in love, are you?"

"My God, Laudie, I only wish I were. But no—I'm not the kind of man who can lust after his own dau—"

"Don't go on about that. You know it isn't so."

He looked at her. "I want to show you something." He grabbed his wallet from the bedside table and flipped through its clear picture holders. He removed a photo of a dark-haired young woman in a sailor blouse and passed it to Laudie.

"That's a darling picture of her. I don't remember her wearing her hair that way, or that blouse, though."

"No reason why you would—it's my mother, taken for her high school graduation."

Laudie stared at him. She turned the picture over and found confirmation. "Why didn't you show me sooner?" she demanded, sitting up in the bed, her hair, blouse, and bra undone, her breasts bared unselfconsciously.

"I don't know. I don't know." His voice caught, and tears welled into his eyes. "I don't know how to refuse you, Angel. I wanted to think it was just a...a sick fantasy. I wanted, I so wanted, to find a way you and I could stay together without the scandal of—without hurting the Captain. I just don't know how, I haven't got the willpower, to say no to you. And now that poor child—"

As if on cue, Zelda stepped forward in the doorway, a half-eaten chocolate chip cookie in her hand. Her brown eyes reflected sorrow rather than surprise. "Mommy," she said, "why are you here?"

Rowe jumped, fastened his clothing, and backed up against the wall as though Zelda had threatened him.

Laudie gave a bemused laugh. "Well, this all unraveled a lot sooner than I expected."

"I'm not a toy for you to play with," Zelda shouted, hurling the cookie at her. "And I used to think the sun rose and set on you, Rowe. I can't imagine how either of you exist, what it must be like to live inside such cruel brains. You're both so clever, aren't you? I'm glad I'm not. I'm going home to Daddy. Oh my God, you've taken away my Daddy," she cried, as the import of what had passed between her mother and Rowe finally sank in. "At least you never fucked me, you bastard."

She went to the closet and pulled out an overnight bag, dragging it to the dresser, from which she removed underthings, T-shirts, and jeans seemingly at random. She threw them into the bag and began scooping makeup, jewelry, and bits of money off the top of the dresser.

Laudie, meanwhile, had pulled a pink Ruger .380 ACP out of her purse and pointed it at Zelda. "Now, sweetie, calm down. There's no point in flying into a snit. There are all kinds of ways of dealing with this."

"You'd call it a snit? A snit is when you lose your temper because the waiter brings you a hamburger instead of a cheeseburger. This is something else. I'm not sure what, because I've never seen anything so disgusting and so awful. I feel like I'm going to be sick. Don't point that thing at me."

Rowe nodded. "She's right, Laudie—put it away, please? It's making me nervous."

Laudie gave no sign she had heard him. "Zelda, come sit down on the bed and let's discuss this like adults."

"I will not," Zelda said. "I will not put my ass there. You've profaned it."

"Well, listen to the child. I do not profane anything; I am God's channel."

"You're an argument for atheism, both of you, that's what you are."

Her declaration completed Rowe's misery. He collapsed onto the bed, his face to the wall, his eyes shut against the catastrophe unfolding before him. But he could hear the two women struggling.

"Mommy, don't! Mommy—"

A gunshot, followed by another, deafened him momentarily, and the evil smells of burnt sulfur and charcoal assailed his nostrils. He forced himself to turn and look. Laudie was standing with the gun in her hand, staring at her daughter's body at her feet.

She looked up at him. "She was pulling on it. It went off. I never meant to shoot her. You know that, don't you? I couldn't shoot my own little girl. It was an accident. You believe me, don't you?"

He nodded wearily. He hadn't doubted anything she'd said in a long while, and he couldn't afford to start now. He doubted only that he would be waking up from this nightmare anytime soon. "I'll call the police," he said, rising to retrieve his phone from his desk.

"What are you talking about? We can't do that. They'll never believe me, not with my record. We're going to have to take care of this ourselves."

"Laudie, no. What do you mean?"

"I have a plan. Don't worry. Here's what we do."

Before he could reason with her, before he could point out that calling the police is what innocent people do, while dumping bodies in the desert shows a distinctly guilty state of mind, she'd laid out the plan. He was to wait until nightfall and then put the body in the trunk of his car. She'd slip the Captain a little Ambien in his orange juice at dinner, and come back here as soon as she could get away. After Rowe pulled his car out of the garage, she'd put hers in, and then they'd drive far away, where no one knew them and there would be no witnesses. Zelda was going away to visit a friend. Being a married lady now, there was little point in her finishing out the school year anyway. If she eventually decided to stay with the faraway friend instead of coming back to her husband, well, that's a seventeen-year-old for you.

"But what about the Captain? He's not going to buy it. They're so close."

"I can deal with him."

"How?" Rowe feared for his old friend, feared for himself, feared for anyone this dark angel might one day touch.

"I'll send him texts from her phone. They'll become less and less frequent."

"But you know they can tell where cell phones are used. If anyone looks at the records..."

"Why would anyone do that? She's just a kid who ran away."

Darkness had crept over the sky while he waited in the preternaturally still house. The cooling body of his child-bride, a clean hole in her innocent heart, lay in the trunk of his car in the garage below. A fear he had to remind himself was psychotic kept intruding into the chaos of his mind: that Zelda would awaken and come to their bedroom, where he lay, the helpless captive of his shock and guilt, forcing him to kill her so his sin would remain secret, turning accident—or what he wanted to believe was accident—into murder. By the time Laudie returned he lay curled in a fetal position on the late marital bed, hugging his knees to his chest.

To his relief, she took charge, speaking to him in low, quiet tones and without passing judgment on his weakness. When she said she could make him feel better, he nodded, expecting she meant she'd go down on him, as in happier days past, with the tongue that could momentarily obliterate the horror of Zelda's death along with his every other rational thought. But instead of slithering between his legs, she busied herself at the bedside table with some simple implements—spoon, cotton ball, lighter— melting a dark, foul-looking little lump of something while he watched dully. Then she brought a hypodermic kit out of her purse, drew the melted stuff up, tapped the works, and came toward him, smiling an anodyne smile.

"Make a fist," she said. "Here's a little bit of heaven for you."

Chapter Thirteen

October 8, 3:45 p.m.

"This is going to be a lot easier than I imagined," said Mary Jane Lewis. She sat with Quirke at a long, glossy oval table in her office suite with a file labeled 'IRMO Quirke' between them. "No visitation or custody issues; both sides waiving support; no property, not even a house, to argue about; each party to bear own attorney's fees. Simpler—albeit less remunerative—for me, but I'm sorry to say it looks like you're facing a major hit. You do remember signing this thing?" She gestured at a multipage document appended to a letter from Eleanor's counsel.

"Dimly. I was most likely loaded at the time, but I don't doubt it's my signature. I won't contest it, in any event."

"And do you remember your attorney explaining what your liability would be if you and Eleanor split up?"

"Yes, and at the time it seemed fair enough. Gene was taking a chance on me, and I certainly disappointed him by not helping him grow his business after I graduated. God, I've always hated that phrase, 'grow a business.' It makes me want to run away and join the Wobblies."

"The corporate world's loss was the people's gain," she said. "They've submitted an accounting of Gene's expenses in putting you through school—he certainly kept meticulous records—with the judgment rate of interest computed in. Assuming the data's correct, I've run the numbers a couple of times and I'm sorry, but I think their bottom line's correct."

Her red-lacquered index fingernail pointed. Quirke took in the number, digit by digit. Only a pained "Oy" betrayed the magnitude of the loss in net worth that would be his reverse bride price.

"You don't happen to have that kind of money lying around, I suppose?" she asked.

"No. It'll have to come out of my retirement savings."

"There may be tax consequences, then. You'll need to consult—"

"A tax specialist? My life is being overrun by specialists: one for the election—I've got to remember to call him one of these days, dammit—, one for my divorce, and now one for my tax situation." He shook his head. "I'm sorry, that outburst wasn't directed at you. I'll try to keep the self-pity to a minimum."

She smiled and patted his hand. "If you only knew how annoying, or worse, most of my other clients are compared with you, Judge. You're a truly nice man. I hope things are trending happier for you since the split."

"Thanks, they are. So how soon can we get a status judgment?"

"You in a big hurry?"

Quirke felt himself blushing. "Well, I am planning to get married again, actually, but we haven't set a date."

"First, congratulations. I'm very happy for you. She's a lucky lady. And second, I'm relieved we're not racing against the clock," the lawyer said. "It's always so delicate when the client comes in with the hall booked and baby on the way. Because after all the court budget cuts in the past few years—I'm sure you know this as well as I do—it could be eight, ten, twelve months, or more, until we get a judgment. The sooner you're able to pay off the billionaire, the better from that point of view, because then we might be able to get a stipulation and waiver of the final declaration of disclosure—you're nodding, stop me if you've heard all this before. Did you ever have a family court assignment while you were on the trial bench?"

"No, the PJ was all set to rotate me in there, but I was saved in the nick of time by a CA appointment. A law school friend of mine who went into private practice and split his work between criminal defense and marital dissolutions used to say his criminal clients were bad people at their best and his matrimonial clients were good people at their worst. Family court's the most dangerous assignment for trial judges, I hear; personally, I'd rather try street gang cases any day of the week. This is all covered by the attorney-client privilege, right? I'd hate for my random musings to become public knowledge right before the election. Say, I hope I can count on your vote?"

"Early and often, Judge. That reminds me," Mary Jane said. "Apropos of the election, we could try to get the court file sealed, but it might give people the wrong idea."

"I'd rather not. I'm all for transparency."

"If she decides to, we can oppose, or so be it. Whatever. Cross that bridge when we get to it. Well, Judge, I wish I could sit here and chat with you all day, but I've got to make a court appearance."

"I should make a court appearance myself. Till later, Mary Jane."

※

October 9, 12:30 p.m.

"It's an honor to meet you, Judge. I was thrilled when my old buddy Ward told me you were interested in working with me." Bobby James, a tall, slim, bearded African-American man who looked to be in his sixties, shook hands with Quirke. Something in his lopsided smile and big, round, hooded eyes put Quirke at ease immediately. Preparatory to getting to work, Bobby poured two mugs of coffee, placing them on the conference table where he motioned to Quirke to sit.

The airy office, above a party supply wholesaler across the street from the train station south of Market Street, less than a mile from the loft, was simply furnished. Framed posters and photographs, evidently of his past campaigns and candidates, as well as of some classic R&B artists and album covers, dotted the walls, and well-nurtured plants occupied most of the surfaces. Quirke was a little surprised it was only the two of them; he'd expected to have to talk over a phone bank, and told Bobby so.

"I work a little differently nowadays. And I don't anticipate having to do much phone banking in your case anyway. Now, Ward hinted at the possibility of a little trouble on the horizon. What's your take on it?"

"I'm not sure what to think. Did he tell you anything about my personal situation?"

"I don't suppose he wanted to talk out of turn."

"Well, my ex-wife just filed for divorce. Let me back up. I'm going to put this in the most negative light possible, so you'll have a sense of what somebody who might want me out could conceivably churn up." He took a deep breath. "Bless me, Father, for I have sinned. Just after she threw me out of the house, my ex-wife discovered I was having what you might call an affair with a member of my staff. It's actually more complicated."

"It usually is."

"Things were bad before that revelation, and it didn't improve them. Apparently a bit cheesed off, she had me served with the suit papers while I was on the bench at the last oral argument calendar, in full view of the audience. I think a few bloggers mentioned it that day or the day after; you can Google me."

"Oh, I will."

"My chief of staff had actually come upon me and the staff member in question—now my fiancée—on the one occasion when we behaved a little indiscreetly at the office, and took a picture. I think he sent it to the ex. And to who knows who else."

"My lord. And he still works for you?"

"Wait, there's more. He also informed me he's filed a complaint against me with the Commission on Judicial Behavior. I haven't heard yet whether they're going to make a case of it. It may be relevant that we were—well, no, I was—pretty intoxicated on the occasion. In my defense, it was after business hours."

"That something that happens a lot?"

"Well, what do you mean by 'a lot'? Compared with, say, Oliver Reed? Not really. Compared with the average American? Quite possibly. But I've been cutting back. Sadie never badgers me about it, so naturally I no longer feel like getting bombed all the time. If I had to describe her in a word or two, it would be as...my resurrection." Quirke paused. "I'll quit drinking. At some point." He wasn't feeling that uncanny feeling; it was more like Saint Augustine's prayer that he might be perfected—one day.

"How's your health? Any worries?"

"Fine," said Quirke reflexively. "Yes, I know I need to exercise, and I should lose some weight, but it's my good fortune she likes me this way."

"I'd like to meet Sadie sometime, if you both don't mind."

"I'm sure she'll want to meet you. But about Sadie, an odd little thing happened a few weeks ago...I don't imagine it's important, but..."

"Whenever my clients preface anything with 'I don't imagine it's important,' that's when I start to worry."

"Sadie belongs to an unusual...sort of spiritual group. I don't know if you're aware of it—I wouldn't have been, except through her—but there are people today who practice...ritual magic. Not the stage variety, and not witchcraft; I mean like John Dee and Edward Kelley, Aleister Crowley, Golden Dawn, like that."

"Yes, I'm aware of it. How I'm aware of it—let's just say that's confidential."

"I find that strangely reassuring. Now, an uninformed person who saw them preparing for their rituals might think there was something sinister going on—a lot of black-robed people going into a temple and performing ceremonies no one's allowed to speak of. It's kind of like what I do: putting on a black robe, assembling with other black-robed people, and going into a temple—of justice, though we conduct more of our rituals in public. But closed-minded people like to toss around such unpleasant epithets."

"Like, for instance...Black magic? Satanism?"

"For instance. But they're really a nice bunch of people. All by way of leading up to the point that, while we were visiting with some of them down in Sant' Amaro back in late August, some intruders who'd been taking pictures were chased off the property. Apparently, this had never happened before. It would be colossally narcissistic to think everything's about me, but I couldn't help wondering. We didn't notice anyone following us on the way down, though, and I have no way to know for sure."

"If someone did take pictures of you hanging with these nice folks, would I be unhappy seeing them in my Twitter feed?"

"Well, that's the thing. The shot of me playing bass guitar in the band at the party might not upset you much, but the ones of me drinking Jack Daniel's out of the bottle and me inhaling probably would. In my defense, everybody there knew me as Sadie's boyfriend, not Justice Quirke. Okay, I hear how feeble that sounds. I know I stepped over the line, Bobby. It's one I hadn't crossed since before I became a lawyer. And yet..."

"And yet—?"

"It was an incredible night, and I don't regret it. If the Commission were to come after me, I'd guess I'd try to convince them otherwise, but I'm sure I'd fail. Actually, I don't think I could even try."

"So, you're prepared to walk away if it comes to that?"

"Prepared? Hardly. I'll be flat broke after I finish buying my way out of my marriage. Aware it might happen? Acutely. If I have to quit, I'd rather do it over something important, but one doesn't always have that luxury."

Bobby sat looking at him like a father at a teenage son who'd just done something slightly stupid and entirely typical. "Just one more question on that topic. You still smoking weed?"

"Not since that night, and no plans to."

"Because if you were going to make a habit of it, we could look into a medical marijuana evaluation. Everybody I've ever met qualifies somehow."

Quirke shook his head. "Let's not go there."

"All right. Now, you just said something that surprised me, given who the ex-Mrs. Quirke is: You're broke?"

Quirke explained the peculiar terms of their prenuptial agreement. "But I want to assure you I'm good for your fee," he concluded.

"Glad to hear it." Bobby laughed. "My point, though, is you're evidently not in a position to lend money to your campaign."

"If we're talking anything beyond a couple of printing jobs at Kinko's, that's true. I mean, I'm staying-at-my-girlfriend's broke. And it's not even her place, technically. It's very nice, but it belongs to her roommate."

"Who's she and what's her story?"

Quirke corrected him and related the few facts he knew about Peter Blake.

"Judge, I'm glad you find yourself surrounded by these kind and congenial people in your time of need, but with your authorization I'd like to look into their background."

"That's pretty creepy, Bobby. Do you have to?"

"It's my due diligence. Tell you what, I won't pass along what I learn unless it's something I think you have to know. Something that casts a whole different light on the person, keeping in mind what you've told me about them. You okay with that?"

Quirke considered. "As far as Peter goes, I suppose so, if you really think it's necessary. But Sadie? Unless she changes her mind, I'm going to spend the rest of my life with her. And don't forget, we've worked together for three years now. I know her to be blameless and upright. Oh, I think she was in some minor trouble as a kid, but you won't be able to get at those records. It's her mother you ought to check on."

Bobby clicked his ballpoint pen and pulled his legal pad closer. "Name, DOB, last known address?"

"Her name is Laudie—Lauds—Mary Norrell. No idea what aliases she may have used. Or uses—Sadie doesn't even know if she's still alive. She was a career criminal while Sadie was growing up. Drug dealing, theft, grifting, and so on. She neglected Sadie, abused or allowed her to be abused, and was all set to exploit her in the most appalling way, but Peter Blake and a teacher intervened. Date of birth? She'd be forty-nine now, that's all I know. Said to have been a very beautiful woman. Went to prison at least once. Sadie's had nothing to do with her in the last twenty years or so. If you think it's worth looking into—"

"She's on my list. Well, Judge, I'll put together the best strategy I can for you—and an exit plan just in case. With any luck, come November 5th you'll be giving an inspiring victory speech. Just remember to thank me."

Chapter Fourteen

October 8, 6:55 p.m.

"I've never seen Papa so agitated, have you? He's twisting in that bed almost like he has a fever. Leave the tray on the table and come look at him in the light. Come here, I say."

Laudie pulled the maid, Carmen, by her sleeve toward the bed where the old man lay muttering and restless. His pallor was worse, waxier and more yellowish than ever, and his eyes were disconcerting slits, allowing him no rest but seeing nothing. Carmen reflexively rubbed her arm where the Missus's fingernails had dug into her flesh, fearing to look at the Mister. She could not understand why they had not taken him to the hospital, for he was clearly very ill. Perhaps he would revive a little if the Missus were to spare him some of the medicines she was giving him—only a big, strong man could tolerate the amount and number of drugs the Missus, and sometimes the son-in-law, were administering daily and hourly, and if at one time he'd been such a man, the Mister was now anything but. He had not been able to speak on his own behalf for days, and still she kept him here. Why could she not see the crisis he was in?

"Why, Carmen, I'd almost forgotten. Tomorrow's your day off. And we made you work on your day off last week, and the week before, too. I can't take advantage of you again this week. You may go now to make up for some of the overtime I owe you."

"No, Missus. I can stay. Mister is not well. I watch him tonight."

"Your staying won't make him well. You're kind to offer, but I insist. We're quite capable of dealing with him, Rowe and I. You're not the only nurse around here, you know."

"Of course, Missus. But you need rest, too."

"How very thoughtful of you. But go. Now." Missus pushed her roughly out of the sickroom and down the hallway, grabbed her purse from the table in the foyer, and opened the front door for her, handing her some crumpled bills. "Here's cab fare so you don't have to wait for the bus. See you on Monday." She shut and locked the door as the maid looked dully—suspiciously?—back at her.

Laudie stood in the foyer, rubbing the ache out of her temples, relieved to no longer be hearing the incessant sounds of her husband's increasing delirium. His illness was really getting on her nerves, and the time had finally come to do something about it. The plan was ready, and it was a good one. But it required two people. The second was due to arrive at any moment.

In her bedroom, she opened her jewelry chest. She had already been wearing a few pieces for Carmen's benefit: the pearl necklace, the emerald ring, the diamond dragonfly brooch, the charm bracelet. Quite a lot of bling for a home health attendant, she reflected. Pity so much more had to stay in the chest, but to take it all with her would leave a huge red flag behind. The rest was simply more to add to the insurance claim, up to the limit of the jewelry rider, when it was all over. She checked to be certain her passport was in her handbag, along with her wallet, which was nearly bursting with the cash she'd been skimming out of the joint account for the last few months—not enough in any given transaction to be noticeable, but sufficient to accommodate her and Rowe for a while after leaving this house.

Likewise, under her bed, out of sight of the maid but at the ready, was an overnight bag containing a couple of outfits, not enough for anything to appear obviously to be missing from her closet—assuming anything recognizable as a closet remained—but enough to sustain her until she had time for shopping. She might work up a sweat burning down the house, and she wouldn't want to have to go around tacky afterward with nothing to change into. Now she took the bag from its hiding place.

The front door opened and shut quietly, and she skipped out to the foyer with the bag. Tall, thin Rowe, olive-skinned and unshaven, his black hair brushed back from his high forehead, was holding a paper grocery sack. "The propane," he said, setting it down and mopping his forehead with a white handkerchief.

She stole into his arms. "We're alone," she whispered. "Except for him." Because the 'him' referred to was incapable of rising from his bed and discovering them, they stood there, embracing openly, fondling one another until matters were at the point of escalating in unplanned directions and threatening to throw off their timetable.

"Later, darling," she said quietly. "Let's take care of business and get out of here first."

"I'll deal with the wiring, Angel. Have you given him a shot?"

"Yes, but he could stand a topping up. Meet you back here."

They attended to their respective tasks, Rowe meddling with the sockets on the wall in the old man's bedroom, plugging in a space heater, sprinkling propane; Laudie filling a syringe and injecting the contents between the big and second toes on her husband's right foot. He was now deeply asleep, or in a state beyond sleep, his wet respirations starting to rattle. The sound filled her with glee.

At last she and Rowe stood in the foyer, ready to make their last departure from this house where he had discovered the amazing truth about her, where he'd recognized her singular, divinely delegated authority over him and the power to be generated and regenerated by his submission to her. Nothing remained now but to release a tiny spark into the night and wait for it to grow.

※

"They're still sitting in the battalion chief's car." The deputy chief sipped takeout coffee while standing with the assistant medical examiner at the margin of the property while the shell of the residence smoldered before them. Fire department floodlights augmented nearby streetlights; dawn was still hours away, and the fire marshal's staff were combing the place. "She was hysterical at first, but now she's practically catatonic. He's doing the talking. I've had three different investigators interview them. Haven't caught them out in any inconsistencies yet."

"Your first impressions?"

"I've learned not to trust my first impressions, but...I don't know about this one. Nothing about the scene screams arson, but I don't get both of them leaving the old man alone in his condition, even for a few minutes. She supposedly had car trouble in a dicey area not far from here, and he thought he could have her fixed up and on her way before Triple-A could get out there. Meanwhile, there was apparently a wiring problem back here. A neighbor saw the place fully engulfed and called it in. This Rowe fellow, the son-in-law, says he couldn't have been gone more than twenty minutes. What do you think?"

"As far as cause and manner, I won't know anything until the autopsy. Or maybe even for a few weeks after, until toxicology comes back. Right now, I want to talk with them about the old man's medical issues and how he was doing when they left home tonight. Son-in-law, you say? From the way they were acting, I couldn't quite tell what the relationship was. So, where's the daughter-slash-wife, then?"

"He's kind of vague on that. I take it there's some marital problems. Maybe you can get more out of him; you've got a better bedside manner than I do."

"We'll see," the pathologist said.

In the back seat of the battalion chief's SUV, the pathologist found the residents of what used to be the house on the property watching the unfolding investigation. She was lying with her head in his lap, eyes closed, apparently in shock, while he silently stroked her auburn hair. A curious position for a woman and her son-in-law, the pathologist thought. "I'm Dr. Meredith," she said quietly. "Very sorry for your loss."

"Rowe Emworth, and this is Laudie Forrester, the widow." Rowe extended a hand, which Dr. Meredith shook, but Laudie did not move.

"I'll be doing the autopsy, and there are some questions you may be able to help me with, if you're able right now."

He nodded. "We'll try."

"I'll get his medical records as soon as I can, but can you tell me, in a nutshell, about his condition? Historically, over the recent past, and tonight? I'm told he was bedridden."

"He was very sick, only intermittently conscious over the last few days," Rowe said. "He had diabetes and kidney failure, and never really recovered from a stroke that happened not quite a month ago."

"Why was he at home?"

"And not in the hospital, you mean? He knew his time was coming, and he'd made it clear he didn't want a lot of interventions. He was seventy-five."

"Did he ever put his wishes in writing?"

"She has—had—his durable power of attorney for health care. They talked a lot about what he wanted—before the last few days, of course, when he'd pretty much lost the ability to talk. He didn't want to spend his last hours hooked up to a lot of machines, and being kept as comfortable as possible in familiar surroundings was what mattered to him. So, we took care of him. The maid spelled us sometimes. I don't know why she wasn't here when the fire broke out; maybe she misunderstood her instructions and left after I did, although I thought she knew we didn't want to leave him alone if it could be avoided. She's from Mexico and isn't very fluent in English. But it's just as well she wasn't here, or there might be two dead."

"And tonight—what sort of state was he in?"

"I don't think he was conscious today at all. The end was very near. In fact, Doctor, I wouldn't be surprised if you found—I hope you do find— that he didn't die because of the fire or smoke, that he passed of natural causes. It would be more comforting to know he didn't suffer."

"From what you're saying, that's entirely possible. Thank you for speaking with me. May I call if I think of any other questions?"

"Of course. My cell number is 655-1122. I don't know where we'll be tonight."

The pathologist made a note and left the pair.

※

October 23, 3:45 p.m.

"Mr. Timms? Laudie Forrester calling again. I'm inquiring about the status of claim number—yes, that's the one...Well, that's what you told me two weeks ago. I don't understand why it's taking—...I know you have to wait for reports. But why can't you disburse at least some of the—...But the policy covers living expenses after destruction of the property. It says so on page—...With all due respect, Mr. Timms, this is not what we paid for. This is unfair, and it's a fraud. It's—"

"*Bad faith,*" Rowe whispered.

"Bad faith," Laudie said, raising her voice. "If this takes much longer, I'm going to have to get my attorney involved...I don't like your attitude, Mr. Timms. You can just take a flying f—"

She hurled the phone across the motel room with a shriek. Rowe dove toward the second queen-sized bed and felt under it, at last retrieving the device. Apart from a cracked screen, it appeared functional.

"We should be careful, Angel," he reminded her. "Funds are a little short right now, and phones are expensive."

"I know that," she said sourly. "We should be on our way to Mexico already with the proceeds of two nice fat insurance policies. It's unconscionable how long the medical examiner and fire marshal are taking. And I really am thinking about getting a lawyer to write a letter. And thanks to your internet sleuthing, I know a lawyer."

She nibbled at a cold, greasy french fry from the paper wrapping on the bedside table as Rowe picked at a takeout salad in a clamshell container.

"Angel, don't forget you haven't seen or heard from her in twenty years, and you didn't part on the best of terms," he began cautiously.

"I'm well aware of that!" she screamed, and began pelting him with fries. Most landed short of him, staining the beige carpeting. He dreaded the thought of the inevitable cleaning bill and sought to calm her by wrapping her in his arms. She struggled like a child in a tantrum, eventually breaking down in tears.

"Do you think we can get her to help?" she sniffled at last.

"I'd like to think she'd help you, Angel, I would. But the estrangement's lasted so long."

"That's true. Though it's possible, isn't it, Sadie's been thinking about me, wondering what became of me? That she's become able to see things in a different light now that she's all grown up and educated and everything? Maybe she's had children of her own and can understand how a mother feels."

"Of course, it's possible. What concerns me is *where* she is. It doesn't get much straighter than the Supreme Court. There's probably not a lot of tolerance for a criminal history in that place. Ironic how hard it'll be, I imagine, to get a fair hearing from her."

"It doesn't matter what a person's past was when you've really reformed. Or discovered your true nature is much more than anyone thought it to be."

"Especially that," he whispered, stroking her cheek. "My angel. I just don't want you to take it too much to heart if—"

"I'm not going to go negative. I'm all positive, Rowe. I believe in the power of positive thinking, positive dreaming. I'm all about affirming, not negating."

Chapter Fifteen

October 10, 8:00 p.m.

Quirke had a few matters to take up with his ex-father-in-law, but had been encountering difficulty in reaching him. One of Gene's minions had left a message saying he would be available at eight o'clock Friday evening at his house in Hemsbridge. Quirke phoned at the appointed time.

Gene's tone was a shade more genial than it had been the last time they spoke. "Quirke? How's it going?"

"Very well, thanks. How are you? And how's Eleanor?"

"Good. Doing fine. What's on your mind? Can I put you on the speaker? Got my hands full here."

"Sure, go ahead. First, I was wondering if your people had had a chance to gather up my things and ship them to my chambers, as I requested in my earlier message."

"Courier dropped them off a couple days ago, I think. I can check, but that's my understanding."

"Really? Weird. I'll check on my end, too. Second, I want you to know I'm working on satisfying the repayment provision of the prenup. It's taking a little while to marshal the funds, but you'll have them soon. I have no intention of disputing your figures."

There was a pause. "Good to hear."

"I'm being as cooperative as I can be because I have no desire to prolong matters. If you need to know anything else, have your lawyer or Eleanor's lawyer call Mary Jane Lewis."

"Will do."

"And finally, Gene, although I have no interest and no expectation of any interest in Marvelocity Industries, I'd appreciate it if you'd keep me apprised of any changes in your related entities, just as you used to, until everything's settled. For my conflicts list. All right?"

"Sure. You bet."

"Take it easy, Gene."

"You, too."

※

Gene hung up the phone and turned to the others in the great room. "That wasn't so bad, was it?"

Eleanor grimaced. "Hearing his voice again made my skin crawl."

Hetford smiled, swirling his brandy in the glass. "He sounded quite lucid for this hour of night."

"He's not more than a half step behind us," Gene said.

"That'll make this even more exciting," Hetford said. "Can you time the acquisition as we discussed? The case is set for argument on October 20th."

"I'll tell the lawyers the deal needs to close the night before, and hope for the best."

"If this works, it'll be well worth it. Gene, have your investigators come up with anything on the personal front?"

"Yes, but I don't think Eleanor needs to—"

"Daddy, I can handle it. What did they find out?"

"Kitten," he said, shaking his head, "I always told you there was something off about that boy. But I had no idea."

Hetford's eyebrows lifted. "We already know he's a philandering drunk. How much worse could it get?"

"Maybe I should just read you the report and show you the pictures. Then you can answer that question for yourself." He unlocked a desk drawer, pulled out a document, and began to read. " 'Farini and Associates, Private Investigators. To: Eugene Scorchner. Re: C. Quirke. Per your instructions, on evening of 20 August subject was followed from office at state Supreme Court building to index block of Gillian Alley in South-of-Market neighborhood. Subject parked in garage of converted warehouse, remaining until following morning. Same pattern was observed on successive days. Subject appears to currently reside in top-floor condo in the Gillian Alley building, owned by artist Peter Blake, also known to be the residence of Sadie Norrell.

" 'Saturday, 27 August, 0815 hours, subject and Norrell were observed to leave Gillian Alley in Norrell's Fiat.' "

"Quirke hasn't seen eight in the morning on a weekend in decades," Eleanor marveled. "What kind of a spell has she cast over him?"

"Funny you should ask," said Gene. "Pray let me continue. 'Subject and Norrell were followed to a house in unincorporated rural Sant' Amaro County owned by one Carleton Matthews, master carpenter. Numerous other vehicles on Matthews' property indicated some type of gathering was in progress. Operatives were able to surveille from woods on periphery of property until chased off late in the evening by Matthews, who fired what appeared to be a Bushmaster .223 semiautomatic rifle in our direction. Per terms of retainer, invoice to include hazardous duty supplement.

" 'At approximately 1620 hours, attendees wearing long black robes began congregating in an outbuilding on the Matthews property. We were unable to approach closely enough to determine what was transpiring therein, but internet research revealed several attendees are published authors and bloggers on occult subjects including ritual magic, sigils, and invocation of angels and demons. We identified three attendees known to be affiliated with an occult organization known as Ordo Argentum Diluculo, which is rumored to have satanic leanings and to engage in animal sacrifice and perverted sexual practices.' These are the kind of people my Supreme-Court-justice former son-in-law is hanging around with nowadays," Gene interjected hotly. " 'Subject did not appear to be taking part in the ritual, but was observed sleeping in a lawn chair ten yards from the outbuilding where it was taking place.' "

"That sounds like Quirke," said Hetford. "Sleeping it *off*, probably."

" 'At 1705 hours, a scream was heard and two black-robed men ran from the outbuilding, the first of whom appeared to be bleeding from a wound to the hand. Subject ran to their aid, then into the house where he apparently retrieved a bag of medical supplies which the second man used to treat the first, subject assisting. As the ceremony concluded and participants exited the outbuilding, subject reentered the house, later returning to the yard to grill food for ensuing party. While grilling, subject was observed to consume five bottles of Anchor Steam beer. Attendees appeared satisfied with subject's culinary efforts.

" 'At 1830 hours, subject left dining area of party with three other participants and went to garage on the other side of the property to rehearse classic rock songs for entertainment of other attendees; subject playing bass guitar and singing backup vocals. At 1915 hours, subject and other band members emerged from garage and set up equipment in yard. At 1925, band was introduced as "Con and the Ay-thers" (correct spelling unknown) and began to play.' Take a look at that," said Gene, producing a photo.

"Oh my God," said Eleanor. "It's the same Quirke I met in college, plus thirty years and forty pounds, minus the mullet."

" 'At 1945, 2010, and 2030 hours, a bottle of Jack Daniel's was passed around and subject was observed to drink out of it.' "

"I hope they got a picture of that," said Hetford.

"Right here," said Gene, proffering it. "But this is the piece de resistance: 'At 2045 lead guitarist passed subject what appeared to be a large marijuana cigarette and subject was observed to inhale twice.' "

"The money shot!" Hetford crowed. "He's toast."

"But how would they be able to prove it was marijuana?" Eleanor asked.

"Well, Quirke doesn't smoke tobacco, does he?"

"No."

"It's prima facie evidence, then."

" 'After the band's last number, subject was warmly congratulated by Norrell and proceeded to socialize with other participants.' Gene spread on the coffee table before them a sequence of photos depicting Quirke and Sadie in close embrace, kissing with passion evident even in two dimensions, his hands all over her body. Eleanor's face darkened.

" 'As stated, at that point host-slash-property owner Matthews heard operatives moving through the brush, retrieved firearm, and forced operatives off the premises, terminating observation on that occasion. Awaiting your instructions re further observation.' "

Gene again shook his head. "Sad, really. I'm thinking we can call off the dogs."

"Why?" asked Hetford. "This is fun."

"This is shooting fish in a barrel," Gene answered. "It's too easy. It's not sporting. And we have enough."

"I've certainly had enough Quirke for one night. Come on," Eleanor said, pulling Hetford off the sofa by the hand. "Let's go for a walk."

They strolled along the artificial brook in the grotto south of the house, which wound, glistening and murmuring, under strands of hanging lanterns. The evening was unseasonably warm, but Eleanor's hand was cold in Hetford's. She stopped and leaned against a century-old magnolia tree, drew him to herself, and kissed him. He responded in kind.

"Wouldn't you like to stay tonight?" she asked after a moment. "I'd so like to be with you."

"My dear, one day—"

"Who's going to know? And really, what difference would it make if—"

"No one and none, of course. But timing is everything in life. Sex can be so much better once you get past the revenge motive. I was watching your reaction to those pictures of him and, darling, you're not ready. Not for me, anyway. I hope you will be, someday soon. Otherwise, maybe you'll return my heart to me semi-intact, provided we haven't made the mistake of sleeping together prematurely."

She closed her eyes as if making a wish, smiling and frowning at once. "You're getting under my skin, Allan—in a good way. The time may be closer than you think.   But I'll defer to you tonight and try again tomorrow to persuade you I'm over him."

"I have a very open mind on that."

Chapter Sixteen

October 14, 7:00 p.m.

"Thursday at eleven. Great, thank you. See you then." Sadie threw her phone into her handbag just as Quirke entered her room after work one evening a week before the October oral argument calendar. Three of Quirke's cases had been set, and he'd stayed late at the office working them up. She did not, contrary to her habit, immediately throw herself into his arms. Instead she turned toward the mirror on the wall, removing her earrings.

"Hello, sweetheart," he said, embracing her from behind and kissing the top of her head. "Got an appointment?"

"Yes, I'll need to duck out of the office for a little while day after tomorrow. Sorry. It should be quick."

"Nothing wrong, I hope?"

"Nope. Purely routine." She turned to face him, abstractedly letting him kiss her for several seconds before responding.

"Tired?" he asked.

"I guess, a little."

"Me, too. Let's lie down."

He tackled her onto the bed without further ado, eliciting a giggle followed by a sigh.

"What's up? You seem...not quite yourself."

"Just tired. It feels like it's been a long week already, even though it's only Tuesday."

"Maybe you should sleep in tomorrow. None of your cases are on next week, so there's no particular reason for you to go to the office, is there?"

"I want to go to work. If I stay here, it's an eternity till I see you."

That sounded more like his Sadie, to his relief.

"Well, then, you rest tonight and let me make us dinner. Judge's orders. I'll see what I can find in the kitchen, okay?" She gave him a wan nod.

In the kitchen, he opened a dusty bottle of zinfandel and poured two glasses. A search of the fridge turned up, among other things, four fennel and asiago sausages in their butcher paper wrapping, a bunch of lacinato kale, a tray of cremini mushrooms, and a leek. A half-full box of orecchiete stood in a cupboard. That would do nicely. He put a pot of water on the stove and lit the burner, returning to the bedroom with the wine.

"For you," he said, offering her a glass.

"For some reason, I don't feel much like wine tonight," she said. "If Peter's around, he'll probably drink it."

"Are you sure you're feeling all right?"

"Really, I'm okay," she insisted weakly. "Thank you so much for making dinner," she added, but looking as though to get up and eat it would cost her a fair effort.

He went back to the kitchen and prepared the ingredients while the water came to a boil, trying not to worry about Sadie's sudden lassitude or take it personally. Everyone was entitled to low moments. And, given the number of times lately they'd found themselves awake in the wee hours and taken advantage of the circumstance to make love slowly, almost silently, into the dawn, that she was exhausted was unsurprising. Studiously he avoided speculating on why he, with eighteen years on her, felt so much more energetic than she appeared to do.

He sautéed the leek with the sausages and mushrooms, chopped and boiled the kale with the pasta, drained it and tossed everything together with some herbes de Provence he found among the spices. A splash of olive oil, a few grinds of pepper, and some black lava salt to finish, and the dish was ready. Uncharacteristically, Sadie had not appeared in the kitchen, and he went to check on her. She'd turned out the light in their room but lay awake on the bed.

"It's ready if you feel like eating."

"In a little while, maybe. Thank you for cooking."

He sat beside her and rubbed her temples. "Headache?"

"Not exactly. Don't know what it is, but I feel wrung out. Maybe if I go to bed early...I wish I could..."

"Could what?"

"Show you how much I love you. Tonight, take it on faith, and tomorrow I'll try to give you what you deserve."

He kissed her and left her to rest.

In the kitchen, he helped himself to food and another glass of wine. Before long, Peter arrived and joined him.

Quirke had yet to overcome a sense of inferiority relative to Sadie's Gorodish. Not only did the impeccably fit Peter move with a dancer's fluidity, not only did his prematurely white hair and understated jeans-and-henleys wardrobe suit him perfectly, not only was he highly successful as a creative artist and teacher and an adept in the magical order, but he had an unshakeable serenity and ease, seemed never at a loss for the right word or gesture, and knew Sadie better than Quirke did. Not to mention it was his home they were living in. Sadie's fatigue having thrown them unexpectedly together on their own, Quirke sensed it was time he set aside his insecurities, tried to become better acquainted with his host, and expressed, once again, his gratitude.

"I hope I'm not overstaying my welcome, Peter. You've been incredibly generous, and I should be doing more to pull my weight around here."

"Nonsense. You're part of the household now, and you are pulling your weight—you made dinner tonight. By the way, it's very good."

"Thanks. Is it like her to collapse like this? I can't help worrying."

"Not really—Sadie always seems to have energy to burn. But I wouldn't be concerned. Change can be stressful, and stress is fatiguing."

"It's good of you to say that—about me being a part of the household, I mean—but I need to start acting like a grown-up and find a place of our own."

Peter shook his head, smiling. "You might want to ask Sadie before you do."

"You think she won't want to come and live with me?"

"Of course, she will. She adores you, you know that. But you're already living together. This is the only home she's ever really had, and if you're determined to make a new one somewhere else, you need to give her time to get used to the idea. Look, I know you haven't been in a communal living situation—recently, at least—and this is a big adjustment for you, on top of everything else going on in your life. So, if my presence is too obtrusive, I can make arrangements to stay away for a while—several friends have been demanding visits. It's no trouble."

"You're way too kind, Peter. I'm not going to kick you out of your own house. You're right, it is an adjustment for me, but it's one I can probably handle as well or better with you around." Quirke poured himself another glass of wine and offered some to Peter, who shook his head. "I don't know if she told you, but I've asked Sadie to marry me. It's impossible now, but when the divorce comes through, sometime in the early summer of next year with any luck, I'm hoping she'll still want me."

Peter smiled. "She told me the night you proposed, down in Sant' Amaro. I've never seen her so ecstatic. As her guardian, I was very happy for her. But as her guardian, I'll tell you this: You'd better take good care of her."

"Any advice on how best to do that?"

"You clearly know what you're doing. But if I see anything you might be missing—"

"Tell me. Please. I'm not proud. I can't bear the thought of screwing up a relationship that's better than I thought humanly attainable."

※

October 16, 11:15 a.m.

Marking up a draft of Lucas's *Jackson Jones* memo late Thursday morning, Quirke answered the phone to hear a familiar brusque voice on the other end. "Quirke? Howard Latimore."

"Howie, what can I do for you? If it's about a case, you know wild horses couldn't drag confidential information out of me."

"It's not about a case. I'm in the process of replacing Minerva. You remember my senior attorney? She's retiring."

"A lot of that going around lately."

"True. So, I'm sitting here with a Miss Sadie Norrell, who says she works for you."

Quirke couldn't speak.

"Quirke? You there?"

"I'm coming down," he said

Quirke tried to compose his face into something judicious as he entered Latimore's chambers in the Court of Appeal and strode past Latimore's secretary. Barely aware of her clucking remonstrance, he let himself into Latimore's office without knocking. There, in a guest chair opposite Latimore's desk, sat Sadie, in her nice gray suit, looking a little frightened—whether at Quirke's uninvited appearance or at Latimore's crusty interviewing style was unclear.

"I wish you'd told me," he said, sitting down in the other guest chair.

"I'm sorry," she responded quietly. "I didn't know you and Justice Latimore—"

"We go way back," Latimore interjected. "See, her resume said 'Supreme Court Staff Attorney,' and I had to pry it out of her that she actually works for you. It's nothing to be ashamed of," he said to her. "But the Brighton Law School thing confused me. I didn't think you guys looked at people from unaccredited schools."

"Not typically, but Sadie…I wish I'd known. I could have—"

"I wanted to find a place myself, and I didn't want to say anything before I knew where I'm going to be. I never wanted to hurt you. Are you okay?"

"No. No, I'm not okay. Give me a little time to get used to this."

She extended her hand into the space between the chairs and he clasped it. For a few seconds, he struggled to regain equanimity. Then he leaned over and kissed her lingeringly on the mouth.

"I see I was wrong to doubt you, Miss Norrell," said Latimore after a few moments. "Quirke, if you don't mind, maybe you can take that up again with Miss Norrell after the interview. Just one question: knowing what you know, would you hire her if you were me?"

"In a New York minute," Quirke answered. "She's made me look good since the day I arrived at the court three years ago. I have no idea what I'm going to do without her on my staff. I'm in mourning already. If I weren't going to marry her, I'd have to kill myself."

"Perfect. Well said. Miss Norrell, I think we'll be able to work something out. Why don't you let me discuss this further with your...with Justice Quirke."

"Thank you, Justice Latimore." Sadie rose and shook Latimore's hand and squeezed Quirke's shoulder fleetingly on her way out.

"I heard what happened in the courtroom last month," said Latimore. "I had no idea things were that bad between you and Eleanor. Alice was upset—she liked Eleanor."

"It's good for me to be reminded there are people who still feel that way," Quirke mused. "Aren't you going to get in trouble for hiring the home wrecker? I hope you know I'm just being facetious; Sadie had nothing to do with it."

"I do enough judging on the bench, buddy; I'm not going to pass judgment on your romantic life, too. But you've certainly cemented your reputation with this, I have to say."

Quirke shook his head. "I wish I knew where people around here got the idea I'm the Great Beast reincarnated, or whatever it is they think I am. Up until the last month or so, I lived like a monk."

"Maybe it's jealousy. So, when can I have Sadie?"

Quirke couldn't let Latimore establish a precedent of tweaking him over her in this fashion. "Objection to the form of the question," he said.

"Okay, let me put it another way," said Latimore. "Minerva's said she'll stick around till the end of November. I might be able to talk her into staying through the end of the year, possibly into mid-January. How about if the two of you figure out when Sadie'll be able to finish her work upstairs, and let me know."

"That makes sense," said Quirke. "Be good to her, Howie. You can be an awful curmudgeon sometimes."

"I don't know about that; Minerva tolerated me for eighteen years. Besides, I know you'll come charging down here if I so much as look crosswise at Sadie, so you can bet I'll behave."

"She's a lot tougher than she looks, but thanks. Well, it's time I let you get back to making law."

As Quirke was about to let himself out, Latimore spoke. "You're one lucky man, Quirke. She's smart and beautiful, for whatever crazy reason she loves you, and you two were obviously made for each other."

Quirke brightened. "You think so? She's everything to me."

"I have no doubt. But be good and be careful, as my mother always used to say."

Chapter Seventeen

October 16, 2:20 p.m.

Bobby James's heart sank. For the first time, an internet search for "Quirke" pulled up something ominously relevant. Following the link, he arrived at a post on a political blog he'd never previously heard of, from the other side of the aisle if a sampling of other recent posts were indicative.

"Two state Supreme Court justices seeking retention face the voters in less than a fortnight, and one of them turns out to lead a more interesting life than most, yours truly certainly included. We knew Associate Justice Conal Quirke, 52, a registered Democrat appointed by former governor Andrew Benfield, was something of a party boy back in the day—he having played bass guitar in a band with Benfield, in fact, while both were attending Crowne Hall law school. Well, Justice Quirke still rocks on and parties hearty, judging from the below pix. Preliminarily, we're constrained to say we've found no evidence Quirke, J., is actually affiliated with the bizarro "magickal" group that hosted the party. (The search, needless to say, continues.) As for the first photo, what do you think, Dear Reader? Should the honorable judge try to squeeze a campaign contribution out of the Jack Daniel Distillery in light of the product placement? Regarding the second, we admit to a deep curiosity about the nature of the smoking material depicted therein. Is that the biggest spliff you've ever seen, or what??? Lastly, it's impossible not to admire a dude of Justice Quirke's age and girth who has such fine technique with the ladies as the third pic proves. Whether one admires his jurisprudence and believes he deserves another term are, of course, a different kettle of fish. We're reading up on his opinions and, frankly, are rather alarmed at what we're seeing (although, fortunately, most are dissents), and will discuss them in a future post. Stay tuned."

Bobby popped an Advil, washing it down with cold chamomile tea, and picked up his phone, punching in his client's cell number. "Good afternoon, Judge. Bobby James here. Hope you're well. Say, I've got some not-so-good news. Would you please give me a call when you can? The number is 819-0662." He considered texting Quirke the link to the blog, but thought he'd better break the particulars gently in person. "Talk to you soon, okay?"

Quirke returned his call that evening. "Hi, Bobby. What's up?"

"I'm glad you were able to get back to me, Judge. I wanted to be the one to tell you about this thing I found today. You near a computer?"

"I'm next to Sadie's laptop. Wait a second. Okay, where should I go?"

Bobby read off the address and waited. Only Quirke's breathing on the other end signaled he had not fainted or succumbed to a heart attack.

"Holy shit, Bobby. It's been shared ninety-five times and tweeted forty times already. Oh well, at least it's funny. Now I think I'll go get obliterated, if that isn't redundant."

"Where are you, Judge?"

"Here at home. Don't worry, I know enough not to add a DUI to the long list of my sins."

"Is anybody there with you?"

"Yes, Sadie's here. Our roommate, Peter, is away."

"Can you put her on the line?"

"Yes. Bye for now, Bobby."

After a moment, a woman spoke. "Hi, this is Sadie. We need to talk. Right now, or as soon as you can get over here; I'm not leaving him alone. Fifty-five Gillian Alley, the code is 0418. Hurry."

※

October 16, 8:20 p.m.

The door opposite the elevator stood slightly open, and Bobby entered without knocking. The vast area and high ceilings of the place disoriented him momentarily; the place was so unlike a typical home he didn't know where to look until he sensed movement ahead of him.

A slight, diminutive young woman jogged toward him. Her strained features told him he'd arrived not a moment too soon. She closed the door behind him.

"You must be Bobby," she said, extending a hand. "I'm Sadie."

"Hello, Sadie. I wish we'd met under happier circumstances. And I'm sorry it's taken me a while to get here. You're a minute away from my office, but I had to park about a mile from here. What kind of a state is he in?"

"I've never seen him like this, or so determined to get loaded. Usually I can distract him, but not tonight. I think he's afraid it's all over. He can't hear us over here. So...what do you think? Does he still have a chance?"

"I'd say his chances are still better than even—slightly diminished, maybe, but we'll have to hold our breath and check the papers tomorrow morning. Of course, I have no idea what other consequences there might be for him, professionally."

"You're not just saying that to make me feel better?"

Bobby smiled sadly. "Making you feel better's not in my job description."

"Thank you. I suppose I've been overindulging my paranoia tonight, but you can't blame me, can you? Well, come and see what you can do with him."

Quirke was sprawled on a sofa in a seating area near the wall under the skylights. On a low table in front of him was a glass holding a finger's width of whiskey next to a nearly empty fifth of Maker's Mark.

"Judge, how are you doing?"

"Sit down, Bobby. Want a drink?"

"No, thank you. So, this thing today—you know, what I learned long ago in this business is that there are going to be ups and downs. This didn't come totally out of the blue; you told me yourself you suspected something went down in Sant' Amaro. True, that blog post was exceptionally mean-spirited; I haven't seen anything like it in a judicial election in thirty years. But I doubt it'll get much traction."

"I'd like to believe you. But somebody out there doesn't like me and they're going to creep on tying to get rid of me. Keep on trying. I'd almost think my ex-wife is running the oppo. You think?"

"I don't know, but I'll look into it. Hell hath no fury, and all that. Meantime, though, you have a sweet woman right here who's worried about you."

"Darling Sadie, come here," said Quirke. "I'm sorry for everything."

She sat beside him; he leaned heavily against her, wrapping his arms around her. "Conal, you have nothing to apologize for," she said, her words muffled in his embrace. "By the time you get over your hangover, we'll be laughing about this."

"You said something like that once before. An' d'you remember what I said? 'Your loyalty is touching, but don' make me happy. What I need is the truth.' "

"Sweetheart, even wasted you have a phenomenal memory. But I believe what I just said. And no matter what fate throws at us, I'll love you. As you know I always have."

He kissed her sloppily, then leaned back, closing his eyes. "Before I pass out, I need you t'do something."

"Anything."

"Call the Chief. She'll want to know about this. She's on my speed-dial. Bobby?"

"Right here, Judge." The consultant helped him off the sofa and supported him, his shoulder under Quirke's arm, pivoting toward the bedroom.

At the kitchen counter, Sadie rummaged amongst their joint collection of pocket detritus and junk mail, at last finding Quirke's phone. In a moment, she had called the Chief's number.

Somehow the last thing she had expected was to hear the Chief's actual voice, but there it was. "Quirke?"

"No, Chief, it's Sadie Norrell. He asked me to call you."

"How is he?"

"He's...indisposed just now."

The Chief paused. "Drunk out of his mind, you mean?"

"That's one way of putting it. He wanted you to know about something unpleasant that happened today."

"I assume you're referring to the Superior Claim of Right blog post?"

"Oh, no—you've already seen it?"

"It was called to my attention this afternoon."

"We only saw it an hour ago. Of course, he's devastated."

"Tell me, Sadie—is any of it true?"

"Basically, all of it, yes. I'm sorry." Sadie choked back tears.

"I was afraid of that. I thought it had to be you in the last picture."

"We were at a party at a friend of mine's down in Sant' Amaro, and some people were trespassing, hiding in the woods, taking pictures."

"Who was at the party, if you don't mind my asking?"

"Members of this...magical order I belong to...and Conal. But he was just my boyfriend, as far as anyone there knew—I don't think he ever told anyone his last name, and I certainly didn't. We were all having a wonderful time until we realized we were being spied on. My friend chased them off, but he didn't get a close enough look to identify anyone."

The Chief was silent for a moment. Then she said, a little wearily, "There'll be no official comment, and the campaign can deal with it however you deal with it. It's no concern of mine or the court's."

"How likely is it, do you think, the CJB will get involved? You know they're already looking into the...the incident in chambers."

The Chief inhaled sharply. "I didn't. That inquiry's still in the confidential stage, apparently. Well, with this new thing, if they think there's any credibility to it, and I suspect they will, they're bound to investigate. I doubt the fact this arose out of a trespass will carry any weight. I'm sorry; I know that's not what you wanted to hear."

"Better to know the truth. Chief, I feel horrible about this." The words began to tumble out of Sadie's mouth even as tears started from her eyes. "I brought him there in the first place, he was only playing in the band because of a stupid mistake I made, and it was my friend who gave him the weed. I'm probably not making much sense right now. I just want you to know it's not like he goes out every night engaging in conduct unbecoming. We actually live very quietly."

"Sadie, I've known Quirke a long time, and I'll tell you something: I really like him. He's one of a kind, and a good man. But he's also a trouble magnet, and nobody was holding a gun to his head making him smoke that joint. Anyway, keep an eye on him tonight. Are you alone there?"

"No, our consultant—Bobby James—is here."

"Good. Don't let him leave until Quirke's sobered up. I won't expect to see either of you tomorrow."

"Thank you, Chief."

"Good night, Sadie."

※

The consultant sat paging through a book on the sofa Quirke had lately vacated. Sadie looked at him inquiringly. "Sleeping like a baby," he said.

In the bedroom, Quirke was snoring. She drew the blinds and pulled a blanket over him, then returned to Bobby.

"You don't have to stay," she said.

"I'm staying. I don't mind. If he were to wake up in a bad mood, there's no way you could handle him."

"That's never happened and I don't believe it ever will. Truthfully, though, I appreciate knowing you're here. Something about you is so calming it makes me think there may actually be a tomorrow. But for now, let me get some bedding so you can make yourself comfortable." She jogged to the wall of built-in cabinets at an end of the loft, returning with an armful of pillows and blankets.

"It's no wonder you stay slim, Sadie. You're on your feet constantly in this enormous place."

She smiled. "Can I get you anything? There's some leftover Chinese food in the fridge."

"I'm good—ate earlier, but I'll take that as permission to forage if I start feeling peckish. Why don't you go to bed? You need to take care of yourself, too."

"I guess I will. I've been so tired lately, and I don't know why."

"If you don't mind a piece of advice from an old man, you should see your doctor. You need to stay strong for the judge."

"That's what I'm always telling him to do, so I can't quarrel with you. Sleep well, Bobby. Thanks so much for being here."

※

The miserable sound of vomiting in the en suite bathroom, followed by a flush and a moan reeking of self-blame, started her out of sleep while the pall of night still cloaked the loft. She vaulted out of bed. The bathroom door was ajar, and she knocked softly.

"Poor darling. Can I help?"

"I hate this. But—" He turned precipitously back to the toilet and repeated the sequence.

She took a washcloth from the shelves, moistened it with cold water from the tap, and dabbed at his perspiring forehead and temples with it. "Can you stand up? Shall I get Bobby to help?"

"He's still here?"

"He insisted."

"Of course he would. I might harm someone."

"He doesn't know you very well "

"—Not you, never you. Oh, I'm afraid he knows me too well. Baby, you ought to follow precedent and throw me out now, before I move my stuff in and it gets complicated."

"Stop." She knelt and lifted his chin, looking into his eyes, or what she could see of them under their drooping lids. "There's nothing complicated about it. You're mine, Conal; case closed. Also, there's plenty of room here for your stuff."

"Sadie, I—if I weren't so fucking sick I'd—" Another bout of unpleasantness interrupted him.

"I'm going to get you something," she said. "Be right back."

She returned with some floor cushions and placed them around him; he moved weakly onto one, still clinging to the porcelain. "By the way," she said, "I called the Chief."

"Thank you. She must've been furious, but she'd never show it."

"What she said was she really likes you, that you're a good man."

"Did she?" He raised his head with some considerable effort. "She wouldn't say that if she could see me now."

"Actually, that was after she guessed you were drunk out of your mind."

"No way."

"Her exact words. Conal, there's a huge reservoir of love in here, out there, everywhere. You have to believe it."

He didn't bother to hide the tears beginning to mingle with the sweat running down his cheeks. " 'Love is the law,' isn't that what you say?"

She nodded. " 'Love under will.' "

"Right. I knew there was a catch."

Chapter Eighteen

October 20, 1:20 p.m.

John Hendershott scanned a printed list of questions as Quirke settled his robe across his shoulders and grabbed the ends of the fabric to engage the zipper. "Close as the vote is, *Bentley Memorial* is in good shape. You did a great job on the case, John," Quirke told his attorney.

"Thanks, Judge. I've got some questions here you can ask or not ask counsel, however you see fit." He handed Quirke the paper.

Quirke read it, nodding. "I was thinking along these lines, too. Are you going to listen to argument?"

"I'll watch it on the CCTV. And you'll find me right here afterwards, if anything comes up that you want to discuss before conference."

"Excellent. Well, here's hoping this session is excitement-free. I'd better go get in line now."

Quirke departed for the robing room, timing his arrival for the last possible moment before the Chief would start to become annoyed at him for tardiness. Since the Superior Claim of Right blogger had broken, and other news outlets had duly run, the story of his errant conduct at Sant' Amaro (the conventional media mostly suspending judgment, in view of concerns about the credibility of the story's unknown source and the blogger's evident bias), he'd been trying harder than ever to avoid his colleagues, and they had returned the favor. Still touched by the Chief's support in his dark night, he was also trying to stay on his best behavior for her sake.

After the justices had processed into the courtroom and taken their seats, the Chief called the first case. All three cases being argued this afternoon were, coincidentally, Quirke's; he and his staff had prepared calendar memoranda for the court and, atypically for Quirke, had gotten a majority of the votes in each.

The first case, involving theft by false pretenses, was a rescue mission, so called because it involved no significant point of law but was one in which the Court of Appeal, Third District, had gone so seriously off the rails that the Supreme Court had granted review to write an opinion ensuring neither it nor any other CA ever made the same mistake again. The Chief must have been feeling charitable the day she assigned it to him. As expected, respondent's counsel scored no points in his attempt to defend the indefensible, and submitted after a gloomy ten minutes of argument.

The second case was a somewhat trickier one involving the correct interpretation of a statute applying a draconian sentencing enhancement to sex offenders; fortunately for Quirke, three of his colleagues concurred in his calendar memo even though the disposition entailed shaving ten years off each of the thirteen counts of which the defendant stood convicted (thereby reducing the sentence, by Quirke's calculation, from 429 years to a mere 299 years, unless the sentencing court could somehow rejigger the various counts and enhancements to reach the former total on remand). As usual, the bloc saw it otherwise.

The last case, *Bentley Memorial*, was a commercial dispute involving the enforceability of a contractual choice-of-law provision. This was the matter he'd conferred with John Hendershott about just before taking the bench; John had written an elegant and scholarly memo agreeing with the petitioner that the dispute belonged in the courts of this state rather than those of the respondent's corporate home state. The Chief and Justices Wiggins and Corcoran had concurred. Again, the bloc, led by Hetford through a thicket of what seemed—to Quirke—impenetrable and even desperate illogic, took the opposite view.

When the Chief called *Bentley Memorial*, counsel for the petitioner did not immediately take his place at the lectern; instead, there was an unusual huddle of suits that prompted the Chief to ask, "Would counsel like to take a couple of minutes?"

At last petitioner's counsel proceeded to the mic. "We're ready, Madam Chief Justice, but I've just had confirmation of certain facts that oblige me to make a motion on petitioner's behalf."

"What sort of motion?" the Chief asked.

Quirke began to feel queasy as petitioner's counsel explained. "I apologize for the irregularity, but I can only emphasize that the facts have just this minute been verified. The problem here is that, in past, unrelated litigation before this court involving Marvelocity Industries or any of its related entities, Justice Quirke has always recused himself, apparently due to some actual or potential conflict of interest. I am now reliably informed that the respondent in this case, Mortarboard Tile, has just been acquired by a subsidiary of Marvelocity Industries. The deal evidently closed late last night or early this morning. We must therefore request that Justice Quirke recuse himself from this case as well."

"Well," said the Chief, "I have to say I'm a bit surprised not to have heard about this previously from the respondent."

Respondent's counsel briefly joined petitioner at the lectern, saying, with a faintly palpable arrogance, "We, too, regret the late notice, Chief Justice."

Suppressing an impulse to hurl his benchbook at respondent's counsel's head, Quirke spoke up in the most measured and judicious tones at his command. "Counsel is correct that I've recused in cases involving Marvelocity Industries and related entities. I'm unaware of the circumstances counsel's described today, but I have no reason to doubt anything you say as an officer of the court. I'll therefore save you the trouble of a motion, and recuse myself."

He got up and went around Justice Kroner, the most senior associate justice, who was seated immediately to the Chief's right, bent toward the Chief's ear, and whispered while a murmur went around the courtroom and the Chief covered her mic with her palm. "You have to believe I'm totally in the dark on this," he hissed. "I asked Gene Scorchner two weeks ago to update me on his related entities, and he said nothing. Not one word. This is being done to embarrass me. No one is sorrier than I am this is happening."

"I believe you," she whispered back. "But you know what I've got to do."

"Of course. If the pro tem goes our way, you can have my majority calendar memo free of charge."

"That's generous. I'll keep it in mind."

Quirke returned to his seat as the Chief addressed the assemblage. "Justice Quirke having recused himself, the motion is denied as moot. The matter is continued to a future oral argument calendar, and a justice pro tempore will be appointed. The court is in recess."

"All rise," Ward Freitag intoned.

The justices left the bench. On the way out of the courtroom, Quirke heard Hetford humming a Cole Porter tune behind him.

※

"What the fuck, Judge?"

Back in chambers, John was livid. "This is insane. I smell a rat."

"Any particular rat?" Quirke asked him. "Because if I get hold of him, I'd like to pour a bromethalin cocktail down his ugly little throat."

"Maybe I'm overreacting," John said, cooling a little. "There must have been some business purpose behind it. I'm not quite so paranoid as to think Justice Hetford somehow engineered a corporate acquisition by your ex-wife's father's company just so he could take over the majority in this case."

Quirke was struck for a moment. "That idea may not be as crazy as you think. But it'll all depend on the pro tem. I wonder who's up next."

When a Supreme Court justice recuses himself or herself from a case, the Chief Justice fills the empty seat by appointing a substitute from the ranks of Court of Appeal justices, going in alphabetical order from, e.g., Justice Alvin Aachen through Justice Yolanda Zelayo. Following that practice, by the end of the day the Chief had entered an order appointing Justice Phyllis Michaels-Massey of the Fourth District Court, Division Five, to sit as justice pro tem on the *Bentley Memorial* case in place of Justice Quirke.

"Ow." Upon hearing of the order, Quirke grimaced. "Phyllis Michaels authored that turkey we just took up in *Sykes v. Korfu Chemical.*"

"We can still hope," said John.

Their informal hallway conference was interrupted by an anxious-looking Sadie.

"Judge," as she always addressed him at work, "we have a 5:30 appointment."

"Of course. Well, John, there's nothing more we can do tonight. Go home and play with Helen and the twins."

※

"First, the good news, Judge," Bobby said, as the three of them settled onto stools in front of steaming mugs of lemon ginger tea and a plate of shortbread cookies on a worktable in his South-of-Market office. "The Lawyers for an Independent Judiciary is raising some money for you."

"Wow, that's terrific. Who are they?"

"Civil liberties organization, mainly. Also active in seeking reform of marijuana laws."

"Aha," said Quirke. "Am I supposed to send a thank-you note or anything?"

"No, and I'll take care of all the reporting. We also received a few individual contributions, which I've listed here." He passed them copies of a printout.

"Just out of curiosity, how does this compare with whatever Kroner's taken in so far? If you know," Quirke asked, taking a second cookie.

"I haven't kept up closely with that campaign—he's working with a guy who handles mainly Republicans—but last I checked he hadn't had much more donation activity than you. He's also had fewer media references than you by a pretty wide margin."

"Is it true there's no such thing as bad publicity?" Quirke asked. "Kidding."

"Another thing to note and file away is—do you watch much TV, Judge?"

Quirke turned to Sadie. "Do we have one?"

"That answers that," said Bobby. "It's interesting to me that, for all the social media hoopla, there hasn't been a single TV ad against you. By this point, I'd have expected something, in a couple of the big markets at least. But—nothing. It could mean they're saving their money to mount something really nasty in the final days, or it could mean..."

"It could mean the opposition is the Wizard of Oz," Quirke mused. "Nothing but a thoroughly nonmagical little man behind a curtain. I hardly dare hope."

"The other news is that—you recall the early endorsements were all standard positive. The MetroNews, the Trib, the Sentinel. I've shared those with you. However..."

"Go ahead. Let me have it, Bobby." Quirke fortified himself with another cookie, brushing crumbs from his necktie. Sadie reached over from her adjacent stool to hold his hand.

"The Times had this to say today." He passed a printout of an editorial to them.

" 'The Times has always supported the independence of the state judiciary,' " Sadie read aloud. " 'We have long maintained that our system, which forces sitting appellate judges to stand for retention at the end of their terms, risks compromising judicial independence and should be scrapped in favor of a state constitutional amendment providing for something more like the federal system of lifetime appointments. We know such an amendment is vanishingly unlikely in the foreseeable future, and in the meantime have endorsed judges who, in the Editorial Board's view, possess the intellectual and moral integrity to stand up for what they believe in regardless of the political pressure we can't pretend doesn't exist. Associate Justice Conal Quirke of the state Supreme Court, who is seeking retention this November, is, we believe, such a judge. In his relatively brief tenure on the high court, he has put together an impressive record of thoughtful, well-reasoned majority and minority opinions—not all of which we've agreed with. But troubling questions have arisen regarding Justice Quirke's judgment in off-bench matters. We do not necessarily credit those who have accused Justice Quirke of flagrant illegalities tending to cast the judiciary into disrepute, but neither can we simply overlook allegations of behavior that, if engaged in by an ordinary citizen, could have led to arrest and prosecution. We therefore regretfully take no position on Justice Quirke's candidacy at this time.' "

After a moment, Sadie spoke again. " 'Arrest and prosecution'? That seems a bit overblown. It was just a quick toke."

"If the police had been lurking out there in the woods with the spies, they could have nailed me on possession while I was holding that reefer, or being under the influence after I smoked it," Quirke acknowledged. "Technically, I'd have to say the editorial's accurate. And, of course, the Times is entitled to its opinion. The tone's pretty reasonable, actually. If I were someone who looks to the Times for advice on how to vote, I'd be giving it some serious thought."

"Whether or not the Times intended it to be, it's a clarion call to the CJB to investigate," Sadie said. "Not that they'll be able to draw any conclusions before the election."

"True. And with the thing today—"

"What thing today?" Bobby asked.

Quirke recounted the recusal incident, omitting mention of its confidential aspects, including his authorship of the majority calendar memo and how the other members of the court stood on the case. "So, by being forced to recuse on the morning the case was supposed to be argued, I ended up looking either shady or stupid," he concluded. "Apparently just what they wanted."

"Stealth forced recusal. That's a new one on me," Bobby said, shaking his head. "I don't know how any of us could have anticipated it. Well, that's about all the news on my end. Oh, Judge—I did want to get back to you on a question you asked me some time back. I finally found the answer."

Sadie looked up inquiringly.

"It's nothing very interesting—unless, of course, you find the nuances of campaign finance under the Political Reform Act interesting."

"I think I'll go home and start making dinner. Good to talk with you again, Bobby. See you in a little bit, love." Sadie donned her leather jacket, kissed Quirke, and departed.

"Not that I don't find campaign finance law totally engrossing," Quirke said, "but I thought we went over that part already."

"I just didn't want to talk in front of Sadie." Bobby pulled a manila file out of a cubby mounted underneath the worktable and spread the contents in front of them. "The background checks we talked about? Peter Blake's clean. Sadie too, of course. Nothing to worry about. Even the Ordo Argentum Diluculo turns out to be a perfectly respectable religious nonprofit 501(c)(3). You were curious about Sadie's mother?"

Quirke nodded, feeling a trace of apprehension.

"Well, Lauds Mary Norrell was everything you said. More aliases than you can count, a bunch of convictions—nothing major but cumulatively impressive—including grand theft, procuring a child, possession of methamphetamine, possession for sale. About eighteen years ago, she stopped accruing criminal history."

"She went straight?"

"So it appears. Not long after getting out of jail on the procuring charge, she married a retired Navy officer, Captain Henry Clayton Forrester. He seems to have some money. They had a daughter, Zelda. And, other than getting sued a few times—neighbor-type stuff: property line disputes, a dog-bite case—there's nothing of record on her. Not to say she's necessarily led an exemplary life—it's hard to get a real sense of her from the paperwork. But there's no obvious red flag."

"Given what Sadie told me, I'm surprised, but I guess people sometimes do reform. When I was a trial judge, I always hoped the folks I was sentencing would one day turn into good citizens. I always gave them a good pep talk right before throwing the book at them."

"Lauds Norrell appears to have become a reasonable facsimile of a solid citizen, at least."

"On the other hand, she never bothered to look for Sadie after she straightened out. Maybe she felt she'd never be able to make it up to her, and she'd have been right."

"Oh, and I almost forgot. You're probably aware that most appellate judicial candidates, especially on your court, do an interview with GovChan, the public access cable channel in the capitol building. It's about the dullest, safest thing imaginable. Good way for you to counter the wild rumors."

"Actually, I think I they called me earlier this week. I'll get back to them."

"Do that."

Chapter Nineteen

October 25, 4:55 p.m.

"Smoking was prohibited in the building last time I checked, Judge," Lucas noted anxiously. "You're sure it won't set off the sprinkler system or something?"

"It might set off a torrent of complaints from Justice Corcoran, but we can deal pretty handily with that by the simple expedient of shutting the door and ignoring him. I just thought a little celebration was in order, since you'll so soon be coming aboard my staff. You do indulge, don't you, Lucas?" Hetford, sprawling expansively on his deep-tufted, rolled-arm sofa, waved his Cohiba Corona in the direction of his soon-to-be-chief of staff, who, unused to cigar smoke, was beginning to feel nauseated.

"Not generally before dinner."

"Good God—thank you for reminding me. I'm expected at six, and I don't want to keep Eleanor and her father waiting." Seeing Lucas's startled expression, Hetford grinned. "Yes? I know you're dying to ask."

"Would that be Mrs. Quirke?"

"She's resuming her maiden name, so it'll soon be more correct to say Ms. Scorchner."

Lucas nodded slowly.

"You're a bit young for that *où sont les neiges d'antan* look, Lucas. Don't you find it gratifying that despite the initial awkward dislocation, everyone seems better off now? After all, Eleanor and I are rapidly becoming quite fond of one another, and her father of me; Quirke and his Sadie are to all appearances blissfully in love despite being mired in their shared poverty; and—now, now. Was that a trace of the green-eyed monster I just saw passing over your face? Don't worry, we can get you fixed up, too."

"I'd just as soon not, but thanks for the thought."

"Maybe it was you who wanted little Sadie, but the big bad boy stole in ahead of you? I had no idea! There's an opera in this somewhere."

Lucas stood. "I should really be going. Have a nice evening, Judge, and please say hello to Mrs. Quirke for me."

"I'm sorry, Lucas. That was awfully crude; forgive me. I've just been feeling so damned happy lately. You know, there are only ten days until the election."

Lucas appeared to relax into the deeply upholstered leather chair on which he was sitting but, had Hetford been paying as much attention to him as to his cigar, he would have noticed a certain unfamiliar wariness in the attorney. "I'm looking forward to it being over with and moving on," Lucas said.

"As am I. Yet I think we need to step up our efforts. There's been nothing really definitive yet, nothing that would grab the typical apathetic voter by the balls and make him say, 'Quirke has got to go.' Although eventually, no doubt, Quirke would sink his own ship, it may not be possible to wait for that to happen in the normal course."

"But Judge, is it right to manipulate the process like that? It's one thing to watch him fumble, another to—"

"Your scrupulousness is touching, but short of filling in a voter's ballot for him it's all part of our glorious system. Say, I've just had another idea for a blog post. Don't worry, it won't involve trespassing or otherwise invading anyone's privacy. I think you're actually going to like this."

※

October 27, 11:30 a.m.

At first Sadie could scarcely comprehend what the caller was talking about. Then, as her understanding grew, outrage replaced confusion.

"I'm not interested in helping you with your investigation. How can I make it any plainer? The incident happened, it's over and done with, and it hasn't been repeated. Presumably you agree I'd be the aggrieved party in the scenario, but I'm not feeling aggrieved. In the slightest. Except by what I consider your highly intrusive questions."

"I'm sorry you're having such a difficult time with this," Special Investigator Jeremy Bains replied in a tone at once unctuous, condescending, implacable, and sanctimonious. "At CJB we take very seriously the protection of the public from judges who reject appropriate limits on their behavior. So, no, actually, I wouldn't agree you're the aggrieved party. Not the only one, anyway."

"Well, I'd urge you to go find a judge who does reject appropriate limits and exercise every last one of your vast powers against him. Or her. I'm sure there are a few of them out there. But you're really barking up the wrong tree here. Justice Quirke isn't what you seem to think he is."

"But you're not saying the incident didn't happen."

"I'm trying to make you understand: He's a good judge. Not perfect, maybe, but about as close to it as I've seen."

"Now, your job there at the court is...what?"

"Staff attorney."

"Which staff?"

"Justice Quirke's chambers staff."

Jeremy Bains could be heard keyboarding. "Serving at his pleasure?"

"I think you know how it works here. We're confidential at-will employees."

"So, would it be fair to say it's problematic for you to make a complaint, knowing you can be fired at any time?"

"Look, the jerk who filed the complaint with you is still on Justice Quirke's staff, so why would I worry he'd ever retaliate against me?"

There was a pause during which Sadie could hear more keyboarding, then Bains asked, "How would you characterize the judge's drinking habits?"

Sadie was taken aback. "Are you investigating that, too?"

"Does he drink to excess? If so, how often: occasionally? Weekly? Daily? Has it occurred during office hours? Can you estimate quantity and describe how it affects the judge? Have you seen him under the influence of alcohol in the office, on the bench, or in any other activity related to official duties?"

"I'm going to have to seek the advice of counsel before answering any more of your questions."

"Please understand, we're not investigating you, Ms. Norrell."

"All the same, this conversation is over. Good day, Mr. Bains."

Shaking with anger, Sadie crossed the hall and knocked at Freddie's office. Hearing a response within, she entered and shut the door behind her.

Freddie, in the middle of a takeout lunch at his desk, took one look at her and stopped slurping his udon. "What happened? You look ready to kill somebody."

"This all stopped being funny a long time ago." She described her contact with Bains. "Their inquiry's still in the confidential stage, but he was dead serious. Now I'm in rather a pickle."

"How so?"

"I can't lie to them, but neither can I help them destroy the judge. I also don't want to be accused of obstruction. They'd probably report me to the State Bar, and then I'd be in seriously deep shit. No staff attorney at this court has ever gotten into disciplinary trouble; I could be put on administrative leave at best, fired at worst. All because of that despicable Lucas."

"You're jumping ahead a little, aren't you? But it does sound like you need to get some expert advice. And if the judge hasn't already done likewise, he should, too. But look on the bright side; it's still possible it may all come to nothing."

"He's weary of experts running his life, but I suppose you're right. I hope you're right."

"Speaking of Lucas," Freddie said, "I think there's something afoot with him."

"What do you mean?"

"Well, he's never around anymore. Used to be you'd walk down the hall and he'd always be at his desk—days, nights, weekends, holidays. It was creepy how much he worked. Lately it seems like hours or even days go by without a sighting."

Sadie shrugged. "Maybe he's in the library."

"Nobody ever goes to the library, you know that. And he's never been the type to schmooze with other staff. Just saying."

"Well, if you hear anything, tell the judge—he has a right to know if his chief of staff is slacking off."

"Should we do a little investigation of our own?"

"After what the judge and I have been through recently, I'm sort of allergic to the idea of spying on anyone. On the other hand, I'd never forgive myself if I left some stone unturned just because of my personal scruples. Freddie, is there any chance you might…"

"You know I will. You'd make a lousy spy, anyway; you've been attracting too much attention. Besides, if you start following him around, he's apt to think you're finally returning his feelings."

"What feelings?"

"Come on, you didn't know?"

"If you're suggesting he had a crush on me, I'm going to throw up."

"Has, not had. As far as I know."

"I'm not even going to ask how you ever learned that. Because, like I said, it makes me want to—no wonder. No wonder he's been so vindictive and horrible toward the judge. If Lucas ever so much as looks at me, I'll file a complaint. No, you've got to be kidding. But it's not funny."

Quirke rounded the corner of the hallway at the same moment Lucas opened the stairway door. He raised an eyebrow at his chief of staff. "Glad you decided to join us today. I have some comments on your *Jackson Jones* memo."

"I'm sorry if you weren't able to find me; I thought I left a note on my door. In any event, I'll get to those revisions as soon as I can."

"Do you have a higher priority?" Quirke couldn't recall another case Lucas was then working on, and found the little lawyer's demeanor even more irritating than usual.

"Did you know, Judge," Lucas suddenly blurted, "that Justice Hetford's dating Mrs. Quirke?"

For an instant Quirke struggled to discern how Lucas's reply followed logically. In the next fractional second, vast explanatory possibilities related to recent events opened before him. And in the succeeding moment, it struck him as hilarious, and he began to shake trying to contain himself.

"Next time you see Justice Hetford," he instructed Lucas between spasms of silent laughter, "tell him no backsies."

Hetford's relationship with Eleanor—the image of their congress, assuming they'd achieved it by now, was one he found terrifying—meant that conceivably he was friendly with Gene as well, rendering John's conjecture that Hetford had engineered Quirke's recusal in the *Bentley Memorial* case something far from a mere paranoid fantasy. That it was not outlandish, however, did not constitute proof. Trying not to succumb to bitterness, Quirke wondered how the CJB would feel about that scenario. As he sat at his desk considering how he might come up with the evidence, Sadie entered his office and shut the door. He got up and embraced her.

"You're warm," he observed.

"Hot and bothered is more the truth. I've just had a very annoying conversation." She described the call from Bains, adding as an afterthought Freddie's revelation about Lucas's rumored infatuation with her.

"Well, if it comes to that, I don't know how I'll be able to convince the Commission I'm not a hopeless inebriate. And, though I can't say I ever noticed it, I totally get Lucas having feelings for you. By the way, after being invisible all day, he just graced us with an appearance. And guess what? He announced to me, out of the blue, that Hetford and Eleanor are dating."

She studied him for a moment. "How do you feel about that?"

"Two people never deserved each other more. And it might explain a few things. But how did Lucas find out, I wonder? Is spying becoming a habit with him? Or is he now Hetford's confidant? How weird is that?"

"He must be—" Suddenly Quirke's arms were all that kept her from falling to the floor.

"What's wrong, sweetheart?"

"I feel a little dizzy," she whispered through white lips. "It'll pass. If you could help me sit down—"

He carried her to the sofa and laid her on the cushions where, some two months previously, they had discovered a new world in each other. "Has that happened before? Tell me the truth."

"Once or twice. Yes, I'm planning to make an appointment with my doctor, but I need to finish the *Bartley* calendar memo before I...have to go to work for Justice Latimore."

"He can wait a little longer. Please do it."

"I will, I will. I'm sure it's nothing."

"Because, you know, I couldn't go on if anything happened to you."

"Don't worry. I'm the healthiest person I know."

He made to kiss her, but she turned her face aside, saying, "It's not you, darling, I just feel a little ill."

Chapter Twenty

October 28, 11:10 a.m.

Under bright studio lights, two chairs, angled slightly toward the camera, faced each other on a Bokhara rug, a glass-and-metal end table between them and two ferns and state and federal flags behind. The host—looking elegantly severe in a belted black sheath dress—winked at her guest, looked at the camera, and launched the interview. "I'm Marilee Clark on behalf of GovChan. We're honored to have with us one of two Supreme Court justices facing the voters for a decision on their retention in the upcoming general election. Tomorrow we'll have a chance to talk with Justice Ted Kroner. Today we speak with Justice Conal Quirke, who was appointed to the state's highest court by Governor Andrew Benfield three years ago after serving as a trial judge for six years and a Court of Appeal justice for five. Justice Quirke, welcome to GovChan."

"Thank you for inviting me here today."

"Justice Quirke, how would you describe the court's role in advancing the values of our diverse society?"

And they were off and running. GovChan had sent him a list of anticipated questions, and he'd watched enough of these public service judicial election interviews to have a sense of the tone that would come across well to the thousand or so voters who might watch the interview at some point before the election. Sadie had bought him a necktie for the occasion, a light blue and silver repp design that went nicely with his charcoal grey suit. He'd even remembered to polish his shoes, although he now belatedly realized he could have used a haircut and a shave. Given the camera's propensity to add ten pounds, he knew he'd look portly on screen next to the birdlike Ms. Clark, but he wasn't expecting a film deal to come out of this. His mission, as Bobby had repeatedly reminded him, was to prove to a few influential, on-the-fence media types who'd seen the Superior Claim of Right blog post that he was a Supreme Court justice, not a substance-abusing heavy-metal bass guitar player. Not that he'd be making the point expressly: GovChan had trademarked an anodyne high-mindedness that excluded any tabloid-style special pleading.

"Hmm. Interesting," said Marilee, as he wrapped up a brief discourse on the people's access to justice in an era of judicial budget cuts. "And now, a topic you may have had occasion to think about recently, Justice Quirke: campaign fund-raising in judicial retention elections. Is the increasing trend toward sitting judges going out and raising funds for their retention election campaigns a good or a bad thing? How do you feel about it and why?"

"I suppose there's the positive aspect of enabling people to express their support for a judge and for the general principle of judicial independence, but on balance I'm afraid the negatives preponderate. A judge might feel beholden to the individuals or interest groups whose donations helped him or her retain the seat, or at any rate it might look that way, and that would affect people's confidence in the fairness of the system generally. If we lose that, it's all over. And the sheer time involved: I've heard some judges in other states complain they have to do official business at night and on weekends because they're forced to spend their days making phone calls. We're lucky we haven't faced that kind of pressure here, but we're certainly not immune. I don't know any judge who doesn't view the prospect of fundraising with horror."

"It'll be interesting to hear what Justice Kroner has to say about the same topic tomorrow. Next, Justice Quirke, could you tell the viewers what about your background makes you right for the position of associate justice on our state Supreme Court?"

"Apart from my having done the job reasonably successfully for the last three years, you mean? Okay. I would describe my qualifications as follows. I graduated from the U of C and Crowne Hall—"

"What subject was your undergraduate degree in?"

"God, that's a long time ago. Philosophy, with a minor in Celtic Studies."

"Interesting. Please go on."

"—and I received my law degree from Crowne Hall Law School. While there, I was lucky to have the chance to work alongside some of my classmates in the legal clinic representing indigent prisoners in state and federal habeas corpus proceedings under the supervision of the excellent clinical professors there. That's where I realized I could make a serious difference in someone's life. It was incredibly exhilarating, and I began to think about trying to become a judge myself one day. After graduation, I spent three years in the local public defender's office, after which I opened my own practice."

"Representing criminal defendants?"

"Mostly, but not exclusively. From time to time I did a little civil work for some of my criminal clients or their family members. I appeared in state and federal courts, did trials, appeals, and writs—a little of this, a little of that. But when the Governor appointed me to the superior court bench I knew I'd found my true calling."

"That was Governor Benfield?"

"Governor Max Benfield, not Governor Andrew Benfield his son, my law school classmate."

"—The latter of whom appointed you to the Court of Appeal and the Supreme Court, correct?"

"Yes."

"Has Governor Benfield senior gotten out of prison yet?"

Quirke shifted in his chair. Marilee had just veered off script, and it seemed a bit unfair to dredge up an old man's twentieth-century scandal. "His eighteen-month term at Lompoc was up quite some time ago, yes; he's long since retired from business and politics. But to finish answering your question, I've always tried, and I think succeeded, in my work on the court to act impartially and faithfully to the law. Sometimes that's meant leading the court in a unanimous or majority opinion, other times it's meant differing from my esteemed colleagues in a dissenting opinion. I call 'em like I see 'em."

"We're running out of time, I'm afraid, but in the minute or two remaining, is there anything else the voters should know before deciding whether to vote yes or no on whether to retain you, Justice Quirke?"

He'd been hoping the last question would be something impersonal, preferably one that would allow him to rattle off an impressive bunch of justice-system statistics memorized for the occasion—five thousand petitions for review! three thousand original writ petitions! forty-four different languages with certified interpreters in the state trial courts!—but Marilee's reference to the elder Benfield's legal problems suggested a desire for a more intimate, soul-baring finish to the program.

In truth, a part of Quirke had dreaded closing the interview with so much left unsaid—or, more precisely, dreaded the aftermath, assuming he won retention, when, months from now, the CJB would announce an official disciplinary proceeding against him and the few, the hardcore, who had watched this GovChan interview all the way through would realize Quirke had known of and hidden from them the allegations of his off-bench wrongdoing then percolating through the initial stages of the disciplinary process. He didn't think he would be able to hold up his head publicly in the face of such a loss of trust. Better to go down to an honest defeat, *pace* Bobby.

"There is something, Marilee," he heard himself saying. "Some viewers may have heard of an agency called the Commission on Judicial

Behavior, or CJB. It's a kind of watchdog, the police of the state judiciary. They investigate and prosecute judges who are alleged to have engaged in wrongdoing of whatever sort. Often, it's some kind of official corruption, like ticket-fixing or doing other favors for friends. There've been a few judges kicked off the bench for that type of misconduct in the last several years. Sometimes it's allegations that judges were mean or insulting to litigants in proceedings before them, or participated in a case in which they shouldn't have because they had a conflict of interest.

"The way the CJB works is they receive a complaint from a lawyer, a fellow judge, a member of the public—someone who has knowledge of a judge's misbehavior—and undertake a preliminary inquiry. That stage is a confidential search for evidence proving or disproving the allegation. The fact they're looking is nonpublic. If they find enough to suggest they can make a case, they open a public disciplinary proceeding. The judge gets a hearing, the commission makes a decision, and my court—the Supreme Court—decides whether to impose the recommended discipline, which can range from a private reprimand, to a public censure, to the judge's being removed from the bench.

"Well, my feeling is that the initial investigation is confidential to protect the judge, in case it all turns out to be a mistake or a false accusation, or the judge operated in a gray area that's later determined to be permissible. And if I'm right about that, then the judge should be able to waive the confidentiality. And that's what I'm doing here right now, because you asked if there's anything else the voters should know. I'm letting the viewers know—because I would want to know if I were in their position—that the CJB is currently looking into an allegation that I did something improper, namely having a romantic encounter with someone in my chambers at the court. Apparently, too, they're investigating whether I have a serious problem with alcohol. It wouldn't surprise me if they also started checking into the possibility I smoked marijuana at a semipublic gathering recently. Such conduct, if admitted or proven, would arguably tend to bring the judiciary into disrepute and warrant some kind of discipline. I think that little red light means we're out of time, Marilee."

She gaped, but recovered quickly. "Oh, no, you don't, Justice Quirke, with all due respect," she said, gesturing off emphatically to the studio technicians to keep the lights up and the camera running. "So, did you? Do you?"

"Are those allegations true, you mean?"

"Yes. Here's your opportunity to set the record straight."

"It's straight enough already, actually."

"So, you—"

Quirke shrugged. "I'm not going to sit here and deny it."

"Any of it?"

"Well, it's hard to either admit or deny an accusation that hasn't been filed yet, and 'serious alcohol problem' means different things to different people, but what I alluded to just now, I'm owning to the people of this state. That's why I brought it up."

"And the romantic encounter—"

"You understand, of course, that to protect her privacy, I won't go into any detail about that in this forum."

"So, it seems you're essentially admitting the truth of the Superior Claim of Right blog post that got a bit of play a couple of weeks ago. Am I correct?"

Recalling his dark night, Quirke sank into his chair and frowned. "It was unnecessarily mean-spirited, I thought, but most of it was accurate. And funny, I have to say."

Marilee shook her head, eyes wide in amazement. "We're going to leave it there. Justice Quirke, thank you for being with us today. You're a courageous man, and I wish you luck."

"Thank you, Marilee."

※

Never before, and never since, had a GovChan voter information video gone viral. By the same time the following day, 722,356 people had watched the interview on YouTube, a number that continued to rise in the run-up to the election. From the comments section, it seemed a majority viewed Quirke's confession favorably. "Finally a real live human being on the bench!" read a typical reaction. "A Celtic mensch!" read another. "First time in recorded history a man in a prominent government position didn't temporize over what the meaning of 'is' is," read still another.

A substantial minority, however, expressed outrage at a perceived double standard ("I'd get fired if I had a 'romantic encounter' in my office, why should he get to do it with impunity?"; "I had to pee in a cup to get my job; he should have to do the same, but I bet he'd flunk the test."). Some descended to vulgarity ("Here cum da judge, lol!"; "hes [sic] sho nuff a JILF"; etc.); others to the sort of breathless fandom usually only accorded pop-culture novelty acts ("Yummy tummy!!!"; "OMG I'm gonna go watch the Supremes live next month"). One viewer was inspired to coin a new slang term meaning to have sexual intercourse with someone ("fix someone's ticket," as in "Judge Quirke can fix my ticket any time") that appeared a few days later in the Urban Dictionary. Of course, as Bobby pointed out, a certain selection bias inhered in the YouTube responses; it was impossible to tell how many of the viewers would be voting in the election, or even lived in the state.

"Judge, I thought I was going to have a stroke as I sat listening to you confess up there," Bobby said, shaking his head, over coffee in his office the day after the broadcast. "But tactically it looks like a brilliant move."

"Jury's still out on that. I just didn't think I'd be able to look at myself in the mirror if I didn't come clean. So, do you need anything more from me at this point?"

"I did want you to look at this mailer. Courtesy of Lawyers for an Independent Judiciary. They've put together three different versions, for different regions of the state. What do you think?"

Quirke studied the colorful rectangle of card stock that Bobby pushed in front of him. Across the top was emblazoned "VOTE YOUR RIGHTS—VOTE FOR AN INDEPENDENT JUDICIARY." Immediately below, there appeared a photo of him, taken just after he'd joined the court, the same official portrait that hung on the wall in the corridor at work. That rakish smile, that sparkle in his eyes, were the emblem of the Quirke who, back then, had yet to confront a professional or political enemy, who was still learning his staff's names and the court's ancient and sometimes unfathomable customs, who, although surrounded by luxurious excess at home, was dying inside unawares.

"Do I look anything like that now?" he asked.

"Of course, you do, Judge. Sadie's putting that gleam back in your game."

Below Quirke's picture was a column of down-ballot Court of Appeal justices also standing for retention in this election. Quirke knew a few of them personally; others he recognized by reputation. At the bottom, a border of stylized marijuana leaves added an artistic touch. "Nice of the Lawyers to do it. May I have this as a keepsake?"

"Sure. You know how it is—you'll probably get a few in the mail in the next few days."

"If not, I'll be picking them out of the neighbors' recycling bins at the loft to send to all my relatives. Speaking of the loft, I need to go home and check on Sadie. I'm worried about her. She hasn't been well lately."

"She did mention she was feeling tired that time I spent the night."

"She nearly fainted in my arms the other day. I can't get her to see the doctor; she claims to be too busy. Bobby, if anything were to happen to her, I'd be a mess. Like you've never seen. And I know you've seen me in a pretty bad way."

"What makes you think anything's going to happen to her? Nothing happens to young women."

"She's different lately, somehow. Not unloving, but...absorbed in something. I'm not making sense, I know, but this not understanding what's going on is driving me nuts. I can't think about anything else."

"Why, you don't suppose she...Never mind. Try to stay cool. You've both been through a lot of changes lately, so be gentle with yourselves. Well, that's enough advice from an old man. You get on home, then, Judge."

Chapter Twenty-One

October 30, 11:55 a.m.

In his haste to flag down a cab to transport him to his 12:05 dental appointment downtown, and distracted by the noisy Code Pink protest outside the federal building across the street, Quirke tripped over the feet of one of seven towering judicial effigies erected on the sidewalk outside the state building by a fathers' rights advocacy group already incensed at a decision the court had yet to reach in a pending child support *cause célèbre*, and went sprawling onto the pavement.

Feeling like a prize idiot, he accepted a hand up from a passerby and was dusting himself off as Sadie approached from Foltz Street. Laden with a tray full of takeout bag lunches from the café on the corner, she could not give way to her natural impulse to embrace him, but stopped in her tracks and asked, "Are you okay, sweetheart?"

"Apart from a bruised ego, fine," he replied. "What's all that?"

"I took lunch orders from the comrades. Got you your favorite: turkey breast with cream cheese and cranberry sauce on toasted nine-grain, sriracha chips and coleslaw on the side. And a rocky road cookie for dessert."

"Thank you for thinking of me, dearest. I shouldn't eat all that—I really am getting too fat, no matter what you say," he said, smoothing his tie over his belly, "but a turkey sandwich without cream cheese is an abomination. I'll eat it after I get back from the dentist. Got to run."

"I love you. See you later," she said, heading for the employee entrance as he began waving his arms at a taxi barreling eastbound on Golden Gate Avenue.

❈

"That's her, I'm sure of it," said Laudie, grabbing Rowe's arm as they emerged from the Inns of Court Hotel, kitty-corner to the state building, and pointing.

He squinted. "Who? That petite girl in black—?"

"The one carrying the takeout who just went inside. I see her taste in clothes hasn't changed. I wonder who she was talking to."

"Somebody she works with, maybe. At least she's in the office today. Are you going to call her?"

"I'll wait until later in the afternoon. Then maybe she'll be more inclined to slip out and meet us. Or even invite us in for a tour, who knows?

This is so exciting. I have a feeling everything's on the point of changing for us."

"I hope so, Angel. But remember, places like this have all kinds of security."

She scowled at him. "You don't have to remind me. Don't worry, I'm not going to do anything to attract attention. We'll get her nice and unobtrusively."

※

Back in their hotel room after a decadent early-afternoon breakfast at Brenda's and a stroll around the gritty environs of the Inns, Rowe busied himself on a laptop while Laudie took several deep breaths and phoned the state Supreme Court.

"Yes, please. Could you connect me with Sadie Norrell? She's an attorney there. I'm her mother." She added, hurriedly: "But I want to surprise her, so don't breathe a word, Miss—? Thank you, Miss Lowe. You're a real dear."

※

Afterward, Sadie put it down to feeling under the weather. The sandwich she'd bought for herself sat untouched on her desk but for a broken-off crust that she'd managed to eat before the nausea returned and, while wondering for the nth time why this bug or whatever it was refused to go away, it didn't occur to her to think who could be calling via the court's general number. Instead, she absent-mindedly stayed on the line as the deputy clerk downstairs transferred the call to her desk.

"Sadie Norrell," she answered.

"Oh, my sweet child. I can't tell you how good it is to find you at last."

No matter how many years separated her from that voice, she could never have failed to recognize its honeyed peril. She hesitated, a vestigial sense of duty competing with self-preservation.

"My gosh, how long has it been?" Laudie went on. "How are you, darling?"

"I don't want to talk with you, and I have to ask you not to call again. Goodbye, Laudie."

"Wait, dear child. I know things were hard for you when you were small. I was a victim, too—"

"Mm—no. That kind of bullshit won't work with me. You thought of nothing and no one but yourself. You were ready to sell my body—"

"Child, I honestly don't know what you're talking about, though I do see you feel very strongly about it. But be fair to me, Sadie—being fair is your business, after all—and try to think of the good times. Like when we lived in Ceres and we'd go to that dumpy little old movie house and I'd treat you to a sundae afterward? Remember the time that old man gave us a lottery ticket and it turned out to be a winner? How we splurged?" Laudie laughed.

Sadie did remember. It was when she was five or six years old and still able to see magic in her heartbreakingly erratic mother. Thanks to a $500 windfall courtesy of a half-soused stranger who may have been—probably was—one of Laudie's johns, there was a two-hour period one day when Sadie got everything she'd ever wanted in all the shops on a tawdry stretch of the main drag in the town they were dwelling in at the time. A red plastic bead necklace, a comic book, clear plastic sandals, an ice cream cone, all were hers just for the asking. She and Laudie laughed together until their sides ached as they walked hand in hand along the street in the hot summer breeze, and life felt silly and precious, and Sadie became, in her own mind, for a brief and shining moment, the princess Laudie kept calling her all that day. After they'd perambulated the streets for a long while, Laudie took her to a converted trailer with an awning under which they ate a greasy hotdog and fries, where Laudie met a man and her attention swerved away from Sadie. She couldn't remember what had come next, except for the fear, a palpable fear beyond any words she had to encapsulate the experience at the time.

"Don't try to reach me again. Don't come near me or I'll have you arrested. Don't—"

"I knew it, I knew you'd never listen to me after the two of them spoiled you and turned you against me. I should never have let them near you, those bitches—"

"If it weren't for Peter and Leila, I'd have turned out like you."

Sadie hung up and immediately called the Clerk's office, instructing the answering deputy under no circumstances ever to connect her with an outside caller claiming to be her mother. Then she ran to the restroom and squatted beside a toilet with wave after wave of dry heaves. When they finally passed, she pulled herself, seeing stars, along the wall to Freddie's office and told him she was going home.

"—Bitch yourself," said Laudie. "Fuck her, then. Damn her to hell." She jumped off the bed and Rowe, looking up from his laptop, saw her begin to search for something to destroy.

He intervened. "I may have figured out who that man was."

"Who?"

"The guy she was talking to on the sidewalk. See this picture of the Supreme Court? The one standing here on the left? I think it's him. Justice Conal Quirke."

Laudie hopped back onto the bed and looked over his shoulder at the computer screen. "This one?" she asked, pointing.

"Yeah, with the Van Dyke and the horn-rimmed glasses. Pretty distinctive-looking, wouldn't you say?"

"I think you're right. Brilliant, my love."

"According to Wikipedia, he's married to Eleanor Scorchner, the daughter of the CEO of Marvelocity Industries."

"He must be worth a fucking fortune."

They exchanged smiles.

Chapter Twenty-Two

October 30, 4:55 p.m.

Days before the election, the popular mind turned toward urinalysis. Quirke's admission to having lately smoked marijuana produced a drumbeat of demands that not only he, but all candidates for public office, submit to the same ritual indignity suffered by thousands of job seekers, student and professional athletes, and others.

The Superior Claim of Right, picking up on a theme echoing in some of the comments to Quirke's GovChan video, took him severely to task for presuming to sit on criminal cases if not personally committed to remaining on the right side of the law at all times: "How much confidence can the parties have that a judge like Quirke can be fair? Given his longstanding criminal leanings, old defense lawyer that he is, the prosecution might well suspect him of undue sympathy toward the defendant, while the latter might expect a tendency on Quirke's part to try to curry favor with the prosecution by exhibiting undue severity toward him. On a more fundamental level, do we even want to be judged by a judge who so obviously has such a problem with self-control that even licit psychoactive substances, of which there are plenty enough on the market, aren't sufficient for him? We will save for another post, while we draw up the indictment against Quirke, the issue of sexual continence and its relation to judicial philosophy. Here we simply add our voice to the chorus of voter-citizens who like to think public servants should live and work under the same conditions we do: If I have to pee in a cup to get a job, why shouldn't Conal Quirke and every other candidate for office do likewise?"

Justice Ted Kroner either shared Claim of Right's views on the matter or saw an opportunity to raise his profile by hitching it to Quirke's notoriety, for, the day after the post excerpted above, his campaign announced that the justice had indeed undergone drug testing, with negative results "except for prescription medication at therapeutic levels." Several Court of Appeal justices followed suit.

A MetroNews reporter asked Quirke in an unguarded moment whether he would support a requirement that candidates for judicial office undergo drug testing. "Would I vote for something like that? Certainly not," he laughed. "We don't operate a lot of heavy equipment here at the court, so the need for it escapes me. Nobody should have to submit to that just to put bread on the table. Hasn't the whole concept of privacy already been eroded enough?" The article appeared on the first column of the paper's front page and was picked up by the national wire services. Lawyers for an Independent Judiciary sent Bobby a check in the high four figures.

Although polling was too expensive for their shoestring campaign, and a reliable index of likely voter support thus remained out of reach, Bobby expressed unflagging confidence to his preoccupied client. Then, as the time before the election dwindled, with the social media attacks on Quirke gaining only modest steam, every uptick in publicity seemingly favoring him on balance, and negative TV ads still conspicuous only by their absence, a new and desperate theme emerged from the still-murky anti-Quirke forces.

DEVIL WORSHIP AT THE STATE'S HIGHEST COURT? screamed the headline in the *San Eligio Banner*'s website and print editions of October 30. Accompanied by screen shots of the Superior Claim of Right photos of the Sant' Amaro party, along with several other previously unseen photos of black-clad magicians entering the temple on Carleton Matthews's property, reporter Phil Crosse, theretofore unpublished in the *Banner*, detonated a bombshell. "Did Supreme Court Justice Conal Quirke and his staff attend a Black Mass in late August under the auspices of a secretive satanic society? The photos above and to the right show the female staff member, whose name is being withheld pending advice of legal counsel, fourth from the left, entering the temple in the society's remote and well-guarded compound in Sant' Amaro, while the photos below depict the justice, far right with guitar, supporting the blasphemous liturgy in concert with other members of the society. Justice Quirke could not be reached for comment before press time."

"This is wrong on so many levels," Quirke, cold with fury, told Bobby, who had called his cell phone as soon as the piece broke. "It's fucking un-American: Religious tests for public office are unconstitutional. Article VI, paragraph 3 and *Torcaso v. Watkins*. It's also fucking wrong as to Sadie's people: They aren't a 'secretive satanic society'; they're actually a solar-phallic sex-magic order. Very different thing. And finally, it's fucking wrong as to Satanism: I had a client who was a Satanist once, and he was a stand-up guy. They don't worship the devil, contrary to popular belief. At least the fucking idiots didn't publish Sadie's name. God, I hope she doesn't see this; she's been so fragile lately. I don't suppose there's anything we can do about it. I'm not even inclined to dignify it with a response, assuming they ever actually do try to get a comment from me, which, by the way, is a fucking lie: they never did."

"You're absolutely right, Judge. Any reasonably intelligent human being could spot this for the bullshit it is. Phil Crosse, huh. I'll see what kind of a journalist he is, though I believe I already know. Judge, I—I don't know if it's my place to say it, but—"

"I'm not going to get wasted over this. I wouldn't give Phil Crosse the satisfaction."

"Thank you, Judge. Thank you. All the same, if you start feeling bad about this, or anything else, call me right away. I'll remind you why we're doing fine."

On ending the call, Quirke discovered a just-deposited voicemail on his office phone number. "Ninety-three, brother Con!" a jovial voice boomed. "Frater Nox, aka Carleton, as in Matthews, here. I suppose it's premature to address you that way, Your Honor, but I feel sure it'll be correct one day. Say, I'm taking the liberty of calling to say it's clear we, you and I, are under magickal attack, and we, the O.A.D., are on it. So, look for striking developments by and by. Over and out. Ninety-three."

Puzzled, Quirke listened to the message a second time, then forwarded it to Sadie's phone, adding a message of his own. "Sweetheart, here's a voicemail Carleton Matthews just left me. What does it mean? Oh, I forgot to mention I'm meeting up with a friend for a drink after work, so I'll be home a little late. I love you, baby. Bye for now."

Chapter Twenty-Three

October 28, 5:15 p.m.

"I'd like to speak with Jennifer, if she's there. Tell her it's Laudie. Laudie Norrell. She'll know who I am."

Over the sound of a toddler's screaming in a space that sounded to be in the shape of a double-wide, the girl who answered the phone made muffled inquiry for too long, as if she were having to cajole Laudie's old friend into taking the receiver. But that couldn't be, Laudie knew. After you've done time and enough drugs with someone, they always take your calls.

And when Jennifer finally came on the line, she sounded as ecstatic to hear from Laudie as Laudie knew she would be.

"Girl, what have you been up to?" Jennifer asked after pleasantries. "I heard you got married."

"I was blessed with eighteen heavenly years with the Captain. We truly adored each other. That's why it was so horrifying, what happened."

"Why, what happened?"

"He was burned up in his bed. I would have died, too, right alongside him, but I was out of the house getting his medication."

"Oh, my God. Laudie, what a nightmare."

"And the damn insurance company's turning it into one of those nightmares you can't seem to wake up from. They keep holding up the policy money. I'm ready to sue—or burn down their offices," Laudie laughed coldly. "No need to pinch me, Rowe. Jennifer knows I'm kidding. Rowe's my son-in-law," she explained. "Without him I don't know where I'd be in all this trouble and turmoil."

"Your son-in-law? But I thought Sadie and you—"

"Rowe was—is Zelda's—my baby's—husband. Zelda married young, like me. Did you ever meet Zelda?"

"Huh-uh. I don't think you ever came back out this way after you got married. I always thought you were smart to leave it behind you."

"I won't dispute I was smart, but I couldn't leave a friend like you altogether behind me. Jenny, honey, I think I'm going to be coming out your way soon. But first I'm going to have a little reunion with Sadie."

After a few beats, Jennifer said, "Well, will wonders never cease. I'm happy for you."

"She's doing well—a lawyer now, would you believe it?"

"Oh, my goodness. She was always the smart one. She married?"

"Not currently." Laudie made it sound unquestionably true. "She works real hard all the time, but I'm going to have her take a look at this insurance problem I've got. After that little piece of business, we're going to come and visit with you."

"It'll be great to see you."

"Likewise. You still dealing?"

"You know I—I don't do much of that any more. The stress, and I had a kid, and..."

"Oh, honey, that's wonderful! How old is she? Or he—I don't know why I assume every kid's a little girl."

"He. He's good. Three and a half. A little fussy now and then, maybe you heard him on your end just now. But a good little boy."

"Well, I can't wait to meet him. But you do have connections out there, right? I can't imagine a Jennifer so straight she couldn't put an old friend together with somebody who can get stuff."

"Sure, I can help you out with that, though I'm not into it...personally...too much anymore."

"Well, bless you, honey. I'll give you a call again when we're on our way out there. Hoping to have good news to tell you by then about the insurance."

"Yeah, I hope you get what's coming to you."

Laudie was silent for a moment. "Thanks, Jennifer. You'll be hearing from me."

※

"So, there we are," she said, smiling, as though the path to their financial security were now smooth and brightly illuminated. "Don't you doubt for a single second that everything'll turn out just fine. But all the same, have you got the Georgia Home Boy?"

"That and everything else you told me to get."

"The duct tape? The line? The zip ties? Syringes?"

"Everything."

"Car going to make it?"

"I think so."

"Well done. Dear one, the day you stepped into my life was the day God finally smiled on me."

He dropped to his right knee, lowering his head into her pleat-skirted lap. Her long, cool fingers stroked his temples like an electric paintbrush, or what he imagined one might feel like on his fevered skin—

166

her touch now purple, now deep rose, now blood-red in the back of his eyes, which he shut tight as he inhaled deeply the mysterious scent of his angel.   Her commands could be inexplicable, but the blessings she dispensed came straight from Almighty God.

Chapter Twenty-Four

October 30, 5:05 p.m.

John was working on Quirke's opinion in the just-argued sex-offender sentence enhancement case, trying to accommodate the concurring justices' every wish and suggestion to the maximum extent possible without undercutting the opinion's basic rationale, hoping the bloc wouldn't go behind his boss's back to somehow carve off another vote and thereby force him once again to turn a majority opinion into a dissent, when the phone rang.

He clicked the speaker button. "Hi there, Alban." Alban Gregory was the Chief's chief attorney, and thought of himself as the judicial staff attorney counterpart to the Sergeant Major of the Army, a view not widely shared among his fellow staff attorneys. "What's up?"

"I just got a call from Kevin Elvington, the chief counsel of the CJB. He asked me if I could explain to him why their website's useless this afternoon."

Alban's response was such a non sequitur that John had to shake his head. "Does he often call you with tech questions?"

"Not previously. But having looked at the site, I'd probably have done the same thing in his place."

"Hang on," John said, clicking over to the CJB site. "Wow."

In the middle of the CJB's cookie-cutter .gov website, superimposed on the usual visually numbing paragraphs of informative text, there appeared the official-portrait face of Justice Quirke, photoshopped onto a picture of the Master Therion as ceremonial magician wearing a triangular hat, his bare forearms pressed alongside his face, thumbs extended outward. Above, in bold: QUIRKE. Below, in italics: *Love is the Law*. None of the links on the page worked.

"Holy God." John bolted out of his chair and yelled down the hall. "Margie!"

The judicial assistant came running. "Where's the judge?" John asked her.

"He left half an hour ago. He didn't say where he was going."

"Alban, this is stunning. Who'd be crazy enough to do something like this?"

"Well, given the imagery," said Alban, "a fair supposition is it's one of the people Justice Quirke's been accused of fraternizing with lately."

"Is Sadie still around?" John asked Margie.

She shook her head. "She went home an hour ago. She was really tired, poor thing."

"Strangely enough, but paling in significance, of course, the Superior Claim of Right blog was also hacked today," Alban said.

"I don't know what to say," John sighed. "Whoever did this is either exceptionally stupid or really hates the judge, because it's obviously terrible from the electoral standpoint."

"That's for his campaign to sort out. I just called because I thought someone over there should know."

"Thanks, Alban. Deeply appreciated."

After ending the call, John turned to Margie and Freddie, who had entered John's office. "First thing to do is find the judge and let him know, and then talk to Sadie. If whoever's behind this is one of her friends, she ought to be able to call it off. Would you mind trying to reach her, Freddie? I'll keep trying the judge's cell."

Freddie nodded. "She's probably at home now, but I'll bet she put her phone on airplane and went to sleep. She was totally knackered. But I'll try."

※

October 30, 5:10 p.m.

The popularity of the Inns was evidently on the upswing, judging from the noise, the crowds around the bar, and the dearth of empty tables. After finally catching the bartender's eye and procuring his double whiskey sour, Quirke turned and surveyed the room. At last he spotted his old friend and office mate Jim Forney, sitting at a tiny round table squeezed along the wall. Forney, waving, looked delighted to see him, and it occurred to Quirke that, among lawyers, he was something of a celebrity, even setting aside recent events.

"Jim, how've you been?" Quirke deposited his drink on the table and they shook hands.

"Great to see you, Your Honor. Sit down, sit down. Sorry about the clown table—it was all I could find. You should have let me buy you a round. But then I guess you'd have to declare it to the Fair Political Practices Commission, huh?"

"Yeah, it's a lot less complicated if I pay my own way. And cut it out with the 'Your Honor' thing—just for tonight, I'm Quirke, like old times. Say, you look terrific. How do you do it, trying back-to-back murders, running a law office, and all that, and still find the time to stay fit?"

"I get up at five and hit the gym. You look great, too."

"You always were a terrible liar. How are Kate and Kimmy?"

"God, you're good, that memory. Kimmy's at Stanford and Kate's gone part-time in her pediatric practice, starting to wind down to retirement."

"Only a matter of time for you, too, I imagine?"

"Not bloody likely. Tuition's over fifty grand a year, and lately Kimmy's been talking about law school. How about you? Of course, I know you're on the ballot this time. I already voted for you—absentee."

"Thanks, I'm honored. You're the first to tell me that." They clinked glasses. "Personally, it's been a roller coaster in the last few months. As soon as my divorce comes through, if a certain cherished young woman hasn't gotten tired of me I'll be getting married again."

"You don't waste time. Congratulations. I shouldn't be saying this, but I never could stand Eleanor. She didn't appreciate you."

"She still doesn't. But I was a terrible husband to her, so we're even." He finished his drink. "You must be wondering why I called you."

"I'm curious, yes."

"I don't know how closely you've been following the political news this election cycle."

"Haven't had much time. It's all so trivial and sensationalized, and ninety percent of it false or exaggerated. Plus, I already did my civic duty."

"Well, there's been an unusual amount of attention paid to my particular candidacy."

"Why? You're running nonpartisan and unopposed. It's a goddamn retention election."

"Some people think I'm running against myself. Long story short— and you can watch the GovChan interview for yourself on YouTube—I admitted to a few things, stuff that'd be pretty mild for anybody except a sitting supreme court justice, but I'm left with a few blots on the escutcheon and a pending CJB investigation. I'm kind of wondering if I'll have a job in a couple of weeks."

"Any likelihood of criminal charges?"

"No, no. I inhaled, but I'm not holding. I just don't know how it's going to sit with the majority of voters. My constituency are the kind who don't turn out."

"I hear you, buddy. Well, damn. Good luck and everything."

"So, what I wanted to ask was, if things do go south, is there room for one more in the old office? I haven't done any trial work in eight years, fourteen if you don't count my time on the superior court bench, but it's really all I was ever good at as a lawyer. I might be rusty, but I know I could get my groove back."

"Quirke, I—it would be too great an honor for our humble chambers to have you take up with us again. We'd have to buy new furniture and get a whole new clientele—white collar criminals exclusively. No more chop shops, drug dealers, or gang bangers."

"I'm not kidding, Jim."

"What about shopping your resume to O'Melveny or Latham or MoFo? You could pull down a million a year. Or maybe one of the litigation boutiques. Look, I'm sorry. You're a great trial lawyer; there's nobody better with a jury. But I also have to think of client relations."

"What do you mean? I always had great client relations."

"You did. That was before you started shipping their asses to the Department of Corrections on a regular basis."

"I could change my name," Quirke mused.

"You're going to beat this thing, my friend. Whatever you did—and you said yourself it was mild shit—it can't take away from the fact you're a great judge. And whatever sensational lies and half-truths they're slinging about you, you're still a great judge. You gotta have faith in yourself. I hope I'm not being presumptuous, but I hate to see you looking so depressed for no good reason. And you have a woman who's probably wondering where the hell you are. Maybe you should call and let her know you're on the way home, instead of getting another whiskey sour like I know you want to do."

"Wise advice. Maybe just one more for the road, and then—what you said."

"Good. Judge, I'm going to follow my own advice and head home now. But when the ballots are counted, I promise I'll be the first one to send an email congratulating you. I know I didn't tell you everything you wanted to hear, but I hope I've been of a little help tonight, anyway."

"You've put things in perspective. You were always the level-headed one in the practice." The two men stood and shook hands again.

"Best of luck to you, Judge."

"Same to you, Jim. Take care."

※

Quirke maneuvered through the throng and signaled to the bartender. Soon a glass was deposited on the bar in front of him, and he wasted no time in addressing himself to it. While he had the barkeep's eye, he ordered another. *And* that's *for the road*, he adjured himself as sternly as he could. *Sadie's waiting.*

The mention of his own name to his left drew his attention away from the whiskey at the same moment that the touch of a hand on his back sent a shiver up his spine: "...you're Justice Quirke."

The speaker, a woman who appeared to be but barely in her fifth decade, had an uncannily familiar face: oval, only starting to show lines, with huge, long-lashed brown eyes and the kind of milk and cherries complexion he always found attractive, under a corona of curly auburn hair. Her clinging jersey dress perfectly outlined her slender figure, which pressed closer to him as other patrons surged toward the bar.

"Have we met?" he asked, casting his mind back. *College? Law school? How do I know her?*

"We have now. Laudie Forrester," she said, slipping her hand into his. "It's such an honor. I saw your picture in some newspaper recently, but I never thought I'd be meeting you so soon. And this is my son-in-law, Rowe Emworth." A tall man with brushed-back glossy black hair, standing a little behind her, nodded.

Quirke was momentarily incapable of making a reply. She was still clasping his hand, and his normal excess of good manners seemed to have absconded.

"How do you do?" he finally said.

She smiled. "It's difficult to talk here. Shall we try to find a table? Rowe can wait for your drink. Come." She led him toward the back of the room and a passageway into which he'd never previously ventured.

"I'm sure you know this," she said, looking back at him as he followed, "but there's another bar in the hotel part of the Inns. It's much quieter and more comfortable, and you can get a decent meal. Are you hungry?"

"I should tell you I have an engagement—" he began.

"I wouldn't dream of taking you away from it. But I have a particular reason to speak to you, if you'll excuse my boldness. Here, this is perfect."

She gestured toward a booth in a dark corner of the hotel bar, sliding into the apex of the deeply cushioned seats. A waiter came and lit the candle in its mirrored holder on the heavily varnished oak table.

"Good evening. Would either of you like a drink, or to see a menu?"

"Yes, I'd like a glass of white wine, and I believe my friend would like a whiskey sour. Double? Double," she nodded. "And yes, why don't you bring a menu when you come back."

Although he could point to nothing about it that seemed overtly other than benign, the intensity of her focus on him gave him claustrophobia. He could see she'd been as beautiful as Sadie had said, and was still arresting, but his intuition clamored at him to escape, and he already regretted following her into the hotel bar.

"What is it you wanted to talk with me about?" he asked, sounding to himself unnaturally gruff and defensive.

"I have a sort of connection to you," she said, and panic now augmented his claustrophobia. He suddenly felt an urgent duty to shield from her as much as possible of his and Sadie's lives, but to do that effectively he had to discover what she knew about him.

"I have a daughter who works at your court. Her name is Sadie Norrell. Do you know her?"

The question suggested she knew rather little, and he could breathe again. "I've met her. She's a good lawyer."

"She's a smart girl, all right. We're very proud of her. I called to see if she could stop by for a drink, but they tried ringing her office and she wasn't in."

Quirke gave silent thanks. The last thing Sadie needed, as weak and low as she'd been feeling lately, was this intrusion of the painful past.

"I'll call her again in a little while, of course, but meanwhile, when the bartender mentioned who you are I simply had to meet you. How's the election campaign going?"

Clearly, she knew very little indeed, and Quirke felt he could relax ever so slightly as the waiter brought their drinks. He quickly pulled out his wallet.

"You must let me—" she began.

"I insist. The record-keeping is unbelievably onerous if I let people pay for me."

"Thank you."

He settled with the waiter, who left menus for them to consider. Quirke ignored his.

"There's a problem I want to consult Sadie on," she said. Leaning closer, she lowered her voice. "An insurance issue. A gross unfairness. Ah, here's Rowe."

The tall man had arrived with a collection of drinks from the public bar, and the tabletop now looked as if they'd been indulging for some time. He slid into the booth beside Laudie.

"I think we need a new law: All insurance claims must be paid within two weeks. Doesn't that seem fair? It's certainly not fair of Fairstate—ironic name, isn't it?—to keep making these nondenial denials. But we're completely at their mercy. Do you know of any way to—"

"I'm sorry, but it's impossible for me to give you legal advice. It sounds like your unfortunate situation might be heading to litigation, and I simply can't help you. Now if you'll excuse me—"

"Please don't leave yet. I understand, and I do apologize. I shouldn't have asked, but it's so easy to become obsessed. So, you know Sadie? Have you worked with her? Or I should say, has she worked with you?"

Quirke's pulse quickened again, and he took a swallow of his drink, trying to plot a course to lead smoothly to a calm and swift exit from the conversation.

"I'm aware of her work," he said. "But I'm afraid the confidentiality rules preclude me from talking about it specifically. The court's opinions speak for themselves, and to protect our deliberations the public's forbidden to look behind the curtain."

"I'm a great decision maker, but I'd never be able to keep anything confidential. Just as well I never became a judge." She laughed as the waiter appeared. "Shall we order some food? I'm absolutely famished. We haven't eaten all day, and I know this glass of wine will make me tipsy if I don't put something in my tummy soon. Rowe, what about you?"

"The club sandwich looks good," he said, after a cursory glance at the menu.

"Swiss steak and mashed potatoes for me," she said. "Justice Quirke, please let us treat you. Oh—you probably won't take me up on that, will you?"

"No," he answered. "Even if the Fair Political Practices Act weren't there to deter me, my engagement is. I really must be going."

"Go, then. I'm sure you have interesting people to see every night of the week, and the last thing you'd want is to spend a half hour with a couple of hicks like us."

The anger in her voice was all out of proportion to the offense. "I'm sorry," Quirke replied hastily. "I didn't mean to imply that. I'll just say goodbye." As he slid out of the plush seat, Rowe grasped his forearm.

"Let me walk you out," he said. It was a statement rather than a request.

"All right," said Quirke, not waiting for him, but moving toward the Lamden Street exit.

On the sidewalk, Rowe spoke up in a more conciliatory tone. "I apologize for Laudie's behavior, Judge. Please understand, the stress of the last few weeks has been terrible. First the trauma of the fire, and being widowed—and her husband had been ill for a long time—and finally the incredible runaround we've been getting from the insurance companies have all taken their toll on her nerves. She's sometimes a bit snappish. She doesn't mean anything by it. Won't you at least stay and finish one of those drinks? I think there's at least two whiskey sours on the table, and you paid for them."

Seen in this light, Quirke's abrupt flight seemed a bit absurd, and the two men laughed simultaneously. *What could it hurt?* Quirke asked himself. "Okay. Just to finish one of them. Then I really must go, or the person I'm seeing tonight will become quite annoyed."

"Of course. Just one."

As Quirke pulled the door, Rowe added: "She's awfully worried about how to get the insurance proceeds; it's what she hopes Sadie'll help us deal with."

At the table, Laudie was already tucking into her Swiss steak, as a pile of sandwich triangles awaited Rowe. "Excuse my lousy manners," she said cheerily. "I told you I was famished."

"Bon appétit," Quirke replied.

As his companions ate, he knocked back one of the whiskey sours. It seemed not quite up to the Inns' usual standard, and to test his observation, he polished off the other, arriving at the same verdict: too salty. This was odd because, to his knowledge, salt was not an ingredient in the typical whiskey sour recipe.

Rowe and Laudie began to chat about inconsequentials: their drive into the city that morning, the weather, the softness of the mattress in their hotel room. Quirke was starting to feel the effects of the bourbon a few minutes later when he noticed Laudie and Rowe blurring together in his eyes. The room began to swim and his stomach to churn, and he suddenly knew he had to get out of the bar or embarrass himself. Oddly, before he could say a word, Rowe and Laudie had him by the arms and were carrying him outside, although not before Rowe had gone through his pockets and tossed his phone onto their abandoned table. The last thing Quirke remembered was losing his lunch on the sidewalk, and then came blackness.

Chapter Twenty-Five

October 31, 4:00 a.m.

Under the bedclothes, at four in the morning with the foghorns distantly sounding, was usually the most secure and comforting place in Sadie's entire world. But that was only when she could nestle back into Conal's warmth, feel his arms enclose her, and listen to his quiet snore. Tonight, their bed was cold outside the perimeter of where she'd lain and the loft was utterly still and dark. Only the rain on the skylights provided a dismal semblance of company. She considered, and tried to believe in, the possibility that he'd stayed out late drinking with the nameless friend he'd referred to in his voicemail message, that they'd closed a bar or two and maybe decided to crash at the friend's place. Or that they'd found a club still open at this hour. Or that perhaps they'd gone to breakfast at an all-night restaurant and he'd soon come stumbling in, still slightly drunk, apologetic.

Except that it was Thursday night—now Friday morning—and Conal had never stayed out late on a work night, never gone unreasonably long without checking in with her. He never failed to think of her.

She tried his cell phone again, but it went to voicemail immediately. Having listened through the outgoing message just to hear the sound of his voice, she ended the call and then texted him once more: *where r u dearest? missing you something fierce*.

With the resumption of sleep an impossibility, she rose and pulled on a fleece robe that did little to fight the chill in the room and sat down on the floor in an asana, adding a simple pranayama technique, trying to clear her head, failing miserably. As well as feeling fatigued and ill lately, she'd been lazy in her magical practice and was now paying the price for her lack of discipline in the form of a runaway mind and overwhelming fear. She wanted to call Peter, her teacher in these matters, but she thought she knew what he'd say; likewise, she wanted to call the police, but knew to a certainty what they'd tell her. She would have to live with this dread for some seemingly interminable hours until it became obvious to everyone that something terrible had befallen Conal.

There was one more thing she could try, although she knew if she couldn't sit still for even five minutes, she was unlikely to succeed in it. Nevertheless, she put on slippers and went into the loft's main living area, all lifeless and bleak this morning, and took her scrying mirror from a shelf. She removed its black velvet wrapping and placed it on the table over which

Bobby had talked encouragement to a drunken Conal the night of the first Superior Claim of Right blog post. She performed, as best she could, first the lesser banishing ritual of the pentagram, then that of the hexagram. The familiar movements and the vibrating of the divine and archangelic names at last brought clarity and tranquility to her mind, like a body of water after its surface had been stirred and become still again, and she knelt before the black mirror.

But some moments passed during which, despite her right focus, nothing appeared, nothing even hinted at appearing. She saw only emptiness in its depths. A legal saying suddenly leaped into her mind: *The absence of presence is not the presence of absence*. But as consolation it was thin, cold stuff.

※

October 31, 11:55 a.m.

Freddie's brows knit in concern as Sadie nibbled a cracker and sipped ginger tea on Friday, just before noon.

"Tummy still out of sorts?"

"Freddie, he didn't come home last night."

"The judge?"

She nodded, touched her forehead to her desk, and looked up wearily. "I've been up since four, going crazy with worry. He doesn't answer his phone. Or texts. I've called hospitals. I called the police. Of course, they laughed at me. They probably get a thousand calls from worried girlfriends every day over nothing. But this isn't nothing. He left me a message around five o'clock yesterday, saying he was going to have a drink with a friend—he didn't say who, he didn't say where—and would be home late. Oh my God, I forgot: he also forwarded a weird voicemail from a friend of mine that I meant to follow up on."

She scrolled down the contact list on her phone, then called Carleton Matthews, reaching only his voicemail. "Ninety-three, Carleton. Sadie Norrell here. Conal forwarded me your voicemail yesterday; what did you mean by 'magickal attack'? And what did you mean that 'we're on it'? Hey, did he call you, by any chance? I'm looking for him. Call me. Please? Ninety-three." The call seemed to drain her of her last reserves of energy, for she again lay her head on her desk.

"I'm sorry you're feeling so lousy, honey. Maybe you should go home and rest; he's just as likely to turn up there as here, don't you think? More likely, I'd say. He'll want to shower and change clothes. I'll take you home if you're too tired to get yourself there; just say the word." When she made no response, he turned to leave, but then added, "You know, you missed some excitement here late yesterday afternoon: the CJB website was hacked, and the judge's face—you really had to see it. The site's fixed today, but I'll bet John took a picture."

"What about his face?" she asked, without lifting her head.

"I'll go see if John got a shot of it."

The moment Freddie stepped out of her office, her phone rang. With monumental effort, she looked over to the caller ID and, seeing who it was, forced herself to answer.

"Chief?"

"Hi, Sadie. I'm trying to convene a meeting of the Committee on Self-Represented Litigants, which Quirke agreed to chair, but he's not here and I can't seem to reach him. Is he by any chance with you?"

Sadie had always prided herself on her professional demeanor—her court colleagues needed no additional reason to be dismissive of Brighton Law graduates—but it failed her now. She found herself sobbing, barely able to speak, as she told the Chief the judge had been missing and incommunicado since the previous night.

"I'm so sorry, Sadie. I believe you: He didn't go on a bender; something's really wrong here. I wish you'd called me right away. Since the local cops don't want to get involved, I'll put the Judicial Protection Detail on it. Trust me, we'll find him. Give me your private numbers so we can stay in touch."

Sadie dictated them to the Chief.

"Lieutenant Grimes will be contacting you," the Chief continued. "Tell him if you hear anything, and do keep me posted, okay? Let me know if you need anything. I'm calling the Lieutenant right now."

The Judicial Protection Detail was a squad of state highway patrol officers responsible for the justices' security in the state building and at their public appearances elsewhere. Rarely did they get a chance to investigate events of such magnitude, and Lieutenant Grimes, whose motorcycle-cop boots and gun holster creaked with an undeniable gravity, and whose broad shoulders seemed to fill Sadie's office, was eager to begin. Although reassuring, his presence made the judge's disappearance even more real, and after giving her report and sending him off to commence the search, Sadie ran to the restroom and was miserably ill.

Seeing her grey, exhausted face as she made her way back to her office, Freddie took her gently by the shoulders. "Are you sure you don't want me to drive you home?"

She shook her head. "I'm sure. Did you find the picture you were talking about?"

"Oh, from yesterday? Here it is," he said, bringing out his phone, opening a text message from John, and showing it to her. He would not have thought it possible she could turn even paler.

"I don't know who did this, but it wasn't one of us," she said.

John stuck his head in Freddie's office shortly after lunch. "Have you seen Lucas today?" he asked.

"Lucas who?" Freddie replied, looking up from his computer. "Oh, the arch-douche? He's been pretty scarce all week."

"Well, the nameplate's off his door, and Justice Hetford just sent an email to the court that we'll all want to archive."

Freddie clicked over and read aloud. " 'I am pleased to announce that, effective today, Lucas Grieber has joined my staff as head of chambers. He can be found in room 4544. Please stop by and welcome him next time you're in the neighborhood.' October 31, 2014: a date that will live in infamy. How long do you think they've been cooking that up?"

"The timing does look suspicious. Let's rattle his cage and send Lieutenant Grimes over to interrogate him about the judge's disappearance."

"It's tempting, but I'd rather Grimes work on finding the judge. Say, what's that?"

The wail of sirens near the Civic Center was nothing new, but a convoy of Sant' Urbano police and fire department vehicles skidding to a halt at the state building's loading dock was something out of the ordinary. Freddie opened the window facing Foltz Street and leaned out.

"It's the bomb squad. Cute robots. Wonder what's up?"

At that moment, the sound of walkie-talkies in the hallway heralded the arrival of more law enforcement officers. John and Freddie exchanged anxious glances and went out to check.

One khaki-uniformed officer, a tall blond man with a buzz cut, stood addressing the staff who had filtered out of their offices, while another officer was going door to door reaching out to staff attorneys too absorbed in writing calendar memos to have noticed the commotion. "We're asking folks to stay away from the windows overlooking Foltz Street until the suspicious parcel is taken care of," the tall officer was saying. "Just to be on the safe side."

"What kind of a parcel? Where did it come from? And where did you guys find it?" Freddie asked.

The officer grimaced in embarrassment. "Apparently, it's been sitting on the loading dock for quite a while, possibly even a few weeks. The label was kind of hard to decipher, and they eventually gave up trying. Today one of the mailroom guys finally made out that it was addressed to the missing judge."

"Justice Quirke? He's our boss," Freddie said. "And our comrade in the office across the hall there is his inamorata. You must tell us everything. Why the bomb squad?"

"The box had started to leak. The joint task force took X-rays and determined it contains a timer and some kind of possible explosive or flammable substance, so they're going to blow it up."

"But aren't you going to try to find out where it came from, and why someone would send the judge an incendiary device? And anyway, who sends a bomb that doesn't go off for weeks?"

"We actually know where it came from. The label says Marvelocity Industries."

"That's the judge's ex-father-in-law's company."

"Right. Investigators are talking to people over there right now. As for why it hasn't gone off, that happens all the time. It's not very hard to make a bomb, but people drawn to doing that kind of thing are often bad at following instructions—fortunately for us, of course. Anyway, for public safety we need to get that thing disposed of."

The officer's walkie squawked. "Excuse me a sec," he said, stepping away to communicate without an audience. Returning, he declared, "Hazard's been cleared. You all can open your windows again."

"I hope you get to the bottom of it," John said. "I for one would like to know who'd do that to the judge."

"Same here. We'll say more about it when we can." With that the two officers rejoined each other and strode off toward the elevators.

John and Freddie stared after them for a few seconds. Then Freddie spoke. "I hate to worry her even more, but she needs to know."

The two attorneys went across the hall to find Sadie lying unconscious on the floor. As Freddie checked her pulse, John phoned 911.

Chapter Twenty-Six

October 31, 6:00 p.m.

It was the pain in his shoulders that finally woke him, although the pain in his head was scarcely less intense. He was sitting on stained carpeting that could only belong in a motel, his legs stuck straight out in front of him and his wrists bound over his head to the foot of the bed on which the man and woman were lying watching TV and smoking cigarettes. He was naked above the waist, but moist with sweat in the overheated room as the radiator clanked mournfully. Feigning continued unconsciousness, he tried to think of something he could eventually say to appease them into releasing him, or at least not provoke a violent reaction. Nothing came to mind.

"I still worry about the coyotes," she was saying. "Haven't you read about cases like that, where animals get at the body and the sheriffs find an arm here, a leg there, and the face all gone?"

"That would tend to work to our advantage," the man observed. "To prevent identification."

Quirke feared hyperventilation would betray his having awakened, and forced himself to breathe slowly, deeply and silently.

"But she was my baby. She was such a pretty girl; you thought so, too, once, didn't you? I just can't bear the thought of her being disfigured like that."

"You wouldn't recognize her now anyway, Angel. Everything dissolves after a while in the ground. And it's been three months. Where we put her, I don't think she'll ever be found."

"You also didn't think anyone would ever have a suspicion about the house fire and the Captain's death, but it's over a month now and we haven't seen a dime out of the insurance company, not even living expenses for this fucking fleabag."

"I'm sorry, Angel. At least we've got this new prospect."

"Aren't you glad we looked him up? He may not have money himself, but he's married to it, sure enough. They can part with a few hundred G without feeling it a bit."

"That's not the same as saying they will, but—"

"Don't you think it's a good idea? I thought you said it's a good idea."

"It's the only one we have right now, so—"

"Well, Jesus effing Christ. What a time for second thoughts."

"Shhh, you'll wake him up."

"That stuff's bound to wear off soon, anyway. So, if he wakes up mean—?"

"I can handle him. He's going to feel like shit after the GHB. And we've got the universal pacifier."

"Don't use it all on him. I want some, too."

"You'll get some, Angel. And we'll get more where we're going."

The sexual interval that followed allowed Quirke to shift his legs slightly and review his situation. He was tied up, half-naked, unarmed and outnumbered, held captive in a motel room in an unknown location by a pair of apparent murderers who evidently intended to demand hundreds of thousands of dollars' ransom for him from Eugene Scorchner—a man who wouldn't ransom Quirke's car out of a parking garage, much less pay that kind of money to the mother of the woman Quirke had cheated on his daughter with. Karma's a motherfucker, he reflected. If the universal pacifier, whatever that was, didn't kill him, no doubt they'd find some more sadistic way to do it later.

What had the Judicial Protection Detail's Threat Management staff told the justices about how to survive a kidnapping in one of the periodic trainings the Chief had insisted everyone attend? Their message was basically *existence precedes essence*, familiar to him from his undergraduate philosophy days. A kidnappee must act independently, must be responsible for his own life, must not helplessly succumb to the meaninglessness and absurdity of the situation. He must decide what the moment calls for, whether compliance or resistance, and act accordingly. There is no instruction manual. Some, Quirke had been told, find that trying to gain the kidnapper's trust by displaying sympathy and complying with all commands enables them to stave off being murdered long enough to find a means of escape or be rescued. Quirke provisionally decided to adopt that tactic. Further: He'd been snatched off a busy city street; someone must have seen it happen, so reason existed for hope. Still further: He was, after all, an important person, a Supreme Court justice, and someone was bound to look for him.

Sadie would look for him. Tears started out of his eyes at the realization this was the first time in their too-brief months together she, unless by magical methods, wouldn't know where to find him. Laudie's cruelty ramified and ramified, even as she loudly climaxed a few feet away. How sickeningly ironic that Laudie was surrounded by both of her sons-in-law in this vile motel room. She could have her way with that one, but she was good for multiple murder—a potential capital crime—and kidnapping for ransom carried a life top, and Quirke vowed never to rest until she was locked up for good.

"Well, well," she laughed, and the sole of a narrow foot slapped the back of his head. "Our friend has awakened at last. So how are you feeling, Judge? You really need to watch that tendency to overindulge. It's not good for you, you know."

Now that it came right down to it, he didn't seem able to drum up much sympathy, and he wasn't in the mood for compliance. "Isn't it time to quit playing this game?" he asked, unable in his bindings to turn his head far enough to see her. "It stopped being amusing a while ago."

"Not yet, I'm afraid," she replied. "This road trip's hardly gotten started." There was a pause, and then: "Jennifer? Lauds here. We're in your neighborhood. Yes, we'll be there in an hour. If not, it's because we're lost. In which case, you'll be hearing from me again. Till then, Jen."

"I'll get our distinguished guest ready," Rowe said. He sat at the nightstand mixing powder and water in a spoon, flicking a lighter, sticking a cotton ball in the resulting hot puddle of liquid, drawing the mixture up into a syringe, tapping it, setting it aside. He came and knelt beside Quirke with a strip of green latex that looked like it belonged in an exercise class, tying it around Quirke's upper left arm until the blue veins stood out.

"Virginal," he observed. "Don't worry, it's a clean needle—this time. You're going to love this. I predict you'll soon be begging for more."

Chapter Twenty-Seven

October 31, 4:30 p.m.

Sadie lay on a bed in a bay in emergency, a nurse having taken her blood and vital signs half an hour before. The dizziness, as she told Freddie, who had come along to the hospital and stayed with her to wait for the attending doctor, generally came and went, but today it hadn't lifted, and she had felt nauseated, sometimes acutely, all day.

"And this has been going on for how long?"

"A month or so."

"And you never thought to get it checked out? Putting us through these tsuris, shame on you."

"The judge is after me constantly to go to the doctor, but I just haven't had—"

Just then, a hand pulled the privacy curtain aside; attached to it, the attending approached the bedside, grabbing her chart from a rack on the wall nearby.

"Hi, I'm Dr. Lucius Senter. And you're Sadie? So, let's see. It says here you fainted today at work, been feeling fatigued and nauseous for several weeks. But good general health; no recent injury or trauma, is that right? Let's take a closer look." He shined a light into her eyes and ears. "Beautiful. Headache?"

"Not really."

He felt along her neck and collarbone. "Nodes unremarkable. Temperature's normal, so I'm thinking probably no infectious process, but we'll look at your white count when the labs come back, which should be shortly. Any abdominal pain? No? You filled out the whole intake form, right, as best you could?"

"I tried."

"So, history of neurological or endocrine problems blank means no problems, correct?"

"As far as I know."

"And LMP question mark?"

"Sorry?"

"You don't know the date of your last period?"

"It was—I don't know, two or three months ago, I guess."

"And you've been sexually active during that time? You're nodding. Well, given all these symptoms, then, I have a pretty good idea what's up: Dollars to donuts you're pregnant, Miss Norrell."

"But—"

"You're going to have a little judge!" Freddie exclaimed.

Dr. Senter turned to him. "Are you the dad? Congratulations."

"No, I shall be Tía Freddie. Honey, this is so wonderful!"

"But I was told I couldn't—"

"I could fill an elementary school with the kids born to patients of mine who were told they couldn't get pregnant. Ridiculously irresponsible thing for a doctor to say to a young woman, in my opinion. First, we should confirm with the lab work, but then we can do an ultrasound—here in the emergency department, if you like. We should be able to hear the heartbeat by now. Or you can schedule it with your ob-gyn later, whatever you prefer. Maybe you want the dad to be here for it."

"Yes, I want the dad to be here. More than anything in the world." She began to sob, while Freddie took the doctor aside to explain the immediate crisis.

"...So, with all the stress, the disappearance, the fainting, and not being able to keep food down, I don't think she should be sent home by herself," Freddie concluded. "I'd go and stay with her, but my husband's the jealous type."

Dr. Senter turned to Sadie. "I want to keep you here for observation tonight, mainly because of the syncope—the fainting. Have you been throwing up a lot, losing weight at all?"

"Some. I haven't been able to eat much. I feel sick all day, not just in the morning."

"There's this condition called hyperemesis gravidarum. The Duchess of Cambridge famously had it, you might remember. It means vomiting excessively during pregnancy. I don't think you quite qualify for that diagnosis from what I'm hearing so far, but we'll keep an eye on you tonight. We'll give you fluids, and that should help the dizziness. Give me a second to write the orders, and then they'll take you upstairs. Good news is most women feel a lot better after the first trimester, so things should soon start looking up. Be sure and make an appointment with your ob-gyn tomorrow, okay?" With a handshake for each of them, Dr. Senter departed for the patient in the next bay.

Sadie had begun to cry again, showers rather than thunderstorms, but the lack of a ready means of lifting the anguish from her drew Freddie's anxious sympathy. "Is there anything you'd like me to do? Or to bring you?" he asked. "I'll stay, at least until they take you to your room."

"Thank you for being here, Freddie. And for remembering to bring my purse along in the ambulance. I can't think of anything else you can do right now; I'm just in shock. I must seem like a ditzy kid, not knowing, all this time, when the signs were so obvious. But since I was a teenager I thought this was impossible. Now all I want, all I need, is Conal. When you say your prayers tonight, include one for him. And me."

"Of course, I will. I'll do even better than that: I'll get *mi abuelita* to pray for you both. For all three of you. She's got a direct line."

"What's her name, your grandma?"

"Araceli. Meaning altar of the sky."

"What a beautiful, perfect name. If it's a girl, she'll be Araceli, then. Araceli Nuit."

"Araceli Nuit Quirke? Not that it isn't a lovely name, honey, but you know the judge—he's apt to dissent."

Chapter Twenty-Eight

October 31, 6:20 p.m.

Rowe clearly knew what he was doing, piloting the needle into the right place, delivering the payload, and bloodlessly withdrawing it from Quirke's arm. He sat for a few minutes, studying his captive's face with a self-satisfied half-smile.

And before Quirke knew it, he was flying—flying and sinking simultaneously, his limbs heavy and inert, his body a raft carrying him along above and somehow at the same time deeply immersed in the river of life. Nothing had ever felt so easy, so warm and blissful, so perfect. He was satisfied to let the life-force pass him along in its current—he had no other will than to be carried like this; forever if possible—and when Rowe untied him from the foot of the bed he saw no need to move. Now and then an awareness that everything was as it should be at that moment welled up into his consciousness, but mostly there was an emptiness filled with contentment. It made no sense, but then everything that had ever seemed to make sense was so far away as not even to exist meaningfully, like an entirely separate solar system on the opposite end of the galaxy, growing ever more distant in the inexorably expanding universe.

His captors busied themselves packing and making phone calls for perhaps an hour while he lay on the floor in this state, until at last Rowe pulled him to his feet. This was a change decidedly for the worse; the motion caused him to have to stumble in a hurry to the motel room door and let himself out to vomit on what looked like a scrubby patch of snow but was more likely a discarded pile of crushed ice from a bar or restaurant, of which several, all advertising pool tables and big-screen TV in their neon-lit windows, adorned the block of this town or truck stop, whatever it was. The sky's darkness meant he must have been unconscious or asleep for close to twenty hours since they'd taken him from the city. The cold air on his bare skin felt deliciously bracing until Rowe pushed him into the car, where Laudie already sat waiting with the heater on and the motor running. After binding his wrists with zip-ties and looping another tie through the wrist ties and under the belt on Quirke's pants, Rowe tossed a shiny baseball jacket over Quirke's shoulders. Then they were off into the night.

Occasionally as a trial judge Quirke had ordered men shackled when they refused to behave themselves in court. Leg irons, belly chains, discreet wrist cuffs to keep a recalcitrant or psychotic defendant from, for example, stabbing his counsel in the ear with a pencil—Quirke in his supreme authority over his courtroom had subjected others to such restraints, and now he was himself subjected to them. The moral symmetry, rotated through all dimensions in the space of his mind, was somehow fascinating. Though he didn't bother to tell his captors, these security measures were unnecessary; he was still too strung out to try to run. In any event, the grip of the nine-millimeter pistol sticking out of Rowe's jacket pocket was more than enough to have deterred him had he been inclined to flee.

※

October 31, 6:30 p.m.

Gene Scorchner listened for the third time to the voicemail his assistant had forwarded to him, straining and again failing to make out, over the ambient traffic sounds punctuated by truck horns on the recording, some of the crucial words the male voice spoke toward the end of the message. "...So be sure to tell Mr. Scorchner we...his son-in-law. He will...upon...and will be in contact...instructions."

At last he gave up and called Eleanor to see if she could tell him what this was about. But after six on a Friday evening, he was more likely to find a giant panda in her office. Particularly since taking up with Allan Hetford, she'd devoted herself to living the good life, taking weekend trips to New York, Hawaii, and the beach house, invariably bringing Hetford along in her train. Gene couldn't find it in himself to blame his daughter for her self-indulgence, after thirty frustrated years with the terminally unsuitable Quirke, but as a taxpayer he wasn't sure he liked the idea of a supreme court justice spending so much time outside his chambers cavorting with Eleanor. Say what you would about Quirke, at least he had a work ethic.

In due course Scorchner decided he'd had enough of the office himself for the week, but the fragmentary message kept nagging at him. He forwarded it to his own cell phone and drove home to Hemsbridge, finally calling Quirke's number on his Bluetooth along the way; he could not have said exactly why. There was no answer, not even voicemail.

His preprandial scotch was another reminder of Quirke. Hardly the intuitive type, Scorchner nevertheless felt impelled to do something with this sense of Quirke on his brain, and called Eleanor.

She picked up promptly. "Hi, Daddy."

"Hello, Kitten. What are you up to?"

"Allan and I were just sitting down to dinner."

"Where are you?"

"At the beach house."

"Not too cold out there?"

"Not for us."

"I'm getting the picture. Say, have you heard anything from Quirke lately? Or of him?"

"No, have you?"

"I'm going to forward you a message somebody left on Delores's phone. Apparently, it was intended for me, but I can't make out much of it. Maybe the problem's my old ears, and you'll have better luck. It seems to have something to do with Quirke. Would you try? I'm going to send it to you right now, so listen in."

"Sure, Daddy."

※

A moment later Eleanor, in the dining room overlooking the ink-black ocean, was making the same vain effort to piece out the message. She handed the phone to Hetford and told him to listen.

He did so, with no more successful result. "Some business between Gene and Quirke? That could only be the marital settlement."

"But why would some strange man be calling Daddy and talking about instructions? There's no need for instructions; Quirke just has to send Daddy the money. And why would this person be referring to Quirke as Daddy's son-in-law? The whole point of the settlement is to put an end to that."

"And calling from a truck stop, apparently."

Hetford's phone rang. Looking at the caller ID, his eyebrows first shot up and then knit together. He rose from the table, holding up an index finger to signal a call that could not be let go to voicemail and a need for silence.

"Good evening, Chief. What's up?"

"Hi, Allan. Is Eleanor Quirke there?"

"Yes, she is. Just a moment." He handed Eleanor the phone with a baffled look. "The Chief Justice," he whispered.

"Hello?" said Eleanor.

"I'm sorry to interrupt, but I'm afraid I have some bad news. Quirke's been missing since yesterday afternoon, and we need to know if you've seen or heard from him."

"Oh my God. Do you know, my father just called and asked me the same question. I haven't, but Daddy got a weird voicemail that seems to have to do with Quirke. It's hard to make out. I could forward it to you, but maybe you'd better speak with him."

"I'll have Lieutenant Grimes do that right away. In the meantime, we'd like to get Quirke's phone records, but Verizon's being a little sticky. You wouldn't happen to be on his account, would you?"

"No, I'm afraid we always had separate accounts."

"Do you know of any reason why he might be incommunicado? Of course, all the hospitals have been called—multiple times. Did he have any health conditions that might have led to a mishap of some kind?"

"Well, everyone knows about his drinking. Have you found his car?"

"It's in the garage right here in the building. Nothing seems amiss."

"I don't know of anything else, but I haven't talked with him in weeks. I'm sorry. I wish I could help."

"You may have done just that. If anything comes to mind, call me or Lieutenant Grimes. May I give you his number?"

"Of course."

"He's at 881-9909. That's in the 515."

"Chief, there was something in this weird voicemail about instructions. It sounds crazy, but maybe we're about to get a ransom demand."

"That thought had occurred to me. Thanks, Eleanor. Stay in touch if anything at all comes up."

※

October 31, 8:10 p.m.

"To be quite honest, Lieutenant, I've seen the judge messed up. I mean staggering, slurring messed up, and just this side of despondent. But when I talked with him Thursday afternoon he was in his right mind. Angry, but not self-destructive."

Bobby had returned to the office late Friday evening to meet with Grimes, and had just finished reviewing pertinent records, turning up nothing that appeared worthy of further investigation. "What was he angry about?" Grimes asked.

"I'll show you," said Bobby, moving to his laptop, clicking to the *San Eligio Banner* website, and searching for "devil worship." The Phil Crosse article popped up and Lieutenant Grimes read it over Bobby's shoulder.

"Nasty, but the average person would probably find it too ridiculous to be believed. *Weekly World News* type of thing."

"That was my take, too. The judge seemed more offended on behalf of the magicians and Satanists than worried about the impact on himself. Funny thing is, I looked up Phil Crosse, the author, today. Until you came by with this awful news, I was hoping to be able to call and tell the judge that this is the first and only article Crosse ever published in the *Banner*; in fact, I couldn't find anything else by him online—anywhere. There are a bunch of guys out there named Phil Crosse, and one Philippa Crosse, but none seems to be a journalist or writer or politico. It's almost as if this Phil Crosse was a persona created just to trash the judge on this one occasion. I have it on my list to call the editor and ask how he happened to publish this shitty little article from a newbie author. You might be able to get more out of him than I could."

"I'm making a note, but, candidly, there are some other things I need to follow up on first. Now, I understand Justice Quirke was going through a rough patch, personally and professionally: getting thrown out of the house, marriage ending, financial issues, having to go through this retention election, some say struggling with substance abuse, and apparently there's a judicial disciplinary proceeding in the works, although not public yet. Well, it wouldn't be public if he hadn't announced it on YouTube, anyway. That's a lot for a man to take."

"True, but it wasn't enough to make him want to hurt himself, if that's what you're implying. There was no love lost between him and the ex-wife for a long time even before the split, and he and his girlfriend Sadie are over the moon with each other. And he doesn't seem to care all that much about money. Like I said, Lieutenant, he has a self-destructive streak, but it's usually buried pretty deeply."

"What does he think of his chances of winning retention?"

Bobby considered. "I know he worries about it."

"What do you think?"

"He'll win."

"You're saying that based on your experience with similar candidates?"

Bobby laughed. "Nobody's similar to Justice Quirke. I'm saying it based on his core. He's a good man and a good judge, and voters will see that."

"That's interesting, because another viewpoint that I've heard is that he's—well, I've heard the word 'wicked' used. You don't hear people called that very often nowadays."

"I'll turn it around and ask you: based on what?"

"Good question. I'm not getting a clear sense of it. Based partly on his recent revelations, but also partly on his history—his colleagues seeing him loaded in bars and at holiday parties a few too many times, going all the way back to his playing in metal bands a lot of years ago—I guess that's something you shouldn't do if you ever plan to become a Supreme Court justice—and his connections to the Benfields—whose name, I'm sure you know, is synonymous with 'crook' to some people—and on rumors of flirtations and affairs that nobody would confirm to me and he never bothered to try and squelch. He dissents a lot, doesn't simply go along with the majority program. He didn't cultivate a conservative façade; I've heard him called a socialist. I suppose he just didn't live up to some people's image of a justice. Even more than that, some people seem bothered that he didn't think it was part of his job to live up to their fantasy of a justice."

"Do me a favor, Lieutenant?"

"Sure, if I can."

"Use the present tense when you're talking about the judge. It'll make me feel better."

"Of course; I'm sorry. It's entirely inappropriate to do otherwise. By the way, there's going to be a news conference on the disappearance tomorrow at noon, if we haven't found him by then."

"Too bad nobody watches the news on Saturday. Are you running it?"

"My boss is, actually. Captain Marshall."

"Thanks for letting me know. I'll probably get calls, but I won't be able to jeopardize your investigation by talking out of turn, since I don't know a damn thing. Say, do you know how Sadie's bearing up?"

"I understand she's still in the hospital."

"What? Why?"

"She collapsed at work. She was taken to St. Mary's."

"I've got to go see if I can do anything for her. Let's talk again later, Lieutenant."

※

Sadie looked tinier than ever, drowning in a sprigged cotton hospital gown in her bed on the medical ward at St. Mary's. "I feel like an idiot," she said, blushing. "You'd think I'd have known, but you figured it out long before I did."

Bobby, clutching a cellophane-sheathed bouquet of carnations, daisies, and roses, shook his head with a smile. "I almost told the judge I suspected you were in a family way last time I talked with him, but I assumed you had a reason for not saying anything."

"Oh, I wish you had told him," she cried. "I wanted him to be the first to know, but, more than that, I want him to have a reason to come back, a reason to hope. Bobby, where could he be? Tell me they'll find him, or I'll go crazy with worry. I *am* going crazy with worry."

His big, gnarled, mahogany-colored hand covered hers. "Now, now, child. He'll be found. Man like him doesn't, can't, just disappear off the face of the earth. Lieutenant Grimes is a sharp guy; he'll figure out where the judge went."

"Don't they say the first seventy-two hours is critical? It's going on half that now without a significant clue."

"We don't know that. Grimes is out there right now, talking to—"

"It's going to take more than one investigator; he could be anywhere. They think he's just unstable, a drunk, overwhelmed. But—"

"Now, I'm going to say something that may sound patronizing, but I hope you won't take it that way. For the judge's sake, for your sake and the baby's sake, you need to tune into a different frequency. Dial past the fear and find that band of love and passion that unites you, somewhere on the cosmic spectrum, and keep beaming it out to him. I believe it'll reach him, and he's surely in need of it. I wouldn't have thought that man could go an hour without you, let alone a day and a half. So, use the power that you have, right here, even as weak as you may be feeling. Make him feel it, wherever he is; wrap him in it. Don't overlook your magic. That's a hella technology."

Sadie's eyes filled with tears. A moment later, her arms reached out toward him. The consultant leaned closer to enfold and comfort her silently.

"You're absolutely right, Bobby," she said at last. "Put it down to hormones. I'll try harder to stay strong. Would you do something for me?"

"Anything, honey."

"Would you be my honorary uncle? That'll make you the baby's honorary great-uncle."

"I'd be delighted. So how can I spoil the two of you today? You look like you could use a good meal. Can I bring you something besides hospital food?"

She made a wan face. "I'm still not feeling up to much—the house graham crackers and Jell-O are all I've been able to handle—but thank you for the offer. I'm sure I'll wake up ravenous one of these days, and then look out."

Chapter Twenty-Nine

October 31, 9:00 p.m.

"Finally. I thought we'd never find our way through this goddamned subdivision," Laudie fumed as they pulled into Jenny's driveway and cut the engine after a half-hour of winding in and out of tantalizingly proximate cul de sacs and straining to read house numbers in the thickening fog. "Why does anybody live in a place like this, anyway? It's laid out like a maze and has all the charm of a gulag. If I lived here I'd feel like I'd died and gone to hell."

"Better street parking for customers," Rowe pointed out.

"True. Jenny says she isn't into dealing much these days, though. Speaking of which, we need to get a connection. The big guy's going to need topping up, and I feel like indulging myself."

"Your friend said she could help with that. Why don't you go say hello, and I'll wait for your signal."

Laudie's heels crunched over the gravel to Jenny's front door while Rowe remained in the car with Quirke, who had drifted off intermittently but was now conscious again, if subdued.

"How was your maiden voyage?" Rowe asked. "You looked like you were having a nice time there."

Quirke nodded. Any voluntary movement seemed to require massive concentration, and in general to be hardly worth the trouble, but if the question implied a chance to score again, he'd make the effort. "People say it's good, but it was really good. Really, really good."

"Dope fiend judge, who knew? Well, there's at least one more trip in your future. So, when was the last time you ate?"

"I don't remember."

"We probably ought to do something about that. Angel's friend has a kid, there must be food in the house."

Laudie stuck her head out of the front door and nodded. Rowe pulled Quirke out of the car and cloaked his bound wrists in the baseball jacket. Had any neighbors peeked out from behind their curtains, they might have wondered why the shirtless stranger was wearing his jacket backwards, exposing his bare flesh to the near-freezing prevailing temperature. They would not have had the chance to contemplate the problem for long, as Rowe hustled Quirke into Jenny's house as quickly as he could get him to put one foot in front of the other.

Once inside, he did not pause to greet their hostess, but pushed

Quirke along a hallway toward the rear of the house, peering inside the rooms on either side, and onto the floor of a tiny bedroom at the end furnished with a battered oak crib, low dresser, and toy box. From his pocket, he drew a length of nylon twine, which he knotted after doubling and running it under Quirke's arm and between two crib slats. The loop was long enough to allow Quirke either to sit against the crib leg—not a tenable position for long— or to lie down, half on a hairy braided rug and half under the crib with lost teethers and dusty beanie babies. Having thus secured his captive, Rowe left the room without a word and shut the door.

Quirke lay in darkness, trying to think as his captors were thinking, trying to think at all. Since the last time he'd assessed his situation, he'd gained no advantage. Still tied up, unarmed and half-naked; growing weaker from deprivation of food and water and the dissipating effects of the narcotic; still outnumbered, it appeared, unless the woman who lived in this house could somehow be made his ally to engineer a rescue. The chances of that happening were remote, he knew.

The scenario reminded him of a case the court had decided in which a sociopathic meth-snorting couple had cut a swathe of rape, sodomy, and murder across the southern part of the state, stopping briefly with a captive at the home of an acquaintance who ended up copping to aiding and abetting a kidnap and testifying against them, the difference being that Rowe seemed considerably more intelligent than the male half of *People v. Donovan and Reese*. Even those defendants had been smart enough not to allow the acquaintance to speak to the captive, to prevent the formation of just such an alliance. Donovan and Reese were alive and well on death row, which was where he fantasized seeing Laudie and Rowe one day. He winced to think his ordeal was turning him into a law-and-order conservative.

Offhand, he couldn't think of any other realistic means of escape, and his chances of rescue by the authorities were unknown. With his reputation and luck, any publicity surrounding his disappearance probably consisted of speculation he'd eloped with a succubus to the netherworld, or of rumored sightings of him, lying stuporous with drink, on skid row. Which wasn't, he recognized, all that far from the truth.

Thinking about his situation thus proving to be ungratifying, Quirke resumed meditating on heroin. It wouldn't be a bad way to go, if that was what Rowe and Laudie had planned for him whenever they finally gave up on their futile efforts to collect a ransom. As its sweet, subduing influence dwindled away, an itchiness—maddening, because he could reach only a few places with his zip-tied hands—began to supplant it, and he could feel himself starting to seethe in spite—or because—of his powerlessness.

All at once, something external to him, like a jolt of electricity or a comet—or another consciousness—sliced through his mind and vanished, leaving in its wake absolute certainty that Sadie had at that moment been contacting him in what he supposed she'd call her body of light—or etheric body, he wasn't sure which was which. He longed to hold her so much he ached. In the instant of contact he'd felt more alive than ever before; the succeeding instant left him feeling more hopeless, hollow and bereft.

In the kitchen, Jenny was arguing loudly and profanely into her phone, as Laudie sat at the table, smoking a cigarette and enjoying the entertainment. "I said I was through with you, asshole! When I want you to come over, I'll tell you to come over. Until then, you better just sit there and wait for me, because if I see you, I swear I'll break your fuckin' arm! All right? Don't call me, I'll call you." She ended the call and put the phone in her pants pocket. "In your dreams," she added.

Laudie applauded. "That's telling him, girlfriend! Some guys just never get the message, do they?"

Jenny shook her head disbelievingly. "And they always seem to find me. Hi, I'm Jenny." She extended a hand to Rowe, who reciprocated. "Nice to meet you. So, who's the dude back there?"

"Let's just say he's our latest project," Laudie said.

"Really, the less you know, the better," Rowe added. "He'll be out of your hair one way or the other in a day or two. For now, I put him in the kid's room. The kid can sleep with you tonight. I hate to cause you inconvenience, Jenny, but is there something to eat around here? Don't go to any trouble."

"I don't need anything," said Laudie. "We ate at the motel."

"Not for us, Angel. I don't think the big guy's had anything in a day or two, and we don't want him getting noisy."

"Oops, I forgot about that. Yes, he probably needs a little something."

Jenny leaped up, opening cabinets and refrigerator. "Tomorrow's my shopping day, so the cupboard's a bit bare right now, but I have Cheerios, graham crackers, applesauce—I'm sorry; it's all Timmy food."

"Doesn't matter," said Rowe. "Maybe graham crackers. That's something he can feed himself. Oh, and some water, maybe."

"I'll take care of that right now," Jenny said. "You guys just make yourselves at home."

"I'll get our suitcases out of the car," Rowe said.

"Need me?" Laudie asked him.

"No, Angel; stay with Jenny."

As Rowe left the house, Jenny smiled broadly at Laudie. "I need to use the little girls' room for a second, and then I'll get a bowl of crackers for the big guy."

In the bathroom, Jenny took out her phone and began typing a text message. *Ofcr Fuller pls disregard that crazy vm except really dont call till I tell u its ok. I still want 2 work as yr CI but that old friend of mine & her BF r here & talking isnt safe. They have a guy in my babys room, theyre planning 2 do something 2 him 2morrow or next day. Didnt get good look at him sorry.* She sent it, put the phone back in her pocket, flushed the toilet, and ran the faucet. She had a hand on the doorknob, but then took the phone out again, set it on airplane mode, and stuck it in a box of tampons under the sink.

In the kitchen, Laudie was sitting at the table, still smoking, regally bored, as Timmy shyly displayed his newest toy. Seeing his mother, he ran to her, wrapping his arms around her thighs.

"Baby's tired," Laudie observed.

"Yes, he is. Would you like to sleep in Mommy's room tonight? Just for tonight." Timmy nodded, still clinging to her. "I'll get him settled," she told Laudie. "The graham crackers are in that cupboard, and the plates and glasses are in this one, if you want to take them to him yourself," Jenny said, gesturing. "Otherwise, I'll go in there after Timmy's asleep."

"Sure. You go take care of the kiddo."

Laudie entered the baby's darkened room, smelling of musk and violets, and sat cross-legged on the floor beside him, her skirt pooling around her. "I've got something for you," she whispered.

Hunger and thirst compelled him to respond. "Can you help me up, then?" he asked.

Her hands—exerting force under his arm, pulling him upright—impressed their chill dampness on his skin, and he fancied they left a mark that would last. He could not repress a shudder at the thought these were the same hands that held (and neglected) Sadie as a baby, that bore responsibility for so much grief and terror, that had committed murder and would likely do it again with less compunction than he would feel to squash a spider.

"You hungry?" she murmured.

"I haven't eaten in a long time," he said. "Can we quit playing games for a little while?"

"You didn't answer my question," she said, a little more sharply.

"All right, yes. I'm hungry." Having said it, he suddenly recalled the story of Persephone and was flooded with misgivings, but the pangs of his empty stomach would not be denied.

Her hand was already under her skirt, and when it emerged she thrust it—wet, salty-sweet and rank-spicy—into his mouth. He recoiled, scrambling, hitting his head on a crib rail. The last thing he'd expected or wanted to taste was her pussy, but there was nothing left in him to come back up, and he had little strength remaining and nowhere to go.

She sat motionless for a second, then hurled the plate across the room and backhanded his face, hard, catching his lip with a ring and opening a little cascade of blood. After getting to her feet and kicking him a dozen times—in the face, ribs, gut—for good measure, she stormed out and slammed the door.

He lay on his side, stunned, until his jaw and chest grew slick from the bleeding and the injuries began to throb. A corner of a blanket protruded between the crib rails; he pulled it down to his mouth to stanch the flow, promising himself that if he survived, he'd send the woman who lived here a replacement. After ruining the baby's blanket, he wrapped it around himself against the cold of the room.

The door opened again, making him flinch. Rowe was momentarily silhouetted in the hallway light, and then the door closed again.

"I hear you're making trouble," he said flatly.

"No—a misunderstanding," said Quirke.

"Well, we want a nice quiet night. Drink this or I'll have to gag you," he said, squatting next to Quirke, pulling him up and holding a glass to his battered mouth. It was cheap brandy with an off-taste, presumably laced with leftover GHB from their first encounter in the hotel bar. "Cheer up," said Rowe. "Tomorrow we're letting you go." His promise was unbelievable, crueler than her brutality. "Sleep tight." He left the room, and Quirke was alone but, mercifully, not conscious for long.

※

November 1, 7:20 a.m.

A tugging, gentle and persistent, yanked him out of a heavy sleep. Out of one eye he could see a curly-headed, runny-nosed little boy, perhaps three years old, in footie pajamas pulling at the bloodied blanket Quirke had curled up in. Daylight leaked through and around the circus curtains covering the windows on two walls of the room. He tried to open his other eye, but it was swollen shut; he felt his lip, fat and crusted with dried blood, in an unfamiliar shape, with the sensation it was someone else's. His face must appear monstrous and his shirtlessness weird, and he marveled the boy could look at him without screaming and running away; but with the matter-of-factness characteristic of children too young to have fully developed empathy, the boy seemed unperturbed.

"Give me my blankie."

"Let's trade," Quirke suggested. His wounded lip made the consonants soft and tentative. "I'll give you your blankie, and you give me something to eat. Okay?"

"Okay." The boy scampered out of the room, leaving the door open.

A few moments later he came back, carefully gripping a bowl of graham crackers. He set it down just out of Quirke's reach and resumed tugging the blanket. Quirke had almost forgotten about his end of the deal, but sat forward to allow the boy to pull it away.

"I'm afraid I got it dirty. Tell your mommy I'm sorry. You'd better use another blankie until she washes it."

"This is my only blankie," said the boy.

"What's your name?" Quirke asked.

"Timmy."

"My name is Conal. It's nice to meet you, Timmy. Could you push that bowl a little closer? I'm tied up and I can't reach that far."

Timmy pushed it, as requested, a little closer, but not quite enough for Quirke to reach it. "Why are you tied up?" he asked. "Were you naughty?"

"I suppose I was. Not very naughty, but a little bit naughty."

"When I'm naughty Mommy gives me a time out."

"Much better than getting tied up. Would you bring your mommy in here so I can say hi to her?"

"She's still sleeping. I like to get up early."

"Good for you. Could you move it a little closer, please?"

Timmy considered. "You might spill. I'll feed you." He began to push crackers at Quirke's battered mouth, generating such an intense throbbing pain he was afraid the wound would bleed again. Hunger, however, took precedence over pain.

"More slowly, please, Timmy. I've got a big owie. Have you ever had an owie?"

"I burned my hand on the stove once."

"I'll bet that really hurt. My face hurts a lot, too."

Timmy fed him more painstakingly, and the crackers, although stale, were delectable. Quirke ate until the bowl was empty.

"Would you do one more favor for me? Would you get me a cup of water? Can you reach the cups?"

"Sure, I can," said Timmy, bounding out of the room.

As the minutes passed, Quirke wished he'd specified Timmy should bring the water at his earliest convenience instead of leaving the delivery time to his discretion. He could little fault a small child for becoming distracted, but the dry crackers and the lack of liquids on top of all his other ordeals over the past couple of days had combined to make him weak and dizzy. By and by he wondered if Timmy was a hallucination, a residual effect of the GHB. Could a hallucination feel sticky and smell of dried milk? Quirke lay back down, half under the crib again, drifting on a memory of the heroin river. If he couldn't get that cup of water, a needle and oblivion would be a fine substitute.

Chapter Thirty

November 1, 12:15 p.m.

Jim Forney was still in his workout shorts and tank top, a white towel slung around his neck, when Lieutenant Grimes walked into the 24 Hour Fitness to interview him. Several of the TVs mounted along the wall in front of the steppers and treadmills and elliptical machines were still tuned to the news program that had just broadcast the press conference announcing Justice Quirke's disappearance and calling on the public's assistance in finding him.

"Wow, that was fast," the lawyer commented. "Sorry, I didn't have time to shower. I don't know how much help I'll be, but apparently I did see him right before he went missing."

"That was Thursday evening? Where?"

"Yes, at the Inns, a bar—"

"We know it well."

"He'd called and suggested we meet there after work. He didn't say why, but we're old friends and practiced law together years ago, and when a Supreme Court justice calls, of course you say yes."

"How did he seem to you? I mean his mood, state of sobriety, anything you can think of."

"He was sober when we met up. His overall mood was okay. He spoke of its having been a rollercoaster year for him—he mentioned his divorce and his plan to remarry as soon as possible. He seemed a little...concerned, though."

"About—?"

"He confided some doubts about the election, owing to a few little peccadillos he'd recently admitted to. I'm assuming you know about the GovChan interview."

"Yes."

"He was aware he may be facing official discipline, but that didn't seem to be the big issue for him. What he wanted to know was...was whether he could come back to our law practice if he loses the election. I hate to say it, but I'm afraid I wasn't encouraging."

"You weren't willing to take him on again?"

"I feel like a complete ass given what's happened, of course, but I'm not John Keker or David Boies, basically—I just thought it would be weird having a former Supreme Court justice in our little office. Clients would freak out if I asked them to trust the guy who might have sent them or a brother to prison, or a symbol of the guy who did. Or so I thought. I suggested he turn his sights toward a setting more appropriate to his talents and background, like a big firm where he could make a shitload of money. You know, he was a terrific trial lawyer."

"How did he take it when you turned him down?"

"He seemed disappointed, but I tried to buck him up. Personally, I still think he'll be retained if he turns up in time for the election; if he doesn't, people might assume he bolted out of fear and vote no. By the way, I don't know if the news conference was all that helpful to the electoral effort. That idiot reporter suggesting the reason the local cops didn't want to get involved in the investigation is because Quirke's unstable and probably just got overwhelmed and took off on his own, that was pretty cheap. And so not true."

"I hope you noticed Captain Marshall tried to defuse that suggestion."

"Sort of. He said, 'I'd be speculating. You'd have to ask the local PD why they're not involved.' That's hardly a ringing denunciation. Anyway, you guys had better find him soon."

"That's our plan. So, getting back to when you shot down his job inquiry, what happened next? Did he leave, did you leave, or what?"

"I think at that point I urged him to go home to his sweetheart, because I could see he was inclined to—I hope I'm not telling secrets out of school, but Quirke likes his whiskey, and he looked as though he was about to go up to the bar and have a few, with or without me. So, he said he'd just get one for the road. That's when we parted."

"So, the judge headed to the bar by himself, and that's the last thing you remember."

"I guess so. I have a vague sense of seeing him turn to a woman standing to his left and starting to talk to her. Or maybe she was the one who started talking to him, I don't know. The bartender might remember more specifically, but it was wall-to-wall people in there and he was really busy. Quirke's the kind of guy he ought to notice, though. The woman, too, it seems to me."

"Can you describe her?"

"Boy, I'm stretching my memory muscles here, but it seems like she was about average height, slender, longish wavy reddish hair, black dress. I saw her only from the back and in right profile, and only for a second; I had no reason to focus on her. I hope this isn't as useless as I'm afraid it is."

"Was it your impression she was young? Middle-aged? Old?"

"Younger than the judge and me, I think. Say fortyish."

"And she was alone?"

"I think so, but I can't really say. I'm describing an impression that lasted about a nanosecond, you understand."

"Thank you, Mr. Forney. This has been extremely helpful. We'll track down the bartender ASAP and see what he has to say."

※

November 1, 2:10 p.m.

"I sure do remember," the bartender, Hank Swofford, said, stretching and sleepily mussing his sandy head. His girlfriend, an unseen presence in the kitchen of their apartment, where Grimes had located him at two on Saturday afternoon, had ground some coffee beans, which filled the place with a bracing aroma, and brewed a pot of strong coffee, of which Grimes had gratefully accepted a mug. "I wish I'd known this was going to be so important; I'd have called you instead of making you track me down. I'm just hoping it hasn't cost too much time."

"So how did it go down on Thursday?" Grimes asked.

"Well, I haven't been seeing much of Quirke lately, so when he does come in I make it a point to say hi. It was nuts that night, but I remember introducing him to a woman who was bugging me to tell her who he was. She was a little scary."

"How so?"

"It was subtle. You could tell she'd been gorgeous back in the day, and she's still sort of pretty, but there was something so intense in her way of looking at you that you kind of feel there's a predator bird sizing you up. A velociraptor. Like she's going to carry you away and eat you at her convenience."

"Why did you introduce her to him, then?"

"I'm not sure. She's the kind of woman who doesn't hear the word 'no' very often, I'd guess. And you know Justice Quirke—or maybe you don't—he's a nice guy, very down to earth. Not one to get upset with you for introducing a citizen to him. She gave the impression she was a bit star-struck to meet him. I recall she said they were from out of town and rarely come into the city. It was kind of a big deal to her. And he was very gracious. He may have agreed to have a drink with them; I don't exactly know, because I had a lot of drink orders to fill right then. If that's what happened, they might have stepped into the hotel bar. It's always quieter in there."

"A different bartender works in there?"

"Yeah, and waiters."

"One last question. Any idea what her name was?

"I wish. I seem to recall it started with L, but ...I'm sorry."

※

November 1, 2:20 p.m.

Peter flew back to Sant' Urbano directly on receipt of Sadie's text message and took a taxi from the airport to the hospital. After several rounds of hugs and kisses, and exclamations about the magical qualities of Conal's sperm, Peter asked how he could help.

"I don't know. If only there were something I could do," Sadie mused. "I feel utterly useless lying here."

"You have your own Great Work for the time being," he said. "When's the baby due?"

"I won't know for sure until the ultrasound, but I'm thinking early June. Conal's birthday's the second of June, so I hope to be able to give him the best present of his life. You know, after what happened when I was a kid, I never thought I'd be having this conversation. I told him, down in Sant' Amaro, that I couldn't have children. It must have been around then, when we were in Sant' Amaro, that..."

"Carleton's place has a very salutary atmosphere. You'll have to tell him—when you're ready to tell people, of course."

"You don't think Carleton would hack a government website and put Conal's face on the Master Therion's, do you?" she said abruptly.

"I don't quite follow."

Sadie described the mischief done to the CJB website and Carleton's voicemail message to Quirke.

"I think if Carleton said he knew that he and Conal were under magical attack and the Order was 'on it,' he meant they were responding by magical means. Carleton's a carpenter, not a hacker. We have some geeks who'd be capable of an attack like that, but I really doubt anyone would use 'Love is the Law' in that parodic way. It must have been some outsider's inartful attempt to make both Conal and us look ridiculous. Someone malicious, but not very knowledgeable."

"That's what I told Grimes. You know what I think? I think it's all related, the Superior Claim of Right blog, the idiotic *San Eligio Banner* article, and the hack attack. The same person's behind it all. But who hates Conal that much? And does he or she hate him enough to kidnap him?"

"*If* it's a kidnapping—"

"What else could it be?"

"I'd expect to see a demand. What are they hoping to get? He hasn't got any money."

"He was connected to money, though. If the kidnappers are as stupid as we're positing, they might not realize that connection's been broken."

"Anyway, the social media attacks and the hypothetical kidnapping seem somewhat at cross-purposes. I mean, if the attacks succeed in their apparent aim, Conal will be out of a job, and then his value as a hostage will go down. I hate to sound so callous, but it's not quite adding up as the work of a single mastermind."

Sadie sighed heavily, tears emerging in the corners of her eyes. "It's too bad, almost. I was starting to think there was some coherent meaning in all this."

"There is. We just haven't discovered it yet."

※

November 1, 4:50 p.m.

Late Saturday afternoon, as Peter was helping Sadie gather her things to get ready for discharge from the hospital, Grimes came by with new information.

"Based on what the bartender told me, I located the waiter at the hotel bar who served the judge and two other people on Thursday evening. We now know he went there in the company of a woman, and they were joined by another man who seemed to be acquainted with the woman. They hadn't been there for long when it appears the judge became ill, and the man and the woman took him outside. Given he seemed fairly sober a few minutes before, when his friend last saw him, it seems unlikely he'd drunk enough alcohol in that short a span of time to make himself sick, although it can't be entirely ruled out. The question is what made him ill, given his normal good health. I'm sure you're aware a number of drugs can be slipped into a drink to make a victim compliant."

"So, you think he was roofied?" Peter asked.

"Could be, although it could have been something other than rohypnol—GHB, for instance. They left his cell phone behind, presumably so he wouldn't be tracked; your number was the last one he called, Sadie. There's some security camera footage of them carrying him down the street. We got lucky: It would have been erased if I'd been an hour later getting there. We're trying to track down where they went after that."

"Do you have any pictures you can show us?" Peter asked.

"Yes." Grimes drew a folder out of his jacket and opened it. "Here's the three of them; in the middle is the judge. Looks like he couldn't even hold up his head, so he may have been unconscious, or nearly so, at this point. Do either of you recognize the man on the left there? What about the woman on the right?"

"Oh, no. Oh, no," Sadie cried.

"Him I've never seen before," Peter said. "But I'm afraid I know her."

※

November 2, 8:30 a.m.

With the knowledge Quirke had most probably been kidnapped, and a strong suspicion as to who was behind it, Grimes put inquiries in motion with other law enforcement agencies and contacted Gene Scorchner again to arrange a meeting Sunday morning at Scorchner's house in Hemsbridge, anticipating that Quirke's captors would soon be transmitting a ransom demand. Grimes drove a marked patrol car through light traffic with mars lights and siren going at intervals down the freeway to the ultra-exclusive suburb. At the entrance to the contemporary-style mansion, a uniformed servant let Grimes in and escorted him to the library, a light-filled, uncluttered space with a wall of windows onto the garden. Scorchner made the introductions.

"Good to meet you, Lieutenant. I'm Gene Scorchner and this is my daughter, Eleanor. And this is Allan Hetford—Justice Allan Hetford, one of Quirke's colleagues and Eleanor's...friend. Help yourself to coffee and something to eat from the table over there, if you like."

Had Sadie not filled Grimes in on the relationship between Eleanor Quirke and Hetford, Grimes might have been taken aback to see him at Scorchner's house on a Sunday morning. As it was, he simply nodded, observing that Eleanor and Hetford both appeared worried—though perhaps not for the same reason. Scorchner, on the other hand, exhibited perfect equanimity as he drank his coffee and, in a few bites, dispatched his English muffin, chasing it down with a glass of orange juice.

"I appreciate your willingness to meet with me, especially so early in the morning," Grimes said.

"Of course, we want to help if we can," Eleanor said.

Grimes nodded. "Based on information we received late yesterday, we're fairly sure we're dealing with a kidnapping, and we have a pretty good idea who's behind it. It seems likely the call you got was intended to give you a heads-up to expect a ransom demand soon. Has there been anything—even a hang-up call—since Friday?"

"Nothing. The recording device you guys installed is in place. I told Delores to answer her phone day or night, and she's been checking in every few hours. There's been no contact whatsoever."

"No physical communication, either?"

"Like a note? No, nothing."

"It's not clear why they've waited so long to pursue this. Maybe they've been in transit. We hope there hasn't been some kind of crisis."

"What do you mean?" Eleanor asked.

"Well, for example, if the judge tried to escape and force was used."

"I don't think he would," she said. "He might try to talk his way out, but not make a break for it."

"You may be right; he's outnumbered, after all. Since they apparently drugged him on Thursday evening, they may have done the same thing again, and he may be in no shape to try running. He's also likely to be restrained. Hopefully, we'll soon hear from them."

"Who do you think is responsible?" Gene asked. "Anyone we know?"

Grimes showed them the stills from the security camera outside the hotel bar. None recognized the man and woman with Quirke.

"Strangely enough," Grimes said, "we think the woman is Sadie Norrell's mother."

Eleanor's mouth dropped open. "Do you think Sadie's involved?"

"No," Grimes said.

"She's well aware of our wealth; she might have—"

"No," Grimes repeated. "Nothing at all to indicate it. She hasn't seen her mother in twenty years. We're looking into what the mother's been up to, and we have no reason to think she or her partner will show up here, but I wanted you to be aware."

"Much appreciated," said Scorchner. "Now, Lieutenant, we haven't talked about what we'd do if a demand comes."

"Your thoughts?"

"I've always believed it's a bad idea to pay, or promise anything, in this kind of situation," Scorchner said. "The last thing you want to do is encourage other criminals."

"You mean you wouldn't pay a kidnapper to get me back?" Eleanor sounded incredulous.

"We're not talking about you, Kitten."

"Quirke's life is valuable, even if he was a terrible husband."

"I'm not disputing that, it's just—"

Hetford drew Grimes aside as Eleanor and her father argued. "On another topic, Lieutenant, have you—or anyone—been looking into the blog posts and mudslinging and all that going on in this election?"

"My job is to find Justice Quirke, not work on political matters. Why?"

"Oh, no particular reason. I'm due to go on the ballot next time, so, you know, the fairness of the whole process interests me."

Grimes studied Hetford for a moment. The justice was looking a little haggard and avoiding eye contact. "I thought it was just people exercising their First Amendment rights. Is there something more to it?"

"No, no. Why would you suggest that?"

"I'm just trying to understand your concern, Justice Hetford. If you want to know the source for the blog posts and articles and such, maybe you should contact the websites. Or Justice Quirke's election consultant might have some insights. His name's Bobby James."

"I've heard of him. The Democrat judges use him, I'm told."

"In case I do get assigned to look into it after we find Justice Quirke, do you have any theories as to who might be doing the mudslinging, as you call it?"

"I didn't call it that. No, I haven't got any particular theories."

"It sounds like you've been thinking pretty deeply about it, though."

"One can't help wondering. But if you want to know what I think, I'd put my money on a party. A disappointed litigant. Look at the losing side in each of Quirke's cases, going all the way back to his superior court days, or even his days as a lawyer, and I'll bet you'll find something interesting. If you'll excuse me, Lieutenant, I think I'll try to settle the dispute on the other side of the room." He nodded and went to join Eleanor and Scorchner, immediately immersing himself in their argument over the advisability of paying ransom demands.

There was little else Grimes could do in Hemsbridge, so he excused himself and set off for the city. The traffic had picked up a little, so once again he selectively deployed his lights and siren to speed up the trip.

As he negotiated the freeway, he mused on Hetford's peculiar interest in Quirke's social media troubles. The issue seemed like the last thing a sympathetic colleague would focus on while the judge was still missing, but perhaps Hetford was less than sympathetic. His conversation consisted of obvious misdirection, leading Grimes to consider the seemingly outlandish notion Hetford may in fact have had something to do with the blog posts and articles. If so, possibly Lucas Grieber, the chief of staff he'd poached off Quirke, was also involved. John Hendershott had mentioned the longstanding antagonism that Hetford apparently felt toward Quirke, which seemed to turn exclusively on disagreements over arcane legal questions, and Grimes wondered if Hetford had let it cloud his judgment to the point of leading him to plant those vicious stories. Still, the odds of that seemed rather long.

The biggest elephant in the room, of course, was Hetford's relationship with the soon-to-be-ex-Mrs. Quirke. Oddly, Grimes saw no evidence it had produced any friction on either side. To the extent anything made sense, the only motive Grimes could imagine for Hetford's engaging in *sub rosa* efforts to make Quirke look bad was a mild case of sadism. He decided to ask the Chief, as soon as he arrived back in Sant' Urbano, if he ought to start looking into it.

※

In Hemsbridge, seated closed to Hetford on the down-upholstered pink loveseat in the sunroom adjacent to her bedroom on the east side of the house, Eleanor couldn't help noticing that the teacup rattled on its saucer as he passed it to her. "What's wrong, darling?" she asked. "You're looking pale. Of course, nobody likes to be interrogated before breakfast. Would you pass the sugar?"

He complied. "I've been thinking, Eleanor. I—this may sound sudden, but it's been on my mind for quite some time. You've been kind, generous, everything I could hope for in a friend. And so, there's something I have to say."

He paused, catching her eye. There, Eleanor saw a nervousness she'd never detected in Hetford before. A boyfriend using the word "friend" in alluding to the relationship usually meant imminent breakup. This she hadn't seen coming at all—she'd thought they were growing closer every day—and her lower lip involuntarily quivered at what she expected him to say next.

"When I first met you, and you began to confide in me, I could only marvel at how blind Quirke was, ignoring the amazing gem he had in you. Then, to my complete surprise, you gave me to understand you were interested in me. Romantically. Well, I've been hurt before. Someday I'll tell you about it. For now, I'll just say I don't bestow my trust easily. And so, I tested you. I'm sorry, darling, I had to. I held you off, I acted noncommittal, I had to see whether you were looking for quick gratification, in which case I knew you'd soon move on to the next man, or whether there was a chance you might embark with me on something lasting.

"Every night I'd go home wondering how long you'd put up with my temporizing about our relationship. But, again to my complete surprise, you've stuck with me, humoring me, never trying to pressure me. You've been absolutely...the top."

"The Tower of Pisa," she whispered.

"More like the Burj Khalifa. And today, sometime between undergoing interrogation and sitting down with you to listen to the birds warbling outside these windows, it hit me like a ton of bricks: I must have you in my life, now and always. So, will you marry me?"

She gasped, and his arms encircled her.

"I promise you that if you'll have me, I'll be more of a husband than you're used to. The work of the court can be hard and lonely and consuming, as you know all too well. If we marry, I'll give it up. Maybe I can help Gene in the business, but my first priority will be to live life to the fullest with you, no matter whatever happens."

Eleanor couldn't speak at first. As she sat, trembling a little, Hetford held on tight. A full minute ticked by. At last, tears in her eyes, she answered him.

"This is the happiest moment of my life; I wish it could last forever. But yes, yes, I want to marry you, Allan. Let's share our lives and grow old together. I've never wanted to think about getting old until now. Suddenly it doesn't scare me anymore."

They sealed the deal with a deep and lingering kiss.

Chapter Thirty-One

November 2, 9:30 a.m.

"WHERE IS THE JUSTICE?"

So shouted the headline in the *Costante Bee*, weekend edition, which rested atop several days' worth of junk mail on the untidy coffee table in Jenny's living room. She took the newspaper principally for the grocery coupons and yard sale notices, and only occasionally looked at the news articles the Bee printed from the wire services. Had she done more than glance at the headline on this Sunday before the statewide general election, she would have learned the article did not, contrary to her hasty impression, concern another of the all-too-frequent instances of a grand jury failing to indict a police officer responsible for the death of a person in custody. Instead, she would have learned the following information of immediate and personal interest to herself:

"State police yesterday announced an investigation into the mysterious disappearance of a Supreme Court justice facing a difficult retention battle. Associate Justice Conal Quirke failed to return home as expected on Thursday evening after meeting with an attorney friend near the courthouse in the Civic Center area of Sant' Urbano. Minutes after saying goodbye to his friend, he was seen in the same neighborhood in the company of a man and woman described as well-dressed Caucasians in their forties.

"Justice Quirke may be ill and in need of medical attention. Anyone with information as to his possible whereabouts is urged to call Lieutenant Grimes of the state police at (515) 881-9909.

"Although well regarded as a jurist, Justice Quirke has been plagued by controversy regarding his behavior off the bench, including allegations of substance abuse and other improprieties. His campaign consultant, Bobby James, dismissed rumors the judge disappeared voluntarily, saying: 'Justice Quirke is a great judge and he loves his work. He's had ups and downs in his personal life, like any of us, but there's absolutely no reason why he'd fly the coop. I'm worried about him.' Justice Quirke married socialite Eleanor Scorchner Quirke, daughter of Marvelocity Industries' founder and CEO Gene Scorchner, in 1984, but the couple separated several months ago. Mrs. Quirke, who recently filed for divorce, could not be reached for comment."

Rowe surfaced into consciousness sometime after noon in the guest bedroom while Laudie lingered on in sleep. He pulled on a pair of jeans and went to the kitchen. There Jenny was kneeling in front of the little boy, forcing his arms into the sleeves of a jacket. "Morning, Rowe," she said, giving him a bright smile. "I'm glad you're up—I'm out of milk and everything else. I was just going to take Timmy to the store and didn't want to wake you."

"That wouldn't have been a very good idea. Is he still asleep?" Rowe gestured toward the back of the house.

"I haven't heard anything."

"Wait a little while and take Laudie with you. I'll stay here with our friend."

"Okay, but, Rowe, I really do need to get some groceries in the house, or make a McDonalds run, or something—the baby's hungry, I need to eat, and I'm sure you and Lauds need to, also."

"Look, I'll get her up now. We'll be out of your hair before long. Get the kid a special treat on me," he said, pulling a five-dollar bill out of his wallet and handing it to Jenny. "I'll tell her to get ready." On his way to the bedroom, he picked up the newspaper from the coffee table. "Mind if I—?"

"Go ahead. Just save me the coupons." She knelt again and pulled Timmy's arms out of his jacket sleeves, and he scampered to his room. A minute later he returned, clutching a small plastic dolphin and his bloody blankie.

"Con-o says bring me some water."

"Who, honey? What happened to your blanket? You mean that guy in there? Oh, my God—he hasn't had anything since they got here, has he? Let me get some water for him." She filled a glass from the tap and started down the hall.

Before she could enter the baby's room, Rowe slid out of the still-darkened guest bedroom, grasping the wrist of the hand holding the glass. "Don't bother. I'll do it."

"It's not a bother, I—"

"Stay out. And keep the kid out, okay? Please?"

※

"It looks like you're missed," said Rowe, trying to pull Quirke to a sitting position. "Hey, here's some water for you. Sit up."

The command seemed to come from a vast distance. He wanted to comply, but his energies seemed to have dwindled to nothing. "Help," he whispered.

Rowe raised him to a sitting position and kept an arm around him, holding the glass to his lips. "You're even more famous than before, Judge. The cops are looking for you. This complicates matters somewhat."

A few ounces of water restored something of Quirke's powers of speech. "If you let me go, I'll say I don't remember what happened. You can get away."

"Somehow I suspect that isn't how it would play out."

"There's nothing to be gained."

"That's true. Nothing either way."

Rowe stood up abruptly and left the room, leaving the glass, still half-full, on the floor a foot away from Quirke.

※

"Jenny, we need to get to your connection tonight," Rowe said. "You told Lauds you could set it up."

"I'll try." Seeing the desperation in his eyes, she said, "I'm sure I can. What do you need?"

"Say an ounce, more if they can get it. H."

"Let me call right now."

※

Jenny ended the call, shaking her head. "He wants me to bring you there to do the deal, but it won't work if you're planning for all three of you to go at the same time. I can't leave Timmy here by himself, and I can't get anyone to come and stay with him on such short notice."

"Well, what if you and I go over there right now, and you introduce me, while Angel stays here to babysit. That way he knows who I am, and tonight the three of us go over there and do the deal."

The idea of Laudie caring for Timmy, even for the brief time it would take to make the introductions with her connection, made Jenny shudder inwardly, but she couldn't think of a better plan offhand. "Okay, but we really have to hurry. Oh, and we absolutely have to stop and pick up a few groceries on the way back. My child's never gone hungry in his life, and he's not going to start now."

"Whatever you say. You've been good to us, and we won't forget it."

※

"Are you my daddy?"

Timmy, who had no relationship with his biological father, had returned to his room after his mother and Rowe went to meet the connection, in hopes of clearing up a point of confusion. The man tied to his crib was old and weak and messy and broken-looking, but he talked nicely, and if he was Timmy's daddy and for some reason had chosen this strange way to enter his life, Timmy could get used to him.

Quirke struggled to sit upright, his wrists still tethered to the crib and his waist by the twine loop. "Timmy, you're such a wonderful boy that I wish I were your daddy. But no, I'm just visiting. I'll be leaving later today."

"Where are you going?"

"Home."

"Are you crying?"

Few things, Quirke realized, get past a small child. He wished now he'd had a chance to put that realization to practical use in his too-finite lifetime. He and Eleanor had never had children, first because they were both young and unready, then because he was unready, then because she was unready, and finally because they could no longer stand each other. With Sadie, he reflected sorrowfully, it was not to be. Then he felt a hint of something uncanny, a glint of something hopeful that he couldn't reconcile with the knowledge that his captors had the power and the intention to kill him tonight.

"I don't know. Yes. It seems silly, doesn't it?"

Timmy shook his head.

"I want you to tell me a story," Quirke said. "Will you do that?"

Timmy clambered onto his lap, laid a small plump hand on Quirke's, and began to speak gravely of dinosaurs and their mommies, of epic owl journeys, of production problems at marshmallow factories, of puppies and wizards.

"I know some magicians," Quirke volunteered. "They're very nice."

"Then they'll probably come and take you home in a magic car," Timmy opined.

At that moment, the front door opened and Timmy, knowing his new friend was, for reasons comprehensible only to grownups, forbidden company, flew out of the room.

※

November 2, 6:20 p.m.

At dusk, Rowe went outdoors with pliers and wire and switched license plates between his car and Jenny's. Laudie sat sullenly chain-smoking in the guest bedroom. She had not looked in on Quirke since the contretemps of the night before. Jenny watched her son watch TV in the living room, too nervous to read to him.

At last Laudie emerged from the bedroom to bid her friend farewell.

"Our little project didn't go anywhere, as luck would have it, but we have to get on the road. Thanks for putting us up."

"Well, sure, Lauds. I hope the next project's more successful."

"It had better be. Maybe I'll call you again before long."

Jenny smiled, silently praying she might never see Laudie's face again unless in a news story about her capture.

Rowe returned to the house and told Laudie to warm up the car. She stubbed out her cigarette in her coffee cup and did as he instructed. He went into Timmy's room, coming out a few minutes later with the man they'd called the big guy.

He didn't seem, to Jenny, particularly big. His wavy hair stood up stiff with sweat and salt, his eyes—red, black and blue all at once—searched hers, his mouth was swollen and raw in his blood- and dirt-streaked, unshaven face, and he moved with a wary meekness. He and his clothes obviously hadn't seen a good washing in days. Rowe held him in a pincer grip by the elbow, his wrists bound together and to his waist.

"Bye, Con-o," said Timmy from the floor in front of the TV.

"Tell the kid to go to his room," Rowe directed her.

"Timmy," she said, "you heard."

The child stood, hesitated, and threw his arms around Quirke's legs for a moment before scampering down the hall. Watching him, Rowe seemed distracted.

Jenny approached the man Timmy had called Con-o as Rowe began to move him toward the door. Just then Laudie, outside, called to Rowe, sounding irritated. Rowe marched the captive to the easy chair next to the coffee table and pushed him into it as he went to see what Laudie wanted.

The big guy tried to smile, or so at least it seemed to Jenny. His visible teeth and gums were stained alarmingly red. He was about to speak when Rowe burst back into the house, startling Jenny.

"Anybody seen her cigarette lighter?" he asked.

"I think it's on the kitchen table," she said.

He had soon retrieved it and went to pull the big guy out of the chair. She could see he found it difficult to stand. As he got to his feet again, he looked down at the coffee table and up at Jenny, and winked. Then they were gone, and Jenny heard their car pulling out of the driveway onto the street.

She ran to the bathroom and retrieved her phone from the tampon box under the sink, tapping in Officer Fuller's number. Her heart sank as his voicemail took the call.

"Officer Fuller, this is Jennifer Mortensen. It's super urgent, so please check your messages, please? The friends who were staying with me, the ones I texted you about, just left my house. They took the man they were holding with them. They're on the way to Armando Kline's out on Avenue 216 to buy heroin, but I think they plan to kill that poor man, maybe by overdose, or maybe they plan to shoot him and push his body into the canal, I don't know. If you get there in time, you might be able to stop it. Or you can at least bust one dealer here in town. Please let me know you got this message."

In his bedroom, Timmy sat cross-legged on the rug, holding his cherished blankie by a corner.

"Mommy, Con-o got it dirty." He pointed to the bloodstains. "Don't be mad, Mommy."

"I'm not, sweetie, but I'd better take this and wash it," she said. *On second thought,* she realized, *this might be evidence someday.* "Next time I do the laundry, okay, buddy? In the meantime, you still have your little baby blanket." From the bottom drawer of the dresser she took the tattered piece of white flannel, striped pink and blue at the ends, that the Costante General Hospital maternity department had wrapped Timmy in three years before. She handed it to her son. He held it to his cheek and inserted his thumb in his mouth, sucking pensively.

"I think it's time for a nap, buddy." She lifted him into his crib, kissed him, and gently brushed the curls off his face. Within seconds, he was asleep.

Not hearing from Officer Fuller was making her increasingly agitated. She tried Fuller's number again and once more heard his outgoing message. Unable to do more, she resorted to tidying up.

In the guest bedroom, she found three sooty dishes—makeshift ashtrays—and took them to the kitchen, tossing the butts in the trash and rinsing the cigarette residues away in the sink. She returned to the bedroom intending to strip the bed, and noticed the newspaper on the coverlet.

Suddenly she focused on the article beneath the headline, realizing the topic was not at all what she'd assumed. "...Associate Justice Conal Quirke failed to return home as expected on Thursday...he was seen...in the company of a man and woman described as well-dressed Caucasians in their forties...Anyone with information as to his possible whereabouts is urged to call Lieutenant Grimes of the state police at (515) 881-9909."

"Oh my God," she whispered. "Con-o."

She rushed to the living room and scanned the coffee table, remembering how the big guy had deliberately looked down and then winked at her. There in the most recent stratum of junk mail was an election flyer urging her to "VOTE FOR AN INDEPENDENT JUDICIARY." Immediately beneath the command was printed a photo of a handsome, smiling, blue-eyed Justice Quirke, who might very well have been a long-ago version of the broken man who'd just left her house.

"Stay here, Angel," said Rowe as they parked in front of the connection's house on Avenue 216. "You wouldn't like it in there."

"Just don't use it all on him."

"Of course not—we'll have a good time tonight, too, as soon as we get to a safe place. Come on, Judge. It's the moment you've been waiting for." Getting out of his seat behind Laudie, who was driving, Rowe walked behind the car and opened the passenger side door, letting the grip of his nine-millimeter poke out of his jacket pocket for its deterrent effect. Quirke remained immobile for a moment, but then gathered himself and exited the car unassisted.

"Why do you call her that?" he asked.

Rowe seemed taken aback. "Call her Angel, you mean? She is an angel. An angel of God. Well, if you don't see it, I'd never be able to explain it. Hey, I'm tired of standing out here; go on in."

As a lawyer and judge, Quirke had watched and listened to plenty of surveillance tapes and heard scores of informants testify about drug deals, but he'd never been within a few feet of a real-time transaction. The ambient sounds and smells in the drug house, and the sight of his torpid fellow users sprawling on the seedy furniture and listening to the unfamiliar music coming over the invisible speakers gave it all a fresh and less morally fraught slant. This scene was simply a variation on the bar at the Inns—or what the Inns might have been like during Prohibition.

Then again, there was no way to normalize his own approaching death. He had no fear of meeting a god who would send messages to the likes of Laudie, but for a conscious mind to fully grasp the permanent cessation of its own consciousness is almost impossible. He tried to conjure the feeling of Sadie's hand in his, so that he might experience his death as merely the sleepy oblivion at the end of a day spent with her, a day like the wonderful Saturday in Sant' Amaro when he had felt more alive than at any time he could remember.

Impossibly soon, it seemed, Rowe had fixed his works and was motioning for him to take his place on the rotting sofa next to the other addicts. "Make a fist, Judge," he said. Quirke complied, remembering the first time and trusting that same bliss lay just around the corner. And in the blink of an eye, it was done, and he was sinking and floating toward heaven again.

Detective Fuller's report, and all his future reports involving Jenny, would identify her as a reliable confidential informant. Fuller's team arrived on the scene to execute their warrant (on which Fuller had, in fact, been working for some time before Quirke happened to visit) in the middle of a deal of rather impressive size, and they arrested Armando Kline and three others for sale of narcotics, possession of narcotics, possession for sale, being armed while possessing for sale, etc., etc., etc. Some of the arrestees would face serious quantity enhancements, and each had an impressive array of priors. It all went down like clockwork, a textbook raid.

Except for Quirke, on the sofa, whose lips had turned blue and who'd stopped breathing with the needle still in his arm. Fuller's timing wasn't ideal for him.

Chapter Thirty-Two

November 2, 10:00 p.m.

"Get the paramedics over here," Fuller told another officer. "On second thought, wait. Give the dead guy a shot of naloxone and see what happens."

The policy of the Costante Police Department was to carry an opiate antagonist on every drug-related call because seeing a miracle happen now and then gave officers a much-needed bounce. On this occasion, the results were gratifying.

Within seconds of being jabbed, Quirke sputtered and sat up. "Fuck, man, what did you just do?"

"Take it easy, Chip. You do like breathing, don't you?" Fuller pulled Quirke off the sofa and tried to get him to stand upright. "Jesus, your face. You and the missus have a disagreement? Never mind, tell it to the booking officer. I'm arresting you for being under the influence of a controlled substance."

"11550," said Quirke, starting to nod again.

Fuller knuckled him on the chest to keep him semiconscious. "What are you, a lawyer? You guys are no better than the rest once you get the taste for skag. What happened to your oath to uphold the law? Or maybe this ain't your first offense?"

"If you're going to keep asking me all these questions," said Quirke, whose reasoning was still somewhat clouded, "then I'd better have counsel present."

"Well, if that's the way you want it, we'll just take you in, then."

※

November 3, 6:30 a.m.

Quirke had been strip- and body-cavity searched, photographed, fingerprinted, and booked, and his mug shots had been uploaded into the database, before Costante PD became aware of his true identity. His judgment was still a bit off, and he was mainly keen to avoid seeming to throw his judicial weight around to escape criminal liability. He'd seen the CJB go after many a judge stupid or arrogant enough to make that mistake in the wake of a DUI or other low-level arrest.

After the booking process was completed, the cops decided he looked bad enough that they sent him to the jail infirmary, where he received first aid, intravenous fluids and, eventually, Grade B orange juice to raise his blood sugar. He was offered a stale bagel, but declined it. He asked if he could make a phone call instead, thinking Jim Forney might be able to get him out in time to go and vote for himself on Election Day.

By that point, Jenny had reached Lieutenant Grimes, who had communicated with Detective Fuller's supervisor, and Costante PD was now, as the sun began to rise on the Monday before Election Day, prepared to release their distinguished guest on his promise to appear. Which, the Chief of Police explained to Grimes, was likely to be unnecessary once they'd had the opportunity to more carefully review Fuller's report.

"There was something in there about zip-ties. Obviously, if they were still on his wrists Judge Quirke couldn't shoot himself up. Then we might be in the realm of a duress defense. And if, like you're saying, he was kidnapped by the pair that Marengo County's interested in for the possible arson-murder, well then, he's just a witness, victim-witness, in my mind."

"Mine, too," said Grimes. He'd dealt with enough local law enforcement to know it would be counterproductive to suggest the Chief quit being such a fucking idiot and just let the judge go; the Chief would get there in his own way, at his own pace.

Peter drove Sadie to Costante in his Audi. They left the loft at 4:00 a.m., when Grimes was finally able to confirm Costante PD was holding Conal, and pulled into the station parking lot around 6:30 a.m. They'd had time only to stretch their legs when a tattered, filthy, and barely recognizable figure emerged from the building. He was walking so slowly and painfully that Sadie was compelled to run to him, her heart pounding. His facial injuries momentarily took her breath away.

She stood in front of him, her hands holding his, which seemed to be the only uninjured part of him. "When I imagined what it would be like getting you back, I thought about crushing you with hugs and smothering you with kisses," she said. "But I'm almost afraid to touch you. What happened?"

"Your mom beat me up. I'm okay, don't worry. I'll explain later."

He took her into his arms, and they held each other for a long time. Finally, Sadie smiled up at him.

"I did what you said. Went to the doctor."

"That's good. Is everything okay?"

"Way better than okay: We're having a baby."

It was almost as if the rush was back. "I thought—"

"So did I. Turns out you're—as I've been saying—magical."

He was silent for a moment. "That makes me all the more sure. Sadie, I'm getting clean and sober, starting now. If I'm lucky enough to have a job after tomorrow, I know I'm looking at censure; the CJB's not going to turn a blind eye to what I did. I used to think my drug of choice was bourbon whiskey, but—have you ever done heroin?"

Her eyes filled with tears. "She shot me up once when I was thirteen. I threw up and spent the next three hours feeling like I'd died. I never felt so powerless, and I've never been tempted to touch it since."

"It doesn't surprise me she'd do that to you. But when they gave it to me, first to keep me quiet, and then to kill me, I felt that same negation as pure bliss. That's the difference between thirteen and fifty-two, I guess. So, I'm in a dilemma: I can't unlearn what it feels like, and I could never be satisfied with chipping. You know me, I go all in when it comes to mind-altering substances. Well, I don't want to live that way. I don't want to lose you living that way. Most of all, I can't inflict it on our child. Our child! Oh my God, Sadie. And somehow, I suspect the CJB would come down harder on a practicing dope fiend. I'm not a heroin addict, not yet. You can't get addicted in a weekend—physically, anyway. But if I drink, I'm just going to want my real drug of choice. That's not the complete truth: I want it right now, I'm sorry to say. And soon enough I'd find a way to get some, and eventually I'd be banging it all day, every day. So, I'm done. Maybe rehab wouldn't be such a bad idea after all. But mainly I love you—more than anything, Sadie—and I'm glad to be alive again. And I can't wait to be a dad. I want at least six kids. Provided you're up for it, of course."

"Ask me when I can keep food down again." She smiled. "Of course, I want more, dearest. I was an only child, I'd have loved to have had siblings."

"Sadie, I learned things. You had a sister—half-sister. I know very little about her, but I'll tell you later. You know what I'd like right now?"

"Name it; anything."

"Soap, hot water and clean clothes. I've been in these since Thursday and puked on them a few times. You really must love me, to get anywhere near me in this condition."

Chapter Thirty-Three

November 3, 12:30 a.m.

After injecting enough heroin to dispatch their captive to his heavenly reward, Rowe stayed in the house on Avenue 216 only long enough to watch him slip into unconsciousness. Pocketing the rest of their drug purchases, leaving the needle in Quirke's arm, and, as an afterthought, snipping the zip ties that bound his wrists with the tiny scissors on his Swiss army knife, Rowe exited into the cold, starry night and the idling car.

Laudie, behind the steering wheel, was drumming on the dashboard to the beat of the music on the car radio. Rowe hadn't yet closed his door on the passenger side when she began backing out of the driveway and onto the road. They continued west on 216 to its first intersection with a wider highway and then headed north, along the floor of the valley, the speedometer edging up past the speed limit.

"Where are we going, Angel?" he asked. From the start, their venture had lacked a workable plan, and she was evidently still improvising. Having cast the die by leaving the judge for dead, he saw no point in now demanding systematic thinking. Nevertheless, he felt a mild curiosity.

"I still want to see Sadie, of course."

"You think she'll have changed her mind?"

"I don't care."

The air inside the car grew intolerably close. As Laudie sped along, he rolled down the window and stared out at the night sky as the cold air's urgent caress reawakened him. They passed car after car on the highway, the occupants all looking as still and artificial as mannequins. The wild thought strayed across his mind that he and Laudie were the only people left alive under heaven, and the unsettling sense of claustrophobia deepened.

He looked across at her and found her profile strange, unrecognizable. Sound sleep had been elusive for the last few nights; that might account for this peculiar feeling he was experiencing. Once they found a temporary refuge maybe he'd find rest, and his senses would return to normal. But would he ever begin to see her as he used to do?

He realized he would not. It wasn't she who'd changed—it was he. He, an ordained minister even if he'd trampled his calling into the muck of Satan, had just killed a blameless man for no reason except to further their futile escape effort. They'd killed the Captain, too, but he was dying in any event, and Rowe hadn't laid his own hands on the man. The moral distinction was minuscule to nonexistent, but he now knew he'd crossed irredeemably into the territory of the damned. Viewed from within its boundaries, his angel lacked the glamour she'd possessed when he stood outside. The cords on her neck, her stale breath, the tunelessness of her humming afforded a hint of the far more serious imperfections in her heart. But as flawed as she was, his fall made him far, far worse.

She'd merged into the westbound freeway, heading back toward where they'd begun this trip three days before. It appeared she really meant to find Sadie, come hell or high water, whether or not Sadie wanted to be found.

"We should find a place for the night," he said. "I have some—"

"Fairwood's pretty close to the interstate. Hang onto it, honey, till we find a place and check in."

Despite recent events, she was bright and chatty to the dull-eyed clerk at the motel, and soon Rowe was carrying their few possessions into their small, dark, low-ceilinged room. He removed his jacket and placed it carefully over the back of the desk chair, as precisely and delicately as if he were still the pastor in the parsonage. Laudie turned on the television, lay on the bed, and spread her arms, angel-fashion. He felt nothing—neither love, nor fear, nor anger; nothing save a progressive sense of being hollowed out.

"What's with you?" she asked, grinning. "Finally, some peace and quiet. Jenny's little brat was getting on my nerves and, frankly, I'm just as glad the big guy's out of our hair. Though it's too bad." He didn't need to ask what was too bad; she could only have meant the failure of her revenue projections to materialize. "Tomorrow we'll—"

"Let's talk about tomorrow." He sat on the edge of the sagging bed.

"That's just what I was about to do before you interrupted me," she said.

"Let me say this. Nothing went quite the way we'd—nothing really worked out. Laudie, I just don't see it happening, and you know why? It's because we've displeased the Lord."

"We've what?" she repeated, sitting up with a sudden rigidity. "You don't see what happening?"

"This enterprise—well, it failed for a reason. We somehow misread the Lord's plan for our lives. It couldn't have been what we thought it was. But we can still make amends." As the words left his mouth, he felt his courage gathering. He was back in the pulpit preaching to his congregation of one.

"I have no idea what you're talking about, and I doubt you do either."

"To the contrary, I've just begun to see it all clearly. I can't explain it any more than I can the fact the Lord chose you to speak through. Because I believe He did, He did at one time, but...a good man doesn't wind up dead with my needle in his arm by the will of the Lord."

"You're presuming to understand His will."

"Either you're wrong, or He doesn't exist."

She eyed him. "So, what's this about making amends?"

He smiled and nodded, reaching to clasp her hand. "I'm going to turn my life over. And you're going to come with me."

"Like hell."

"It's the only way to find peace."

She snatched her hand away. "But Rowe, honey, there's no such thing. Chaos is all there is or ever was. It's in my blood. It *is* my blood. You and I are bound forever. My Jenny'll keep her mouth shut. Nothing's changed, nothing at all. You've gone insane to think of turning yourself in. I can't let that happen."

"Just give it some thought," he said, gently. "And now, for the first time in a long while, I feel like I can go to sleep. Here." He pulled a baggie out of his pocket and tossed it onto the bed. "Do what you want with this. We can speak more about it in the morning."

He lay down next to her and, within minutes, had relaxed into a deep slumber.

Next to him, Laudie seethed in outrage. Where was this bland blasphemy coming from? It certainly didn't spring from fear; his face was as tranquil as an infant's. The prospect of the law catching up with them had him inventing a reconciliation in the embrace of his mythic Jesus. And now he'd convinced himself not only that it was the proper thing for him to do, but that she had to throw her life away right along with him. She knew better than he what would happen if they handed themselves over; she'd seen quite enough of prison life, and she wasn't going back.

There was another way. The only way. She slid lightly off the bed, baggie in hand, tiptoed to the bathroom, and shut the door. Kneeling beside the bathtub, she took a deep breath and brought her head down hard onto its ceramic rim, biting her lip to stop herself from crying out. The pain momentarily stunned her, but she knew she'd succeeded in blackening her left eye. Next, she stood and raised her arms as if the tub were a pool and she were about to dive in with a butterfly stroke; then, violating a lifetime's practice of muscular control, she let herself fall. She'd have screamed, but the impact had knocked the breath out of her. As soon as she could move again, she took her hairbrush from the counter beside the sink and raked it across her right cheek and arm. The face of a domestic abuse victim now stared back at her from the mirror. Finally, with a sigh, she dumped the contents of the baggie into the toilet bowl and flushed. The baggie itself she stuffed into Rowe's shaving kit, which she zipped closed. Returning to the room, she reached silently into the pocket of his jacket, retrieving his nine-millimeter pistol.

Looking down at him as he lay asleep, she disengaged the safety, held it at arm's length against the underside of his jaw, and pulled the trigger. The loud report made her cry out—all to the good, for verisimilitude's sake. Then she took a tissue from the box on the bedside table, wiped the grip, and wrapped the lifeless fingers of his right hand around it as voices stirred outside the room.

"Help!" she called. "My husband just shot himself. Oh, help me, please."

※

November 3, 1:00 a.m.

"We've gone this far, Judge. You don't want to take the final step?"

Hetford, phone at his ear, his mind roiling at Lucas's proposal, moved away from his bed, where Eleanor was sleeping, and into the hallway of his apartment. Now that he thought of her as his betrothed, he was beginning to open his life to her, but he couldn't bear the thought of her learning the full truth about his conspiracy with Lucas to cost Quirke the election.

"Good God, how did you find it? I haven't seen anything in the news yet."

"I've set it up to search the law enforcement databases every five minutes."

"That's not only illegal, Lucas, it's insanely obsessive. So are you sure it's—"

"There's no doubt. He was arrested late last night in Costante for being under the influence of a controlled substance. His mug shots look like somebody was using his head for a soccer ball. Look at my text message."

Hetford looked at it. Despite his feelings toward Quirke, the sight of a fellow judge beaten practically to a pulp made him ill. "It's appalling. But you know there must be more to it—he didn't get into that state voluntarily. Grimes thinks he was kidnapped. By your little Sadie's mother, no less."

"Not mine, Judge, not mine. Whatever. All I'm saying is it would make a hell of a blog post on the day before the election. Makes all the rest of it look like child's play."

Hetford was sweating. "I don't know, I...If it's traced back..."

"It hasn't been."

"No one's started looking yet."

"I know what I'm doing."

Eleanor stirred under the bedclothes, and Hetford suddenly wished he'd never started pranking Quirke. Posting the mug shot would be simply too brutal, and Hetford's life had already taken a new direction. "Look, Lucas," he whispered, "it's moot. I planned to tell you soon, but—but I'm leaving the court. Eleanor and I—"

"What?"

"I'm going to be the GC at Marvelocity."

"I quit my job to work with you. What am I supposed to do now?"

"I'm not going to leave you high and dry; there'll be a place for you. As for the pictures, don't. It's—"

"Too late," Lucas replied. "I sent it."

Hetford ended the call. He stood in the hallway for a few minutes, feeling powerless, bargaining at some level of his mind with a silent supreme being with whom he'd not lately been in contact. Finally, he slipped back under the covers and, his skin icy, lay motionless so as not to disturb Eleanor. Still asleep, she reached for him, whimpering once at his cold touch.

※

November 3, 4:00 p.m.

"JUSTICE FOUND. State police announced Monday that Supreme Court Justice Conal Quirke, who had been missing since Thursday and who is believed to have been kidnapped from Sant' Urbano, has been located. After undergoing medical treatment, the judge, whom voters in tomorrow's election will decide whether to retain, is resting at his home. He is expected to make a full recovery. No other information has been released, and police spokesman Lieutenant Edmund Grimes asks that the public respect Justice Quirke's privacy."

Bobby James studied the news release for the umpteenth time. Although he had approved it himself, to his political eye it was unsatisfactory, too guarded, as though the judge had something to hide. Unfortunately, he did. Until the 11550 charge was dropped and, more importantly, until his kidnappers were apprehended, the less publicly said about his ordeal, his condition, and his whereabouts, the better.

Bobby began to surf, searching the internet for references to his candidate, as he routinely did multiple times a day. At last he clicked on the Superior Claim of Right, a site he dreaded visiting but could not afford to ignore.

"Jesus Lord have mercy," he gasped. Bobby had spoken with the judge on the phone, but had not gone by to see him yet, thinking he needed time alone with Sadie, and so was unprepared for the images he saw on the blog. There, under the line "A TYPICAL WEEKEND FOR JUSTICE QUIRKE," were his mug shots, full face and profile, battered, black-eyed, bloodied, and obviously strung out.

※

Bobby phoned Sadie on his way to his car. "Hey, Sadie. How are you two? You three, I should say."

"Hey, Bobby. We're doing all right, just lying low."

"That's good. I want to drop by for a few minutes, if this isn't a bad time."

"What's up?"

"I need to tell the judge—and you—something. Keep him away from the computer in the meantime, would you, honey?"

"Is it anything like—"

"Worse. I don't know where these jackals come from, but I'm afraid it could set him off like the last time."

"Bobby, he quit."

"What are you saying, quit what?"

"Drinking. Drugs. He'll tell you about it. Bobby, forgive me if this is too personal, but I have to ask: are you—"

"I'm so glad to hear it. And yes, baby, you guessed right. I'm an addict and alcoholic myself, twenty-seven years clean and sober. I'll tell y'all the drunkalogue—Reader's Digest condensed version, at least—when I get there; it might help him."

"There's parking space in the garage. Call me again when you get to Gillian, and I'll let you in."

"Thank you so much. Be there in about ten."

※

At the loft, Bobby's initial reaction to seeing the judge mirrored Sadie's: an urge to throw his arms around him out of sheer joy and relief, tempered by a fear of inflicting further injury.

"It looks worse than it is," Quirke said, "although there's a little cheekbone fracture and a lot of pain. I haven't taken the Vicodin they gave me for it, but I don't know how much longer I can hold out."

"Judge, it takes huge courage to do what you're doing. But there's no rule against taking advantage of the medical help you need to heal. Have you talked to your doctor about this?"

"Not yet. I don't want to tell him what I'm afraid of and have him write in my chart I'm an addict. Depending on what happens tomorrow, I might need to buy health insurance soon."

"I hope I'm not overstepping my place, Judge, but Sadie must have told you I've got a little experience in these things, and it seems to me you're more likely to relapse if you're in constant physical agony."

Quirke sank defeatedly into the sofa. "I wanted today to count."

"It does count. It's great you feel the desire to put using behind you; without that, you'd surely have gotten loaded by now. But as I always tell folks in this situation, you can't get a year's sobriety in a day."

"What was your drug of choice?" Quirke asked him.

"Brandy and cocaine. It was VSOP and me, early in the morning and late in the evening. I don't think I drew a sober breath between '76 and '87. Man, those were times."

"What did you do for a living back then?"

"Not much. Nothing legitimate, anyway. I wrote a lot of bad poetry and did odd jobs in the drug trade for a guy in the neighborhood. Lived off my girlfriends when money was tight and my mom when things got really desperate. Taking real employment would have compromised my art, you see." Bobby laughed. "Of course, one night I got sloppy and a cop pulled me over for failing to indicate a right turn. One thing led to another and I ended up pleading to a deuce and possession of cocaine. That was down from transportation and possession for sale. I got lucky. But I did six months in county as a condition of probation, and that's when I found the program."

"It took right away? That's unusual, isn't it?"

"First thing I did when I got out was to relapse. My girlfriend had quite reasonably decided she'd had enough, and rolled up the welcome mat. So, naturally, first night back at Mom's, I put away a pint of E&J's. She was a good tee-totaling, church-going lady, and took my girlfriend's point of view, which made me feel sorry for myself. Yeah, I was sorry, all right. When she tossed me out, I spent a night or two on the street, trying to find a friend to take me in. Looking back, I don't know why I was surprised none of 'em would when they found out I was no longer in the drug trade. Well, though I had to change my feckless ways and work hard, it's been pretty much uphill from there. When I became eligible, I got my convictions expunged. Did you know Judge Morton Willard?"

"He was a legend. Before my time, though."

"He turned me around. Having to account to him made me want to be accountable generally in my life. It's because of him I work on judicial campaigns. Him and the program."

"Still go to meetings?"

"Most every day. Feel up to coming with me to one tonight?"

Quirke considered. "I knew this was coming. It's been coming for a long time. Sadie, do you mind if I go?"

"Not at all, as long as Bobby takes good care of you and brings you home right after. You need as much rest as you can get."

"You can count on me, honey," Bobby assured her.

"And you're sure it's okay if I have one of these to take the edge off?" He picked up the vial of Vicodin that had sat, untouched, on the coffee table.

"We both know you're not doing it for recreation. You'll heal faster if you're not dealing with so much pain."

Quirke swallowed a tablet and handed the vial to Sadie. "Don't let me have another until—what does it say there?—six hours from now, please, sweetheart. Okay, Bobby—let's go."

"Wait, Judge, there's one more thing I wanted to tell you. I don't want you to see or hear about it from another source. The Claim of Right has another item on you, and it's nasty."

"They've picked on my drinking, pot-smoking, magical connections, guitar playing, love life, judicial opinions, even my weight. What more could they possibly find to write about?"

"Well, somehow they got hold of your mug shots from Costante PD and posted 'em with a caption. I'll warn you, it's cruel."

"Let me have it."

" 'A typical weekend for Justice Quirke.' "

Sadie and Bobby watched anxiously as Quirke began to shake.

"I have to put it out of my mind," he said.

"That's right, there's no point in torturing yourself—"

He shook his head. "My face hurts too goddamn much when I laugh."

※

November 4, 9:15 a.m.

"Wow, that looks nasty," Dr. Singh marveled. "How'd that happen?"

As Quirke had feared, his injuries threatened to upstage the mother-to-be at this first prenatal appointment. "It's not as bad as it looks. I was the victim of a crime recently, and I don't mean to be churlish, but I'd rather not talk about it."

"Of course. My sympathies," said the doctor, a slender, white-coated young South Asian woman with a glossy black ponytail to the small of her back. "So how are we doing, Sadie? I have the records from your hospitalization. Not fun. You should have come to see me sooner."

"I wish I had," she said ruefully, lying on the cushioned table and gazing at the acoustic tile on the ceiling of the exam room. "It was stupid, but I just never guessed I could be pregnant. I'm starting to feel better. Finally."

"Getting your appetite back?"

"Yes. I'm taking vitamins, avoiding sushi and—and there's something I've been wanting to ask."

"Sure, of course. Something's worrying you?" Dr. Singh asked, seeing Sadie's suddenly anguished expression, which concerned Quirke likewise.

Sadie nodded. "Before I knew, I used to have a glass or two of wine with dinner. I think I know the answer, but I want to hear you say it."

"If it was really only a glass or two, and you stopped by—would you say, week eight? Week nine? We'll know more precisely after the ultrasound."

"Probably. It's a few weeks now since I could even think about drinking alcohol."

"Then it's unlikely to have caused any problems. So, don't worry. Worry is not healthy. Now, do you want to hear your baby's heartbeat? Of course, you do. Let me get my wonderful Doppler." The doctor adjusted the volume on the equipment and passed the cold wand over Sadie's belly.

"I hadn't noticed it before, but you've grown a little bump," Quirke said, laying his palm there before making way for the wand.

In a moment, the doctor's experienced hands found the optimal place for listening, and a strong, fast, swishing beat filled the room.

"Oh my God," Quirke and Sadie said in unison. He saw on her face the identical terror he himself was feeling, then her recognition he was mirroring her. Bubbles of nervous laughter escaped them both.

"Conal, I have to confess something," she said. "I don't know the first thing about babies. I've never babysat a baby, or even held one."

"That makes two of us," he said. "So, Doctor, this parenting thing—is it something we can sort of pick up as we go along?"

"My advice to Sadie, by the way, goes for you, too: Worry isn't healthy. I think that's the way humans have always learned parenting—picking it up as we go along, unless there's a granny handy who can tell you what to do, in which case I imagine you'd simply have to test her advice by figuring it out for yourselves anyway. If you come up with a new method, just think of the bestseller you'll have on your hands. So, shall we see if we can get a picture? We'll do this again later, but because you're unsure exactly when you conceived it would be good to do a dating ultrasound now. This jelly I'm smearing on you feels weird, I know, but it helps the probe move smoothly."

They fell silent, all eyes glued to the monitor, where a grainy image that looked half head took shape. The little figure turned and wriggled and danced solo to its heartbeat anthem.

"Beautiful," said Dr. Singh. "I'm seeing a normal, healthy-looking ten-week fetus. I can't tell the sex yet, but if you want to know, come back in a couple of weeks. Here are the first snapshots for your baby book.

※

The plan had been for them to go in to the office after the appointment, but, feeling themselves overwhelmed, they instead sat in a café a block from Dr. Singh's office—he over a latté, she over an herbal tea—holding hands, saying little but nestling as close as the bench seat would allow.

He wanted to call Mary Jane Lewis and tell her to hurry up with the divorce—not that nagging the lawyer would make any difference; state law allowed entry of a decree no sooner than six months from the filing of the petition, and it was still not quite two. As well, he had to finish assembling the funds to pay off Gene Scorchner under the terms of the prenup.

But these were, in his view, the merest minor irritations in the grand scheme. Less than forty-eight hours previously, he'd gone to sleep thinking he'd never see Sadie again, never even awaken again, not knowing of the existence of his child. Even the uncertainty over the result of the election paled in significance.

The thought reminded him of something.

"Sadie, darling, today's Tuesday, right?"

"Mm-hmm."

"We should go and vote."

November 4, 3:00 p.m.

Later, his mind still consumed with attempting to comprehend the existence of the baby, Quirke was pretty sure he'd made a mark on the ballot for each of the contests, but all he knew with certainty was that he'd voted yes on the judges, in particular himself. The idea of engaging in productive work under the circumstances seemed fanciful, but Sadie insisted they try.

John, Freddie, and Margie were on hand to welcome him back with an extravagant floral arrangement and a banana tres leches pie from the Three Babes Bakeshop (Sadie having forewarned Freddie not to order the chocolate bourbon pie, which the judge had formerly been capable of eating nearly all by himself). Margie solicitously kept refilling his coffee cup until he asked her to stop, as he could feel himself beginning to vibrate with the caffeine.

"Comrades, you're tremendously kind, and the best staff a judge ever had," Quirke began. "I hope we all have jobs tomorrow. I would like to announce that, even if it's only for the remainder of my current term, I've appointed John as my new head of chambers. That ought to have some resume value, and if not, at least it comes with a minuscule raise."

"Thank you, Judge," said John. "I'm seriously honored, and I'll stick with you for the next twelve years and beyond." He returned his attention momentarily to the pie, and then looked up. "Oh, we almost forgot to tell you. There was a little excitement around here Friday afternoon: The bomb squad blocked off Foltz Street outside the loading dock, right below our chambers, and blew up a dodgy-looking package addressed to you. It was mailed from Marvelocity Industries, but sat around the loading dock for a while, possibly weeks. I guess the label got a bit smudged and they had a hard time reading it. Doesn't inspire a lot of confidence, I must say. Apparently, it had a timer and some kind of fuel in it."

Quirke sat motionless for a few seconds. "Well, it's good to finally learn where that went."

"Where what went?" Sadie asked.

"The residue of my past life. That 'timer' must have been my alarm clock from the old place, and the fuel was probably that bottle of A.H. Hirsch Reserve Bourbon whiskey I was saving for a special occasion. Just as well. In a few months Sadie's going to give me the greatest little alarm clock I can imagine, and I have no more use for the whiskey. Unfortunately, they probably also blew up my birth certificate, family photos, and college yearbooks. But we're alive, comrades. Never forget we're alive."

※

November 4, 3:30 p.m.

Hetford brushed past Margo's desk and strode into the Chief's office. "I've only got a minute, Chief, and I'm sure you're—hello, Ward; Lieutenant Grimes." Seeing the Chief had another meeting in progress, presumably something to do with the Quirke situation—perhaps brainstorming on security improvements for the justices generally—Hetford stopped short. "I see this isn't the right time. I'll call you later."

"No, please sit down," the Chief said, pointing to the sole remaining guest chair near her desk. "We wanted to have a word with you."

"With me? What about?" he asked, his eyes darting from one to another of the three. They sat silently looking at him, without so much as a nod, much less a smile. "Great news about Quirke, eh?"

"It is, indeed. This whole episode has been the most upsetting thing I think I've ever encountered, professionally," the Chief responded. "Naturally, we were so focused on getting him back that the other stuff took a back seat."

"By 'other stuff' you mean...the social media—?"

"Of course. None of us have ever seen tactics like that in a judicial election in this state. Last time there was such intense opposition to a justice of this court was back in the pre-internet era."

"I found it disturbing, too," said Hetford.

"I could tell you did, Justice Hetford, when we talked Sunday morning down at Mr. Scorchner's place," Grimes said. "You seemed quite focused on the media issue."

"Well, I don't know if I'd say 'focused'; I—"

The Chief cut in. "It's not for me to intrude on a colleague's staffing decisions, Allan, but I was curious about the timing of your hiring of Lucas Grieber. It seemed so sudden, and I wondered if you or he'd been able to let Quirke know before he was kidnapped. It just seems like the sort of basic courtesy one colleague would extend to another."

Hetford's smile froze on his face. Where were they going with this? "I assume so—I mean, I assume Lucas told Quirke; he and I'd agreed on it some time before."

"Really?" The Chief's brow wrinkled. "Quirke never mentioned it to me. When exactly?"

"Well...now that you ask, I don't remember the precise date. Several weeks, a month, couple of months...is it important?"

"It may be," she said. "If Lucas had an arrangement with you while still purporting to be working for Quirke...it raises questions in my mind."

"What kind of questions? How does this relate to what we were talking about, the m-media attacks?"

"Your question assumes there's a connection. But that's what I've been trying to puzzle out. Do you know what Lucas used to do for a living, Allan?"

"I—no, I—"

"He was a computer security analyst for the FBI. An ethical hacker type."

The Chief looked across her desk at him as calmly and evenly as though she could sit there all afternoon. She would make a hell of a poker player, Hetford thought. Ward and Grimes were trying to wear the same expression, but Hetford saw that Ward was fighting to hide a glimmer of something triumphal behind his eyeglasses. Clearly it was time to go nuclear and end this interrogation session.

"Chief, this is fascinating, but I'm afraid my mind's elsewhere—on matters of the greatest personal import. I came to tell you I'm leaving the court. Eleanor Quirke—Eleanor Scorchner and I are planning to get married, and I'm going to be the general counsel at Marvelocity Industries. Of course, I'll stay on here until all the cases I've participated in are filed. Incidentally, I've made an offer to Lucas to join the company, and I expect he'll accept."

The Chief said nothing for a moment, although she allowed herself a smile. "That sounds like the best possible outcome," she said at last. "Good luck to you, Allan."

※

Quirke was sitting at his desk in chambers, trying to read a draft dissent but failing on multiple attempts to get past the first paragraph, when Grimes phoned him. A few minutes later, the lieutenant came in, trailing law enforcement agents wearing the uniforms of at least three jurisdictions.

"You're looking much better, Your Honor," Grimes said. "Sorry to disturb you, but there've been some developments. We picked up Mrs. Forrester yesterday morning at a motel in Fairwood."

Quirke's stomach lurched. Fairwood was only ten miles from Sant' Urbano. "She must have been on her way here."

"She hasn't admitted it, but that's our working hypothesis."

"What about Rowe? Was he with her?"

"He was. He'd been shot. Her story is he shot himself, but we're, let's say, skeptical and very interested in the autopsy report whenever it becomes available."

"So he's dead."

"Yes. We'd like you to ID them, if you can possibly spare the time."

"You're holding her in Fairwood?"

"Yeah, in the county jail; he's in the morgue there. If you could ID him today, it would really be helpful. We'd also like your girlfriend to ID her; we understand she's the daughter. We just want to dot all the i's."

"Sadie's down the hall; you can ask her yourself."

"Thank you, Your Honor. By the way, I hear Parmenter County dismissed your 11550."

"That's good news. I'd hate to leave a loose end like that."

In the end, Quirke rode up to Fairwood with the cops and picked Laudie out of a lineup, while Sadie declined to make the trip and instead identified her in a photo array. The body in the medical examiner's drawer was Rowe's, as best Quirke could tell, given how little remained of his face.

Snatches of certain conversations Quirke overheard in the Fairwood station led him to think Laudie was working on a coercion or battered intimate partner defense to all the charges—the arson-murder of Captain Forrester, which the Marengo County DA had finally decided to prosecute while continuing to investigate Zelda's disappearance; the kidnapping of Quirke from Sant' Urbano; and, upon consideration of all the evidence surrounding Quirke's overdose, an attempted-murder charge by the Parmenter County DA.

The cases would eventually be consolidated somewhere, but the various jurisdictions were still fighting over which one would try them. Sant' Urbano was going to lose that fight, Quirke knew, since the hometown DA had a policy against ever seeking the death penalty, while her Marengo counterpart, in his last campaign, had made a point of ridiculing Sant' Urbano's soft-on-crime attitude.

Snatches of other overheard conversations, recounting how Laudie claimed Quirke had made sexual advances toward her at Jenny Mortensen's house, led him to inform the Parmenter County DA that under no circumstances would he testify concerning Laudie's assault on him, so that offense appeared to be the only one she would get away with.

Chapter Thirty-Four

November 5, 7:30 a.m.

Wednesday after Election Day dawned brilliant and clear. Sadie awoke with a ferocious appetite and went to her computer to check the results while Quirke made her a plate of bacon, eggs and toast. She came to the table looking bemused and reporting that, although all the other judicial elections had been decided by comfortable margins, the Secretary of State's website was saying his was too close to call. Pockets of precincts here and there around the state where technical problems had precluded sending in vote counts would have to fix those problems before his retention could be decided.

He and Sadie walked, arm in arm, to the courthouse; she stopped in the cafeteria to buy yogurt and fruit salad while he went up to chambers. All morning, well-wishers within the court stopped by to congratulate him on his electoral win, and he grew as tired of telling them their felicitations were premature as he was of explaining that his injuries were not as bad as they appeared.

Between visitors, he checked the Secretary of State's website, which continued to report inconclusive results, until he grew sick of looking. He called Bobby to inquire whether he could take him to a meeting after work; Bobby was eager to oblige. Finally, he interrupted Sadie to declare he'd sworn off checking the Secretary's website, and asked her if she would simply come and tell him when the election was called, one way or the other.

Before leaving her office, he sat on her desk, lifted her from her chair and—as she put her arms around his shoulders and kissed him gingerly, avoiding his lip wound—caressed her firm little bump, the seal of their future together.

※

About noon, as he'd finally gathered his attention sufficiently to read conference memos with normal comprehension, there was another knock at the door.

It was Hetford, who'd never before, in his years at the court, stepped over Quirke's threshold. Quirke found himself tensing until he noticed the absence of the aggression that had always emanated from his nemesis, who looked strangely downcast.

"Come on in, Justice Hetford. Kind of you to drop by. Sit down, if you like."

"Thanks, but I feel like pacing, if it's all right with you. Look, I know your race hasn't officially been called, but I'm sure you've won."

"Thanks for the vote of confidence."

Hetford continued to move about the room, studying the books, papers, pictures, knickknacks—everything except Quirke.

"I know I'm not pretty, Allan, but, really, can't you look at me for a second? Is there something you wanted to talk about? Lucas told me you're seeing Eleanor, and I think it's wonderful. You two are very well matched."

Hetford finally directed his gaze at Quirke. "Yes, it's the best thing that's happened to me in—just the best thing. We're planning to marry."

Quirke felt astonishment and happiness so extreme that his face hurt. "I wish you both all the best. You'll be a much better husband to her than I was. You know, Sadie and I are going to get married, too, as soon as the decree comes through, and it can't happen fast enough for me. Yesterday, for the first time, we heard the baby's heartbeat."

It was Hetford's turn to register surprise. "Quirke, congratulations. I know your joy must be boundless, and you have my very best wishes— Eleanor's, too, I'm sure. Is it okay to let her know?"

"It's okay. Oh, and I've been meaning to tell you, it's fine with me that you took Lucas. In fact, if you don't mind my saying so, it's another instance of two people finally finding the right match in each other. He and I never had the optimal working relationship."

"So he said. But, as luck would have it, Lucas and I won't actually be working together, and that brings me to the first of the two things I came here to say. I've written to the Governor, I've told the Chief, and now I'm telling you: I plan to leave the court. As soon as all the cases I've participated in are filed, I'll become general counsel at Marvelocity Industries. I'm bringing Lucas to the firm, but he's going to be based in Abu Dhabi."

Quirke whistled. "Given the pleasure you seemed to take in our jurisprudential battles, I must say I'm surprised, but it makes perfect sense. Not only are you going to be the husband I wasn't, but you'll also be the son-in-law I couldn't be. Just be sure and read the prenup carefully."

Quirke had thought that would elicit a laugh, but Hetford managed only a fleeting and rueful smile.

"What's the other thing?" Quirke asked.

Hetford balled up his firsts and began to breathe so rapidly Quirke was afraid he was going to hyperventilate. "This is probably the most difficult thing I've ever said to anyone, Quirke," he panted, between inhalations. "It doesn't reflect well. It may even open me up to liability."

Quirke cast about mentally for anything that might relieve Hetford's evident distress. "Do you want me to sign a release?"

"I have no right to ask you for anything. There's no way to sugarcoat this, so—the fact is, Lucas and I were behind all the social media attacks on you. The Superior Claim of Right, the CJB hacking, the *Banner* editorial. Not to mention serving process on you in the courtroom and the surprise recusal motion. We were—I was—responsible for all that ugliness, which I've no doubt cost you considerable unhappiness."

"And maybe the election."

"I just can't believe the voters would reject you even after all that, but—maybe."

All the frustration, fear, and anger of the past few months flew past Quirke's mind's eye. Sitting at his desk perfectly sober, he felt intensely how he had struck back—not at the real target, his now-unveiled attacker, but at himself—by getting wasted, obliterated with drink, over and over again. Had he allowed himself to get up from his desk at that moment, he would have staggered across the room under the vividness of the memories and tried to mess up Hetford's face the way Laudie had messed up his.

But the moment passed and he said to Hetford, "Thanks for telling me. I see it's bothered you a lot, and I don't mind telling you it bothered the fuck out of me, too, but now it's over."

Just then a radiant Sadie burst into the room and, as he rose, ran straight into his arms. "It's official, Judge," she exclaimed. "You won."

Chapter Thirty-Five

January 4, 2015, 8:50 a.m.

Regretting having acceded to the Chief's request that he address the Committee on Self-Represented Litigants on the same day he was to be sworn in on his new term, Quirke hustled down Ninth Street from the loft to the courthouse. The fifty-degree temperature, chilly for Sant' Urbano, motivated him to step lively, and the ease with which he was now able to do so, having lost a good twenty-five pounds between his kidnapping ordeal and quitting drinking, still surprised and gratified him. Sadie missed the belly, now and then rubbing his planar middle and asking, "Where did it go?", to which he invariably replied by rubbing her swelling bump and saying, "I lent it to you, remember? I expect to get it back eventually." The bump would, in due course, be known as Ruairí Norrell Quirke, pronounced more or less like Roorie, though Gaelic purists would quibble. If he inherited his mother's punctuality, he would arrive on his father's birthday.

The walk to work was one they usually made together, but Sadie was staying at the loft this morning to attend to the city's annual backflow prevention inspection and would come in later, in time to stand at his side as he took his oath. He discouraged her from coming this way by herself, it being populated chiefly by residents of the street, most of them dually diagnosed, but she laughed and reminded him it was her neighborhood and she'd been walking in it at all hours for years without ever having been victimized. She was probably right, but Quirke's recent experiences had oversensitized him concerning issues of personal safety.

Go home and get it yourself, the voice, altogether clearly and pointedly, said. Quirke looked around and, seeing only a homeless guy sitting on the sidewalk looking bored and holding his penciled pitch on a bent piece of cardboard, asked him, "Did you say something?"

"Spare change?" the guy replied.

Quirke retrieved a dollar from his jacket pocket, handed it to the man, and continued along Ninth. Looking down to adjust the flap on his left pocket, he noticed he was wearing the wrong necktie. He'd meant to put on the silver and blue repp tie Sadie had bought him for the GovChan interview, but had absent-mindedly knotted one with a purple floral design around his neck instead. Not suitable for a solemn occasion, he chided himself.

So, go home and get the other one, the voice nudged. He was relieved to understand what it was referring to, but the sudden emergence of auditory hallucinations, months after he'd quit taking mind-altering substances stronger than caffeine, was troubling. He hoped he hadn't survived kidnapping and attempted murder, won a retention election, and negotiated the CJB down from censure to a public admonishment only to be stricken with late-onset schizophrenia. "It'd make more sense to call Sadie and ask her to bring it," he said to no one in particular. Just then a disheveled guy pushing a loaded shopping cart on Harrison Street crossed his path and said, "When my voice talks to me, I generally pay attention."

Go. Home. Now. As fast as your legs can carry you.

Quirke turned around and jogged back in the direction he'd come from. Pulling out his phone on the fly, he speed-dialed the Chief and left a voicemail. "Chief, Quirke. I'll be a few minutes late. Have to run back home and take care of something. Have 'em start without me." He began to sprint for all he was worth, hoping the voice was simply a weird byproduct of living with magicians and that he'd be feeling stupidly overprotective in a few minutes.

As he stepped into the lift, he undid the knot of the purple tie and yanked it off his shirt. His heart thudded almost painfully from the exertion and from apprehension. He found himself rolling the ends of the tie around his fists, then told himself not to abuse it so—the cleaner might not be able to reshape it. But he tiptoed into the loft—that the door was ajar scarcely registered at that moment—still holding it ligature-fashion.

Peter's side of the space was dark; he was in New York on art business. The door to Quirke and Sadie's bedroom stood open, and Sadie was nowhere visible. He approached. From the bathroom, he could hear a voice—not Sadie's, but familiar, although he could not place it immediately—petitioning, wheedling, reciting a litany of grievances, all with an undertone of menace.

Then he realized who was speaking: Lucas Grieber. Quirke padded soundlessly to the bedroom doorway, then through it and to within a yard of the bathroom door, and saw the back of Lucas's balding head. He was talking to Sadie, whose magnificently angry face was just above the water line in the full and sudsy tub.

Lucas's left hand held one of their chef's knives. It trembled as he continued his harangue.

"I know you don't have the same feelings for me that I have for you. I can't pretend to understand what you see in Quirke, but I accept that you care for him. I'm just asking you to think about it. Think carefully. Do you really want to be his caretaker when he's in his dotage and you're still a relatively young woman? When his clerks call and confide to you that he's losing it? Remember what happened forty years ago, when Justice McPhee was removed from the bench for senility in hearings so humiliating their existence isn't even noted on the spine of the official report volume that contains them?"

"You're so full of shit, Lucas."

"Just saying. Think of the brain cells he's killed over the years. And when he can't wait until five o'clock, or even noon, to start drinking, what then? I hear he's sober now. How long is that going to last, I wonder? What I'm saying is don't just brush off someone who could be a good friend to you when you need one. And you're going to need one. I'll be far away from here for a long time, but all you have to do is email, call, whatever, and I'm at your service."

"It's best if you just leave. You won't get what you want from me. But if you need help, we'll see that you—"

"Don't talk to me in that patronizing way! I don't need help, I'm offering it to you. Sadie, get up out of there. I need to see you. I need to see for my own eyes if what I heard is true." Lucas raised his arms, and the knife, supplicating, stepping toward the bathtub.

She didn't move, but continued to eye him evenly, except for a split second when she glanced toward the bedroom and, Quirke was sure, caught sight of him.

Later, Quirke didn't remember closing the space between himself and Lucas, but in another instant, he became conscious his purple tie was looped around Lucas's skinny neck. In a blind rage, he'd crossed one end over the other and was pulling both with all his strength, dragging Lucas backward into the bedroom.

"Drop the knife. Drop it, or this time I will kill you," he said. Still Lucas gripped the knife, jerking his arm backward, slicing wildly at the air and at his human restraint. Quirke felt the blade penetrate his thigh, but in the adrenaline rush there was no immediate pain. In falling, Quirke's knee at the small of Lucas's back pushed him to the floor and held him there for a moment before Lucas rolled and threw Quirke off. Lucas ran from the bedroom. Quirke followed, trailing blood and starting to feel the wound throbbing. Behind them, Sadie stepped out of the tub and, dripping bathwater and suds, ran to the bed and rifled through her handbag for her phone.

Lucas had sprinted out the entrance to the loft and down the hallway toward the open window at the end. There he hesitated. Sounds of traffic rose from the alley below. Turning back, he stared at Quirke limping toward him.

"Why, Lucas?"

The attorney shook his head. Half-smiling, he sat on the window sill, drawing his legs up.

"Don't. It's salvageable," Quirke said. He pressed his palm against his thigh, over the wound that kept leaking red through his fingers onto the concrete floor. Seeing such a quantity of his own blood made him feel faint. As pain began to claw at him worse than any he'd ever felt, save after the beating he'd suffered while in captivity, Quirke moved slowly toward Lucas, trying to keep looking straight at him. "This was a misstep, but it doesn't have to be the end of the line."

"Wrong, Judge. That's exactly what this is. I didn't come here to hurt Sadie. Or your baby, God damn it. I didn't even come here to hurt you."

The approaching sirens nearly drowned out his words.

"You made your point," said Quirke. "So, get down from there and I'm sure the paramedics can find rooms for both of us at General. Ha! Maybe the same room, depending on how good or bad the insurance is. That'd be a hella way to recuperate. Hang on there, buddy—" Quirke reached for him just as Lucas launched out the window into the air.

Leaning over the window sill, trying not to bloody the wall, Quirke saw Lucas's twisted form lying still in a dark, spreading pool on the Ninth Street sidewalk. Sirens were already signaling the fire department's approach. When the trucks pulled up, blocking off Gillian, he waved to the paramedics who were jumping out of their vehicles and then, feeling loss of consciousness to be imminent, lay down on the cement floor.

※

January 4, 3:20 p.m.

"Sorry to put you to the trouble, Chief. I could have come in and taken the oath tomorrow. I'm sure they'll let me out of here tonight."

The Chief smiled and shook her head as Sadie stood on the other side of the hospital bed holding Quirke's hand. "Tomorrow's too late; your term's expiring, and I need your vote on a stay request today or I'll have to get a pro tem. Before I forget, here's the memo," she said, tossing a file onto the bed. "Anyway, I wanted to see how you're doing. Everyone at the court's in shock, to say the least, and I'm expected to report back. And, of course, I wanted to wish you well. To say it was a long road getting here would be an understatement, and after that nail-biter on Election Day...did you know your race was the closest judicial election in state history? Alban told me—he likes digging up obscure facts like that. But in the end, all that counts is you got more yeses than nos. So, are you feeling up to it?"

"Absolutely, Chief."

"Great. Let's do it. Repeat after me—you've been sworn in a few times; this should sound familiar. Wait: Do you swear or affirm?"

"Swear," he said. Sadie placed a small leather-bound volume under his left hand, and he raised his right hand.

" 'I, Conal Quirke, do hereby solemnly swear that I will support and defend the Constitution of the United States and of this State against all enemies, foreign and domestic; that I will bear true faith and allegiance to the Constitution of the United States and of this State; that I take this obligation freely, without any mental reservation or purpose of evasion; and that I will well and faithfully discharge the duties upon which I am about to enter.' "

Quirke repeated the oath.

" 'And I do further swear that I do not advocate, nor am I a member of any party or organization, political or otherwise, that now advocates the overthrow of the Government of the United States or of this State by force or violence or other unlawful means; that within the five years preceding the taking of this oath I have not been a member of any party or organization, political or otherwise, that advocated the overthrow of the Government of the United States or of this State by force or violence or other unlawful means except as follows:' "

She paused, lifting an inquiring eyebrow; Quirke shook his head.

" 'No exceptions. And that during such time as I hold the office of Associate Justice of the Supreme Court of this State I will not advocate nor become a member of any party or organization, political or otherwise, that that advocates the overthrow of the Government of the United States or of this State by force or violence or other unlawful means.' "

Quirke duly repeated after her.

"You're good to go for twelve more years," said the Chief. "I wish I could stay and celebrate with you two, but I have a conference call with the Department of Finance. The Governor's budget's due out next week, and the questions DoF had for me suggest it won't be a pretty sight."

"Totally understood. Thanks for coming down here. One of these days, Chief, I'm going to have you marry us."

"It would be a great pleasure. So, what's this book you swore on? Liber AL vel Legis? Sounds vaguely legal. Let's see." Opening at random, the Chief recited: 'Every man and every woman is a star.' I'll bet the self-represented litigants would find that inspiring." Reading a little further, she smiled. " 'For pure will, unassuaged of purpose, delivered from the lust of result, is every way perfect.' Boy, there are days when I really need to remember that. Quirke, see you back at the court. Bye, Sadie."

After the Chief had departed, Sadie leaned down and kissed him. "I hope you were serious, sweetheart. A magical oath is peculiarly binding."

"I'm entirely serious. You'll see how faithful I am to my promises. How are you holding up?"

"We're all right. I can't wait to tell Ruairí the story of how his papa, the brilliant judge, became an action hero one morning to save mama's life."

"Are you sure you want to throw away your credibility with the boy like that?"

"And I'll tell him it wasn't the first time, either. Because I know that when my mother and her lover came into town, they were looking for me. I could have been the one taken instead of you. I know you could have saved yourself by leading them to me. But you were ready to die rather than do that. I've never known a braver man than you, Conal, love of my life."

Quirke smiled, both at the extravagance of her praise and at his own delight at being known and called by name. "Every family has its mythology," he said. "We may as well start creating ours."

Acknowledgements

Here I express my thanks and deep appreciation for the thoughtful feedback given me by beta readers Amy Haddix, Jason Marks, David Kaiser, Paul Lufkin, Sarah Plotkin, Mary Jameson, and Michael Nava (whose Henry Rios mystery novels and *Children of Eve* historical novels, the first of which is *City of Palaces*, are not to be missed). Many thanks, too, to cover artist Mark Ziemann.